ALLAN LEVINE

THE BLOOD LIBEL

GREAT PLAINS FICTION

An imprint of Great Plains Publications Ltd.

Great Plains Fiction
An imprint of Great Plains Publications Ltd.
3-161 Stafford Street
Winnipeg, Manitoba
R3M 2X9

Design and typography: Taylor George Design

Printed in Canada by Friesens

Canadian Cataloguing in Publication Data

Levine, Allan Gerald, 1956-

The blood libel

ISBN 0-9697804-5-1

I. Title.

PS8573.E9646B4 1997   C813'.54   C97-920131-4
PR9199.3.L4745B4 1997

In memory of my grandparents

Sam (1902-1958)
and Sarah Kliman (1908-1995)
&
Aaron (1885-1941)
and Clara Levine (1893-1954)

Pioneers and immigrants, whose names I have borrowed but whose rich lives fortunately bear no resemblance to the characters in the fictional tale that follows....

Medieval woodcut depicting a blood libel

F rom then on the Jews conspired together to hunt the innocent child out of this world. For this they hired a murderer, a man who had a secret hide-out in an alley. As the child passed by, this vile Jew seized firm hold of him, cut his throat and threw him into a pit. Yes, they threw him in a cesspit where the Jews purged their bowels. Yet what may your malice profit you. O you damnable race of new Herods? Murder will out, that's certain; and especially where the glory of God shall be increased. The blood cries out upon your fiendish crime...

Thereupon the Provost caused each of the Jews who had been concerned in the murder to be tortured and put to a shameful death, for he would not tolerate such abominable wickedness. 'Evil must have its due reward.' So he had them torn apart by wild horses and then hanged according to law.

The Prioress's Tale in The Canterbury Tales
by Geoffrey Chaucer (1390)*

*Translated into Modern English Prose by David Wright (1964)

Acknowledgements

More than two and half years ago, I received a telephone call from Gregg Shilliday, publisher of Great Plains Publications. He asked me if I would be interested in writing a chapter on early Winnipeg for the second volume of the Manitoba history series that he was putting out. I immediately agreed and I have never regretted it.

Later, Gregg and I began discussing the possibility of a mystery novel set in Winnipeg's famed North End immigrant quarter in the years before the First World War. At that time, the North End was a vibrant but impoverished area of the city, confronting all the various problems of early twentieth century Canada: slum housing, prostitution, crime, and prejudice. Still, with a booming immigrant population, the place had a unique character, as it still does to this day. In short, it was the perfect setting for a story about ethnic tension and survival.

I had always wanted to write historical fiction, and with Gregg's prodding, *The Blood Libel* was eventually born. But it was not an easy birth. I do owe Gregg and his staff my sincere thanks. Gregg, in particular, pushed and led me in the right direction. He is an astute publisher, a talented editor and a good friend.

Thanks also to Jack Templeman, curator of the Winnipeg Police Service's museum, who answered my many questions about police work at the turn of the century. Bryan Schwartz and DeLloyd Guth of the University of Manitoba's Faculty of Law helped with legal issues; Gitel Morrison, Nina Thompson and Esther Nisenholt provided me with much-needed assistance with Yiddish phrases; Marshall Carroll answered my science and chemistry queries; Eppy Rappaport instructed me on kosher rules and regulations; and Frima Wright, my aunt, was an invaluable source of information about growing up in the North End.

As always, my family lived through the various ups and downs of seeing this book to publication. My children, Alexander and Mia, gently urged me on, while my wife Angie listened to my problems and interminable griping (generally with a smile). Then, she advised and instructed me accordingly about medical issues, human nature and love. The novel benefitted enormously from her keen insight, knowledge and support.

AL

Winnipeg, August, 1997

Author's Note

This is a work of fiction. The events described in this book did not happen, nor were the major characters real people. I have, however, used names of famous Winnipeggers, such as Police Chief John McRae and *Free Press* editor John W. Dafoe, among several others, to give the tale some historical flavour. In reconstructing life in the North End in 1911, I relied on the newspapers of the day, and in particular, three books by popular historian James Gray, *Booze* (1972), *The Boy From Winnipeg* (1970) and *Red Lights on the Prairies* (1971). Other useful reference sources included: Harry Gutkin's history of Jewish settlement in Western Canada, *Journey into Our Heritage* (1980); *Winnipeg: A Social History of Urban Growth, 1874-1914* (1975) by Alan Artibise; *The Blood Libel Legend: A Casebook in Anti-Semitic Folklore* (1991) edited by Alan Dundes; *Heritage: Civilization and the Jews* (1984) by Abba Eban; *Blood Accusation* (1990) by Gavin I. Lanqmuir; and *In War's Dark Shadow: The Russians Before the Great War* (1983) by W. Bruce Lincoln.

Prologue

The body was exactly where the agent had been told it would be — behind a grain shed and loading dock belonging to a Jew he knew named Schiff. The young girl had been dead two, maybe three days. The naked, mutilated body was stiff, gray and beginning to decay. Her eyes, once blue and wide, were gone.

It was easy to see that she had been stabbed more than twenty times. But two things caught his attention: the circular pattern of slashes on her stomach and the absence of any blood.

Covering his nose with a handkerchief, the agent examined the corpse more closely. Her dress and underwear had been shredded. There was skin under the fingernails on her right hand and the inside of her legs were bruised. A deep gash bisected her throat. He suspected that she had been raped first, then killed. But where was her blood?

The wounds on her shrunken abdomen were deep, yet carefully placed. It was too precise, the agent thought. Too neat. This is not the work of just any drunken murderer. He stared long and hard at the girl's nude body, conflicting emotions rising up and disturbing his concentration.

Shaking away the thoughts in his head, the agent glanced around the loading dock. Unable to make out anything in the gloom, he got to his feet and searched the yard for a weapon or any other clues. He found nothing. Damn, this stupid girl was definitely going to ruin his stay in Odessa.

The agent had hoped his annual visit to the city would be straightforward. He always looked forward to coming south, even if only for a week or two. The warm spring breeze from the Black Sea invigorated him. His relatives had urged him to stay at their house, as they always did, but he had politely refused them, as he always did. He preferred the elegant service at the Hotel de London, on the south side of the Nikolayev bulvar, and enjoyed the fine food in its restaurant; for two rubles, you couldn't find a better five-course meal anywhere in Russia.

Unlike most Russian cities, Odessa was a cosmopolitan centre and home to a diverse population of Greeks, Jews and Italians, most of whom made their money in one way or another from the grain trade. The Port of Odessa was a hub of activity fifteen hours a day, exporting grain to Europe and beyond.

Mostly though, he was glad to be out of St. Petersburg. In the capital, the work was dreary, the hours long. There was little glory in reading other peoples' mail and following potential enemies of the state. But, like most Russians, he had been taught to obey orders. Subverting authority could have serious consequences.

Two years earlier, anarchists proved that point. On March 1, 1881, Czar Alexander II, while out for his regular Sunday ride through St. Petersburg, had been assassinated — blown up by a band of revolutionary terrorists who had been stalking him for at least three years. Both his legs had been severed from his body. The Autocrat of All the Russias died one hour later in his blood-soaked bed at the Winter Palace. Massive arrests and executions followed. Alexander III showed no mercy towards his father's killers.

Like all the other officers of the Okhrana — the Czar's security police — the agent's job had been clear. He was ordered to target certain individuals and take them from their homes in the middle of the night. "Mousetraps" was what they called such actions. People were held for days without ever being charged. Some were tortured, others executed immediately.

There were widespread attacks on Jews which began soon after the Czar's death. From one end of the Pale of Settlement (the western area of European Russia where nearly all the Jews of the Empire lived) to the other, pogroms broke out. Angry mobs used the assassination as an excuse for random violence and bloodshed. Local police did nothing and hundreds of innocent people were killed. Thousands more fled for their lives.

Thus, when he had been ordered suddenly to report to General Mikhail Perov at the Odessa Okhrana headquarters, he was apprehensive. At least a quarter of the city's 350,000 people were Jews; many were prosperous grain exporters and brokers. He had heard rumours that the attacks were to start again. There had already been trouble recently in Odessa, when Jews were blamed for the destruction of a Greek Orthodox Church. A bloody, senseless riot ensued. Was he expected to investigate yet another "conspiracy"?

When the agent had finally been ushered into the general's office, he found the local head of the secret police sitting behind a desk piled high with papers and discarded plates. As far as the agent could determine, the general was a dissolute fool who ate too much caviar and drank too much vodka. Fat, pompous and slyly stupid, he had been promoted quickly through the ranks of the Okhrana only because he was the first cousin of General Pavel Zavarzin, commander of the security force. In fact, at thirty, Perov was the youngest general in the Russian military. Behind his back, his subordinates referred to him as *maladoy* or youngster. In his past dealings with him, the agent had found it difficult to respect a superior officer who was his contemporary.

Standing at attention in front of the general's desk, the agent tried to hide his distaste. "Excuse me, " he asked, "but isn't a murder investigation the responsibility of the local police? I was under the impression that we are called in to assist only when there are extenuating circumstances."

"I have complete authorization," Perov wheezed. "You are to go to this address and retrieve the body. I want a full report by tomorrow morning. Do you understand?"

It was odd, the agent thought, that his question had upset Perov. More to the point, if the general knew where the body was, why didn't he just contact the Odessa police? But it wasn't in the agent's character to disregard a direct order, even if it was from someone like Perov. From the first day of training school, he had been taught the code of the Okhrana, a code that governed his life: obedience, loyalty and discipline. He went directly to the waterfront.

By now, a crowd of curious onlookers had gathered near the murder scene. The agent could hear muttering about "killer Jews". Several policemen held the crowd back as a young sergeant approached him and gave him the results of the initial investigation. The dead girl turned out to be Katrina Vasilev, the fifteen-year-old daughter of a Russian dock worker. A medical examination confirmed that she indeed had been first raped and then stabbed to death. The police doctor's report offered no theories about the meaning of the circular wounds, and less about what happened to the girl's missing blood.

The agent dismissed the sergeant and walked slowly to the home of the young girl. This was not his favourite part of the city. No matter what the weather or time of day, Odessa's slum neighbourhood was always dark, dingy and damp. Black smoke from coal-driven grain barges hung over the area in dense, stagnant clouds. Row upon row of dilapidated wooden tenements lined the muddy streets, home to foreign dock workers, whores, thieves, and beggars. Half the population here, the agent figured, was either destitute or suffering from tuberculosis. And the other half were too drunk to know just how wretched their miserable lives actually were.

After a chat with her neighbours, it became clear that young Katrina was no angel. She had lived nearby in one of the small wooden sheds with her family. Her bereaved parents were not much help, but the locals were more than willing to talk to him.

"The girl was a whore, plain and simple," a toothless Greek woman named Scouras told him. "Every night, I see her, dressed like a slattern on her way to the bars." Other neighbours more or less confirmed Scouras's observations.

From Katrina's shack, it was only a few blocks to the strip of seedy taverns near Odessa's waterfront where, it was said, a man always watched his back, guarded his rubles, and never took his eyes off his woman. Each tavern was favoured by one of the city's various ethnic groups and each group respected the others' territory.

Katrina's last movements were easy to follow. Around nine o'clock of the evening in question, she had been seen first in the Greek tavern (actually run by a Russian named Zubatov). Later she moved next door to the Decembrist House, so-named, the story went, because its owner, Serge Pestel, claimed to be a remote descendant of the infamous Colonel Paul Pestel, who had led an ill-conceived rebellion against Czar Nicholas I on December 14, 1825. A small hand-drawn sketch of the executed rebel leader hung above the glasses behind the bar.

Wary Russian officials didn't approve of Serge Pestel or the name he had chosen for his tavern. After the Czar had been assassinated, authorities kept a close eye on the proprietor. Pestel didn't worry much, however, since the Decembrist House was the favourite drinking establishment of General Perov.

The general's affections for under-age girls was well known. He had been caught more than once in the company of girls thirteen and fourteen years old. His position and status had always protected him.

Further questioning of Pestel and the bar's patrons that night led the agent to conclude that Perov was the last person to see the girl alive. He had noticed scratches on the general's face the other day, but thought nothing of it. Now, they made sense.

Needless to say, when he submitted his report, the general was not happy.

"Is this a joke?" Perov demanded, slamming a glass of vodka onto his desk. "Do you know who I am? I could have you shot for this kind of accusation."

"Yes, sir," the agent said, "but all the evidence points directly to this office and we both know it. How do you account for the scratches on your face?"

Perov raised a damp hand to his face and traced the scabbed scratch above his mustache. He smiled thinly. "None of your business."

The agent could barely hide his disgust. The way the general dressed in his uniform that was clearly too small for his large body; his unkempt appearance, and his greasy black hair and beard all repulsed him. He decided, with barely suppressed satisfaction, that he would report this incident to his superior as soon as he returned to St. Petersburg. Obedience, loyalty and discipline did not mean protecting a deviant killer like General Perov.

"What about the Jew Schiff?" asked the general. "Wasn't the body found behind his grain shed? Wasn't he involved somehow?"

"No. I'm sure he was not," the agent replied. "Sir, again, how did you get those scratches on your face?"

The general ignored the question. "And how can you be so certain about the Jew?"

"My father knew Schiff. I have broken bread with him and his family and we have drunk wine together."

He was certain that the general was guilty and that his father's acquaintance was not responsible in any way for the murder of Katrina Vasilev. The fact that her body had been discovered behind his shed was a coincidence, nothing more.

Perov stared at him with a blank look on his face, his long, dirty fingers twirling the hair of his beard. "So you know the Jew. No matter. This is what will happen," said the general, pulling a three-page document from the top drawer of his desk. He handed it to him. "Here is the report that will be filed."

The agent glanced at the report without interest. "And it says...?"

"It says that the girl was murdered by the Jew Schiff. There are eyewitness accounts testifying that Schiff was seen with the girl near his grain shed. Furthermore, I have a signed statement from the police surgeon that states that the girl's blood had been drained by a special ritual knife."

The agent almost laughed. The cover-up was so transparent that no one in St. Petersburg would take it seriously. Besides, it offended his sense of rationalism to bring up such a medieval concept. "With all due respect, General, I will not be a party to a blood libel."

The general sneered. "You think it is barbaric? But don't you see — that's the beauty of it. You are probably the only person in Russia that isn't eager to blame the Jews for something like this. There was a hailstorm yesterday. I'm sure the local peasants blamed the Yids."

"I have only one suspect and your name will stay in my report."

With that, the agent stood and walked out of the room, not bothering to turn around when Perov called to him. It was a calculated and dangerous gamble, but what choice did he have? He had done many things that he was not particularly proud of in the employ of the Okhrana — beatings, abductions — yet blaming an innocent Jew for a blood killing was too much.

He thought about warning Schiff, but at the last minute decided against it. Okhrana agents had already been ordered to watch Schiff's house.

That evening, he left Odessa and returned to St. Petersburg by train, where he filed his report. He left no doubt as to the circumstances surrounding the death of Katrina Vasilev: she had been raped and murdered by Perov.

He heard nothing for two days. Then a note was pushed under his door late one evening. The message was anonymous but direct: "You must leave now, they are coming for you within the hour."

The agent was not particularly surprised; in Russia, you learned to expect the worst. He burned his private papers, packed what he needed and fled the city.

A day later, Schiff was arrested in front of his pregnant wife and infant son. He was immediately put on trial for the murder of Katrina Vasilev. The prosecutor charged that Schiff killed the girl as part of a Passover ritual. Unwilling to wait for the court to reach a verdict, a mob broke into the jail, took Schiff from his cell and hanged him in the city's square. Before they did so, however, his head was shaved and iron spikes were hammered into his left and right eyes.

I

Winnipeg, Canada
April 10, 1911

At first, they did not see each other. Anna was busy playing behind the shed. She was mad at her mother.

How could she say that? How could she say that I couldn't wear that dress? It's my favourite one. I will show her, I will show all of them. I'm never going back. Never.

She picked up her doll and rocked it in her arms. "Shush Lilia," she whispered, "Mama will come for us soon." Lilia's right leg was hanging by a thread. That made no difference to Anna because Lilia was her best and only friend right now.

Although she would not have admitted it, Anna was a little frightened. The sun had disappeared below the city skyline and darkness was descending on Winnipeg's streets. Spring had yet to arrive and the winter wind returned each night with a vengeance. Dressed only in a red cotton dress and a light wool jacket, Anna was cold and hungry. Her small brown shoes were wet from the mud.

Why wasn't her mother looking for her? Doesn't she want me to come back?

Then she heard the voices. Loud, angry voices. They were talking to each other in English. Anna could not understand what they were saying. They were speaking too fast. Her initial reaction was to cry out for her mother, but her mouth made no sound. Ever so slowly she peered around the wooden shed.

There were two men. The man doing most of the talking was large. He was wearing a dark brown suit and a bowler hat. Inside his jacket, a thin gold chain dangled from his vest. But Anna noticed his hands; they were much larger than her father's and almost twice the size of hers put together. She could not make out his face very well in the fading evening light.

The other man was immediately in front of her. He was thinner and dressed in clothes of a finer quality. In his splendid suit, he would have stood out in any crowd.

The second man was holding his bowler hat in his right hand. Anna stared at his black hair, which was combed back and matted against his head as if it had been soaked in grease. He was listening to the first man, nodding his head every so often. Her eyes focused on his yellow teeth.

Neither of them, in Anna's opinion, appeared to be friendly. She pulled her body back and just as she did so, her arm knocked a tin can that lay on the ground beside her.

The two men were suddenly silent.

"Did you hear that?" the larger man asked.

"Forget about it, it was nothing," said the other man. "Now what about this stuff in the crate, is it worth anything?"

"I can't believe you're trying to fence this. This is low, even for you."

"Do we have a deal or not?"

"I don't think you're in any position to tell me what to do. Forget that shit. I want my goddamn money. And if I don't get it within the week, I'm going to hurt you. It's as simple as that."

The well-dressed man laughed. "You wouldn't do that. We're in this together, remember. If I get caught, the first thing I'd do is tell them about you."

The larger man moved closer and grabbed the man by his coat collar. "Don't ever talk to me in that tone, and don't try to scare me. I'm warning you."

Anna sneezed. It had come too suddenly for her to cover her mouth. Her heart skipped a beat as the men stopped talking and exchanged an alarmed look. The larger man stepped forward and called out in Anna's direction. "You, behind that shed. Come out right now."

Slowly, the tiny, blond, blue-eyed girl crept out from behind the shed. Her dress and shoes were covered in mud and she clung to an old, worn-out doll.

"What were you doing there?" the large man demanded.

Anna tried to speak, but could not.

"I said, what the hell are you doing here?" the man asked again, his voice hardening.

"Oh, leave her alone, she's a kid," said the other man.

"A kid maybe, but she has ears, don't she?"

He walked closer to Anna, putting his face so close to hers that she could smell his breath. It was foul, a mixture of tobacco and garlic. "Did you hear us talking, kid? What did you hear?"

Anna started to whimper and then she cried out as loud as her tiny lungs could muster. "Mama, Mama," she wailed.

"Shut up," snarled the man. "Shut the hell up."

But Anna kept on crying in a shrill, hysterical voice.

"See what you've done," hissed the other man. "Leave her. Come on, let's get out of here."

The large man grabbed the girl's face with a giant hand and squeezed. "Be quiet, you little runt! Let me finish my business."

Anna let out a shriek of fear and anger, then bit down on the man's thumb with all her might.

Suddenly, his large hands were around her throat. "You Galician bitch. I'll shut you up!"

Anna thrashed about, desperately trying to breathe. The man's hands were too strong and he would not, or could not, let go of her. After a few moments, her eyes closed and her body slumped. The man shuddered, once, twice, then released his grip. Anna fell to the ground.

"You stupid fool," the other man said. "Look what you've done. Christ, what a mess. I'm clearing out of here." Without waiting for a response, he turned and walked briskly into the night toward the crowds of Main Street.

The large man opened and closed his hands. Damn. But what if she had heard? There could be no witnesses. Too much was at stake.

He tried to think, to focus on what to do next. He eyed the crate his partner had brought with him and knew suddenly what he had to do. He walked over to it and took out one item: a large, sharp butcher's knife with a silver handle. There were engravings on it. He walked back to the body. Even in the night cold, he was sweating and his heart was pounding. Did she move? No chances. No mistakes.

He bent down and cut what was left of her dress. Then he grasped the large knife in his right hand and quickly carved a circular pattern on her stomach. It took only a few moments. The blood was next. He pulled up her blond hair and with one clean swipe, he drew the knife across her neck. Blood poured out of her little body into the black, wet mud.

He wiped the knife clean, both the blade and the handle, and threw it down beside her body. Then he walked back to the crate and pulled out a blue sack with strange markings on it. He opened the sack and removed two long black leather straps. He returned to Anna's body and tied one strap around her arms and the other around her bloodied neck.

Satisfied, he picked her up, careful not to get any remaining blood on his suit, and placed Anna's body behind the shed. He glanced around and saw a pile of wood nearby. Working quickly, he piled one piece after another on top of the body.

By the time he was finished, she was no longer visible. His eyes scanned the area, as he once had been trained to do. No clues, except the ones he wanted to leave. The police in this frontier city were stupid. They would take the path of least resistance, following clues that led inexorably away from him to some other innocent. Without a backward glance, he picked up the crate and walked into the night.

A person could not walk down Rachel Street without noticing number 118. It was a red two-story wood frame house with address numbers that were almost two feet high. A white picket fence encircled the property and a verandah with one hammock and four swinging chairs fronted the entrance. The roof was in need of repair, a few of the wooden shingles had given way during the winter, and the back yard was cluttered with old bed frames, bottles, and discarded furniture. A medium-sized woodshed, where fuel for the furnace and stove was stored, stood at the far end of the yard. The winter of 1910-11 had been especially cold and the woodpile that had been six feet high in October was now nearly gone.

In the early morning, this neighbourhood in the north part of the city, surrounded on three sides by the Red River, was like most working class areas in Winnipeg. Men in blue overalls, many of them recently arrived immigrants from eastern Europe, made their way to work at the nearby CPR rail yards and shops. Their wives got their children ready for school before they too left for work in downtown garment factories. Other women in long dark coats and tall Cossack hats ran to catch the morning streetcar traveling south to take them to jobs as maids and housekeepers for the families of the city's Anglo elite.

In the distance could be heard the distinctive sound of the Crescent Creamery milk wagon pulled by a sturdy brown hackney clip-clopping down the back lane. The driver hardly had to pay attention since his horse knew precisely where to stop for deliveries. Patiently, the horse would wait at each house as his master poured the milk from large ten gallon containers into smaller cans that could be more easily carried into his customers' kitchens. Then the milk was transferred again into quart-size bottles. The whole process took a couple of minutes, unless the dairy driver stopped to chat or play a game with one of the children who usually trailed him on their way to school. At that point the horse grew more anxious, aware that bread and ice wagons would soon be behind them with goods to deliver and no time to waste. The traffic on the city's back lanes was constant six or seven hours a day, six days a week.

In the stillness of a crisp spring Winnipeg morning, 118 Rachel Street might have been mistaken for just another Point Douglas family dwelling. Like every building in the area, it was covered in a thin-layer of black dirt, the result of smoke and cinders from the nearby trains and dust from the road. It was in the evening, however, that this section of Point Douglas, specifically Rachel and McFarlane Streets, came alive with the excitement of men from all walks of life seeking female company — and willing to pay for it.

Sam Klein opened the gate to 118 Rachel and walked up the brick sidewalk to the front door. A cigarette, his second of the morning, dropped from his right hand and he ground it into the dirt with his boot. With his sharp face and tall angular body, Klein looked as rough as any CPR yard boss. Indeed, the girls in the house always bragged that their Sam could handle all types of trouble-maker. Even though he never picked a fight, if there was trouble, Klein usually had the last word. It had always been that way, even when he was just a kid surviving on the mean streets of this frontier New Jerusalem.

Klein reached into his pants pocket trying to find his key and then remembered that he had left it in his room. That wasn't like him; he was not the kind of a person to forget things. He stood before the door, then noticed the pieces of glass beneath his boots. He looked to his immediate right and saw that one of the front windows had been smashed. It was covered with a red satin sheet. More glass had been swept beside the wall of the house.

He knocked lightly on the front door and waited. No one appeared, so he pounded harder. "Come on," he growled, "open the damn door."

"Go away, we're not opened until this afternoon," said a female voice from inside the house.

"Melinda, it's Sam. Open the door."

"Sam! It's not even eight o'clock. Everyone is still sleeping."

Klein could hear the lock being unbolted. The wood door swung open and a large woman in a long black satin negligee stood before him. The top of her ample breasts was visible.

"Morning, Melinda."

"You forgot your key."

Klein shrugged.

"Where were you last night? I went to bed at four and you weren't here yet."

Klein ignored the question. His trouble with his family was his own business, always had been. He stepped inside the foyer. "What happened to the front window? I'm away one night and there's trouble."

"Oh, it was those bloody moral reformers. They decided to hold a protest outside my house last night. I don't know what they want. They should go talk to Chief McRae. He's the one who told me to set up shop here, and that was two years ago." Melinda's breasts heaved as her voice rose. "They hounded me out of my place on Thomas Street and now they want me out of Point Douglas as well. I paid a good price for this house to that bastard Beaman. He took me for five thousand more than his property was worth. So I say screw them. Screw them all."

Klein had heard Melinda's rant about civic politics before. "I'll fix the window this afternoon," he said.

Melinda took a deep breath and suddenly smiled at him. "You got anything to smoke?"

Klein reached into the inside pocket on his jacket and took out his silver-plated cigarette case, a gift from the girls on his twenty-eighth birthday last February. He handed a Player's to Melinda and put another one in his mouth. He lit hers first and then his own. The two of them stood together side by side, silent for a minute, inhaling the tobacco. A white haze of smoke hovered above and around them.

"You want some coffee, Sam?" she asked sweetly, back in her role as successful madam and legendary pleaser of men.

He nodded, his eyes wandering over Melinda's finer features. Even at forty, and a little heavy, she was still a beautiful and voluptuous woman. In her prime twenty years ago, according to the stories that made their way around the Main Street bars, men had lined up for hours to spend some time with her. Melinda charged as much as ten dollars in those days — almost half a week's pay for the average Winnipeg worker. Now, however, she was content to manage her house and keep her clientele happy. She did the odd favour for only her wealthiest customers.

Klein trailed closely behind her through the maze of rooms and hallways to the kitchen at the back of the house. Other than the creaking of the floorboards under their feet, the house was silent. Yet within a few hours, Melinda's would again be noisy, thick with smoke, and alive with revelry and entertainment.

Men visiting Melinda's were first led into the parlor, ostentatious as a whore's vision of wealth — gaudy tapestries on the walls, black velvet drapes over the windows, and overstuffed turquoise sofas. There was a mottled player piano in one corner that nightly bellowed the ragtime tunes of Scott Joplin ("Maple Leaf Rag" was a particular crowd favourite) and Eubie Blake. Tables and chairs for poker games were set up in an adjoining room where girls waiting for business flirted with the players and enjoyed some whisky. Melinda maintained that her decorating tastes matched those of the famous bordellos in Paris, but Klein wasn't so sure.

Because of Melinda's stature as head madam in the city — Queen of the Harlots as she was often referred to by the press — the clientele who frequented her establishment were of a higher quality than the railway labourers, farm workers and hustlers who drank at the nearby Main Street bars. On any given evening, it wasn't an uncommon sight for fine horse-drawn rigs as well as a few automobiles to be parked in front of the house. Melinda and her girls attracted the city's professional classes: doctors, lawyers, grain traders and brokers from the Exchange, and a regular contingent of police officers looking for favours.

They were greeted by a dozen or so of the loveliest women in Winnipeg, dressed in flimsy red silk chemises or black satin laced corsets that — together with their black patent leather pumps — accentuated their finer qualities and made the men's mouths dry. Satisfaction cost two dollars; for five and more there were treats beyond one's imagination.

All of this activity took place in the small dimly-lit rooms on the second floor of the house. In each, there was a pitcher of water, a bar of soap, a white towel, a stock of rubber sheaths (ten cents extra), and a single bed, usually with clean sheets — it all depended on which time of the night you were there. Melinda was very fussy about keeping a clean house and insisted the girls regularly visit a doctor on Selkirk Avenue. And if there were complications — gonorrhoea and pregnancy were the most common — she or Sam looked after them.

Melinda was strict but fair. She didn't mind some fun now and then, but refused to tolerate her girls carousing in public. Last week, several girls from a brothel three doors down had had too much whisky and decided, at four o'clock in the morning, to take a ride on their horses wearing nothing but high-laced boots. Their screaming had the entire neighbourhood outside and provided more ammunition for the detested reformers. The next day, Melinda had spoken to the girls' madam, a slatternish woman named Ida, but she refused to listen to Melinda's lecture on correct business procedures. According to one *Free Press* reporter who had staked out Ida's for a story, more than three hundred customers a night were being entertained at her house. Ida was making lots of money and as far as she was concerned, she could do as she damn well pleased.

"I warn you," Melinda had told her, "take care of your girls or I will do it for you. Your foolishness will shut us all down."

Sam Klein owed Melinda a lot. Neither of them ever spoke of it; Klein did his work, no questions asked, and that was enough for both of them. Besides, public displays of gratitude were not his style. Melinda had taken him in when he needed a place to stay and given him a job when his only other option was working for his mother's friend Isaac Hirsch.

Klein respected Isaac and was grateful for all he had done over the years for the Klein family. Nevertheless, he wasn't about to spend the rest of his life as a clerk in Hirsch's hardware store fetching hammers, shovels, and bags of nails. Long ago, Klein had decided that there had to be something more to life. Money and power did not interest him. Freedom to make his own way was his only goal.

He had been with Madam Melinda now for nearly three years. Working out of her house, Klein had earned a well deserved reputation as a problem-solver. As time went on, the word on the street was that there was nothing Sam Klein couldn't fix or find. He liked his new status, even if it was slightly exaggerated, and he did nothing to dissuade opinions about his talents.

In fact, he knew the streets of Winnipeg like no one else. In this booming frontier city of 136,000 people, there was not a hotel owner, pool hall hustler, bootlegger, whore or cop that Sam Klein wasn't familiar with. Up and down Main Street and across the railway tracks into the North End, Klein knew everyone and everyone knew him.

And so it was that in exchange for room and board at the back of Melinda's house, he worked as her handyman and bouncer. Klein ensured there was always enough liquor and beer for the customers, and he watched over the girls, especially Sarah.

He couldn't put his finger on it. But lately his heart raced more than he liked when he thought of her. These were feelings he had never had for any woman. Many of the other girls in the house were quite beautiful. He had an open invitation to visit a half-dozen rooms and occasionally, when he was in the right mood, he accepted their offers. But it was only for the sex, nothing more, despite what a few of them thought.

With Sarah, however, it was different and that troubled him. He would often lie awake at night thinking of her — how her long brown hair swept the back of her neck and how her sweet, intoxicating smell unnerved and excited him. Such feelings were foolish, he knew; she slept with a dozen men each night. But —

"Here's the coffee, Sam," said Melinda, setting a hot mug before him. He put his cigarette in a metal ashtray Melinda kept on the long pine kitchen table in the middle of the room. There was a wood-burning stove to his right and pots, pans and an ice box across on the far side. A row of cupboards was beside the kitchen sink to his left.

When Melinda purchased the house in 1909 it already had electricity, but she had wisely paid the city the two thousand dollars required for water and sewer hook-up. Still, that meant that there were about a dozen people using one bath and toilet; Klein preferred the quieter confines of the backyard privy that Melinda maintained (contrary to a city bylaw) for her customers.

On most days, the same dozen people also sat down for lunch and dinner. A few years ago, Melinda had hired a young Chinese cook by the name of Lee to look after meals. Klein had never tasted food prepared like that. His mother Freda was an excellent cook when it came to roast chicken, soup and fish. But Lee's exotic dishes were something else: noodles with vegetables and meat in a variety of sauces that Klein had never tasted before. If Lee had the right spices — pepper, ginger, and garlic — he could make horse meat taste great. He confided once to Klein that his secret ingredient was a spice called *veh tsin*. It enhanced the flavour of Lee's dishes and sometimes made Klein and everyone else feel dizzy. Lee only laughed when Klein asked him about it. "Do not tell anyone," he said. "Family secret."

Klein reached across the table and picked up the stick of white rock sugar that always was kept there. He broke off a small piece and popped it between his teeth, then took a gulp of his black coffee.

Melinda lowered herself onto the chair opposite him and glanced at the previous day's newspaper. After scanning the headlines, she passed it to Klein.

"I want you to call Fred Dunn today and order another cord of wood. I see he's got a special on, five dollars a cord, and I figure there is enough left for two weeks. But hell, if I can save two dollars on each cord, we'll get it now."

Sam nodded.

"Also", continued Melinda, "I want you to keep an eye on Ida's place. She is the reason those reformers were here last night. Stupid woman. She lets her girls do as they please, never shuts her blinds. She'll be the ruin of all of us."

"I'll take care of it," Sam said, taking another sip of his coffee.

Ten minutes passed without another word between them. "Anything exciting in the paper?" Melinda asked, trying to engage him in conversation.

Klein looked up at Melinda. The way she was sitting across from him at the table, his eyes, through no fault of his own, were directly aimed at her cleavage. She hardly minded the attention and pretended not to notice. After a moment, he glanced down at the paper. He hadn't had the time to read the *Tribune* for a few days, though without looking he was certain he would know the lead items: stories from Ottawa on trade issues between Canada and the United States, boring accounts about British politics, and the usual pieces about how immigration, foreigners, and poverty were destroying the fabric of Canadian society. It was curious, he thought. If the English did not want people like Klein in the country, why had they invited him in the first place?

"Here," he said, as he slid the newspaper across the table, "Help yourself."

Melinda turned to the local news on page three. "Woodsworth is at it again," she said. "He spoke last night at the Trades Hall on Higgins."

"Yeah, what did he have to say this time about us 'foreigners'?"

Melinda chuckled. She knew how Sam detested the Methodist minister's message of wanting to create the "Kingdom of God" on earth for the city's helpless and impoverished immigrants. Granted, J.S. Woodsworth's work at the nearby All People's Mission on Stella Avenue was impressive. He had provided much needed aid for many newcomers and clothed, fed and educated their children. But his stubborn insistence that salvation for European immigrants was to be found only in total assimilation to "Canadian ways", that was to say adherence to British values and customs, angered Sam and other newcomers who wanted to choose their own path in life.

"It was his usual speech," said Melinda, "more promotion for his new book, *My Neighbour*, about the evils of city life. I guess I'm a major contributor to that problem."

"I suppose so," said Sam, only half-paying attention.

"Now, he wants to change all of you immigrants and clean up the city at the same time. The man is ambitious. Sam, are you listening?"

"Yeah. I have decided to ignore the rantings of Reverend Woodsworth. Though, I suppose I should be thankful that he thinks so highly of Jews. How did he put it? 'Naturally religious, temperate, home-loving, intelligent, industrious and ambitious, the Jew is bound to succeed'," Sam recited from memory. "You should hear what he has to say about Galicians, Negroes and Indians. There is absolutely no hope for them."

"Forget about it. Woodsworth will be dead and buried and Winnipeg will still have serious problems. Look, this other article is more interesting. You know that guy Harry Jones, he's been here a lot lately."

"Yeah, the Welshman, he's a fool. I've had to throw him out for being drunk. So what does it say about him?"

"Two nights ago, he was arrested by the police for hitting his wife in the face. Right on the street, for God sakes. The cops also found brass knuckles in his pocket. He says he carried them for years in England."

"Why did he hit her?" asked Klein distractedly, knowing that most men in Winnipeg hardly needed a reason to hit their women.

"Apparently, they were down at the railway office and when he came back from the clerk's desk he found her talking to another man. So he slugs her. Daly fined him a lousy five dollars. He should've got the lash, if you ask me. Sam, you hear what I said?"

Klein was looking at Melinda, but he was not listening to her. He had his cup of coffee in one hand and the butt of a cigarette in the other. "I'm sorry Melinda, I was thinking about something else. I agree, the bastard should've been whipped."

Melinda and Klein had been friends long enough for her to know exactly what was on his mind. "She's in her room, still sleeping, I'd guess."

Klein shrugged and got to his feet. "I need some air. I'll see you later."

"You will have to come to terms with this eventually," replied Melinda. But Klein was already out the door.

Old Ben Goldberg did not sleep well during the night. For some reason, he had dreamt about his parents. His family was together again. It was the Sabbath. They were sitting at the wooden table in their small hut, close to the marketplace of Lutsk in Russia where he had been born. His father was chanting the prayer for the wine. *Baruch atah adoni, eloheinu melech aholam boreh pree ha gaffen.*

His mother had cooked another delicious meal: roast chicken, *kugel*, and a hot pot of carrot *tsimiss*. If he closed his eyes, he could almost smell the food and hear his mother's sweet voice calling him to the table. Those were happy times, but long ago in another life, in another time.

Ben sighed as he roused himself from his bed. Though it was the middle of April, the mornings were still cold. He reached for the kerosene can he kept on a wooden shelf near the door and poured the few remaining drops into the hole on the base of his rusted lamp. Good, he thought, the wick was still long enough. He secured the glass top and lit the wick with a wooden match. For a few moments the strong and distinct smell of burning kerosene filled his small shack, then it gradually dissipated.

Ben had lived in Winnipeg for more than ten years, and in this hut on Dufferin Avenue for about five. It wasn't much — one small room, a table, two wooden chairs and a slab of wood for a bed. Yet, it was affordable and there was a place at the back where he could keep his cart. A nearby well supplied him with water for drinking and washing. His neighbours, the Kowalchuks, a Polish family, were pleasant enough and the synagogue was only a few blocks away.

He dressed in his black suit, his only suit, and pulled on his leather boots. The left one was nearly worn through. But who had the six dollars for a new pair? He would have to manage, as he always had, until *Rosh Hashana*, the New Year.

That morning, not only did his dreams bother him, but he had again awoke with an upset stomach. He had been having sharp pains in his belly for longer than he cared to remember. At first, he ignored the problem. But when it finally became unbearable, he listened to Mrs. Kowalchuk who recommended he spend sixty cents for a large bottle of Abbey's Effervescent Salt.

"Frank had the same problem," she had told him. "A daily dose of the salt and his stomach troubles vanished in two weeks." Much to Ben's satisfaction, Abbey's Salt also helped ease his pain. He mixed a concoction of salt and warm water and drank it down quickly. It kept his "stomach sweet and bowels regular" just as it promised on the bottle label.

The wood stove in the middle of his one-room shanty was barely burning. If Ben was to have his usual breakfast of rolled oats porridge and a cup of tea, he would need more wood. He dressed, opened the door and stepped outside. The sky was a bright blue and the air crisp. The mud beneath his feet had frozen hard over night.

He checked his wagon, contemplating the day's business. Passover was to begin at sunset; there might be some good opportunities for selling a few shirts or tablecloths. His father had wanted Ben to be a rabbi, a man of high distinction respected by the entire *shtetl* community. Instead, Ben eked out a living as a North End peddler.

Each day, except Saturday of course, was the same. Awake at six a.m. and on the streets an hour later. The first stop was the farmer's market by Dufferin Avenue and Derby Street to see what he could trade for. George Brown from Teulon was always eager to swap vegetables for a dress or cloth for his wife. Then it was back down Main Street, towards Selkirk Avenue.

Ben had regular customers — Mrs. Fineman at 237 Selkirk, the butcher, Fred Blutstein next door, and Jacob Luteski, the tailor near Selkirk and Andrews. Along the way he would cut over to Stella and Flora for a rest or to chat with the neighbourhood children on their way to and from school. "Ben the Peddler," they would yell, "Maybe you have some candy for us." And he usually did. In all, he was out for ten or eleven hours a day, bartering, trading and gossiping.

He may not have been a rich man; nevertheless, Ben Goldberg enjoyed life. His only regret was that he had no children of his own. Once, many years ago, there had been a woman, Chana. A more beautiful woman never walked the earth, Ben used to say. The Goldbergs, however, were from Lutsk and Chana's family from Pinsk. There could be no match, her father had decreed. After Ben left for North America in 1889, he never saw Chana again.

Assured that his wagon was ready, Ben walked over to the woodpile so he could heat up the stove for a cup of tea. He reached down for a large log, pulled it away and stopped. The log dropped from his hands. He leaned forward, hardly believing what he saw. At the bottom of the pile, he could see small, thin fingers protruding through the pieces of wood. "*Ich shtarb,*" he exclaimed in Yiddish, his hand over his mouth. "I'm going to die!"

He began to throw off the wood, slowly at first and then more frantically. It took almost a minute to reach the body. There lay a little girl. Her blue eyes were wide open and her neck was brutally slashed. A mask of terror remained on her small white face. A pool of reddish mud encircled her lifeless being.

Shaking his head, Ben pulled her small body out of the mud and then suddenly recoiled in shock by what he saw around her head and arms.

"No, no, no!" he cried, his hands shaking. Then, standing over the body of the nine-year-old Catholic girl, Ben started to recite feverishly the *kaddish*, the ancient prayer for the dead. *"Yisgadal, vyskadash sheme rabah...."*

"Good morning to you officer," said the man in a dark brown overcoat and flat tweed cap.

Bob Stewart tipped his tall navy blue helmet. It had been the same routine every morning since he had been transferred to the Magnus Street station five months ago. Politeness was both rampant and contagious among the North End's residents. A person couldn't walk more than a block without someone greeting you or wishing you well — and almost always in broken English.

At first, Stewart had found it irritating; now he merely accepted it as part of the job. He hadn't asked for the transfer that had brought him here. He had preferred his stint downtown, patrolling the business district. On most days, he had started at McDermot Avenue, walking with the bankers, newspapermen, clerks and secretaries on their way to work. By ten o'clock he'd have been all the way to Eaton's on Donald and Portage and back to the Leland Hotel on Main Street for a coffee. Except on Tuesdays. Every Tuesday, he'd meet his sister Claire at the coffee shop at the Royal Alex instead. She worked at a book shop in the palatial CPR railway station next door. Often his wife Amanda and their five-year-old son Garth would join them.

Life as a constable in Winnipeg meant long hours and lousy pay. Stewart had been on the downtown beat for nearly six years. He had broken up more than a few fights between drunks and mediated his fair share of domestic squabbles. All in all, however, the work was tolerable. There were no strange smells, no broken English, no dilapidated tenement slums like he now encountered every day.

Having grown up in St. James, what did Bob Stewart, a thirty-year-old Protestant of British stock know about East European immigrants from places with names like Galicia, Serbia, Croatia, and Bukovina? His superiors in the department had assured him that working out of the North End station, he would be dealing with English-speaking Winnipeggers as well. And though it was true that the neighborhoods on the other side of the CPR tracks contained many Brits and Scots, Stewart's day seemed to be occupied with foreigners whose last names ended in 'ski', 'stein' and others he could not pronounce.

He had thought about requesting another transfer, and had even filled out the proper form. But when the moment came to submit it, he changed his mind. Bob Stewart had plans. Unlike many of his colleagues, he stayed away from the whorehouses in Point Douglas and didn't ask for under-the-table favours from Main Street bartenders. Too risky to do such things in uniform. There were too many unsavoury characters out there waiting to blackmail a cop. So, he obeyed the rules while on the job and decided that there was no point complaining about his assignment. He'd put in the required time in the North End, and the promotion that would send him back downtown would come soon enough. If not, well, there were always other options.

In fact, he was certain that his recent after-work activities would result in some much needed extra money. He knew it was fraught with danger, that he was walking a fine line, but his wife deserved the best and he aimed to give it to her and Garth. He reasoned that out of uniform, he had a bit of latitude. Who cared what the official rules stated about off-duty life? He knew that he was not allowed to drink and gamble, but did so regularly. The room at Melinda's was private and Sam Klein ensured that no one saw him enter or depart. He stayed away from the women, as difficult as it was sometimes, and never lied to Amanda about what he was doing. When he was approached with this other idea a few months ago, he decided that for the amount of money that was dangled before him, some chances were worth taking. He just wasn't sure yet how far he was prepared to go.

Stewart had not walked farther than a block before he heard the commotion. Jesus, he thought, glancing at his watch, it's not even eight in the morning.

"Hurry, constable," said a woman in a long dress with her head covered by a scarf. "A man is in asking for help over there," she said, pointing to the alley behind Dufferin Avenue.

"Yeah, yeah. I'm coming," said Stewart, slightly picking up his pace. What is it now, he thought, some cat get stuck in a tree?

As the cries for assistance got louder, he could see an old man with a white beard in a black suit pacing back and forth, among a small crowd of North End residents. Stewart strode forward. "So, what's the problem, old timer?" he asked.

Ben Goldberg said nothing. He turned, with his brown eyes wide and his hands shaking, and pointed to the limp body of a young blonde girl beside a pile of wood.

"What the hell," muttered Stewart. He moved closer to the body. Nothing he encountered in the North End surprised him any more. He tolerated the slums, the dirt and poverty and usually overlooked the strange manners and customs he witnessed. If these foreigners wanted to bring up their children in these shacks, that was fine with him. But the sight of the small mangled body shocked him.

Stewart lifted his eyes and gazed at Ben. Then he took out his whistle and blew.

Almost before the shriek had stopped echoing, two more policemen arrived on the run. Then, another constable who had arrived by motorcycle was quickly dispatched back to the station so that Chief McRae at the Rupert Avenue police headquarters could be notified by telephone.

"What's your name, sir?" Constable Stewart asked firmly. Because Stewart had been the first officer on the scene, it was his right to assume command of the investigation until his superiors arrived.

Ben Goldberg could not understand or speak English well at the best of times. With three large policemen hovering around him, he froze.

"Sir, your name. What is your name?" Stewart asked more slowly, but still in the same firm tone.

"Uh, Goldberg...Ben Goldberg," the old man stammered.

"And this is your house?"

Ben nodded.

"Please tell us what happened."

"*Ich hob gegangen in droisen tsu nemen holtz...*"

"In English. Can you tell us what happened in English?" He looked at his fellow-officers for sympathy.

"Bloody foreigners," growled one of the constables.

Ben attempted to continue, speaking very slowly. "I came outside to get some wood for my stove and that's when I saw the little girl lying there."

"Did you touch her?"

"No. I only took the wood off her body," Ben replied.

"You go sit down there on the step and don't move," Stewart ordered.

Ben did as he was told. By this time, the small crowd had grown much larger. There were the Kowalchuks from next door and the Litvacks from across the alley. Small groups of men and women on their way to work wandered over from Main Street.

When Mrs. Kowalchuk saw the body, she cried out. "My God, it's Anna."

"Ma'am, do you know this girl?" asked Stewart.

Mrs. Kowalchuk nodded her head, her hand over her mouth.

"What is her name?"

"Anna Rudnicki," she blurted out. "That's little Anna. She lives on Stella, near Charles. She's the daughter of Igor and Eva Rudnicki. He works for the railway."

"Are you sure, Mary?" asked her husband.

She ignored him and continued speaking to Stewart. "Yes, I'm positive. It's Anna Rudnicki."

Stewart pulled a yellow pencil out of his inside jacket pocket and jotted the information down in his black note pad. He thanked Mary Kowalchuk for her assistance and returned to the body.

A few feet away, two of the other constables were preventing the crowd from getting any closer to the scene of the crime.

"Clear the way," boomed a voice from behind the mob.

Immediately, as if Moses himself were there, a narrow path appeared. A hush fell over the crowd. Leading the way in full uniform was big John McRae, the city's Chief Constable. His flat blue police cap was pulled low down on his head, though his dark brown eyes, blazing ahead, were clearly visible. His bushy grayish moustache nearly hid his mouth. Ignoring the crowd, he walked through to where his officers were standing.

McRae had been the chief of the Winnipeg force since 1887 and had a reputation for being very tough. He had been shot at more than once, made deals with prostitutes, solved countless murders, and waged war on gambling dens and bootleggers. He was set to retire at the end of the year, though at fifty-two years of age, he remained such a commanding figure that most city aldermen never would have dared to cross him.

McRae took a long, hard look at the body, but said nothing. If the gruesome scene bothered him, he didn't show it.

Two plainclothes detectives accompanied him — Michael Stark and Bill McCreary. Both men were as large as McRae and dressed in checked three-piece suits. They too had mustaches, though Stark's was nearly white whereas McCreary's was as black as shoe polish. That, plus the wisps of gray hair protruding under Stark's hat, made it obvious that he was the older of the two detectives.

"Stewart, report please," barked McRae.

Constable Stewart stepped forward to inform the chief as to his findings thus far, every so often pointing his finger at Ben Goldberg who was still shivering on his broken wooden stair.

"And you think he is telling the truth?" asked McRae.

"Pardon me, sir?"

"Stewart, wake up. Do you think he is telling the truth?"

"I'm not sure, sir. He is a Hebrew peddler, who barely understands English. You know these people, it is hard to tell what they are thinking," he said.

"Agreed. Now this is what I want done. Detectives Stark and McCreary will be in charge of this investigation. I want the four of you," McRae ordered, pointing at Stewart and three other constables, "to assist them in speaking to neighbours and searching the area."

The chief looked in the direction of a young constable standing in front of the crowd. "You, Robertson."

"Yes, sir."

"Return to headquarters and have the ambulance wagon come here to deliver the body to Dr. MacDonald at his office at the McIntyre Block. And constables, don't disturb anything. Do you understand?"

"Yes, sir."

McRae knelt down next to the body. The Chief took out a pencil from his jacket and poked and prodded Anna's body. Rigor mortis had set in.

Her body was stiff and an ashen gray. The gash below her chin was partially hidden by the leather straps, but it was easy to see that it was deep and extended from ear to ear.

"Judging by that cut," said McRae pointing with pencil to the girl's neck. "I'd guess she was killed by a butcher knife. But look at those circular wounds on her stomach. I've never seen anything like that before. And what the hell are those leather straps around her neck and arms?"

The policemen shook their heads.

"Well, men," McRae continued, "I want to know what they are."

"I think they...." Michael Stark stopped himself.

"What's that Michael?" McRae asked.

"Nothing, Chief," Stark said. "Bill and I will look after this."

Because of his odd accent, it was sometimes difficult to figure out what Stark was saying. The detective blamed it on his German upbringing and his Irish ancestors.

"It's a strange mix," Stark once admitted to McCreary, "My dad was hired to work at the shipyards in Hamburg. We left Belfast when I was two. By the time I was ten, I knew German better than English. I'm still not sure sometimes if I'm a mick or a kraut."

The chief turned to his two detectives. "What do you think, gentlemen, should we take the old Jew in for questioning?"

Stark and McCreary looked at each other for a moment.

"I doubt if he knows much more than he told Stewart," said Stark, looking in Ben's direction.

"Let me spend a few minutes with him," McCreary declared. "I'll find out what he does or doesn't know."

"Take it easy Bill. I want no rough stuff. By the book, remember."

"Of course, Chief. You know me, I never break the rules."

McRae laughed, in spite of himself. And as if a row of dominoes had toppled over, the other constables all laughed as well. When was there a case that Bill McCreary did not break the rules? If roughing up a suspect or paying off a crooked informant helped solve a crime, so be it. He certainly had little use for the "alien riffraff", as he regularly referred to the city's immigrant population.

"They smell funny, most of them will steal from their own mother, and they live in dirt," he'd declare. "What good are they? They add nothing to this country."

Most of his fellow policemen were not as troubled by the city's burgeoning foreign population, though they agreed that McCreary had somewhat of a point on crime. Criminal activity in the North End seemed to be getting worse every day — robberies, drunkenness, brawling, and even murder were becoming commonplace. It would never have occurred to them that there may have been a connection between the amount of trouble they had to deal with and the intolerable living conditions of the area. The streets were unpaved, the drinking water dirty, and a proper sewage system non-existent. Typhoid epidemics were all too common.

McRae thought for a minute. "All right, Bill. Take the peddler in for a few more questions. See what else he knows. Maybe he heard something."

He called the rest of the officers together.

"Gentlemen," he began slowly. "This is a bad one. We have the death of a child. When the mayor and aldermen find out, they will want us to solve this and quickly. The newspapers will be watching us closely, so be careful. Nobody talks to reporters except me. Everybody got that?"

"Yes, sir," they said.

He looked at Constable Stewart.

"Where did you say that little girl lived?"

"On Stella, sir, near Charles."

"Right. As soon as the body is removed. I want you to track down the girl's parents and bring the father to the station. I will speak with him and take him over to Dr. MacDonald's so that he can identify the body. And Stewart."

"Yes, sir."

"Get rid of this crowd."

"Right away, sir."

Joined by two other constables, Stewart ordered the crowd of neighbours to disperse. Some began to move away, most just continued to stare. At the back of the crowd, a man dressed in a cheap gray suit was pushing his way through, trying to get a closer look at the body. The top two buttons of his long-sleeved white shirt were open and he wore no tie. He was nearly six feet in height with a full-head of wavy brown hair that curled at the back. A patchy black stubble covered his face. He had a long, slender nose that was slightly crooked. An unlit cigarette dangled from his mouth.

Stewart saw him first. "Sam, you dog, what are you doing here?"

"Nothing. I was out getting a morning paper when I saw all the excitement. What happened?", Sam Klein asked casually, taking a match from his inside pocket. With a flick of his right hand, he deftly ignited the match and lit his cigarette.

Bob Stewart did not know many Jews. True, he had worked in the North End for several months and visited many of the Jewish shops on Selkirk Avenue. He had bought lunch at Fishman's delicatessen where they served the best pastrami sandwiches in the city, and last week had had a pair of boots repaired by Joe Guravitch. But Sam Klein was the only Jew with whom he had ever had a beer or played cards.

"A little girl was murdered. Pretty ugly too. Her throat was cut and she was tied up in some kind of leather rope," Stewart said in an official-sounding voice. "I've seen a lot of dead bodies before, but this one is more gruesome than most. I've got a little boy myself, about the same age as her."

"Know who did it?" asked Klein, offering Stewart a cigarette.

"No thanks. Do we know who did this? Not yet. But we will. Stark and McCreary are in charge. They'll figure it out. They always do," he said proudly.

Klein had met Michael Stark only once, when the policeman had visited Melinda's house on official business searching for a thief named Johnson. He seemed like a decent fellow and a honest detective. More importantly, Melinda had known him for many years and trusted him.

"A bit strange," she'd say. "Not a big talker and he has never shown any interest in the girls. But he leaves me alone so what else can you ask from a cop?"

Bill McCreary was another story. Klein had had a recent run-in with him and did not have much use for the big brutish cop. But he said nothing to Stewart.

"Do you know the old Jew sitting there?" Stewart asked, pointing at Ben Goldberg.

The way Stewart tossed around the word "Jew" bothered Klein, even if he wouldn't have readily admitted it, nor understood exactly why. Nevertheless, it touched a raw nerve. He wanted simply to be a 'Canadian'; his family as well as everyone else insisted on treating him as a 'Jew'. Klein, however, understood that it was best to keep his feelings to himself, especially around the police. He had known Bob Stewart for several years. He figured he didn't mean anything by it. That was just the way he talked, it was the way most *goyim* talked. Besides, he had been called worse.

"I've seen him around. His name is Goldberg. He's a peddler, a harmless guy."

"Maybe. We're going to question him some more."

"Stewart, get over here," said McCreary, who saw the constable talking with Klein.

"You're not mixed up in this, are you Klein?" McCreary said loud enough so that everyone standing nearby could hear. The other policemen turned their heads to stare at Klein.

Klein glared at McCreary, not hiding his contempt for the detective. After what McCreary had done to Sarah, he had no use for him, no matter what kind of tough reputation he had. For a moment no one said anything. Several of the other police officers had heard about Klein's brief altercation with McCreary and the story had been making its away around the station house.

Finally McCreary laughed, and the tension broke. He turned his back to Klein as he walked over to speak with Stark. The group of police officers around the body dispersed. Now Klein could see the grisly sight for himself. He moved closer and then gasped at what he saw.

"She's tied in *teffilin*," he whispered, shock tightening his voice.

Stark's head jerked around. McCreary looked up. "What's that, Klein? Tied in what?"

It was too early in the morning for this, Klein thought. If McCreary wanted to pick another fight with him, he would oblige him. It wasn't Klein's fault the detective couldn't hold his liquor, or that he behaved like an animal when he was drunk.

Klein could not take his eyes off the girl. How could he tell the police that she was tied in *teffilin* or phylacteries, the leather thongs used each morning by observant Jews in their first prayers of the day? He couldn't believe it himself.

"Okay, clear away from here," McCreary ordered. "All of you, go about your business, we have police work to do."

Klein turned with the rest of the crowd and started walking back towards Main Street and the red light district beyond. He had to find a quiet place at Melinda's to sit down and think. He knew it was none of his business, but there was something terribly wrong about this murder.

2

Sarah Bloomberg tugged at the large, heavy blanket that covered her. Since childhood, Sarah had been a restless sleeper. Her dreams had always been troubled, mixing her subconscious fears with the barely suppressed anxieties of her daily life. Most mornings she'd wake up with her sheets and blankets in a tangled heap on the floor beside her bed.

The banging on the front door earlier had roused her. Her first instinct had been to run down the hall to see what the commotion was about, but the cool temperature in her room quickly changed her mind.

For the next hour, she slipped in and out of sleep, her eyes opening and then shutting. Exhausted from a night of hard work, Sarah figured she was entitled to lie in bed as long as she wished. Naked under the covers, she wrapped herself like a mummy in her white Hudson's Bay blanket with the distinctive black, yellow, red and green broad stripes across it. This, she thought, was just one of the simple comforts money could buy. There had been a time in her life, a time she tried hard to forget, when she had had nothing but the rags on her back. Now things were different.

Lying on her side, she surveyed her room and her various prized possessions: white lace curtains, a music box from Eaton's, and a closet full of fine dresses and frilly garments favoured by her clients. Men were lining up to see her now, the way they used to for Melinda. Her fee had risen accordingly, from two to five dollars, and now seven dollars. No woman in Winnipeg charged more than Sarah. She enjoyed the status of being the most expensive whore in town.

The strong aroma of coffee sitting in a pot downstairs on the kitchen stove stirred her. Outside of her room, she could hear familiar voices, sounds that comforted her, made her feel safe. Melinda and Klein. One had presented her with opportunities and a home; the other was her protector, her friend, and perhaps some day, her lover.

Sarah was intrigued by Sam Klein. She was especially intrigued by the way she occasionally caught him looking at her. In her line of work, she didn't like to let men get too close. But Klein was different. He excited her. It wasn't only his strong features and lean body, or his smooth style — the manner in which he handled himself in a crowd and the way he let a cigarette droop from his lips — it was also that, underneath the swagger, there was a quiet kindness. Sarah did not know too many men like that. Still, she understood that in relationships, timing was everything. And Sarah was not yet prepared to give up the financial security that she had worked so hard to acquire.

She had often felt Klein staring at her from the other side of the parlour, his brown eyes smouldering, as she talked with other men. Sarah wanted to tell him that her clients only had her body, not her heart, but she suspected that he would never accept that. So she said nothing. She didn't want to be cruel, it was merely the way her life had unfolded. Soon, if matters went according to plan, there would be some changes, and she would not have to worry about money for a long time. A very long time. Maybe Sam would like that.

"That coffee smells so good, Melinda, it got me out of bed," Sarah said, brushing lightly against Klein as she walked by. He nodded to her, but did not acknowledge her gesture. His eyes remained focused on his coffee cup. She sat down at the table and poured herself a cup of coffee.

Even after a short night's sleep, Sarah looked sensational to Klein. He tried to avoid eye contact, but it was difficult. Her hair was tangled and hung partially over her face. She wore no make-up, but her eyes were bright and her complexion clear. Sarah had a look about her that distinguished her from other women he knew: a slender nose, high cheekbones, full lips. A small red scratch was all that remained on her neck from where McCreary had bruised her. Wearing a short flowery Japanese-style kimono, he could plainly see the outline of her slim but full body. It stirred him, as it always did.

Melinda reached for the newspaper, acting as if she did not sense the sudden tension around the kitchen table. It usually happened when Sam and Sarah were within ten feet of each other. Melinda had decided that it was best to keep her advice to herself. What right did she have to interfere into the private and personal affairs of others when she did not appreciate, in fact objected to, other people interfering in her own life. As head of a household of young and carefree women, however, she sometimes didn't have a choice but to act in what she considered to be a girl's best interests.

Melinda had watched Sarah grow more confident and accomplished each day, reminding her of herself not so many years ago. Melinda's life had not followed any preconceived plan. People like her, she believed, were presented with various paths. Events and circumstances happen. Often choices are made without thinking much about future consequences.

In a city burgeoning with optimism and money, how many options did a single woman have to make it on her own? When Melinda had first arrived in Winnipeg back in the '80s she was forced to beg for food. Then she met a man in a Main Street diner who introduced her to Madam Clarice Dubois and the rest, as she was fond of saying, was history. Within a brief time, guided by her new mentor, Melinda became Winnipeg's most famous, most desired, and most highly-priced prostitute.

Like Clarice had done for her, Melinda had taken Sarah under her wing, introducing her to the finer aspects of her trade, teaching her the tricks that drove men to ecstasy and kept them coming back for more. Sarah was an excellent student; the twenty per cent Melinda took from her and the other girls each week was enough to run the household. She had watched Sam and Sarah's infatuation with each other, never saying anything to either of them, hoping perhaps it wasn't as serious as she first thought. Yet over the past few months it was obvious to anyone with even the remotest understanding of human emotion that Sam Klein was miserable.

When she asked him about it, she got nowhere.

"Melinda, we get along, right?" he asked her.

She nodded.

"So why ruin it by bothering me about my private life. Sarah is one of your whores, plain and simple. I watch her like I watch the rest of the girls."

Her talk with Sarah was about the same. Maybe it was time to move on, Melinda had told her, painfully aware of what Sarah's departure would do to her finances. Had she talked to Klein about how he felt? The conversation had not gone particularly well. Sarah politely, but firmly, told her to mind her own business. She said she was handling things, that she would deal with Klein in her own way and on her terms. Melinda did not pursue the issue after that.

The three of them sat around the kitchen table in silence: Melinda pretending to be engrossed in the newspaper; Klein sipping his coffee and smoking, deep in his own thoughts; and Sarah stirring a cup of coffee, wishing Klein would pay more attention to her.

"What a group," Sarah finally said. "Did someone die? Hey, Sam, is there nothing to be happy about?" Klein ignored her. Sarah shrugged and turned to her madam. "Didn't we have a good night last night, Melinda? I think I must have seen at least ten clients myself."

"Eleven," Melinda murmured, looking up from the paper and catching Klein's eyes. They revealed little. He shifted in his chair and reached for his coffee cup.

"You know, Sam," continued Sarah in Yiddish, "my boss over there has given me the evening off. Maybe we can take in the show at the Orpheum. I hear the Five Armanis put on a great show. They have come to Winnipeg all the way from Paris. Their harmony and singing voices are supposed to be beautiful. Four of the brothers sing a selection of opera melodies, while the fifth plays the mandolin. Or, if you don't like that idea, how about some comedy at the Walker? The show is called 'The Midnight Sons'. It's a Lew Field's production from New York. There is dancing, singing by a company of long-legged women, a great vaudeville performance, as they say. What do you think? I'm sure Melinda will let you out too," she said looking in Melinda's direction.

"Are you talking to me?" Melinda asked with a bemused frown.

Sam glanced at both of them, but said nothing.

"I want to go to the theatre tonight," Sarah explained in English. "I could wear my new hat. Have you seen it yet Melinda?" she asked like an excited school girl. "I picked it up for nine dollars at Carsley's. The sales lady told me it's what they are wearing in New York and Paris. Wait, let me show you."

She left the room, ran down the hall and a moment later returned wearing a hat with a brim at least two feet wide. It was curled at the end and decorated with a large clump of red silk roses and strips of blue ribbon. Sarah's face was barely visible.

"It's beautiful," said Melinda, "Maybe I'll go have a look in the store myself. I need something new for Easter."

"What do you think, Sam?" Sarah asked in Yiddish. She turned around to face him. "Will it be the Walker or the Orpheum?"

"Neither," said Klein, also in Yiddish. "I was away all day yesterday and I have some work to do. The front window needs to be fixed." His words were measured and his tone without emotion.

"So what about tonight?" asked Sarah, savouring Klein's obvious discomfort. "I suppose you want to go to the Queen Theatre for a Yiddish play. I prefer English shows, they are more fun."

"Will you two please speak in a language I can understand?" asked Melinda.

"I'm sorry," offered Sarah. "I was only teasing Sam about wanting to attend the Yiddish theatre on Selkirk. Personally, I have no interest in seeing 'The Jewish Hamlet' or "The Greenhorn". Vaudeville is best. It's alive. Besides at the Walker or Orpheum, I can learn many more English words."

"You speak just fine, Sarah," Melinda assured her. "I can't believe how much better your English is now than when you first arrived here. You could hardly put two sentences together. Now listen to you."

"Thank you," said Sarah proudly. She turned to face Sam. "Are you going to give me an answer? Do we have a date for tonight?"

"Can't. I have personal business to attend to."

There seemed to be no point, in Klein's view, in explaining to Sarah about his family obligations. The truth was that the thought of yet another confrontation with his mother and sister made him both anxious and angry. He knew that Isaac would attempt to act as a mediator, as he always did, but he nonetheless anticipated the worst. Why couldn't people just accept that his life was his own to live?

"I see," Sarah said, running her fingers through her hair. "Well, you have a good time doing your personal business. I'll find someone else to spend the evening with."

Few people Klein knew could feel as sorry for themselves as Sarah Bloomberg. He accepted that she had some legitimate reasons for acting the way she did. Her memories from the old country were tainted by ugly experiences with an abusive stepfather. And until recently, her encounters with people in the New World were no better. But life was hard. In Klein's opinion, this self-pity was not one of her better qualities, though he usually tolerated it. Sometimes her pouting was even amusing. Not this morning, however.

"What's your problem, Sarah?" asked Klein, his voice rising slightly. "I said I have some personal business to look after, can't we leave it at that?"

"You know Sam," she said in Yiddish, "with that arrogant tone, you sound just like Meyervitz, before he used to beat me."

Klein shook his head. "Why does it always come back to that?" he replied, switching back to English. "I am not, nor will I ever be Meyervitz. If you can't tell the difference, well, there's nothing more to talk about."

He rose from the table, knocking his cup of coffee over. The lukewarm liquid dripped on to the floor. Cursing, Klein grabbed a rag from the counter.

"Forget about it, honey, accidents happen," Melinda said, looking at both of them. "To be honest, it's a bit too early for this. All of this arguing is going to wake everyone else up and there is nothing worse than a house full of cranky whores."

Sarah snickered, but Klein ignored the remark. He carried the soaked rag to the kitchen sink. "Listen," he said in Sarah's direction. "I don't have a choice. I have obligations you would not understand."

"And I have to get dressed," she said, getting up from the table.

"Right. Run back to your bedroom. That's what you do best," he muttered to himself, but loud enough for Sarah to hear.

She turned in the doorway and glared at him, yet said nothing. With other people, Klein knew when to keep his mouth shut, but with Sarah he couldn't resist getting in the last word.

"Well, that's a nice way to start your day," Melinda said after Sarah left. It bothered her to see Klein so miserable. Even though she had never given much thought to her relationship with Sam, she had grown fond of him over the years. There had never been anything physical between them, though the thought had crossed Melinda's mind from time to time. She wished she could advise him how to deal with women like Sarah, but she knew that he would have to sort that out for himself.

"You don't know the half of it. Damn, I don't know what happens to me when that woman is around."

Melinda laughed. "Let's just say, she gets under your skin."

"I suppose so."

"This personal business tonight. It has something to do with your family?"

Klein nodded. "You know what Passover is, Melinda?"

"Isn't that the holiday that you eat that cracker bread? I thought you liked all those Hebrew holidays," she said, stirring another piece of sugar into her coffee.

"Maybe when I was a kid in Russia. My mother forced me to go to *cheder*, Hebrew school, where the town rabbi, this huge man with a long white beard, taught me and my friends the Hebrew alphabet and instructed us on the stories from the Bible. At home, we kept the Sabbath and celebrated all the holidays."

Klein looked out the kitchen window. "I think I told you that my father died when I was very young."

Melinda nodded, a little surprised by Klien's sudden volubility.

"So I was the man of the house," continued Klein, "I had extra responsibilities. I used to like that."

"So what happened?"

"Everything changed when we left Mezherich and arrived in Winnipeg. I was fourteen years old and the man of the house — or at least I thought I was. The city was more exciting than anything I had ever imagined. So much to do, so much to buy. And I suppose, I was kind of embarrassed by the shack we then lived in over on Jarvis, by my mother's old country ways, her broken English."

"But you still feel like you have to take care of her?"

"Not so much take care of her as keeping in contact with her and Rivka. She is a tough woman, you know, bringing Rivka and me up by herself. Sure, Isaac was there to help her, but it mostly fell on her shoulders. It's funny when I think about it now, all I can remember about my mother from those early days is her sitting in a cold dark kitchen at her black

Singer sewing machine churning out gloves. Lousy piecework, it practically killed her. Life is too short. Sometimes, I think my sister Rivka is right," Klein said, lighting another cigarette, "the workers have to take responsibility for their own lives. Because no one else gives a shit. Look, women were burned to death last week in New York in a fire. Children are murdered in the streets..."

Rather abruptly, Klein stopped himself. Melinda too had read in the newspaper about last week's tragic fire in a New York City garment factory that had killed more than a hundred immigrant women, but she had not read or heard about any children being murdered.

"Sam, what are you talking about? Which children were murdered?"

Klein inhaled deeply on his cigarette and for a moment, he hesitated. "A little girl was murdered," he said quietly. "They found the body behind a shack on Dufferin. You know that old peddler Goldberg, he comes around here sometimes. He found the body and it wasn't pretty. Her neck had been slashed. I can't get the image of her lying there in the mud out of my head." He took a final drag and ground the half-finished cigarette into the metal ashtray.

Melinda shook her head. "You know, I can't figure out what's happened to this city. The North End has always had trouble. I can accept the drunks, the overcrowding, even the occasional theft, but a kid murdered.... Who would do such a thing? Do you know who she was?"

"No. But..."

"But what?"

Klein was certain that he had seen *teffilin* wrapped around that girl's neck, but it seemed so unlikely that now he began to doubt himself. He knew the way Melinda liked to gossip with the other girls. Why start a rumour about something that could, and probably would, turn out to be false?

"Nothing," he explained. "I did see McCreary there. I think he's in charge of the investigation."

"That son-of-a-bitch. Did he say anything to you?"

"Nothing important. He asked me if I knew anything about the killing."

"He's an asshole. After what you did to him last week, I'm surprised he didn't run when he saw you."

"Forget it. He was drunk. I just threw him out of here, that's all. He probably doesn't remember what hit him. But I should have been here sooner."

"It wasn't your fault, Sam. I asked you to find some booze. If anyone is to blame it was me. He seemed nice enough downstairs, but once he got up to her room...Christ, that bastard was an animal, biting her like that on her neck. Sarah could have been seriously hurt."

Klein looked out the window. "You ever think about why you keep doing this?"

"You mean why I run a whorehouse?" Melinda smirked.

"I guess," replied Klein quite seriously. "And put up with all this crap from the police, the reformers who smashed the window, the low-lifes."

"Money."

Now Klein smiled.

"No, honestly, I used to think about it, but not anymore," said Melinda sipping her cold coffee. "I figure that this is the way things were meant to be, and if that includes dealing with assholes like McCreary from time to time, so be it. I like my house, I like my girls, and I make a decent living. Believe it or not Sam, I'm happy."

Klein stared at her. Melinda truly didn't take abuse from anyone, including Bill McCreary. It was a good thing that McCreary was a cop, otherwise, Klein might have done something he would have regretted. As it was, he had to restrain himself to one clean punch in the face. And if anyone in Winnipeg deserved a worse fate, it was McCreary.

The Rudnicki family lived at 211 Stella Avenue in the upper floor of a small dilapidated two-story tenement that they rented for twenty dollars a month. In the house resided Igor, his wife Eva, and their three children, Michael, John and Anna. Eva's mother and Ivan Kopecki, a newly-arrived relative from the Polish village of Grodzisk, (outside of Warsaw) also lived with them in their three rooms.

It was as bad as any immigrant home in the North End: dark, dingy, and crowded. The soot from the wood stove blackened the walls and a variety of clothes and pots hung from rusted nails and a rope strung across the main room of the apartment. There was running water but no electricity. The combined smell of kerosene, sweat and garlic was pervasive throughout the dwelling; in fact, throughout the entire neighbourhood.

Since they arrived in Winnipeg five years ago, Igor had been employed as a labourer for the CPR lifting track and hauling freight. When he worked, and it wasn't every day, he averaged about thirty dollars a month. Eva worked as a cleaning woman four days a week for an English family on Stradbrook Avenue on the south side of the city. They paid her one dollar a day. With their expenses for rent, heat, food, street car fare, among other items, the Rudnickis barely made a living. But it was the way things were in the North End and they accepted it. Their children meant everything to them. When Anna ran away last night after she and Eva had an argument, her mother was sure she would return as soon as it became dark. But when she did not, Igor and the boys spent the night searching the streets. Their efforts were to no avail. Little Anna was nowhere to be found.

By the time Constable Stewart arrived at the Rudnickis', a small crowd of neighbours had gathered in front of the house silently standing in a vigil. Some of the women, wrapped in shawls with their heads covered by dark babushkas, held lit candles. The only sound that could be heard came from the upstairs window. The painful sobs of Eva Rudnicki echoed throughout the street. Men standing nearby in blue overalls and muddied black work boots quietly paced back and forth. News travelled fast in the North End, particularly if it was bad.

The crowd parted to allow Stewart to get through. He walked up the muddy path leading to the house and knocked on the side door. Within seconds, a tall muscular man with thin black hair came to the door. He was wearing dirty black pants held up by gray suspenders over a long-sleeve white shirt. He looked tired and his eyes were bloodshot.

"Mr. Rudnicki?" Stewart asked.

"Yes," he replied, his voice quiet.

"Are you the father of Anna Rudnicki?"

"Yes," said Igor, staring down at the ground.

"Mr. Rudnicki. I'm sorry to have to tell you this, but we believe your daughter has been killed. You will have to come with me."

Igor stood motionless. Then he heard his wife behind him. Eva Rudnicki was a thin, frail woman with long stringy blond hair. When she saw Stewart, she began to cry. Igor said something to her in Polish and she ran upstairs to her own mother, calling out Anna's name.

Igor Rudnicki turned back to Stewart. "A moment, and I will come with you."

Stewart hated this part of his job. Who wanted to tell a mother that her child had been murdered? During his police training, he had received lectures about dealing with the public and about the fine art of delivering bad news. "Be kind and considerate," he had been told, "remember you are there to serve the citizens of Winnipeg." But he had learned that such situations were usually worse than what he expected. He turned to look at the crowd and they stared right back at him. Still no one said a word. The silence was awkward and uncomfortable. Then, one man, maybe twenty years old, called out from the back.

"Is it true that you've arrested a Jew?"

"Yes, is it true?" several more asked.

"Now, folks," said Stewart. "We don't know who did this yet. We are questioning several people about the murder. The best thing for you to do is remain calm."

"The dirty Yids," the young man said again, "it had to be them."

There was a general grumbling among the group. The door finally opened and Igor Rudnicki, now wearing a suit jacket over his shirt, stepped out of his house. The crowd grew silent again as he walked into the street with Constable Stewart.

At the alley behind Ben Goldberg's shack, Detective Michael Stark and three police officers — Constables Robertson, Douglas and MacDonald — were conducting a search of the crime area. A wagon from the station had arrived and taken Anna's body. Stark had delicately removed the leather straps with the two small boxes and wrapped them in a white cloth. As soon as they turned the dead girl over, Stark saw a large knife with a silver handle. He picked it up and placed it on a piece of cloth. As he did so, he inadvertently allowed the cloth to rub the handle. Constable Robertson stood right beside him.

"What do you make of that, sir?" Robertson asked.

"I'm not sure, looks like some kind of engraving."

Using a stick, Stark turned the knife over several times so that he could get a closer look.

"You know, Robertson, I'd say that's a miniature of the ten commandments right there at the top," he said pointing at the handle with his stick.

Robertson nodded. Every officer on the force was aware of Stark's perceptiveness and success when it came to solving murders. "I'm sure you're correct, sir."

"Wrap it up in this sheet," Stark ordered, "and we'll examine it and the leather straps more closely after we check for prints."

Constable Robertson did as he was told. Stark knelt down to study the mud around the body, hoping to discover a footprint. A shout from Douglas interrupted him. As he stood up and turned, his right foot slid on the mud.

"Detective, over here, I've found something."

Stark quickly walked over to where the constable was standing. "What is it?"

The policeman pointed at an object half-buried in the mud. Stark took his stick and fished it out of the gumbo. Out came a muddied small blue silk bag. The detective held it up for a moment, but it was too dirty to examine properly. He took another piece of cloth from his inside pocket and wrapped the object.

A close check of the area near Ben Goldberg's shack revealed nothing further. MacDonald had canvassed the neighbours. Did they see or hear anything suspicious during the night? What could they tell them about Ben Goldberg? None of them heard or saw anything, or if they did, they were not talking about it. Everyone, except Mrs. Gertrude Bell who lived four houses away from the scene of the murder, vouched for Ben Goldberg's honesty and integrity. Mrs. Bell, on the other hand, was not so certain. "He lives alone in that hut, never has any visitors," she told MacDonald. "And, well, I don't like his kind, never have."

MacDonald thanked Mrs. Bell for her time and reported to Stark. "The fact that he lives by himself and is a Hebrew doesn't mean much," the detective mused.

"I guess not, sir, but you never know."

Stark ordered MacDonald to remain where the body had been discovered. He glanced around one final time and then, satisfied that he had done a thorough job, headed for Main Street. In his right hand, wrapped in cloth, he carried a knife and two ropes, the only clues to the grisly murder of Anna Rudnicki.

As fate would have it, Igor Rudnicki and Constable Stewart arrived at the Rupert Avenue station at precisely the same moment as Bill McCreary and Ben Goldberg. The four men stood opposite each other directly in front of the main entrance.

"Mr. Rudnicki, I am sorry for your loss," said McCreary, "Don't worry, we will solve the case."

Igor Rudnicki mumbled thank you and then noticed Ben, dressed in his tattered black suit. "This man, he killed my little Anna?"

"We don't know," the detective replied.

"You kill my little girl?" Igor asked Ben.

Ben shook his head several times. "No! No!"

But Igor didn't hear a word he said. Stewart quickly pulled Ben by his coat sleeve. Just as they reached the top of the stairs leading into the station, the distraught father leaped at the peddler. He grabbed him by the jacket and started yelling at him in Polish.

"*Morderswo, morderswo, ty zesh zabiw mojam czorkie!*"

Stewart ran back down the stairs and grabbed at Igor's arms. "Mr. Rudnicki, this is not the man. This is not the man."

But Igor refused to release his grip. "Murderer, murderer you killed my little girl," Igor repeated in English. "Yid, you will die too."

Ben was choking and gasping for air, his weak, thin arms flailed away in every direction. Finally, Stewart wrapped his arms around Igor's waist and tackled him to the ground. They both fell hard on to the sidewalk. Ben collapsed to his knees, trying to regain his breath.

McCreary did nothing. "Oh Stewart, you should've let them go at it," he said chuckling. "It was beautiful. A brawl between a Polack and a Jew. What a sight. Even the show at the Walker doesn't provide such entertainment."

"What ever you say, Bill," said Stewart, rubbing his bruised knee. "Maybe you could escort Mr. Goldberg inside while I try to calm Mr. Rudnicki."

McCreary yanked at Ben's arm and dragged him into the station. "C'mon, peddler." Stewart followed right behind with Igor.

Nearly one hundred members of the Winnipeg Police Force had moved into the new headquarters at the corner of Rupert Avenue and Louise Street three years ago. It was a large red-brick three-story building surrounded by police cars, motorcycles, horse-drawn paddy wagons, and dozens of bicycles. Inside amidst the oak chairs and mahogany desks there was plenty of office space, containing the most up-to-date police equipment, including a finger print lab and material for making moulds of footprints.

Most recently, the Board of Police Commissioners had decided to spend some money on a signal system. Using whistles obviously had limitations. McRae had heard of a call box system set up in Berlin and after some letter writing back and forth to Germany, he was convinced that it was the way to go. City electricians, with assistance from the Siemen's Dynamo Company in Germany, were busy drawing up the plans for an underground telephone cable system. The work was expected to take upwards of two years.

McRae's only real problem was keeping his men happy and in uniform. The average constable was required to work seven days a week, twelve hours a day — nine of which were spent on the streets. McRae figured that seventy-five per cent of his constables' time on duty was spent dealing with public drunkenness. Last year's crime statistics that the poker-playing troublemaker Colonel Porter had published in the *Telegram* in January had told it all: Of the six thousand crimes committed in the city in 1910, more than three thousand were for being drunk in the street, on the railway, even while driving an automobile. Who could blame his men for being fed up with their work? At a salary of $80 a month, many of the men were tired and frustrated — which was why so many of them frequently visited the ladies in Point Douglas. The force's morale was low and two or three constables were quitting each week. On top of this, McRae now had the murder of a child to solve.

Stewart led Igor to the second floor. The chief's office was the third door on the left. The constable told him to sit out in the hall in one of the wooden chairs. Now calmed down, Igor obeyed the policeman's command.

Ten minutes passed before Chief McRae entered the hallway, with Stewart right behind him. He extended his left hand towards Igor.

"My condolences on your loss."

"Thank you," mumbled Igor.

"So, Mr. Roodnowski...."

"Rudnicki, Sir," noted Stewart.

"Yes, of course. Mr. Rudnicki, I will have to ask you to accompany us to the doctor's office so that you can identify the body."

"I loved little Anna. Please find the people who did this terrible thing."

"I promise you we will do our best. Please come with me."

McRae led Igor Rudnicki out to the side of the building where his car was waiting, a red 1908 Model F McLaughlin-Buick. Igor hesitated.

"It will be fine, Mr. Rudnicki," said Stewart. "Autos are very safe. They don't buck or bite and certainly don't leave manure on the streets."

Igor nodded and forced a smile.

The chief had had the car shipped in from Oshawa two years earlier. It was a five-seater with a movable cloth roof and rubber wooden-spoked tires. It could reach a top speed of twenty-five miles per hour, but the chief rarely drove faster than fifteen miles per hour on muddy city streets. The Model F cost $1,400 and though it put a dent in the chief's bank savings, it was worth it. He enjoyed nothing more than taking a leisurely Sunday drive down Portage Avenue, the brass headlamps gleaning brightly in the sunlight. He kept the car at the police stables but spent as much time as he could caring for it as he would a child. The headlamps and trim constantly needed to be polished and the engine parts oiled regularly. Usually he'd send one of his younger constables to fetch him a can of gasoline from Ashdown's hardware store.

Igor reluctantly climbed into the backseat. The chief turned on the ignition.

"All right, Stewart, crank her up."

The constable walked around to the front of the car. He bent down and reached for the crank. "She's not in gear, Sir, is she?"

"Go ahead," demanded the chief, growing impatient.

"You'll recall last time I did this, the car was left in gear and when I cranked it, I almost was run over."

"Stewart," the chief bellowed.

Cautiously, the constable took hold of the metal crank and turned it twice before the engine sputtered to life. The auto jerked but stayed put. Stewart crawled into the left front seat beside the chief who was sitting behind the extended steering wheel on the right side of the vehicle. "Don't worry Mr. Rotowski," McRae shouted above the rumble of the car's noisy engine, "this will be a short ride."

The chief drove towards Main Street and the McIntyre Block at a steady speed of fifteen miles per hour. Igor Rudnicki sat in the back seat. One hand held onto his cap which was blowing in the April wind, the other tightly gripped the side of the car as the automobile putted along Winnipeg's muddy roads.

Detective Bill McCreary's desk was on the second floor in the middle of a medium-sized office, large enough for five other detectives besides him. Along the far wall, behind McCreary, was a bookshelf that ran from the floor to the ceiling. It was stacked with several rows of black leather bound binders. There was paper and newspapers strewn about the floor and a few lights hung low overhead.

McCreary sat down at his chair, removed his jacket, and lit a Roxboro cigar, the only kind he smoked. They were sweet, smelly and cheap—a box of fifty could be purchased at the Hudson's Bay Company store for two dollars. The chief frowned on smoking, though McCreary hardly cared. His desk was cluttered with papers and files. And, except for the ringing bell of a telephone every few minutes and the tapping of typewriter keys from the office next door, the station was relatively peaceful.

Two other detectives worked quietly in the far corner of the room. They glanced up when they saw McCreary, but continued with their work. There were only two windows in the office and both were closed. Before too long, the room was filled with cigar smoke and Ben found it hard to breathe. He undid the top button on his shirt collar.

"Don't die on me now, Goldberg," McCreary growled.

"Maybe you open a window?" asked Goldberg politely.

"Maybe. Hey John," McCreary yelled in the direction of the detective closest to the window, "can you open the window. Mr. Goldberg doesn't like my cigar smoke."

"Sure, Bill," answered the detective with a smirk, then walked out of the office.

McCreary fumbled around for a blank piece of paper and a sharp pencil. "Now, I want you to tell me once again exactly what you saw, in English, and don't leave anything out."

Slowly and methodically, Ben repeated his account of the discovery of Anna Rudnicki's body. Every so often, he lapsed into Yiddish, and each time McCreary scolded him to "bloody well speak Canadian". Ben said nothing about the phylacteries around her neck and arms.

"May I go now?" he asked once he was finished. "It's Passover tonight and I have many things to do."

"Not quite yet, old man. I have a few more questions and I don't give a damn about your holidays."

In fact, McCreary was quite certain that Ben was telling the truth; the peddler had not killed the girl. Neither Ben's personality nor his demeanour were those of a guilty man, let alone a murderer. McCreary had learned from years of dealing with liars and cheats that while they initially might be able to conceal the truth from him, they could rarely disguise their fear. Nevertheless, he suspected that there was something that Ben Goldberg was hiding from him. It was nothing Ben had said or done, just a lingering feeling in McCreary's gut. Call it detective's intuition.

"Now, you're sure that you did not hear anything the night before," asked McCreary again.

"Already, I've told you. I did not hear anything. I was asleep by about nine o'clock and did not wake until six the next morning."

"I see..."

At that moment Michael Stark walked into the office. He sat at his desk, next to where Ben Goldberg was sitting. Stark's working space was the exact opposite of McCreary's. It was as tidy as a desk could be: a pile of paper was to one side, files were neatly stacked, pencils were sharpened, and a grainy black and white picture of his son Christopher sat proudly in a gold frame.

Stark placed three wrapped objects gently on his blotter and removed the cloth sheets.

"This," he said holding up the long knife by its silver handle, "is the murder weapon. We found it right under her body." He pointed to the handle. "Look here, Bill, I believe this an engraving of the ten commandments with some strange markings."

"Michael, did you check that knife for finger prints?"

"It was in the mud. There wouldn't be prints."

"And I think you should know better than that. What's with you lately? Your mind doesn't seem on the job. Maybe you're getting too old for this line of work?"

"Don't worry about me," Stark snapped.

McCreary had worked with Stark since his promotion to detective seven years ago and despite the age difference between them they were an excellent team. Their status as the department's top two detectives was confirmed about four years ago when they had solved the murder case of Thomas Murray, a Winnipeg Street Railway employee who had been robbed and killed.

It had been late in the evening during the last run. The car was empty and Murray was on his way back to the garage when he picked up a man named Jake Tyson, a local gambler and hood. When the car reached McDermot and Main, Tyson, as he later confessed, jumped Murray from behind and ordered him to stop. The conscientious streetcar operator refused. Tyson pulled out a small pistol out of his pants pocket and before Murray could say another word, shot him through the heart. In all the confusion, the streetcar abruptly stopped, throwing Tyson out on to the street and his gun under a seat on the street car. Panicking, Tyson grabbed the money that Murray was so valiantly protecting — $47.12 — and ran, leaving his pistol behind.

Once the gun was discovered, it did not take Stark and McCreary very long to solve the case. Utilizing the new fingerprint system (brought into the city by Chief McRae after he had seen a Scotland Yard exhibit at the St. Louis World's Fair in 1904) the two detectives identified the prints on Tyson's gun. The gambler was arrested, convicted and hanged.

McCreary conceded that without Stark's expertise and knowledge of the city's underworld, this crime as well as many others they worked on together, probably would have gone unsolved. Yet lately, Stark had been slipping up, making mistakes and using poor judgment.

Only two weeks ago, Stark had forgotten to question a key witness in a robbery that they were investigating. Before McCreary could do anything about it, the man skipped town. When he asked Stark about it, the older detective told him to leave him alone — "to mind his own bloody business" were his exact words spoken in that distinctive Stark accent. Such a display of anger and impatience was also not Stark's style, or at least McCreary thought so. Now he was mishandling evidence in the biggest murder case to come along in Winnipeg in years.

The truth was that while McCreary had worked side by side with Michael Stark for seven years, he did not know him as well as he thought. Everyone in the department recognized that the two detectives were as dissimilar as night and day. Stark had spent his long career as a Winnipeg police officer doing everything by the book; McCreary was more than willing to bend the rules if it meant getting a conviction.

Unlike Stark, who lived in a small house in St. James with his wife, McCreary lived alone in a boarding house on Kennedy Street. He had no wife or children to come home to at the end of a shift. He had emigrated to Winnipeg from Glasgow with his family in the early 1880s and had spent six years walking the beat before being promoted. He was rougher around the edges than Stark; he worked hard, drank as much as he felt like, and answered to no one but himself.

Yet what distinguished McCreary from every other detective on the force, including Stark, was his acute understanding of the criminal mind. His years on the street had taught him how to read men. Instinctively, he knew when a suspect was lying. He also grasped the deviant personality traits that made men turn bad. Whereas Stark succeeded because of his dedication, keen sense and intelligence, McCreary ruled the streets of Winnipeg by instinct and intimidation.

Chief McRae, of course, knew all about McCreary's antics and while he did not always approve, he appreciated the detective's abilities. In an era when paying off a cop was all too routine, and when too many officers spent their coffee breaks at Winnipeg's infamous whorehouses on Rachel Street, the chief needed all the help he could get. So he put up with William McCreary.

"Now let me see this engraving." McCreary moved his face closer to the knife. "Appears to be Jew writing to me," he said with a tone of authority.

"Is this or is this not Jew markings?" McCreary demanded. Tentatively, Goldberg leaned forward and peered at the knife. "This," he said pointing to the engraving, "is a picture of *Asarah Hadebrot.*"

"In English," ordered McCreary.

"The ten commandments," Goldberg repeated.

"And that?" McCreary asked, pointing to three other markings.

"Those, I think, are Hebrew letters," answered Ben, "Yes," he said, after a closer examination, "I'm certain these are the letters *raishe, aleph,* and *daled.*" The detectives had no idea what he was talking about. "Like the letters R, A, and D," he explained.

"Is this some kind of special Hebrew knife or is it just a regular everyday one?" McCreary asked.

Goldberg hesitated. "I'm not sure."

There was always a moment in every interrogation, when McCreary could sense that the person he was questioning was about to break down and reveal their inner most secrets. Ben Goldberg was nearly at that point. A few more tough questions, and McCreary was positive that he and Stark would learn what the peddler was hiding from them. Then suddenly, and quite uncharacteristically, Stark interrupted McCreary's attack.

"Could I get you a glass of water, Mr. Goldberg?" Stark asked.

Ben nodded gratefully.

McCreary closed his eyes. "Stark, what the hell are you doing?"

"What does it look like? I'm getting the old man a glass of water."

Stark walked over to the window sill where there sat a jug of water. He poured Ben a drink and gave it to him.

"Could I speak to you, please," asked McCreary, his voice rising.

The two detectives left Ben with his glass of water and walked to the far side of the office.

"Will you tell me what the hell you're doing?" McCreary asked again.

Stark said nothing.

"First you tamper with the knife and now this. I am in the middle of an interrogation. This guy is about to talk. So why in God's name are you interfering?"

Now McCreary was speaking loud enough so that the other detectives in the office looked up from their work. It was not like Stark and McCreary to be arguing with each other. They were the team that everyone else tried to emulate.

"We both know the old man is not guilty," said Stark, "why not leave him alone? I don't think he knows anything more than what he has told you."

"And I think you are a damn fool," said McCreary, turning on his heel and marching back to his desk.

"All right, Goldberg," said McCreary, "what about this?" he demanded, holding up the blue silk bag with a pencil. Stark looked on in silence.

Ben hesitated. "I don't know. I don't know what —"

"— I think you do," barked McCreary. "And we are going to sit here until you tell me."

"I don't...."

McCreary grabbed Goldberg by his shirt collar and began to shake him. "I want to know what this is, you stupid Hebrew fool."

From the corner of the room, Stark moved quickly and pulled back McCreary's arm. "That's enough," he snapped. "Leave him alone. You want to know what this is, I'll tell you. It is a bag to hold *teffilin*. Now get your damn hands off of him." He pushed McCreary hard into his desk.

For a moment there was absolute silence in the room. The other detectives had stood up to watch the altercation between their two colleagues and were dumbfounded by what they had just witnessed. McCreary stared at his partner with a look of astonishment. Taking a deep breath, he straightened out his jacket and walked back to Ben.

"Is that what this is old man? A bag to hold *ta-fill-en* ?"

Goldberg nodded and looked into Stark's eyes. The detective glanced away.

McCreary grinned. "Very good guess, Michael," he said without turning his head from Ben. "Now which one of you wants to tell me what a *ta-fill-en* is ?"

Goldberg hesitated and glanced at Stark, but the detective remained silent with his arms folded. The peddler continued. "Leather thongs worn each day in morning prayer."

"Finally, we're getting somewhere," said McCreary. "Is that what these are?" he said, pointing to the leather straps on the table, "*ta-fill-en?*"

"Yes, yes, yes," Ben blurted out.

By this time, the mud on the bag had dried sufficiently and it was clear that there were markings on it similar to those on the knife. McCreary told Ben to remain in his chair for a little while longer.

"But there is nothing more I can help you with, and I must get ready for tonight," Ben pleaded.

McCreary turned to Stark. "Are you going to tell me how you knew what this bag was used for?"

"I've been around," Stark said quietly.

"That's it?"

"That's all I have to say about it right now."

"Have it your way, Michael. I would like to finish up with Mr. Goldberg. Why don't you take these three items to the fingerprint lab," he said pointing to the objects on the desk.

Without another word, Stark wrapped up the clues in the cloth and left the office.

The office and laboratory of George P. Hicks, the Winnipeg police department's resident finger print expert, was on the third floor, directly above the detectives' room. Finger printing had been widely used in China and later in India, long before European civilization discovered it at the turn of the century. Then Scotland Yard in London instituted the "Henry System", by which the ridge formations on the thumb were imprinted, collected, and classified. Such methods were first used in Winnipeg in 1905 and three years later Ottawa established the National Bureau of Identification.

A diminutive man, prematurely bald, with a neatly trimmed black moustache and round wire-framed glasses, Hicks was busy concocting a formula for a new powder when Stark arrived. Hicks's office was tiny, filled with all manner of bottles, vials and glass tubing. Off to one corner, a large test tube of some strange smelly liquid sat boiling slowly on top of an alcohol burner. Stark cautiously entered the lab, careful not to disturb any of Hicks's experiments.

"Be right with you detective," the chemist said, lifting his head for a moment before continuing with his work.

"What is that awful smell?" Stark grumbled, still upset by his confrontation with McCreary.

Hicks laughed. "Oh that, it's a mixture of sulphur and coal. I'm trying to develop a new kind of rubber."

"Does the Chief know you're doing this on his time?"

"No, and don't tell him."

Hicks set down the bowl he was mixing and looked up at Stark. "What do you have for me?"

"Items from a murder, discovered early this morning in the North End."

"Yes, I heard about it. A little girl."

"Throat slashed with a knife."

"What did you find?"

The detective unwrapped his sheets of white cloth to reveal the knife, leather straps and blue silk bag. "They're used in Jewish prayer," he said, noticing Hicks staring at the leather straps.

"Yes, I know. I've seen men wearing them in synagogue before."

"You've been to a synagogue?"

Hicks peered at Stark. "Don't sound so surprised. It's quite safe you know."

"I just never figured you knew any Hebrews, that's all."

"Our cleaning woman is Jewish. Part of the family really. She's been with us for years, helped raise George Jr. She invited Betty and I to her son's bar-mitzvah a few months ago. A bit strange, but a fascinating ceremony nevertheless. Did you know that until a Jewish boy reaches the age of thirteen, he is not actually responsible for his actions? Once he has his bar-mitzvah, however, he is considered an adult with all the responsibilities that entails."

"I have heard that."

Hicks paused, looked down at the three objects on the table and rubbed his chin. "You think a Jew committed this crime?"

"It appears so."

"As far as I know, they're rather law-abiding people, not like most immigrants, if you know what I mean."

Stark frowned. "I've spent a lot of time walking up and down the streets in the North End and I'll tell you something, all people commit crimes."

"I suppose so. Well, give me a few minutes and I'll check for prints."

As Hicks worked away, Stark leafed through the chemist's library, trying to forget about his altercation with McCreary. He wasn't sure what had come over him. Maybe it was that Ben Goldberg reminded him of his own grandfather. Whatever the reason, the murder of that little girl and McCreary's heated interrogation of the old man had troubled him, adding to his already tense and irritable state of mind.

He tried to put these thoughts out of his head as he continued to examine Hick's books. He was surprised to discover a collection of Arthur Conan Doyle's Sherlock Holmes stories nestled amongst the various chemistry tomes. He opened it and was astonished to see a personal inscription to Hicks from the author. Then Stark remembered that Conan Doyle had been in Winnipeg the previous year to visit a famous medium at Hamilton House who specialized in ectoplasm apparitions. The inscription read: 'To George Hicks, a rare man who understands the limits of science.' Stark was pondering the meaning of that statement when Hicks suddenly clapped his hands.

"We're in luck, detective. There isn't much on the bag or knife, but look here on the strap."

"Let me see," said Stark, walking over to the table.

Hicks picked up a brush with chemical powder, applied a little to the leather strap, and gently blew the residue away. "There, see that," he said to the detective, pointing at the strap.

Stark moved in closer. "Not much there, if you ask me."

"Nevertheless, it is a verifiable print. I can check the files to see if anything turns up. It will take until tomorrow, though."

"I understand."

"One more thing, before you leave," said Hicks.

"Yes?"

"I cleaned off the bag and found some markings sewn into the lining." He turned the bag inside out and showed the detective.

Stark nodded slowly. "Those are the same kind of markings as we found on the knife. They're Hebrew letters."

"Mr. Goldberg, " said McCreary, turning the bag inside out and holding it in front of Ben's face. "Can you tell me what this is?"

"I think so," replied Ben, his eyes avoiding contact.

McCreary handed him the blue bag and Ben examined it for a few minutes.

"*Daled, aleph, vav, vav, yud...*"

"So what does it say?"

"Wait. It is a name. Davidovitich, yes, Davidovitch." Then Goldberg realized what he was saying, and he gasped for air.

"Please, may I have another cup of water?"

"No, you cannot have water. Tell me, old man, who is Davidovitch?" demanded McCreary.

Ignoring McCreary, Stark handed Ben a glass of water.

"Thank you." Goldberg tried to calm down. "I...I know the name."

"You know who Davidovitch is?" McCreary demanded.

"Yes."

"Well?" snapped McCreary. His patience for both Ben's refusal to answer and Stark's odd behaviour had reached its limit. "Goldberg," he began slowly, "I'm asking you one final time, who is Davidovitch?"

Ben stared at the floor. "Rabbi Aaron Davidovitch. The *teffilin*, the bag, the knife, they all belong to Rabbi Davidovitch. He is the leader of the Shaarey Shamim synagogue on the corner of Pritchard and McGregor. I know him well, everyone does. He is a very important man in the community. He couldn't possibly...."

McCreary grinned triumphantly. "Very good, Mr. Goldberg. You are free to go now. We will be in touch later. And don't leave town — you will have to testify in court."

Goldberg did not hear a word the detective said. He looked out the window into the horizon, murmuring an ancient prayer.

3

He had slept little since that night. Even after he had thought about it carefully, he wasn't quite sure what had come over him. It had been a mistake, an accident. But long ago, he had learned that one plays the cards one is dealt. There was no looking back. He had a established a life for himself that he was not prepared to surrender. True, things had not been going as well as he had planned but the new money was going to fix all his problems.

They met in a secluded area of Victoria Park around dusk by an old oak tree. The spring air was damp and the ground wet. The large man was still in the dark brown suit he had worn the night of the murder; the other thinner one had changed to something more casual for this second meeting — gray cotton pants, a long-sleeved white shirt and a bowler hat.

Like the evening before, the conversation was not pleasant.

"So what about the money?" asked the large man.

"What about it? The way I see it, after what you did to that girl, I figure we're even. I wonder what the newspapers would pay for such a story."

The large man laughed, his eyes scanning the park for passers-by. Off to the right, an elderly man, surrounded by a collection of empty White Horse Whisky bottles, was sleeping soundly. Further away, a woman in a dress and shawl pushed her newborn baby in a creaky carriage. He waited until she was out of sight. "Are you threatening me?" he asked in a calm tone. Without waiting for a reply, he grabbed the thin man by the collar of his white shirt and drew him so close that their faces were only inches apart. The thin man could see speckles of dirt in his assailant's moustache and smell the same foul breath that Anna had.

"Listen to me, you son of a bitch," the large man whispered. "If I go down, you go down with me. You have one week to come up with the money you took from me. And if I hear you mentioning my name around, so help me God, I'll strangle you as easy as I did that girl. Do you understand?"

The thin man sneered, but his eyes revealed the fear within him.

"Good, then we are clear with each other." He released the man's collar. "Now what about the woman? Can she be trusted?"

"I think so."

"You think so? Well I don't. I have already hired your friend Smitty to keep an eye on her. He may have to deal with her."

"You really think that'll be necessary?"

Without bothering to reply to the question, he jabbed the thin man hard on the chest. "And another thing, I want you to call in every morning around seven o'clock. We may have further problems."

He strode away abruptly, leaving the thin man standing there frowning and rubbing his chest. Half-way across the park he passed the young mother and her baby, who had stopped to rest on a park bench.

"Evening, ma'am," he said tipping his hat.

"Evening, sir," she smiled back.

There wasn't a head that did not turn when Sarah made her grand entrance into the Walker Theatre that evening. She wore a frilly silk dress that accentuated her finer features. And the new wide-brimmed hat with the floral design that she had purchased at Carsley's nicely complemented her outfit. She did not normally consider herself to be vain, but that night she doubted that there was a more stunning woman in Winnipeg.

Unaccompanied, she made her way to the section of the theatre in the first balcony reserved for Winnipeg's "ladies of ill repute", as they were often referred to by the press ("ladies of the red glim variety", "members of the elite sorority of sisters", and "inmates of houses of ill fame" were other favourite euphemisms for journalists who couldn't bring themselves to use the term prostitute in print). She ignored the spiteful looks directed at her by the prim and proper wives of the middle class. Instead, she accepted the furtive glances of their husbands.

A half-dozen prostitutes from other houses in Point Douglas greeted her arrival in the balcony as if she was royalty. They, too, wore colourful and revealing dresses and wide-brimmed hats of every size and variety. But Sarah stood out, first among equals.

"Please, ladies," she implored them with a smile, "I want no special treatment tonight."

"Nonsense," they roared. "Sarah, you are the princess. There is no finer whore in all the land."

Laughing with them, she took her seat just as the curtain rose. Sarah loved vaudeville and there was no better place to see it in the city than at Corliss Power Walker's luxurious theatre which he had opened in 1907. The show that evening, Lew Field's "The Midnight Sons", was a musical performance featuring beautiful dancing girls in silk tights, burlesque comedy routines and spectacular stage settings. It also included a magical banquet scene in which more than fifty performers — singers, dancers, acrobats and comedy actors — participated all at once, mesmerizing Sarah and every other member of the audience.

Amidst the theatre's Edwardian decor with its rosetted lights, crystal chandeliers and crimson plush seats, she began to feel more at ease. She wished Sam had accompanied her, but he had, once again, stubbornly refused. To hell with him, she thought, and his personal commitments. It was his loss. Soon, the hilarity and lively music on the stage allowed her to forget her earlier argument with Sam.

Unfortunately, her other more pressing problems were less easily dismissed. She was playing a dangerous game, she knew that. But the payoff was too tempting. Besides, she couldn't stop things now even if she wanted to. Still, she wondered how she had got mixed up in such a venture and with such a partner. She felt ill every time she was close to him. She had hoped an evening at the Walker would be a good distraction.

During the intermission, she left her seat and was on her way to the Ladies restroom on the main floor when she noticed a heavy-set man with a black beard staring at her. He was standing by himself in a corner of the theatre not far from the rear exist. In his dirty coveralls, he hardly looked like a typical theatre patron. Nevertheless, out of habit, Sarah smiled at him, but he did not return her friendly and flirtatious gesture. She thought nothing of it, powdered her nose and returned to her seat to enjoy the second part of the show.

An hour later, she was out on the street milling about in the crowd and reviewing the highlights of the performance with her friends. Then out of the corner of her eye, she saw the bearded stranger again and this time, he began to move towards her. From the grim look on his face, Sarah did not think he was a potential client. Her first instinct was to get far away from him. She wasn't sure what he wanted, but she had a bad feeling about him. She quickly bid farewell to her friends and began to walk down the street. She glanced over her right shoulder and could see the man aggressively pushing his way through the crowd.

Half a block away, Lyle Korsen was patiently waiting for her behind the wheel of his black Packard. An old friend of Sam's from Flora Avenue, Lyle often drove Melinda's girls around the city. Melinda paid him $20 a month to be on call and Sarah often used his services.

Sarah ran towards the car. "Lyle, over here" she called out.

Seeing Sarah, the chauffeur immediately got out of his auto and opened the rear door.

"Thank you," she said, out of breath as she climbed into the back seat. "Quickly, let's go. There is a man following me and he doesn't look friendly."

Lyle was not a large man, but he could handle himself in a fight if he had to. He surveyed the area. "There's lots of people, Sarah, but I don't see anyone running after you. You drink too much whisky tonight?"

Sarah searched the faces of the crowd herself, but the bearded man was now nowhere to be seen. "Forget it Lyle, just take me home."

"Anything you say Ma'am."

As the Packard putted along Main Street, Sarah stared into the darkness. She had not had a drop of whisky that night and she knew what she saw. That man was after her and she was certain that she had not seen the last of him. Just as she was sure about who had sent him to watch her.

A few minutes later, Lyle stopped the car in front of Melinda's house.

"Thank's Lyle. Guess I was imagining that stranger," Sarah said. "Maybe he was just an anxious customer."

She hardly sounded convincing but the driver merely nodded. "Good night Ma'am. You go into the house. I'll wait until you're inside."

"No need. I'm fine."

But Lyle stayed put.

As Sarah made her way down the walk and into the house, she did not see the figure lurking in the shadows across the street.

"Why is this night different than all other nights?" asked young Alexander Silverman in Hebrew. "Because," answered Isaac Hirsch in Yiddish, "tonight is the night we remember the exodus of our people from Egypt."

Klein would have given little Alexander another answer. Tonight is different, he thought, because he had already sat around the table for more than a hour with his family, and no one had questioned him about his ill-chosen, misbegotten life. But he knew there was still time for that.

The Passover *seder* at his mother's home on Flora Avenue was a typical Klein family gathering. The Silvermans, Lou, Sybil and their two children, Alexander and baby Mia from next door, were invited as they always had been since they had moved into the neighbourhood a few years ago.

Sam's mother Freda and her cousin Clara Hirsch, both resplendent in their new T. Eaton Company dresses with silk lace yokes and pleats trimmed with buttons and braid, had prepared a meal fit for the King of Israel — *gefilite* fish, chicken soup with *knaidalch*, turkey, Passover *kugel*, *tsmiss*, and Freda's famous *farfel* apple pudding. Freda, who had always sewn her own clothes for as long as she could remember, had reluctantly accepted Isaac's Passover gift: a shopping trip downtown to any store the women wanted. They chose Eaton's with its wide aisles filled with all types of merchandise — clothes, hats, jewelry and French perfume. For both of them, long time residents of the North End, the journey to Eaton's was a like a trip to another world, a Gentile world of high fashion and strange tastes and sounds.

Normally, Freda Klein preferred to shop in the small, noisy and crowded stores along Selkirk Avenue. There, like in *di alte heym*, the old country, merchants spoke Yiddish, Polish, Ukrainian or Russian —languages Freda had mastered as a young child — and it was possible to purchase goods on credit. She would spend an afternoon buying kosher chicken from Harry Blutstein, visit with Clara at Isaac's hardware store, maybe even have a cup of tea at Sam Magid's sandwich shop.

In any event, the day at Eaton's with Isaac and Clara had been delightful. She had chosen a beautiful rose coloured dress with a floral pattern, while Clara had opted for one in a deep King's Blue. Still, Freda had nearly refused the present when she saw the price tag; Isaac paid a total of thirty dollars for both garments. No matter how much she protested, Isaac insisted she accept it and Isaac had a way of winning an argument. The two women proudly carried their white wrapped packages on to Portage Avenue.

Nothing was ever said, nor was there ever any discussion, but each year at the Klein *seder* everyone sat in exactly the same place around the table. The hierarchy was clear. The Silvermans were at the end, because they were both young and had children. Klein's sister Rivka sat next to Sybil Silverman. It had taken Lou, who worked as a salesman at Meltzer's furniture store on Selkirk, more than a year to save the twenty-five dollars for the outfit. But it had been worth the effort when he saw the look of astonishment on Sybil's face the day he presented it to her. The long narrow skirt reached the floor, but the jacket was much shorter, reflecting the latest trend in women's clothing.

Only Rivka — much to Freda's dissatisfaction — arrived at the *seder* wearing the drab grey blouse and ankle-length skirt she wore to work each day at the Dufferin Avenue garment factory. Both Rivka and Sybil were close to the kitchen door so that they could more easily serve the food. Freda and Clara were beside them supervising. At the head of the table, like the master of a royal household, sat Isaac Hirsch, a looming presence with a thick black mustache. He wore his finest black suit. Klein sat to his immediate right as his prince consort. Though not an orthodox Jew, Isaac nevertheless wore a *yarmulke*, day and night. Isaac claimed it was to honour his grandfather. But when they were younger, Klein and and his sister Rivka used to joke that Isaac merely wanted to hide his bald patch.

As usual, Yiddish with a sprinkling of Hebrew and English was spoken around the table.

"So, Isaac, did you hear?" asked Freda in between mouthfuls, "Rivka has been dating Saul Schwartz."

"The son of Misha Schwartz, the cattle buyer?"

"Yes," Freda beamed.

"A fine family. I know the father well. He's a good businessman."

"Mother, please," said Rivka from the far end of the table, "we are only friends. There are more important things in life besides marriage."

"Such as?"

"The plight of the workers who toil for for capitalists and get nothing for their labours."

There was a groan from Isaac.

Ignoring the reaction, Rivka continued. "In Russia, only six years ago, the workers nearly overthrew the Czar. There are strikes by workers breaking out all over North America. In New York, twenty thousand women, nearly all Jews, challenged the owners of the shirt-waist makers factories. And even here in Winnipeg, the Street Railwaymen's Union walked out."

Everyone around the table stared at Rivka in silence. Klein grinned to himself. He was proud of his sister, proud of how hard she worked and how she had educated herself. Rivka worked ten hour days as a sewing machine operator for a grand total of one dollar and sixty cents. Though she and Freda argued incessantly, Rivka was devoted to their mother. Klein was not as committed as Rivka to the idea of a socialist utopia, but he respected his sister for sticking to her principles.

"Did you hear that?" asked Freda looking at Isaac. "Where does she get such ideas? In my day if a girl had *mazel*, she found a husband and raised a family. Period. Twenty-seven years old and not married...It's all that reading you do, Rivka. It puts these strange thoughts in your head. When was the last time you were at synagogue?"

Isaac raised his right hand and the conversation immediately halted. Klein had long been amazed at this power Isaac wielded, particularly over his mother. As a teenager, he admired Isaac for both his strength of character and his success as a businessman and community leader. With no children of his own, Isaac was the closest thing he and Rivka had for a father. No problem was too great for him to solve. Nonetheless, both he and Rivka were often troubled by the way their mother deferred to Isaac's authority.

Rivka suspected that Freda was in love with Isaac and may even have had an affair with him, but Klein would not speak of such things. He did notice, of course, that Isaac and his mother spent much time together at the store, not doing anything in particular, just enjoying each other's company. And he could not help but wonder what Isaac's wife Clara, Freda's cousin alone at home, thought of this.

From his perspective, though, it was not the mutual attraction — the touching, laughter, and warmth — that stood out in Klein's memory. Rather it was an inexplicable feeling Sam had that Isaac acted out of love as well as obligation. On the subject of Isaac Hirsch and her relationship with him, however, Freda Klein was silent.

"Hush," she would tell her children whenever they questioned her about it, "if it was not for the kindness of Isaac Hirsch, we would still be in the old country and you, Sam, would be serving in the Czar's army." With that bromide issued, she would return to her small stool by her sewing machine in the corner of the kitchen.

And it was true. Isaac had provided the Kleins with the necessary funds for their journey from their home in Mezherich, a small town in the province of Volhynia not far from Rovno, to Winnipeg. At the time, in the winter of 1897, Sam was fourteen years old, Rivka a year and a half younger. The trip had been long and dangerous. A local farmer had taken them in his wagon west to the Austro-Hungarian border. They had waited until nightfall to run to the village on the other side. Three hours later, they were on a train heading for Vienna. By the next morning they were as far as Hamburg.

With the assistance of one of Isaac's contacts there, a German named Mueller, Freda was able to purchase tickets for the trip to America. It took another week for them to get out of Germany and they almost lost Rivka. Yet even then, Sam was clever and resourceful. Mueller had told them to go on without her; he promised to send Rivka once the authorities had released her from quarantine. But Sam refused. To keep the family together he bribed an official with the little money his mother had left and secured Rivka's release. A month later, the Kleins were in Winnipeg.

"I think," Isaac began slowly, "that Rivka has the right to decide her own life." Freda Klein shook her head. "But," he continued, "a Jewish daughter should also respect the wishes of her mother." Now Rivka remained silent, while Freda nodded in agreement.

"How is it that you are so wise, Isaac?" asked Klein, with a hint of sarcasm.

"And why is it you bring so much shame on our family?" asked Freda. "Living and working in that house, with those dirty women." She made a gesture with her lips as if to spit on the floor.

"This is not the time to talk of such things," Klein declared. He took out his silver cigarette case from his inside pocket, selected one and lit it.

"Shailek," Isaac said, using Sam's Yiddish name, "I love you like a son, but I have to agree with your mother. What would your father, *a la vashulem*, say if he could see you now? He was a good man your father, a hard worker and a decent provider."

Isaac stood up and walked beside Freda, placing his hands on her shoulders. She patted his hands and looked up at him. "Sam, why not leave that house, that brothel, and come work with me, as a partner. The hardware store will be yours one day, you know that."

Klein shook his head. "Isaac, please do not misunderstand me. I appreciate the offer," he said, inhaling on his cigarette, "but like Rivka, I have to live my life the way I see fit. And if that upsets my mother or you, so be it."

Amidst the white smoke hovering over the table, Freda rose from her chair, glaring at her son. "Shailek, this is a terrible thing to say. I'm thankful that your father is not here to see this."

"Mama, don't say that," pleaded Rivka.

Without another word, Freda Klein marched into the kitchen, with Clara Hirsch right behind her.

"Enough," ordered Isaac, resuming his place at head of the table, "we must finish the *seder*."

Alexander Silverman sang a Hebrew song about Moses that he had learned at *cheder*, while his proud parents beamed. The boy's voice was melodic and soothing and seemed to have a calming effect on the group. Klein butted one cigarette and lit another. He contemplated how different his life might have been had his father not been killed. Klein did not remember him, nor even knew what he looked like. He had only been a young child when his father had died in a freak accident. All Klein knew was that he had been trampled by a runaway horse pulling a wagon. His mother rarely spoke of it or about his father's family.

The moment had arrived in the *seder* to offer a prayer and open the front door of the house for Elijah the prophet. This was Freda's job. Upon Isaac's command, she began walking to the door, when suddenly and unexpectedly there was a loud knock.

"It is Elijah," joked Lou Silverman.

Freda froze, unsure what to do. She looked at Isaac for direction.

"Go ahead," he smiled, "open it."

She turned the handle and pulled the front door open. There before her on the porch stood half the members of the Shaarey Shamim Synagogue board: Ruben Sokolov, Louis Finkelman, Joe Abramavitch, and Avram Zelkin. Isaac rose from the table to greet them.

"Come in gentlemen, what are you doing here? It's *Pesach*. You should be with your families." The men said nothing. "Ruben, Lou, are you going to tell me what this is about?" demanded Isaac.

Ruben Sokolov, a short bald man with a gray beard, stepped forward. "Isaac, as president of the board, we thought you should know immediately—"

"—Know what?"

"It's the police. They have arrested Rabbi Davidovitch."

"Arrested Aaron Davidovitch! For what reason?"

The men looked at each other. Sokolov raised his voice in indignation. "They say he murdered a little Polish girl."

The next morning, his head aching from a late night of too much wine, smoke and arguing, Klein pulled himself out of bed and stepped on to the cold wooden floor in his room. "Could've been anywhere in the world, but Siberia is where I end up," he muttered. He dressed in a pair of brown pants held up by suspenders over a navy-striped shirt. He found the jacket Sarah had bought him at Eaton's as a peace offering after one of their recent altercations, and tip-toed out of the house in search of a newspaper.

The events of last evening still bothered him. How could the police have arrested Rabbi Davidovitch for the murder of that girl? He had seen the mangled body. There was no possibility that any rabbi he knew had done this terrible deed. He lit a cigarette, determined to push the whole episode out of his mind.

It was a brisk walk to the corner of Main and Euclid. As usual, he found Gus standing there shivering with his bag of newspapers.

"Morning to you, Sam," the old man said. "A bit nippy out, don't you think. It's the kind of day you need something strong to drink."

"Sorry Gus, I didn't bring anything with me. Just want a paper. The Trib will be fine."

Klein threw him a dime and told him to keep the change.

"That's very generous of you Sam, you're a good man. You hear about Caponi's fight with McLaglen?"

"Yeah, I'd say the better man won."

Any other day, Klein would've been glad to chat with Gus about the Winnipeg boxing scene, about how the city's own Tony Caponi had beaten Fred McLaglen, the self-proclaimed middleweight champion of Canada. Klein was a boxing fanatic. Since he had come to Canada, he had followed the sport religiously, attending bouts in the city whenever they were held. He was well-acquainted with promoter Jack Cancilla and knew most of the local fighters as well. But this morning, even if he refused to admit it, he had other things to think about.

The story Klein was searching for was impossible to miss. It took up the entire top half of the front page, headlined in big, bold letters: NINE YEAR-OLD POLISH GIRL MURDERED, POLICE ARREST RABBI. It was written by the *Tribune* reporter with the initials, "J.M." Klein knew that this had to be the work of John Maloney, once one of the most prominent journalists in the city. But a failed marriage and a lot of liquor had nearly ruined his career. Now Maloney was a regular at Melinda's — he had a standing appointment with Amy, twenty-two, blonde, and buxom — and the short, balding journalist had not impressed him. He drank like a fish and he once tried to leave without paying (though as Klein later heard from Amy that night, he wasn't up to the task under any circumstances).

According to the *Tribune's* story, Detectives William McCreary and Michael Stark arrested Rabbi Aaron Davidovitch, leader of the Shaarey Shamim synagogue on Pritchard Avenue, at his home last evening during the Passover *seder*. "Though the police as yet will not reveal the evidence against the rabbi," read Klein, "Police Chief McRae said that the decision was not made lightly and that more details will be made available to the public once the suspect has been formally charged in court."

They must know about the *teffilin*, Klein thought, but what is the connection to Davidovitch? It didn't make sense.

To the right of the main story under a hazy photograph of Anna Rudnicki was a sidebar on the murder itself and the Rudnicki family. In vivid detail, it described how Anna's throat had been slashed and a strange circular pattern carved on her stomach; how she had been tied in leather straps, left in the mud, and how her young life had been snatched from her.

There were interviews with her teachers and neighbours. It was all routine, except for the last two paragraphs.

"The crowd outside the Rudnicki house on Stella grew larger as the day progressed," read Klein with mounting horror. *"Told at approximately 10:00 p.m. that Rabbi Davidovitch had been arrested for the crime, the crowd turned ugly. Screams of 'kill the Yids' and 'Jews suck the blood of our children' could be heard. If not for the presence of several Winnipeg constables, matters could have gotten out of hand."*

"Asked why he thought a rabbi could have committed such a crime, Ivan Podolski, a Polish businessmen in attendance, replied: "For centuries, Jews have been murdering our children. Why not in Winnipeg? It is the blood. They want their blood; they need the blood of Christian children for their Passover bread. They use our children's blood in their strange rituals. That's why Anna was killed."

Klein sat down on the curb. He reread the last paragraph several times before it sunk in. He knew what Podolski's blood accusation meant. Every Jew feared the blood libel. Klein, himself, had lived through the terror once many years before.

He had only been eight or nine at the time. A week before Passover that year, the mangled body of a ten-year old Christian boy had been discovered twenty miles outside of Rovno. His neck had been slashed and the blood drained from his body. When a Jewish liquor merchant was arrested for the murder, there were riots in Rovno and the surrounding villages, including Mezherich. Klein's mother kept him and Rivka locked up for days. The nights were especially frightening. Stones flew through the windows and there was banging on their door. Klein remembered thinking it was the end of the world. Months later, it was determined the young boy had been killed by a gang of thieves, though that made no difference to the peasant population who had taken out the frustration of their miserable lives on the local Jews.

And now, Klein thought, the tribal memories of the blood libel were being raised in Winnipeg. If Maloney was any kind of reporter, he should have repudiated such nonsense immediately. Besides the sheer absurdity of the charge, Klein well knew from his lessons at *cheder* that according to Jewish law, Jews were not permitted to consume blood. That was why kosher butchers went to such lengths to drain all blood from the animals they slaughtered. Instead, Maloney printed the accusation without qualifications which, when Klein thought about it further, was not that surprising. As Klein heard it, Maloney was desperate to restore his tarnished reputation and a blood libel story was both sensational and dangerous. It was bound to get him a lot of attention.

By the time Klein returned to the house, Melinda, Sarah, Amy and a few other girls were having a breakfast of Cream of Wheat and white bread soaked in molasses.

"Where have you been?" asked Melinda, sipping her coffee, "The phone has been ringing all morning for you."

"Who's looking for me?"

"Isaac Hirsch."

"Isaac? I wonder what he wants."

"Say, honey, you look like you've seen a ghost. What happened?"

"Here, see for yourself." Klein threw the newspaper down on the table and lit a cigarette. The tips of his tobacco-stained fingers were raw and cold from being outside. He warmed his hands near the kitchen stove.

"Sam, you okay?" asked Sarah.

He shrugged.

"The police arrested a rabbi for killing that girl!" gasped Melinda.

"What girl? Who was murdered?" asked Sarah.

She was about to read the story in the paper when the phone rang again.

"Sit there. I'll get it," Klein told her. He picked up the black receiver and held it to his ear.

"Sam, is that you?" Isaac asked in Yiddish.

"It's me," he replied in English, "What's going on?"

"You've seen the newspaper this morning?"

"I've seen it."

"I have called a board meeting for two o'clock this afternoon at this store. Some of the members would like you to be there. Will you come?"

Klein hesitated.

"Shailek," Hirsch said. "We need your help. The police will not listen to us. Think of the rabbi and his family, not to mention every Jew in Winnipeg."

"I'll think about it."

"Two o'clock, Sam. Please be there."

"Again, I want to hear it one more time," demanded McCreary. He hovered over his suspect, a slight man with a salt and pepper beard who was dressed in a black suit. White fringes called *tsitsis* hung down the man's pant legs, and he wore a large black *yarmulke* on his head.

"I've told you everything I know," said Rabbi Aaron Davidovitch. He spoke impeccable English, one of seven languages in which he was fluent. As a young man, he had studied at the great *Yeshivot* in Grodno and Slabodka in Lithuania. At the age of twenty-one he been ordained a rabbi and had emigrated to Chicago, where within a few years he had learned to speak English like a native American. He arrived in Winnipeg in 1902 to take up his post at the Shaarey Shamim. "Please detective, let me call my family and friends."

"Were you or were you not in the vicinity of Dufferin and Main Street at approximately 6:30 p.m. the night the girl was killed?"

"And if I was?"

"Rabbi, please, just answer the question," said Michael Stark, sitting on a stool in the corner of the small room.

The interrogation had been going on for about two hours and McCreary had to admit that little progress had been made. He had done everything by the book — so far. No shouting and nothing physical. The chief had made it clear that this was one case that had to be handled carefully.

The arrest of the rabbi was carried out in the late evening. According to the plan approved by the chief, McCreary and Stark — accompanied by a group of a dozen constables — had barged in on the Davidovitch family's Passover celebrations. The rabbi was handcuffed, brought to the station, fingerprinted, and placed in a small windowless room on the third floor close to the jail cells. They left him there alone for four hours. Most men would have been intimidated, but it was becoming increasingly clear to McCreary that Rabbi Davidovitch was stronger than he looked.

"In answer to your question," said the rabbi. "Yes. Every day after our dinner I make it a habit to take a stroll by myself. It is true, I was near Dufferin and Charles around 6:30, though I saw no one and heard nothing."

"I see," said McCreary, bringing his chair closer to where the rabbi was sitting in the middle of the room. "You're the religious leader at the, what's the name of that Hebrew church?"

"It's called a synagogue," said Stark.

"You are just a wealth of information about Hebrews," McCreary said. "You related to any? That's it, isn't it? You've got Jew blood running through your veins."

Stark ignored the remark.

"Gentlemen, if I may answer the question," interrupted Rabbi Davidovitch. "I am the rabbi of the Shaarey Shamim congregation."

"Right. And your duties include?" asked McCreary.

"I perform duties similar to any priest. I am the spiritual leader, and involved in the education of the young. I am also responsible for overseeing that meat and chicken are properly prepared according to Jewish dietary laws."

"Yes, tell us about that." McCreary's voice was calm, but there was an obvious tension in each word he spoke and every question he asked. The inner struggle to control his anger and the hostility he felt towards his Jewish suspect was gradually rising to the surface.

The rabbi shifted his body, trying to draw himself away from the detective's face. "There is nothing to tell. At certain times each week, I visit the kosher butcher shops in the North End to ensure that the killing is done properly. A prayer is said before the animal is slaughtered. In Hebrew, it is called the *shechitah.*"

"How exactly is the animal killed?"

"The animal is placed in a wooden stock so that its head is locked. The *shochet* or ritual slaughterer then swiftly cuts the animal's throat. It is raised by its hind legs, the head is removed and the bleeding completed. The body is then split open and the lungs are checked for any defects. If there are none, the meat is declared to be kosher."

"And you check the lungs yourself?"

"Often, yes. Such inspection is necessary, detective," explained the rabbi, "an animal with a lung defect is unfit and cannot be eaten."

"That's fine," said McCreary. "And this slaughtering is done with a special ritual knife, correct?"

"Yes, a *challaf.* "

"Rabbi, you are trained to kill the animals in this way. Is that right?"

"Most rabbis are."

McCreary picked up a white bundle next to his feet. "Now, rabbi," he said, unwrapping the cloth. "How do you explain the fact that these three items, all of which you have already admitted belong to you, were found at the scene of the crime. These *ta-fill-en* as you call them, around that little girl's neck and arms. And most importantly, this knife, this *cha-laff* used to slice her neck. This is a ritual knife used to slaughter animals, is it not?" he asked, holding the silver-handled knife in front of the rabbi's nose.

For a moment, a look of astonishment swept the rabbi's face when he saw his belongings, then he relaxed again. "Yes, that is my *teffilin* and my *challaf.* That knife has been in my family for generations. It belonged to my grandfather's grandfather."

McCreary leaned forward, his voice almost friendly. "Is it not true, rabbi, that you cut the neck of that little girl precisely how you slice the neck of a cow? For some sick reason I haven't figured out yet, you murdered her, didn't you?"

The rabbi's expression did not change. "No, I did not do this. About a week ago, there was a robbery at the synagogue, at which time I notified the police. I went to the station and an officer took down the information. I checked two more times, but was told that nothing had been found."

"Because, Davidovitch," McCreary said standing up, "there was no robbery and there is no police report, we've already checked. You're a damn liar. I know about your kind. Liars, cheats and moneylenders."

Rabbi Davidovitch stared directly into McCreary's eyes. "Let me ask you this, detective," Davidovitch began, speaking slowly and clearly. "What possible reason could I have for killing that girl?"

"The newspapers say its some sort of twisted Hebrew ritual. That you need the blood of Christian children."

"Medieval nonsense."

"Perhaps. But, to be honest, it makes no difference to me. We have the murder weapons and an eye-witness placing you at the scene." McCreary reached for his note pad. "A Mrs. Doris Szchoweski of 290 Dufferin claimed she saw a man matching the your description walking the street at about 6:30 p.m. on the night of the murder. It'll be enough to convict you."

For McCreary, the interrogation was over. "You got anything you want to add?" he asked, looking in Stark's direction.

Stark shook his head. "No," said the older detective, his face closed and unreadable. "Just like you said. Open and shut case."

The rabbi gazed at Stark, but remained silent.

"My feelings, exactly," said McCreary. "Stewart," he shouted. "Get in here."

Constable Bob Stewart appeared at the door to the interrogation room.

"Lock the prisoner up," ordered McCreary.

Stewart helped the rabbi to his feet. "A moment please, officer." Rabbi Davidovitch turned and walked directly to Stark. He moved close to him and whispered in his ear. Neither McCreary nor Constable Stewart could hear what was said.

A moment later, Stark pushed the rabbi away. "You don't know what you're talking about, leave me alone. Stewart, what the hell are you waiting for? Get this man out of here."

"What's going on, Michael?" McCreary demanded.

"Nothing, the man is crazy. Forget about it." Stark fixed his bowler hat and walked out of the interrogation room.

McCreary slumped in a chair. "I need a drink," he said to no one in particular.

Constable Stewart led the rabbi down a dimly-lit corridor to the jail. He glanced down at the older man, a look of pity on his face.

"Do not feel sorry for me, officer. It is the Lord's will that I be here. So be it."

Following Stewart, Rabbi Davidovitch passed through one barred black steel door and into the cell block. The smell was foul and the air was thin. The rabbi covered his mouth with the end of his black suit jacket.

In the first cell, a drunken man had passed out on the floor, a pool of vomit by his head. Rabbi Davidovitch looked straight ahead. The constable stopped in front of cell number three.

"I'm sorry about this, rabbi. Why don't you make yourself comfortable," he said as he led his prisoner inside.

"Constable Stewart, isn't it? Do I know you? I have the feeling we've met before."

"No, sir," said Stewart.

"Well, constable, this is not your fault."

Stewart opened his mouth to say something, then shrugged and walked out. He closed and locked the cell door.

The cell was tiny. There was a small filthy basin for water and a crude toilet, just as dirty. The rabbi sat down on the bottom bunk chained to the wall. It was covered by a gray thin blanket on top of a piece of board. There was a thin pillow covered with a thin black and white striped cloth. There was one light high above the bed fastened in a wire mesh.

Aaron Davidovitch had been detained only once before in his life and that was many years ago. As a boy, he had witnessed a robbery of a shopkeeper in Zhitomir and was brought in for questioning by the local authorities. It had not been a pleasant experience; he had been cuffed on the face and threatened. Now, as then, he placed himself at the mercy of God.

He stroked his beard and stared through the barred door at the constable. Before this terrible day, he had had little contact with the Winnipeg police. The stench of whisky and tobacco that hung in the air were foreign to him, the smells of a Gentile world that he did not participate in.

For him, like so many North End Jews, the life he had made in Winnipeg with his wife and daughters stopped at the CPR tracks. There, within the boundaries of New Jerusalem, his daily needs were met; it wasn't necessary to look any further. To think that he, so dedicated to his people, could be accused of taking another life — a little girl, no less — was beyond reason. It was madness.

He stood up and faced the back of the cell. Rocking back and forth, his lips swiftly repeated words he had said a thousand times before.

"*Shema Yisrael Adoni Eloheinu Adonai Echad.* Hear O Israel, the Lord is my God, the Lord is One."

Just before midnight, there was a rattle on the cell door. The rabbi looked up from where he was lying on the bottom bunk. In the darkness, a shadowed face peered at him through the bars. The rabbi moved closer to the cell door. "Ah, the mysterious detective."

"How could you possibly have known?"

Davidovitch smiled. "A rabbi knows many things."

4

It had been a long time since John Maloney felt this good. Today, for a change, his suit was pressed, his black boots were shined, his moustache trimmed, and his thinning brown hair combed. The girls at Dolly's coffee shop on Hargarve Street where he ate breakfast each day hardly recognized him.

He drank two cups of hot black coffee and devoured a piece of bread topped with Dolly's homemade strawberry jam before setting off for work. The morning air was crisp, but Maloney hardly cared. With a sense of purpose in each stride, he turned left on Main Street and headed toward the newspaper's offices.

The *Tribune* was located in the heart of "Newspaper Row" on McDermot Avenue. Next door was its bitter rival, the *Free Press,* and across the street was the *Telegram.* Each day, reporters from the three papers swarmed over the city in an attempt to outdo each other with local exclusives or "scoops" about the latest robbery, bawdy house raid or city hall scandal. Maloney's blood ritual stories fit the bill perfectly; not to mention the Trib's sales figure for the month of April were already on the way up.

As an independent Liberal, Maloney's boss, publisher Robert L. Richardson was all over the political spectrum, though usually he was content to take pokes at the CPR, the Grain Exchange, and any other institution or issue that the hated *Free Press* supported. If he could, he also went after the city's establishment, those wealthy, influential citizens who resided in their mansions at Armstrong's Point and on elm-lined Wellington Crescent. That most of them regularly read the *Free Press* was besides the point, claimed Richardson.

A few years earlier, he had caused a stir by giving page one to the outspoken Reverend C.W. Gordon of St. Stephen's Presbyterian Church. The preacher, also known in local literary circles by his pseudonym, Ralph Conner, wrote a series of explosive sermons in which he condemned "the flirtation of single men and married women," "the slavish serving of intoxicants at social functions," and "the self-indulgence of young girls." It was the best reading in any Winnipeg paper in years, though it had little effect on public attitudes.

Richardson had purchased the McDermot Avenue building, an old run-down theater, about a decade earlier. It had been renovated and a new rotary press had been installed. Lately, the newspaper had been doing so well that Richardson had his eye on a piece of property a few blocks away closer to Eaton's department store at the corner of Smith Street and Graham Avenue.

Maloney sauntered into the dirty, smoke-filled newsroom. His two sensational stories on the murder were the talk of the paper. The moment he made his entrance, colleagues patted him on the back for a job well done. Better still, Richardson had already told him that the Davidovitch trial was his if he wanted it. He had yearned for such a high-profile assignment for months.

Maloney knew the gossip in the newsroom: that if he did not soon produce something decent he was going to wind up working the grave-yard shift as a "rim-rat", a copy editor. Now he had the blood accusation and it made his mouth water; it appealed to both his sense of melodrama and morbidity. It didn't matter whether the rabbi was guilty or not — Maloney, himself, thought the whole idea of a child being murdered for her blood was improbable — what counted was that the story had suddenly seized the imaginations of the entire population of the city. On the streets, from Selkirk to Osborne, from the North End to Tuxedo, no one was talking about anything else.

Both the *Free Press* and *Telegram* had decided to run the story about the murder on their respective local pages hidden inside after the supposedly more important news from London, Washington and Ottawa. But Maloney had learned many years ago, when Richardson had first hired him, that local news was what sold best. "Think Main Street, not Mongolia," Richardson had told him and every other news reporter.

In those days, Maloney knew Main Street better than any other reporter. City aldermen couldn't wait to share with him the latest inside information. There were no such things as obstacles to a story. He was aggressive, resourceful, and most importantly, hungry. And it paid off. He single-handedly exposed real estate swindles, and reported on more robberies and assaults than he could remember. Unlike most newspaper reporters who had to be content with anonymity, Richardson allowed Maloney to sign his story with his own initials. Other than theatre reviewers, Maloney was the only news reporter to have this honour. And for some unknown reason, Richardson permitted the practice to continue, even when Maloney's work had deteriorated.

His decline was slow and painful. He started drinking too much when Irene packed up and went home to her mother. That was five years ago. Since then, he had moved through the motions of his job, churning out just enough copy to keep Richardson and other editors satisfied. He used to think that one day his life would return to the way it had been — Irene would come crawling back, asking for his forgiveness, he would expose a major political scandal and be the talk of the town. Lately, he wasn't so sure that was possible anymore.

The truth was that as a journalist John Maloney was washed-up and there wasn't a damn thing he or anyone else could do about it — at least that's what he had convinced himself.

This morning was different, however. Maybe it was the arrival of spring in the city; after six months of bitter cold weather. There was nothing in Winnipeg quite like the sight of melting snow and a cool April breeze to change a person's focus and improve their disposition. The streets were slowly coming alive again as if a mass hibernation had finally ended. You had to live on the northern plains, Maloney thought, to appreciate the true value of spring.

Also, it was the murder of Anna Rudnicki and the arrest of a rabbi that stirred and excited him. For the first time in a long time, his reporter's nose was twitching. This story would provide him the opportunity to show everyone that John Maloney was back.

Maloney walked briskly along Main Street. He liked the North End for two simple reasons — booze and women. There was a small hotel and bar on the corner of Jarvis and Main, the Royal, a few blocks from the more popular establishments, where Maloney could drink in peace. For some reason — maybe it was a big German bouncer named Hans — the Royal's bar was not as rowdy and crowded like those further down the street.

And then there was Amy at Melinda's on Rachel Street. She was young with short dirty blonde hair, a small nose and luscious lips. She had breasts that were so firm they didn't move when she walked, and slender long legs that didn't quit. She was too good for Maloney, and both of them knew it. But business was business and Maloney was a regular customer. He usually treated her well and she kept him content.

As Rabbi Aaron Davidovitch prayed in a jail cell in the Rupert Avenue station, John Maloney sat at his desk planning his next story on the Rudnicki murder. He had scheduled two stops that day, one at Wesley College and then later at a Polish church on Burrows Avenue. He knew he'd never make that day's one o'clock deadline for the newspaper's first edition, but he anticipated that he'd have something ready for tomorrow morning's second edition.

Normally, the *Tribune's* first edition hit the streets just after four o'clock in the afternoon when young boys raced from school to get their supply of newspapers. They would buy their papers from the circulation manager for one and half cents each and sell it on street corners for three cents a copy, or two for a nickel. Extras put out for special stories like the death of the Queen in 1901 and the coronation of the King George V, were purchased for two cents and sold by the boys for five cents. If they were fast and strong, the 'newsies' could make a tidy profit. Many of the more ambitious ones would return the following morning before classes to hawk or deliver the morning second edition. This was mainly the same newspaper they had sold the afternoon before, but added in were a few national and international wire service items and the latest sports results.

On any other day, Maloney would have hopped a streetcar for the fifteen minute ride to Wesley College, but given his new positive outlook, he decided to walk. By 9:30 that morning, Portage Avenue, as wide as any street in the West, was already crowded with businessmen, merchants and shoppers. Dozens of horse-drawn wagons moved steadily in both directions. Streetcars on their way east and west noisily clanged by. Usually Maloney enjoyed stopping to gaze at Eaton's and Hudson's Bay window displays (and chatting with the young mothers out for a morning walk with their children). Today, however, his pace was brisk. He was a newspaper man on a mission.

Wesley College was located far down Portage Avenue, about ten blocks from the Main Street business district. It was a large brick edifice set far back from the street. Among the city's various colleges and institutions of higher learning, it was the most notable as the intellectual headquarters of Methodist social gospellers such as the Reverend Salem Bland who, like J.S. Woodsworth, wanted to create "a kingdom of heaven on earth".

Richardson had arranged for him a brief interview with Professor Leon Fredericks, the author of a dozen books, and a recognized expert in the fields of biblical studies and medieval history. Unlike many of his colleagues, Fredericks did not have much interest in aiding farmers or saving over-worked labourers, but that didn't matter much to the college's board of directors. This esteemed body of academics and businessmen felt fortunate having someone of Fredericks's stature on faculty. Thus they put up with his eccentric behaviour and his curious intellectual pursuits.

Just before ten, Maloney found the professor in his second floor office buried among a pile of books and papers. The curtains on the lone window were drawn and only a single light hanging over the professor's cluttered desk illuminated the room.

"Mr. Maloney, isn't it? Come in. I think there's a chair for you somewhere in here," clucked Fredericks.

Maloney could barely see. In the shadow, he could make out a thin man with a white beard pointing to a chair.

"Sorry about the light situation. I find it easier to work like this."

Maloney's eyes adjusted. Sweeping off some scraps of paper, he settled into the chair and reached for his pencil and notepad. "I assume, sir, that you've read about the murder of the little girl in the North End?"

"Yes. A terrible tragedy. Terrible," Fredericks nodded.

"As you may know, a rabbi has been arrested and there is talk on the streets that the girl may have been killed for her blood."

"The blood accusation, the blood libel," interrupted Fredericks, shaking his head.

"You're familiar with it then?"

"Of course, Mr. Maloney. Just a minute."

Fredericks turned in his chair, studied the crowded shelf behind him. "Now where is it? Ah."

He pulled a thick, dusty book from the third row and handed it to Maloney. "All of the nonsense started with this," he said, "The Life and Miracles of Saint William of Norwich by Thomas of Monmouth published in 1173. That's not the original, of course, an English reprint you understand."

"Who was he?" asked Maloney, leafing slowly through the book.

"A Benedictine monk. According to his version of events, in 1144, William was a young boy supposedly kidnapped by the Jews of Norwich. Before he was crucified and killed, his Jewish kidnappers cut him open for his blood. It was generally believed that this was all part of a ritual described in the ancient books. Then they buried him before he was dead. All nonsense, of course. Nevertheless, the tales of Jews murdering Christian children for their blood so it could be used in the making of the Passover *matzot*, or unleavened bread, spread throughout Europe. First in Blois, France in 1171, and then in Saragossa, Spain in 1182. Later Chaucer made matters worse by including a blood libel story in the Canterbury Tales. Are you familiar with Chaucer's work, Mr. Maloney?"

"Can't say I am. An English writer, correct?"

"Ah yes, exactly, he was a renowned English poet of the fourteenth century. In a story he wrote late in his life called The Prioress's Tale, he relates how a young Christian boy has his throat cut by a group of Jews for singing a hymn to the Virgin Mary in the streets of a Jewish ghetto — beautifully written but quite preposterous from a historical perspective. Perhaps he was only trying to reveal the ingrained bigotry and superstitious nature of medieval Christianity." Fredericks reached for a glass of water hidden under a pile of papers on his desk.

"That's all very well, professor, but could you explain why children were targeted?" asked Maloney, as he scribbled in his notepad.

"That is the fascinating part and quite simple," continued Fredericks. "It was believed that Jews could not endure purity, thus their imagined obsession with killing innocent Christian children. Nothing but medieval mumbo-jumbo suggested, I would argue, by myths about the mysterious power of blood. In any event, despite a denunciation of the blood charges by Pope Innocent IV in 1247, the cases have continued right up to the present time. Russia has been especially bad. Even the Czar Nicholas's ministers and advisers have spread the foolishness. You are aware that just last month a Russian Jew named Beilis was charged with a blood murder.

It was after the body of a thirteen-year-old Christian boy was discovered near the brickyards in Kiev where Beilis was employed."

Maloney leaned forward in his seat. "Are you telling me that a few weeks ago there was a murder of a Christian child by a Russian Jew?"

"No, Mr. Maloney. I said that charges have been brought against a Jew for a ritual murder. The indictment was ordered by Ivan Shcheglovitov, the Imperial Minister of Justice. Nevertheless, I expect that the court will dismiss the case. I'm surprised you don't know about it. There was a story in the *London Times*."

"I don't read the *Times* much," Maloney said, standing up.

Fredericks stood up as well. "I'm glad I was able to help you, Mr. Maloney." They shook hands and Maloney turned to leave. "There is no basis to the charges in Kiev or Winnipeg," the professor called out. "If that little girl in the North End was murdered by a rabbi, it had nothing to do with her blood."

But Maloney was already out the door and not paying attention. His head was swirling with anticipation. He hadn't been this excited since he broke the McWilliams scandal fifteen years ago. The story would write itself. He would get ahold of the *Times* piece on the Russian murder and run it side by side with one about Anna. The comparison would be dynamite.

Twenty-five minutes later Maloney was in front of the St. Mary's Polish Catholic Church on Burrows Avenue a block east of Salter, where the Polish community was about to bid farewell to Anna Rudnicki.

Travelling north on Main Street was a visit to a foreign land; a world of exotic sights, smells and people. Most days, Selkirk Avenue, four blocks south of Burrows, could have passed for any muddy marketplace in Eastern Europe. The street resembled a bazaar with small wooden stores built closely together, each displaying their various wares on tables and boxes in front of their shops. On the wooden-planked walkways strolled women with baby carriages, wearing long, flowing dresses and flowered hats. Groups of men stood idly by, smoking cigarettes and talking in Ukrainian, Yiddish, and Polish about events in the old country thousands of miles away.

This morning, however, the street was silent. A few children played on the corners and some elderly women were sitting on a bench. Jewish storekeepers had opened their doors, though only a few customers wandered in and out.

St. Mary's Church had a high domed ceiling that was covered in a gold cloth. Three large and brilliantly colourful painted stained glass windows nearly covered the front main wall of the sanctuary. The middle window depicted the Virgin Mary, the other two, Joseph and the town of Bethlehem. Below the windows was a small cross and upon it the figure of Christ, at once in agony and in peace. It was placed high enough in the centre of the front wall so that it was visible throughout the church.

The crowd was large, even by North End standards. Maloney had a difficult time pushing his way through the main entrance.

To get to a seat on one of the church's long wooden pews, Maloney first had to walk by the small open casket. Dressed in all white, with her long blonde hair combed and clean, Anna looked angelic. The shadow of a dozen flickering candles placed around the coffin illuminated her innocent face. The mortician had wrapped her neck in a white cloth, so that the wound from the knife attack was not visible.

Maloney squeezed into a seat beside an elderly man dressed in a suit of a slightly finer material than most of the male congregants. He held in his left hand a black bowler hat. A bushy gray moustache was his most distinguishing feature.

"You are not from this neighbourhood, are you?" asked the man.

"No," replied the reporter, "name is Maloney from the Tribune."

"Yes, of course, Mr. Maloney. I've read your work and....."

"And what?"

"And, Mr. Maloney, your recent stories of the blood ritual have stirred up dangerous emotions. You know that you are playing with fire?"

"Perhaps. And what makes you such an authority on these matters?"

"Oh, excuse me. My name is Kowalski, Joseph Kowalski, I am the president of the Holy Ghost Fraternal Society. We have our own parish and school over on Selkirk."

The two men shook hands and Maloney could not help but notice Kowalski's firm grip and large, powerful hands. They were the hands of a labourer, not a churchman.

"Yes," continued Kowalski, "my experience in the old country is that such accusations about the Jews can only lead to trouble, serious trouble. You have to keep in mind that Poles and Jews have lived side by side in the great Pale of Settlement for hundreds of years, often oppressed by the same Czarist master, yet still separate. And always the relationship has been brittle. Unfortunately, we Poles have a long memory."

"You mean about Jews killing Christ," interrupted Maloney, glancing at the cross high above Anna Rudnicki's casket.

"Yes, that was important," Kowalski agreed. "But it has been more than that. By their very nature, Jews are outsiders. Socially and culturally, they have chosen to isolate themselves from the Christian world. This arouses suspicions. They have no faith that some day Poland will be a free and independent nation. The real question is — to whom does the Jew owe allegiance?"

Maloney shrugged.

"I will tell you," said the old man, his voice rising enough so that people sitting within three rows were able to hear the conversation. "The Jew owes allegiance ultimately to his God and to his Torah. But from the perspective of generations of Polish peasants working in the fields fifteen back-breaking hours a day to feed their families, the Jew, a town-dweller, is loyal to whomever happens to be in charge. They will never be true citizens of the new Poland because the political loyalty of a Jew is fleeting."

"Maybe that is how they have survived for so many generations," Maloney suggested.

Kowalski took no notice of the reporter's comment. "Finally, and I believe most significantly, throughout our history Jews have been the rent collectors and merchants to whom the peasants have owed money. Who is the landlord demanding money? Where does a Polish wife find her husband late at night? Drunk at at a Jewish tavern. Such are the realities which have produced the unfriendly relations of today," Kowalski said, shaking his head sadly.

"So then, what is the solution?" asked Maloney.

"I don't have all the answers, Mr. Maloney," said Kowalski. "At our church, we promote understanding and friendship with all Canadians."

"Obviously, you have a ways to go."

"Perhaps, Mr. Maloney, but I assure you, your writing has been of no help."

"Just doing my job," Maloney said. "I don't invent the news, I just report it."

Their conversation was interrupted by the words of the heavy-set Catholic priest. He spoke in Polish and then began the prayers for Anna's soul with a Latin hymn. For nearly a hour, the service continued as the priest switched back and forth from Polish to Latin.

"Don't they ever speak English here?" Maloney whispered to Kowalski.

The community leader shook his head. "I am afraid not. That is, in fact, one of the reasons why this is an independent church. Its members are as Roman Catholic as we at the Holy Ghost, only they have opted to follow the lead of our brethren in Chicago." said Kowalski, ignoring the ceremony at the front of the church. "Several years ago, a group of Polish immigrants living in the United States were dissatisfied with the leadership and demands of the Irish and German authorities and decided to establish their own congregation. There was too much emphasis placed on the use of English, disagreements about education. To be honest, I'd say most of the problems in the United States had to do with control of parish funds."

"And in Winnipeg?" asked Maloney, as the priest launched into another prayer.

"In Winnipeg, it was more a matter of miscommunication. Several years ago, some former, and might I add argumentative, members of the our church objected to the work of the Polish Oblate Fathers who continue to minister at Holy Ghost. There was some nonsense about them being more German than Polish and accusations that they did not support using the Polish language in services. I can tell you that it was not true. Nevertheless, they appealed to the officials of the National Church in Chicago who sent Reverend Blazowski to Winnipeg. He proceeded to establish this church in which you are now sitting. I am hoping that someday, the two congregations will merge and again be one..."

"Excuse me," said a middle-aged woman sitting in the pew directly behind the two men.

"Yes?" asked Kowalski, clearly annoyed at the interruption.

"I am sorry to trouble you, Mr. Kowalski," the woman said in Polish, "but this is the funeral of a young child and I cannot hear the words of the priest."

Kowalski turned and stared directly at the woman's husband sitting beside her. The man grabbed his wife's arm and ordered her to be silent.

"Anything wrong?" asked Maloney.

"Nothing I cannot handle."

"You have a lot of influence in the community then?"

"There has to be someone in charge. You can't have just anyone of any background assuming leadership, can you Mr. Maloney?"

The reporter smiled, impressed by Kowalski's knowledge but nevertheless troubled by his arrogance.

As the priest leading the service mentioned Anna's name once more, the church suddenly reverberated with the aching cries of Eva Rudnicki. Igor sat by his wife, stoic and stiff, his bloodshot eyes staring straight ahead.

Outside, following the burial, Maloney approached a group of about a dozen men standing near the entrance of the church.

"Name is Maloney, from the Trib. Mind if I ask you a few questions?"

The men stared at the reporter, until one man, clean shaven and dressed in a brown suit, stepped forward. "What do you want?"

"You know the family?"

The man nodded. "We all work with Igor Rudnicki at the rail yards. He is a good man, hard worker. He keeps to himself. Doesn't deserve something like this. And the worst thing is that a Jew is responsible for this tragedy."

"You know that for a fact?"

"The police arrested a Jew, a rabbi, isn't that true?"

"It's true. But in Canada as I'm sure you know, a man is innocent until proven guilty." The hypocrisy of Maloney's words eluded him.

"Listen, Mr. Reporter, all of us have lived among the Yids for many years. They cannot be trusted, it's as simple as that."

"And what about this business of the blood? That they kill Christian children for their blood."

"True, all of it. In my own town in the Ukraine a few years ago, a young boy about Anna Rudnicki's age was also murdered by a Jew. He was hanged before he could be brought to trial. He was guilty, as guilty as the one the police have arrested here."

The other men nodded their heads in agreement.

"You are all fools," a familiar voice cried out. Joseph Kowalski pushed his way through the crowd, past Maloney, and began talking sternly to the men in Polish. The men scowled but remained silent.

"Excuse me," interrupted Maloney, "what is going on?"

"As I told you Mr. Maloney, your investigations will continue to stir up trouble. I would like to make it clear once again that these men do not speak for the Polish community in this matter. We are quite satisfied with the efforts of the police and hold no grudges against the city's Jews. If the rabbi arrested did indeed commit the crime that he is accused of, well, that is a matter for the courts to decide."

"For the record," Maloney said, leafing through his notebook. "Do you believe he may have killed her for her blood?"

"I wouldn't know."

"Come now Mr. Kowalski, I would've expected something more definite from you."

"I am just being honest."

"Kowalski, you know nothing," someone called out in English. "Go back to the Holy Ghost where you belong. This is our church. Our children and grandchildren will be the true Polish nation and the Jews are as guilty as they always have been. I say, if they want blood, let it be their own."

Kowalski suddenly moved closer to the man and grabbed the collar of his jacket. He spoke in Polish in a low voice. "You dare insult me like this in front of a newspaper reporter. I built this community and you and your kind will ruin everything."

With a wave of his hand, Kowalski began to walk away. "You are all foolish and young and do not realize just how much damage you are capable of causing," he said in English. " And you Mr. Maloney, you, too, be careful what you write."

Maloney said nothing.

"Forget what he says. He's an old fool with a temper," said the young man who Kowalski had grabbed. "The Yids will pay for this, as they always have."

The other men shouted their approval, as Maloney scribbled furiously in his notepad. He had not been among such an a tense crowd in many years; the emotions were raw and the convictions passionate. These weren't the statements of madmen, Maloney felt, but a simmering enmity passed down from generation to generation. Besides, it didn't matter whether or not he believed what they were saying. A quote was a quote.

"Is everything all right, Joseph?" asked Irena Kowalski, speaking to her husband in Polish. She was a distinguished looking woman with a long straight nose, high cheekbones and brown eyes. When they had married in 1888, Irena had been a stunning bride.

"Fine my dear," her husband replied.

"And the funeral?"

"It was a funeral. I really hate going to that church. Those foolish independents. If not for my position, I would have gladly missed it. The girl's mother did not stop crying the whole time, I..."

"Yes?"

"Nothing. I did speak with a reporter from the *Tribune*. The same one who has written about the blood accusation. I explained to him the damage he could cause, but it was of no use. We are headed for trouble."

"Why worry yourself so much Joseph, you know what Dr. Hodur told you."

"I have tried to calm down. But I hate to see so much of our hard work vanish. We have an opportunity to build a model Polish community here and I fear this business with the Jews will ruin everything. Trust me, I have seen these things happen before. The situation can turn extremely ugly."

"It is not as if it is your fault, my dear. You must accept that some things are beyond the control of Joseph Kowalski."

A faint smiled appeared on his face. "You are right, of course," he said touching her hand. "I must try not to carry the burden of the world's problems on my shoulders."

"I have prepared some *bigos*, the way you like it with *kabanosy* and prunes. Come, we will eat."

"In a minute, my dear."

He picked up a copy of the *Tribune* in which Maloney had outlined the findings of the police investigation into Anna Rudnicki's murder. He read over one paragraph several times. Was it a coincidence, he asked himself.

His heart hoped it was, but his instincts told him something different. He would have to investigate further.

"Joseph, the food is on the table," his wife called out.

Kowalski walked towards the kitchen, determined to forget all of his various troubles, past and present, at least until after dinner.

Klein could hear the argument from outside the store. He felt like turning around; in fact, he was not sure why he was there. For the rabbi. For himself. For Isaac. Melinda had convinced him to at least hear them out. He reluctantly had agreed, now he wished he hadn't.

He stepped through the front door of Isaac Hirsch's shop. The smell of sawdust hung in the air, reminding Klein of the many hours he had spent in the store as a young boy. Nearly everyday after school, he had stocked shelves, waited on customers. By the time he was fifteen, Isaac had permitted him to handle the cash and accounts. It was a big responsibility, one that he had not taken lightly.

There was a crowd of customers, as there usually were standing at the front near the order desk. "They're in the back," said Isaac's wife Clara from behind the counter.

"Yeah, I can hear them," said Klein.

Clara was a short, handsome woman. Her long gray hair was kept under a shawl exposing her strong features. Unable to have children of her own, she had treated Sam and Rivka with a rare tenderness as they were growing up. Once, Klein remembered, when his mother had became very ill many years ago with influenza, Clara had moved into their home to nurse his mother back to health. She was always friendly and kind; and she worshipped her husband.

Despite her cheerful demeanour, Klein had long ago concluded that Clara Hirsch was not a happy person. There was an underlying sadness about her; it was as if she carried some great burden on her shoulders. Klein had decided that living and dealing with Isaac for more than thirty years was probably reason enough for any woman to be a little miserable. Few outside the immediate family circle knew of Isaac's quick temper or his periodic bouts of depression. To the Jews of the North End, Isaac Hirsch was a prosperous businessman and generous community leader — the president of the Shaarey Shamim Synagogue and a man who contributed much to local charities.

Isaac and Clara had arrived in Winnipeg from the old country at least ten years before the Kleins. They had been married in 1880 in Lodz, where Clara's family lived. Once in Canada, he had become a merchant — only Ashdown's had a larger inventory than Isaac Hirsch's hardware store.

Isaac preferred to look ahead and, unlike most of the other Jewish men Klein knew in Winnipeg, refrained from talking about either Russia or his youth.

"Please Shailek," he would say, "It's history, ancient history, forget about it."

All Klein knew was what his mother had told him, that the pogroms of 1881 had forced Isaac and Clara to flee Russia like so many other Jews.

He turned down the first long narrow aisle to the right of the counter. As he passed shelves filled with all types of nails and screws, the wood floor covered with sawdust cracked like ice beneath his feet. Three large bundles of metal chain were neatly stacked on the top shelf and below it, there were padlocks, knives, and a variety of tools.

At the end of the aisle, Klein pushed his way past a white canvass drape. The men were sitting around a large wooden table barely visible from the thick cigar smoke which lingered over them, like a rain cloud on a misty day. A pot of tea sat in the middle of the table, beside a plate of Clara's cinnamon *rogelach*.

From what Klein could gather, the ten or so men present, all members of the synagogue board, were discussing lawyers. And typically, they were not making much progress.

"What about Brodsky's son Izzy?" asked Ruben Sokolov, tugging on his long beard. "I've heard he's pretty good in court."

"He's just a boy," countered Avram Zelkin.

"There is also Frank Wolsh," added Lou Finkelman, "when I had that problem with the cattle buyer from Selkirk, he sorted the whole thing out."

With that comment, a great Yiddish debate raged around the table about who exactly was the best Jewish lawyer in Winnipeg and why. Besides Izzy Brodsky and Frank Wolsh, the names of Joseph Asper, Feivel Weinstein, and Benjamin Wolinsky were also mentioned.

"Enough," demanded Isaac Hirsch, speaking English. He noticed Klein and reached out to him.

"Sam. I'm glad you decided to come. Please sit down, have some tea," he said, taking him by the arm.

Klein took a seat beside Isaac. "All right Isaac, you wanted me here, so I'm here."

Isaac poured him a cup of tea and passed it to him with a piece of sugar. "You look well, Shailek."

"Isaac, you saw me two nights ago at the *seder*. I look the same."

"I know. But you still look well."

Klein shook his head. "Did I come here to drink tea or is there something else?"

"Yes, of course." He surveyed the men at the table. "Gentlemen, please we have something to discuss." The room immediately became silent. "As you know, I was asked by several of you to invite Sam Klein to attend this meeting, in the hope that he may be able to assist Rabbi Davidovitch in this terrible mess."

"Just a minute, Isaac," said Avram Zelkin. Zelkin owned a grocery store a few blocks away. Klein had known the family for many years; in fact, he and Sonya Zelkin, Avram's daughter, had been friends in school.

"Yes, what is it Avram?" asked Isaac, annoyed that he had been interrupted.

"Again, I would like to record my disapproval of this decision." He looked in Klein's direction. "With all due respect, Sam. I and several other members of the board object to you being here. I have known you since you've been a young boy. But you work in a house with women, dirty women, and it's shameful."

Without a word, Klein stood up to leave.

"Sit down, Sam," said Isaac.

Klein remained standing.

"Please, Shailek, let's talk. Zelkin does not represent the majority view. Is that not right gentlemen?"

"Exactly," added Lou Finkelman. "Hear us out, Sam. Then if you don't like what we have to say, you can leave."

"Fine."

Avram Zelkin stood up. "I'm sorry Isaac, I cannot support this idea. The boy is a pimp, for God's sakes."

"That's enough Zelkin," said Isaac in Yiddish, slamming his hand on the table. "The decision has been made. You can go or leave, I don't care."

There was silence for a moment. Then with a slight shake of his head, Avram Zelkin resumed his seat.

"Good," said Isaac switching back to English, "now we can get on with business." He turned to Klein.

"I take it you are familiar with what has happened thus far."

"I've read the papers."

"You know then that they have charged the rabbi with the murder of the little Polish girl and that there is much talk about a blood killing."

Klein nodded.

"I don't have to tell you how devastating this has already been for the rabbi, his family and the entire community. Relations here with the *goyim* have always been much better than in the old country. But now, well, we all fear the worst."

Several of the other men slapped the top of the table in agreement.

"Sam," Isaac continued slowly, "we all know that you are much more familiar with the outside world than we are. You know who to speak to and where to look. You speak their language. And, we believe that you could ask around and help us figure out what is going on."

"We are, of course, convinced that the rabbi is completely innocent of this heinous crime. But the only way we are going to get him out of jail and clear his name is to find out what really took place that night. In other words, Sam, we want you to find the person who murdered that little girl. Will you help us?"

Klein removed a cigarette from his silver case and lit it. He inhaled deeply, then blew smoke in the direction of Avram Zelkin who coughed in annoyance.

"As Mr. Zelkin has pointed out, I already have a job," he said.

"We know that," said Isaac patiently. "We would like you to ask your employer for four, maybe five days off and we will pay you whatever you wish."

"I see. Can I think about it?"

"Damn it, Shailek," said Isaac. "There is no time to think. An innocent man, a rabbi, the finest man I know is rotting in a *goyish* jail and you want time to think. Is this how your mother and I raised you?"

"Isaac, I know I owe you a lot, but you didn't raise me. And you're not my father."

"No, I'm not, but I knew your father and he would've agreed with me. There is something I'd like to tell you."

Klein sighed, but Hirsch carried on. "Once, many years ago in a small Russian *shtetl*, there was a Jew about your age, with a wife and young family. He was a peddler, who worked hard and minded his own business. One day, the Czar's soldiers invaded his home in the middle of the night and stole away his eldest daughter, a very beautiful woman. He did not hear from her for two years. Finally, word reached him that she had been adopted by a Christian family, had been converted, and was to be wed on her fourteenth birthday to a local official in a village many miles away."

Hirsch paused to catch Klien's eye. "Using all the resources at his disposal, this man searched for his daughter until he finally found her in a remote northern village. He attempted to buy her freedom but was unable to do so. Unwilling to give up, he kidnapped his daughter and returned her to his family who then went into hiding. Soon the Czar's soldiers returned to the *shtetl*, except this time there was no one there but this man. He was arrested and tortured. Still, he would not reveal the whereabouts of his family. He died fighting and for those he loved and believed in. That man was your great-grandfather, also named Sam. His daughter, Rivka, was your grandmother, your mother's mother."

Klein shrugged. "That's a nice story, maybe it is even true, but it does not change anything here."

"I disagree. You come from a family of fighters, Sam," Isaac continued. "You're stubborn, but you have a spirit within you that pushes you forward. I have seen it in you, since you've been a boy. I know that you can do this thing we ask. If not for me or your father, then for the legacy of your great-grandfather. Please, a rabbi's life is at stake, maybe the future of the entire community."

Klein sat quietly for a moment. "All right, Isaac, you win. As long as Melinda doesn't have a problem with me taking some time off, I will see what I can find out. But I'm not promising anything."

"She doesn't have any problems with it. We've already talked to her," Isaac said with sly smirk.

* * *

"Smitty, are you paying attention?" demanded the large man with the bowler hat.

Smitty nodded, but said nothing. He took one last drag of his cigarette before flinging it into the river under the bridge connecting Maryland Street with Academy Road. Smitty knew this area of the city well. A short distance away, on either side of the Assiniboine River were the grand homes of Winnipeg's elite on Wellington Crescent and in the upscale neighbourhood known as Armstrong's Point. The properties were large and the possessions inside plentiful. On more than one occasion, Smitty had climbed through an open window and helped himself to fine linen, silver cutlery and anything else he thought he could pawn. Once he had even managed to steal a crystal chandelier.

"You've been keeping an eye on the woman?" asked the man.

"I scared her at the Walker the other night, but since then I don't think she's seen me."

"Well, keep following her. I want to know where she goes and who she talks to whenever she steps outside of that whorehouse."

"I know my job. But I wouldn't mind seeing her at work."

"Maybe later. For now, keep your distance. We may have another more urgent problem."

"What?"

"Our friend in the police department. I think he is getting nervous. He may ruin everything. I want you to speak with him. Scare him a little. Tell him to keep his mouth shut and there will be more money for him in the future."

"And if he refuses to co-operate?"

"Then deal with it. But try not to get carried away. I don't need any more complications. You got that, Smitty?"

"Like I said, I know my job."

"I know you do, that's why you're working for me."

"Whatever you say," said Smitty.

5

"**E**xcuse me, sergeant, I'd like to speak with a prisoner." Politeness had never been one of Klein's strongest characteristics, but he made a special effort in the police station. It was a lesson that he had learned many years ago: it paid to be respectful to those people who believed, rightly or wrongly, that they were in positions of authority. Klein used the same approach with street car operators and city hall clerks. Such an attitude of deference usually produced the required results.

"And who might that be?" asked the desk sergeant, a red-faced Irishman. He sat at an elevated desk wearing a department-issue white shirt and black tie. His face was puffy from too much drinking and his belly bulged out of his navy uniform pants.

"The prisoner's name is Davidovitch, Rabbi Aaron Davidovitch."

The sergeant peered down at Klein. "You his lawyer?"

"No."

"His son or a member of his family?"

"No. I'm a friend."

"Well, I'll tell you, friend, I have strict orders from the chief that this particular prisoner is only allowed visits from either his lawyer or wife and family. Nothing here about any friends."

"Can I speak with Constable Bob Stewart? Is he on duty right now?"

The sergeant searched his desk for the day's roster. "Stewart. Yeah, he's here."

"Can I see him, please?" asked Klein, his voice even.

"What's your name?"

"Sam Klein."

An eyebrow raised. "So, you're Klein. I've heard about you."

"All good, I hope."

"You don't want to know."

Klein looked him directly in the eyes, but said nothing.

"Okay Klein, you go sit over there on those chairs in the corner. He'll be down in a minute."

Klein had visited the Rupert Avenue station several times in the past, and it was never an experience he enjoyed. Other than Bob Stewart, his opinion of the Winnipeg police was not favourable. He had seen too many of them act like boors at Melinda's. Most of them, in his view, drank too much, cheated on their wives, and were not above looking the other way for a few dollars.

Ten minutes later, lanky Bob Stewart barged through the oak doors at the end of the hallway. Klein stood up to greet him.

"Sam, what are you doing here?"

"Is there somewhere we can talk, Bob?"

"Here's as good as any place. What can I do for you?"

Klein looked around doubtfully, then lowered his voice. "I've been asked by some friends to sort out this mess with Rabbi Davidovitch. There is no way in hell he killed that girl. I've known the man for years. He's a good man. The whole thing is preposterous."

"Maybe," said Stewart, "but there is evidence and —"

"—What evidence?" Klein asked.

Across the room, the desk sergeant looked over at the two men, clearly straining to hear what they were saying.

"Come with me," said Stewart. He led Klein through the oak doors and into a small interrogation room.

"Sam, you have to understand," Stewart began quietly, "this is a very sensitive case. The department is being pressured from all sides. The mayor is up in arms. The chief wants this thing solved right away. McCreary has already told the police magistrate that he has enough evidence to convict. I'm telling you, they are out to get this guy. It's all that stuff in the paper, yesterday. The blood ritual. Your people don't really practice that, do you?"

"It's horseshit, Bob, pure and simple. Superstitious nonsense. Can you tell me about the evidence?"

Stewart hesitated for a moment.

"Bob, I assure you, it won't go beyond this room."

"I guess there's no harm. It's all going to come out sooner or later."

Stewart proceeded to tell Klein about the discovery of the rabbi's belongings — his religious artifacts and his knife — at the crime scene.

"And he says they were stolen from the synagogue some time ago?" asked Klein.

"That's right. But..."

"Yes?"

"There is no police report and..."

"And what?"

Stewart abruptly stood up. "Nothing. I have to get back to work. Maybe we can play some cards later this week."

"Sure, Bob. Listen, I have one more favour. I need to speak with the rabbi."

Stewart shook his head. "Can't do it, Sam. Only his family or his lawyer. The chief's orders. I'd lose my job."

Klein was about to push the issue, but realized he wasn't going to get anywhere with Stewart. The police constable was too anxious. "All right, Bob. Thanks for your help."

Waving cheerfully to the scowling desk sergeant, Klein left the station and headed for Main Street. Along the way, he stopped in at every hotel bar, pool hall, and cafe on the strip. He spoke with bartenders, hotel managers, maids, whores, drunks, and anyone else he could find. By the time he had reached Selkirk Avenue on the other side of the CPR tracks, the word was on the street: Sam Klein wanted information about Anna Rudniki's murder and he wanted it fast.

At about two o'clock, he backtracked to the Brunswick Hotel on the corner of Higgins and Main. He had stopped there earlier, but his contact had not reported for work yet. There was no more reliable source of information on the strip than 'One-Arm' Eddie, the Brunswick's rugged bartender. Eddie (Klein didn't know his last name) had lost his left arm in a freak accident with a shotgun when he was boy growing up on a farm near Winnipeg. If it hadn't been for the help of a Jewish peddler, who happened to be visiting at the time, Eddie probably would've died. The peddler bound the wound and stopped the flow of blood. From that time forward, there was always a soft spot in Eddie's heart for people of the "Hebrew faith", as he put it.

"I hear you're looking for information, Sam," said the bartender.

"That's right, Eddie," Klein pulled out a cigarette and lit it. "You got something?"

"There's been a lot of talk about the murder, but nothing in the way of real information you could use. It was that story in the Trib, the other day. It upset a lot of people, especially the Galicians."

When Eddie used the term "Galician", Klein knew that he meant any immigrant who might have come from eastern Europe. Like most Anglos, he didn't make much of a distinction between Poles, Ukrainians, Rumanians, Bohemians — in his view, they were all Galicians. It was a generic term, but the meaning was clear.

"Forget about it, Eddie. It's not true, trust me. You think I would drink the blood of a Christian girl?"

"I guess not. Nevertheless, it sounds mighty strange, you got to admit."

Klein nodded. He puffed his cigarette, while Eddie poured him a cup of coffee.

"There is something," added the bartender.

"Yeah?"

"Old Joe James. I don't know how reliable he is, but I understand he's been telling some people that he heard something."

"Is that so?" Klein sipped his coffee thoughtfully.

A husky man wearing dirty blue overalls who had been standing at the end of the bar walked to where Eddie was speaking with Sam and ordered another glass of beer. While the bartender was pouring it, the man bent down towards the floor spittoon and a large wad of tobacco juice poured out of the left corner of his mouth. The splash hit Klein's boots.

"Hey friend, watch your aim," said Klein.

"Did I hit you?"

"As a matter of fact, you did."

"I guess you shouldn't have been standing there," the man laughed.

"And I guess you owe me an apology."

"I owe you nothing. Why don't you just shut up." The man took his beer from Eddie, turned away and resumed his place at the end of the bar.

"Sam," said Eddie, "he's not worth it. Leave it alone."

Klein mulled it over for a minute. "I suppose so. I think I'll go find Joe. You have a good day."

As he was leaving, Klein passed the man in the overalls who was standing alone. Klein stopped, leaned forward and spit right into the large man's beer. With a roar, the man turned to confront Sam, only to be met by a quick left cross to the chin. He dropped to his knees, then fell forward unconscious.

Klein waved towards the bar. "Sorry, Eddie, I've been in a bad mood all day."

For as long as anyone in Winnipeg could remember, Joe James could be found at the corner of Logan and Main, day or night, no matter what the weather. Rumour had it that he was once a successful grain trader at the Exchange, but lost everything in the early 1890's. Liquor had beaten him down further. He lived in a tiny room at a run-down boarding house on Elgin and spent his days peddling pencils, doing odd jobs — anything to pay for his room, food, and drink.

"Sam, how you doing? It's been a while."

"I'm fine, Joe." said Klein, slipping a quarter into Joe's breast pocket.

"You're a good man, Sam. What can I do for you?"

"I heard from Eddie at the Brunswick that you might know something about the murder of that young girl that happened a few nights ago."

"That's right, I heard something."

"What did you hear Joe?"

"Come closer."

Klein moved as close as he dared. Joe probably hadn't taken a bath in a month. He stunk of alcohol, tobacco and urine.

"What have you got?" Klein asked again, pushing another quarter into Joe's pocket.

"People are scared to talk. Whoever killed the girl. It wasn't who the police got in jail."

"How do you know?"

"I'm telling you, Sam. I got ears. You know I got ears."

Klein nodded patiently.

"That nice girl who works for Melinda?" Joe continued, his eyes turning sly.

"There are a lot of nice girls who work for Melinda, Joe. Who are you talking about?"

"She's real pretty, long legs, wears those dresses with the slit right up to..." Joe pointed to his hip.

"You mean Amy?"

"Yeah, Amy," said Joe. "You ask her. I saw her talking to this guy, real greasy looking, but wearing fine clothes. Didn't recognize him. They were arguing about something. He kept mentioning that little girl's name."

"Anna?"

"Right, Anna. Anyway, this guy, he told her that he had to leave the city for a while. He looked real upset. So did she. You talk to her, Sam. Bet she can help."

"Is that it?"

"I figure that's plenty."

"Thanks Joe, you've been a real help. I won't forget it." said Klein, pulling a dollar from his jacket. "Why don't you get something to eat? It's on me."

"That's mighty generous of you, Sam. Thanks kindly."

Klein continued down the street. How could Amy be involved in this, he wondered. He didn't know much about her. She had come to Melinda's about a year ago, looking for work. She had the looks and the body Melinda liked and was hired on the spot. It was a good business decision; Amy proved to be popular with the clientele, especially that troublemaker Maloney. But as far as Klein could recall, he had not seen her with any man matching the description Joe provided.

Klein walked between the horses and wagons parked along the street and ran to catch the north-bound street car. He was back at Melinda's in twenty minutes. It was already 5:30 p.m. and there were a few men sitting in the parlour, chatting with the girls. Klein arrived in time to watch Sarah climb the stairs arm-in-arm with a tall, finely-dressed elderly gentleman. As she reached the top, she turned and saw Klein. She smiled. He pretended not to notice, reached for a cigarette and turned to his left towards the parlour and Melinda's private office/boudoir.

Decorated with a flowery wall paper and red drapes, the office was as gaudy as the rest of the house. There was a small desk, where Melinda did her paper work and in the far corner, a brocade couch where she entertained her very special clients.

"Sam. Where've you been?" asked Melinda. She was sitting on a plush velvet chair behind the desk, wearing a sheer negligee that did not leave much to the imagination. Her lips were ruby red and her eyes thick with a blue liner.

"You weren't wearing that when Isaac Hirsch was here to speak with you, were you?"

"I was indeed. And I'll have you know, he couldn't take his eyes off me."

Klein laughed. "I bet! He'll be talking about you for the next five years."

"Listen, I offered him a free consultation."

"And did he take it?" asked Klein, playing along.

Melinda stared at him, trying to keep a straight face. "Don't worry, honey," she said with a smirk. "I didn't do anything to embarrass you. But I'll guarantee that if I had, he would've said yes."

"How do you know?"

"Honey, I know the type and that man is it. A bit strange isn't he?"

"He is a bit eccentric. I've known Isaac all my life and deep down, I think he means well. He just has to do things in his own way."

"Sounds a lot like you."

"Me and Isaac, we get along, but I've had plenty of arguments with him. He can be pretty stubborn."

Melinda smiled.

"Don't say it."

"Okay, I won't."

"Forget about Isaac. I have to speak with Amy."

"Well, that makes two of us. I haven't seen that girl all day. In fact, she had the evening off yesterday and I don't know if she's even come back."

Their conversation was interrupted by the ringing of the telephone. Melinda answered it.

"Whitehall ten-ten," she announced. "Sam? Yes, hold on."

A familiar voice was at the other end the line. Klein listened, then smiled. "Sure, I'll meet with you. At nine o'clock in the alley behind the Brunswick. I'll see you then."

"Who was that?" asked Melinda.

"A friend. Wants to see me later. It's probably nothing."

"Be careful, Sam."

"I always am."

An hour later, Klein stopped in at his mother's house. It was dark, except for the kitchen which was illuminated by the flickering light of a single kerosene lantern. Ever since electrical hook-up was available for city residents from the Winnipeg Electric Railway Company in 1905, Sam had tried to convince his mother to switch over. He had argued that it was safer, more efficient, and much easier. But his case for modernizing the Klein household fell on deaf ears. Freda had reluctantly paid for a sewer line, only when city officials had ordered her to do so, and she wasn't about to waste her hard-earned money on some fancy new idea like electricity. Sam had even offered to pay, but she would not hear of it. "I have lived like this all my life, why change now?" she had stubbornly asserted. "There is nothing wrong with kerosene. The light is fine." After a time, Sam simply resigned himself to the fact that he was fighting a losing battle.

"Shailek, what are you doing here? You just missed Isaac," Freda Klein said in Yiddish. "He managed to get in to the jail to see the rabbi."

Klein nodded. "That's good. How is he?" Sam would have rather spoken English, but he knew it was easier for his mother in Yiddish.

"Holding up. Isaac brought him a kosher supper the *rebbetzin* had prepared. The rabbi says he must get out of there. He's supposed to be in court in two days. But it is going to be difficult on him until then."

"Did the board decide on a lawyer?"

"Yes. Isaac has an appointment with Alfred Powers tomorrow afternoon."

"Powers. He's going to cost them. I've heard he likes cases that are high profile. And I doubt if there is as high profile a matter in the city right now than this murder."

"Isaac says Powers is the most respected lawyer in Winnipeg. Isaac seem very confident about this."

"I'm sure you're right," said Klein with just enough sarcasm in his voice to upset his mother.

"Shailek, please. I don't want to have another argument. If not for Isaac...well, I don't know what I'd do with myself."

Klein sighed with exasperation. "And what about Clara? The great man's own wife. She is the most miserable person I've ever seen. Don't you think you owe her anything?" As the words came out of Klein's mouth, he realized he had stepped beyond that invisible line that children — no matter how old they are — should not cross when they speak to their parents.

"If you were younger, Shailek, I would slap your face. How could you ask me such a question? I've told you, my relationship with Isaac and Clara is my own affair and none of your business. But you know I love them both." Her eyes welled up with tears. "I would never hurt Clara, its just that, Isaac has told me...."

"Please. You don't owe me an explanation."

Klein's sister was standing in the doorway. "I see you've come for your semi-annual visit," Rivka said coldly. "Ignore him Mama, he didn't mean anything. Sam can be insensitive sometimes."

"Thanks, Rivka. But I've already apologized."

"Is that what you call it?"

Klein glared at his sister. "If you're so interested in other people's business, why don't we talk about your love life?"

"And I think you've overstayed your welcome," retorted Rivka, "As usual."

Main Street was unusually quiet for a Thursday evening. Most shops were closed and even the hotel bars seemed silent. The evening air was cool. Klein buttoned up his jacket and walked briskly the seven blocks to the Brunswick for his meeting.

As he crossed the street which headed to the alley behind the hotel, he could hear shouting. Then as he turned the corner, a sudden scream broke the silence of the night. Klein ran into the darkness.

"Is anyone there?" he yelled.

"Over here," a voice cried out.

He ran further ahead and there lying in the mud was his friend, Bob Stewart. He was bleeding from a knife wound to the chest. Klein bent down on his knees and cradled the policemen's head in his arms. "Bob, what happened?"

Stewart gasped, spitting up blood. "Sam, I'm sorry for this."

"Sorry for what, Bob? Who did this to you?"

"My fault."

"Bob, what are you talking about? What's your fault?"

"Money. I know it sounds stupid, but I did it all for money," he whispered. " Tell Amanda that..."

"Did what? What money are you talking about?"

Stewart reached for Klein's jacket collar and tried to speak. But his mouth filled with blood and with a gurgling moan, he closed his eyes and died.

Gently, Klein let the police constable's head to the ground. He was stunned. Who could have done this? What did he mean when he said that he had crossed the line? As far as Klein knew, Stewart was a honest cop. Now that judgment appeared to be wrong. Had Stewart, like so many of his colleagues on the Winnipeg Force, been corrupted? And if so, for what reason and by whom? What money was he referring to? Stewart had telephoned him to arrange a meeting in the alley. The constable said he had some information that would help him free the rabbi. But what was it?

As Klein attempted to sort out the confusion of the last few moments, he heard the distinct sound of a twig cracking under the heavy weight of a boot. He stood up, turned slowly to his left and searched the darkness. Then he saw it, a movement, ever so slight, behind a pile of firewood. Klein stepped forward.

"You want me," Klein declared in a clear voice. "I'm right here, you murdering son-of-a-bitch."

Ten seconds passed without a sound. Then the figure in the darkness emerged into the moonlight and moved swiftly towards Klein. The attacker swung at Klein's head with a thick piece of firewood, but missed. Sam's fist slammed into the man's face, sending him sprawling. He quickly stood up and moved at Klein again with the firewood, this time hitting him on the shoulder. Klein rolled onto the ground. He turned and lunged for his assailant's leg, grabbing and twisting it.

The stranger let out a sharp yell. He kicked at Klein's face, but still Klein would not release his grip. Then with both hands, the man swung his club once more, this time finding his mark. Klein's fingers dropped from the man's pants as he fell foreward, unconscious. The stranger straightened his jacket. His nose was bleeding. He reached inside his pants pocket for a handkerchief and wiped the blood from his hands and face. Then he calmly took out a cigarette and lit it. Satisfied that Klein was out cold, he sauntered down the alley, around the corner and out of sight.

As a young child, Klein always had the same nightmare. It was the image of a man with a black beard crying out for help as he was surrounded by a group of strangers who were attacking him. Just as the besieged man was being dragged away, he tried desperately to say something. "Tell me, please tell me," Sam would plead. But as the man opened his mouth to speak, no words could be heard. It was at that point that Sam's mother would be there to comfort him, to assure him that the world was safe.

He was nearly twelve years old when the dream finally stopped disturbing his sleep on a regular basis. Yet now as he lay in a dark alley in a pool of cold, wet mud, the image of the bearded man returned. Klein twisted, moving closer to him wanting to hear his words....

"Hey, mister. Are you okay?" asked a boy, perhaps fourteen years old.

"What? Yeah, fine," said Klein, "just a little sore, that's all."

In fact, Klein was still groggy. "That nightmare again," he muttered. "I thought it had left me for good."

"What's that?" asked the boy.

"Nothing. Here help me up."

Once on his feet, Klein surveyed the area. He glanced in the direction of Bob Stewart's lifeless body and the events of the past hour returned immediately. He had been certain that he'd had his attacker beaten. He wasn't prepared for a shot to the head and was angry at himself for allowing the stranger to flee so easily. Even with a bright moon, he could not make out the man's face, only that he was certain his opponent had a black beard. But given that many men in Winnipeg sported beards, that bit of information would not be of much help in solving his problem. Nevertheless, Klein's gut feeling told him that what had just transpired was inextricably linked to the murder of Anna Rudnicki. Find Stewart's killer, Sam thought, and he was one step closer to getting Rabbi Davidovitch out of jail.

He looked into the wide blue eyes of the boy standing beside him. The young man was lanky with ears that stuck out like wings. A flat wide nose sat crookedly on his face. He had clearly outgrown his brown trousers which, Klein noticed, only reached the top of his black laced boots. On his head, like most boys his age, he wore a flat gray cloth cap.

"I work across the street at the Bell," the boy said. "I was just walking past the alley when I heard you moaning. You in some kind of fight or something?"

Klein reached into his jacket pocket for a cigarette. "What's your name, kid?"

"Charlie, Charlie Watson. Like I said, I run errands and clean up around the Bell."

"You live around here?"

"Yeah, a few blocks away in a room with my mother. You're Sam Klein aren't you?"

"Good guess."

"So what's going on, Sam?"

"Kid, I wish I knew."

Klein walked towards the dead body of his friend, with Watson just behind him.

"Jesus," Charlie cried out, stumbling backwards.

"Easy kid, don't get scared. The guy who jumped me did this."

"I've never seen a dead body before, that's all."

"It's not pretty is it?"

"He a friend of yours?"

"We knew each other."

"You got a line on who did it?"

"Not yet. Listen Charlie, I think you'd better be going. First, I want you to do me a favour. Can you do that?"

Charlie moved closer to Klein. He was trying to remain calm, but his blue eyes were wide. "Name it, Sam."

"My friend over there," said Klein, pointing at Stewart, "is a police constable."

Charlie inhaled sharply.

"There's going to be a lot of questions about what happened here tonight. For my own reasons, I would prefer it if the police did not know I was involved. Can you forget you saw me?"

Watson did not hesitate. "No problem, Sam. Never saw you. Didn't see anything."

"Thanks, Charlie. Listen, you come see me at Melinda's house in a few weeks, you know where that is?"

Watson nodded, his eyes glued to the corpse.

"Good, you come see me there, I'll fix you up with a friend of mine. Now get out of here, and keep your mouth shut."

Klein needed to get back to Melinda's to sort things out. He knew that he could not be around when the police found their colleague, especially with McCreary on the case. He propped Stewart's body up on a wooden plank. He would have to walk back to Melinda's without being seen and then he could send an anonymous tip to the police.

Stumbling out of the alley, Klein was hurrying toward Main Street when he heard the first crack of glass. It was loud and echoed through the night air like a bullet. He looked first south towards Portage and the business district. All was still. Then he looked to his left toward the North End. Again, he heard the sound of glass shattering. In the distance, he could see shooting flames, red and hot, slicing their way through the moon-lit sky.

By midnight, the crowd that had gathered in front of the Rudnicki house on Stella had grown large and unruly. Small groups of men who had sat for hours in nearby bars drinking beer and stewing over the day's events wandered over to offer their support. A few brought burning torches with them. They flickered in the brisk wind of a Winnipeg April night. A small contingent of police constables stood by, holding their billy clubs. Another three officers on horseback paced their animals up and down the street. Sensing the tension in the evening air, the snorting black horses grew more anxious as each moment passed. Their riders, dressed in the traditional blue uniform of the Winnipeg force — except for the black leather high-top boots which rose to their knees — settled their mounts by pulling back hard on the reigns. The animals jerked their heads with each tug, momentarily stopping before they resumed their forward march.

The spark that ignited the mob was the arrival of a wagon with copies of a *Tribune* extra edition. Sensing the impact of Maloney's story, the newspaper pushed ahead its nightly printing schedule. In essence, it was the same paper that had been on the street earlier that afternoon. Except there in black and white on the front page had been added Maloney's two stories: one on the likelihood of the ritual murder of Anna Rudnicki by Rabbi Davidovitch; the other detailing the arrest of a Jew named Mendel Beilis for the murder of a thirteen-year old Russian boy in Kiev. Maloney had totally ignored what Professor Fredericks had told him. Instead his sensational story suggested that centuries of blood accusations were true.

"The Yids did this and they should pay," a man said from the back of the crowd, waving a newspaper. "They killed Christ, now they have killed little Anna!"

A few men in the crowd hooted and shouted their approval. "The kikes must leave us. They must vanish from our neighbourhoods."

"That is utter nonsense," said Joseph Kowalski, the head of the Holy Ghost Fraternal Society. Hearing rumours that there might be trouble, Kowalski and his four-man executive had made their way to the Rudnicki house. They pushed their way through the crowd towards the Rudnicki's front steps.

"My friends," Kowalski shouted, his voice firm despite his age. "When I came to this land, I left many things behind: my mother, my relatives. I decided to leave the old hatreds and beliefs behind as well. No matter how you feel about the Jews, they too are entitled to all the benefits this new land has to offer. And one of the most important is justice. I have said before that the charges of the blood accusation are unfounded; I maintain that. Nevertheless, it is for the courts to determine, not some mob. Otherwise we go back to the ways of the Czar, not of Canadian citizens."

As Kowalski stepped down, a few people clapped. The man who had waved the newspaper now made his way forward to the front steps. "Now it's my turn, Mr. Kowalski," he declared. "My name is Stephan Zabrow. I am married with two daughters. I live across the street and I work with Igor Rudnicki at the rail yards. Our families knew each other near the town of Otwock. Mr. Kowalski told you what he knows, this is what I know.

"I happen to be working in Kishnev eight years ago when the same terrible thing happened. A little boy was stabbed to death. Why? I will tell you. For the same reason the Yids have been murdering our children for centuries. For the blood. That is the reason they killed little Anna. That's why another child has been murdered in Kiev. They are our enemies. They are the enemies of our children!"

Kowalski attempted to speak again, but a loud cry drowned his words out. His face grew red; he was not used to being ignored.

"We demanded justice then and we demand justice now," continued Zabrow. "Shall we wait for the judges and lawyers to be paid off by the Yids? No! Never! I say to you, we must avenge Anna's death now before more of our children meet the same fate."

"Yes. Yes," several members of the crowd said over and over again.

"*Bei zhidov,*" added a group of Russian men wielding clubs, "Smash the kikes as we did in the old country!"

Kowalski attempted to grab Zabrow's jacket collar, but the younger man, with the aid of a friend near him, pushed the large hand out of the way. Zabrow quickly distanced himself from the community leader.

"This is not finished between us," Kowalski declared.

Now the crowd began to move. Three more police officers on horseback had arrived to ensure that there was no trouble. The six riders lined up side by side up across the street, forming a wall of horseflesh, so that the mob could be contained. Their horses continued to jerk and thrash as the noise from the crowd grew louder. The police on foot, clutching their billy clubs, moved to a point just to the right, about ten yards from the Rudnicki's front steps.

Then, from out of the darkness, a rock flew through the air crashing into the window of a house two doors away.

"Yids live there, smash the house, smash the windows," a woman urged.

More stones flew and the sound of breaking glass reverberated throughout the neighbourhood as more Jewish residences were targeted.

"They murder our children. They grow rich on our labours. They suck our blood dry! Destroy them," Zabrow said. "Come follow me."

"Stop," shouted Kowalski. "I order you all to stop. You don't know what you are doing." He called to the four other members of the executive and the five men linked arms in front of the mob. But it was to no avail. Zabrow and about a dozen other men rushed at them. Kowalski and the others were easily pushed out of the way.

"Halt," urged Kowalski. "What has happened?" he said under his breath.

Led by Zabrow, the large crowd ran up Stella towards Charles. There were maybe eighty men and another twenty women, some with young children. Finally, the police reacted. The six constables on horseback urged their animals forward.

"Steady boy," one of them ordered. "All of you," the same constable said to the half-dozen officers standing to his right. "Fall in behind." With their clubs at the ready, the police did as they were told.

The mob was now only a few feet away. The lead mounted policeman tugged on his reigns as he separated himself from the pack. His horse waded into the middle of the mass.

"Out of our way," a woman said. "Get out of our way."

"Stop," the constable demanded from high atop the saddle. "Stop or we will have to arrest you.."

Before he could finish speaking, two or three hands had grabbed at his uniform, pulling him down onto the ground. His own horse nearly trampled him.

"Charge," yelled another officer. "Get that man out of there." As the police on horseback rode into the crowd, those on foot attempted to free their downed comrade. But the mob of labourers, farmers and rail workers would not be intimidated. Hands and arms flew wildly around the constables' heads. In a split second, several of the officers were on the ground, their billy clubs gone. Feet kicked at them and hands beat them with their own weapons.

The five other officers on horseback swung with their clubs at the heads of those who had encircled them. Though their black "billies" found their mark, they were waging a losing battle. Before long, two of them were on the ground, beaten and bleeding.

"Fall back," shouted one of the constables still on his mount. The three riders pulled hard on the reigns, turning their animals and moved back towards the Rudnicki house.

Joseph Kowalski, who had watched the melee from a safe distance, gathered his executive around him. "Come gentlemen quickly," he said. "I know where they are headed. We have one more chance to prevent a disaster."

Sensing victory, the crowd moved quickly, gathering momentum as it got closer to Selkirk Avenue. The police left standing and on horseback regrouped and assisted the injured officers.

"There, look, the star," a woman said, pointing to a sign on a kosher butcher shop. "Smash it."

More rocks and sticks flew through the air, breaking windows and destroying property. One of the torch-bearers, seeing a wagon of hay beside Frankel's tailor shop, set it on fire. Within minutes, the entire wooden building was engulfed in flames, illuminating the street for further violence and destruction.

Many of the Jews of the North End had experienced such violence before in another lifetime, and as in the past, their reaction to the carnage outside was instant. If the pogroms in the old country had taught them anything, it was how to protect themselves and their young. Antagonizing the mob was not the answer. They would just have to wait it out.

This seemed to make sense to everyone but Rivka Klein. Imbued with the spirit of the Bund, the Jewish Labour Union that had been created in 1903, Rivka refused to back down from anyone. Bundists felt that the future of Judaism was not to be found in the synagogue, but in the shop and on the picket line. Rivka believed that in order for Jewish immigrants to survive and prosper in the new world, they had to establish their own unique identity. It wasn't one based on religion and taught to them by rabbis bent on preserving the old ways and traditions. No, it was the spirit of the Jewish union that was to be the immigrants' guiding light.

Rivka Klein smiled grimly at her mother as the noise outside in the street grew louder. "Mama, stay here. You will be safe." She picked up a shovel and walked toward the front door.

"Rivka, where are you going with that thing? I forbid you."

"I'm sorry, Mama. I have to try to stop them. There are others like me. We have talked of such an event happening. Don't worry, I will be fine. We have a plan."

"Plan? Who has a plan? Rivka, are you *mishigina*? Don't leave me, Rivka..." It was too late, her daughter had slammed the door.

By the time Klein reached the corner of Selkirk and Main, he could hear the mob in the distance, its path of destruction in front of him. There was broken glass everywhere. The windows of most shops, Jewish or not, had been smashed so that there was nothing left but the frames. Dozens of pairs of shoes from Rosenbluths' were strewn about in the mud on the street. Dresses and suits from Finkelman's next door were shredded and five of their sewing machines had been broken into a dozen pieces.

Klein walked quickly through the rubble west towards Salter Street. Isaac Hirsch's hardware store looked like it had been hit by a raging storm. The entire front of the shop had been pulled out and every imaginable item looted. The mob had used Isaac's own tools to destroy a life of hard work. Sensing the worst, Klein ran towards his family's house a block away. He saw the smashed windows first and there, maybe fifty feet away, lying face down on the mud, was his sister. He ran to her.

Klein knelt on the ground, turning his sister over, cradling her head in his arms as he had done for Bob Stewart only hours earlier. Except Rivka was still alive. She had been beaten badly. Blood flowed from a deep gash on her head.

"Don't worry, Rivka, you'll be okay. I'll get a doctor."

She was unable to speak. She looked into his face and briefly smiled before her eyes closed.

The mob had now split into two groups. One led by Zabrow headed down Main towards the police station; the other in the opposite direction towards McGregor Street.

Word of the rioting already had reached Chief McRae who immediately left his home on River Avenue and headed back to the station. He arrived moments before the crowd. He ordered every available police officer outside with pistols at the ready. Five more constables were told to guard the rabbi's jail cell and shoot the first person who tried to attack him.

Guns were not normally part of the Winnipeg Police Force's daily arsenal, but each constable had been trained in the use of a firearm. In fact, two years ago, after a spate of violent robberies, McRae had authorized his constables on the night shift to carry a pistol tucked inside their tunics. Though most Winnipeg officers, like their British counterparts, prided themselves on being able to keep the peace without a gun, the rowdiness of the city's night life sometimes demanded a change in tactics.

Outside in front of the station, there was mass confusion. Flaming torches burned in the wind, amidst the cries for quick justice.

"Will we wait for the charade of the courts?" asked Stephan Zabrow.

"No" came the loud reply.

"String him up now," a man said.

"Hang the Jew before he kills anyone else," shouted a young woman.

With two constables at this side, McRae waded into the middle of the mob, towards Zabrow. He grabbed him by the collar of his jacket. "You have exactly one minute to leave here or I will arrest you and your friends."

"We're not afraid of you!" said a man standing beside Zabrow.

The constables beside the chief were nervous. McRae had ordered them to holster their pistols before they accompanied him into the crowd. The last thing the chief wanted was an accidental shooting. The officers grasped their clubs with two hands, ready to strike. Chief McRae looked behind him just as the first blow came. A tall heavy-built man of about thirty years of age, wearing a flat gray cap with a thick black moustache, charged at him with a club. He hit the chief on the head and McRae fell to his knees.

Then bedlam. Whistles blew and several officers fired shots into the air. "No guns," a sergeant yelled. The constables placed their pistols back inside their uniforms and ran forward waving their clubs at any heads or bodies in their path. There were screams of pain as billy clubs found their marks. Two officers reached the chief, who was bleeding from a wound on his temple. As more constables arrived, the mob ran in every direction.

Inside in his dark cell, Rabbi Aaron Davidovitch could hear it all. He grasped his *tsitsis*, the long white fringes at the end of his prayer shawl, and asked God to forgive those who wanted to murder him.

The other half of the mob had now reached the corner of McGregor and Selkirk, leaving a path of destruction behind it. Still, the crowd's blood lust was not satiated. There was one final desecration to commit.

The large gold Star-of-David, high above the street, was visible from blocks around. On this night, the light of the moon hit the glass at just the right angle so that its reflection glowed far off into the horizon.

Rabbi Aaron Davidovitch's synagogue was a structure of graceful design. The building was all white with three pillars jutting upwards towards the sky. The middle pillar, with its circular starred window, was the highest, the other two rose slightly below it. Three massive arched windows, one in each pillar, were spread across the front. A canopied doorway, like a *chupah* used by a bride and groom on their wedding day, led into the synagogue's lobby and sanctuary. Engraved above in stone were the black Hebrew letters of its name — Shaarey Shamim, the gates of heaven.

There was no stopping them now. A dozen or so men began to throw rocks at the large windows. Then others joined in and within minutes, they had smashed them to nothing. They charged the door, but it would not give way.

From behind them boomed a voice of authority. "What are you doing?" demanded Joseph Kowalski. His tone was firm and uncompromising. Anticipating that the mob would attempt to loot Rabbi Davidovitch's synagogue, Kowalski and his group had used a horse-drawn wagon belonging to a member of the Holy Ghost Fraternal Society executive to reach the steps of the Shaarey Shamim only minutes before the unruly crowd.

A man wielding an iron rod approached him. "What do you want, Kowalski? You have no business here."

Without warning, Kowalski's right hand slapped the man's face. The force of the blow sent him tumbling to the ground. The crowd immediately grew silent, stunned by the power wielded by the older of the two men. "Get up, you fool," Kowalski ordered in Polish. The man got to his feet. "What's your name?"

"Schwartz, Henry Schwartz," the man muttered.

"Speak up, Schwartz. Tell me where are you from?"

"I was born in Drohobych. It's in the Galicia," he said more clearly.

"A lot of Jews live there, don't they? Ten, fifteen thousand?"

"That's right. Maybe half the town's population."

"Ever have any problems with them in Drohobych?"

"No, but..."

"How long you've been in Canada?"

"About ten years. What do you want from me?"

Kowalski ignored the man's impatience. "You work in the rail yards?"

Schwartz nodded.

"They treat you well? Pay you a decent wage?"

"I can pay the rent."

"Your boss Jewish?"

"No. English, I think."

"Let me make sure I correctly understand the situation. Jews have never done you any harm before, here or in the old country, but you and your friends want to destroy this synagogue because...?"

"Because of what they did to Anna Rudnicki. They killed her for her blood." Several members of the crowd shouted their approval.

"You believe they use the blood of our children in their ceremonies, don't you, Mr. Kowalski?" asked a petite woman, her head covered by a white scarf.

"To be honest, Miss, I don't know. Maybe they do. But I do know that this is not the way to deal with it. If you destroy this synagogue, all of you will be no better than the Cossacks who pillaged our ancestors."

"So what would you have us do?" the woman asked.

"Leave now. As I have said already, let the courts mete out the punishment to the rabbi. He will get what is coming to him. Have faith in the Canadian justice system, it might surprise you."

Police whistles could be heard in the distance.

"I think it's time you all went home and back to your families," said Kowalski. The crowd had lost its momentum. Schwartz turned on his heel and walked away. Silently, one after the other, people dropped their stones and clubs and the crowd dispersed.

Kowalski took out a handkerchief from his suit jacket pocket and wiped his brow. Good, he thought, the damage has been contained.

6

"That's the most senseless thing you've ever done, Rivka!" claimed Freda Klein with the authority only a mother could muster. "*Mishigina*," she affirmed as the Yiddish words flowed from her tongue fast and furious. "A *shlemiel* would have had more brains."

For the past hour, Freda had not stopped moving or talking. She paced back and forth in the kitchen, fetching her daughter a cup of tea and a piece of honey cake Rivka did not want.

"Mama, will you please sit down. I'm fine. Sam, tell her that I am fine."

"She's fine. Leave her in peace," Klein declared.

Freda ignored both her children and returned to the kitchen for more food.

"You're lucky that mob didn't kill you," Klein said, glaring at his sister.

"Anti-Semites, all of them," said Rivka. "I just couldn't stand by and do nothing."

"Regardless, your death would have destroyed the family. Next time you find yourself in the middle of a pogrom, stay put."

Rivka knew that this was Sam's way of letting her know that he cared about her but at that moment, she wasn't interested in his lecture .

"Tell me, what were you doing in the street before you found me?" she asked him. "Who hit you on the head?"

Klein ignored the questions. He still was uncertain about how Bob Stewart's murder fit into the events of the past few days. What did the police constable have to do with the Rudnicki murder? Was the attack in the alley linked to the riot? These were the questions that Klein needed to solve, but by himself.

"It's over now, why not lie back and rest," he advised her.

Rivka looked terrible. The whole left side of her face was bruised, her right arm was fractured, and she had a deep gash on her forehead that had required a few stitches. Klein was not surprised by the violence — he had been certain that Maloney's *Tribune* articles would incite old hatreds — but the intensity and damage inflicted upon the Jewish community was out of the ordinary, even in a case like this.

Soon the house on Flora Avenue was crowded with friends and relatives who came to visit with Rivka and reassure Freda that her daughter would recover. At such times, ideological differences which normally divided the city's Jewish community were pushed aside. Rivka's Bundist comrades, dressed in the simple and plain uniform of a seamstress and tailor, mingled easily with Rabbi Aaron Lev from the nearby Beth Yisrael, a distinguished looking man of forty with a long beard as black as the fine suit he wore. His wife, Bayla, the *rebbetzin*, in a long-sleeved blue blouse and matching skirt and a *sheitel* covering her short-cropped hair, sat in the far corner of the small room with the prim and proper ladies of the Shaarey Shamim sisterhood. They spoke of their friend Freda's troubles, of the terrible plight of the Davidovitchs and of the tragedy which had recently burdened their *shtetl* community.

To the left of the women, Alter Cherniack, Joseph Guravich and several other smartly dressed young Socialist Zionists conversed easily with their rivals from the Poale Zion. For the moment, it was agreed that discussions about the future of Palestine would be halted.

"You are certain, Freda, we cannot be of assistance?" asked Meyer Erenberg, President of the Mezericher Society. "You know," the short and heavy-set man assured her, "that as a Mezericher, you are entitled to health benefits. We are here to help you. Despite our misgivings about your son's work, we still consider you our *landsman.*"

Freda smiled. "I am honoured Meyer. I know coming from you such treatment for a woman is not so routine. But Rivka will be fine and I do have Isaac's support. Please have something to eat and a cup of tea."

The past twenty-four hours had taken their toll on Freda. After a few hours of gossiping and running for food, she was exhausted. She collapsed on a chair in the living room. Beside her, as usual, was Clara and Isaac Hirsch.

Suddenly, Isaac stared at his wife. "Clara, what are you doing sitting here? Go fetch Freda a cup of tea," he announced in Yiddish. He raised his voice loud enough for other people nearby to hear. Clara Hirsch immediately stood up, embarrassed by her husband's tone.

"Don't bother, Clara. I can get it myself," said Freda.

"Nonsense," said Isaac. "Clara, tea."

As soon as Clara was in the kitchen, other conversations resumed. Freda turned to Isaac. "Why do you treat her like that? She cares so much for you."

"It's peculiar that you of all people should ask such a thing. And how do I treat you?"

"Isaac, you know how I feel about you, but I still think that...."

"Clara is your friend. She is my wife. I will continue treating her in the fashion I choose." He reached for Freda's hand. "Don't worry, everything will be fine." Freda lightly brushed her hand against his cheek.

Watching this scene from across the room, Klein was troubled. Did his mother not know what people said about her? That she was Isaac Hirsch's prized possession, his concubine. That she had betrayed her friend and cousin Clara.

Klein needed a cigarette. He appreciated the community support and the good wishes bestowed upon his family, but he had little patience in particular for the rantings of the Zionist intellectuals. Life was here and now, not in some far off mythical land in the desert. More outrageous, he thought, was the notion fostered by Cherniack and his group that a Jewish state could be built in Uganda, of all places. It was even more absurd than believing there would one day be a homeland in Palestine. As far as Sam understood the complex issues there, the British and Arabs would never permit it.

Outside on the porch of his house, he could smoke and think about more pressing matters. Alone in his thoughts, things finally began to fall into place. He was convinced that someone had framed the rabbi for Anna Rudnicki's murder and then stood back while ancient hatred ran its ugly course. That was why Rivka had been assaulted. Except now there was also Bob Stewart's guilty conscience to deal with and perhaps a beautiful prostitute named Amy. Maybe there were others.

"I'm sorry for intruding, Sam, but we have to talk," said Isaac speaking English.

"No problem."

"Shailek, You know how upset I am about Rivka."

"She will be back on her feet in a couple of days."

"I know, but I still cannot believe she went out into the street."

"She was determined to stand up for herself and I can't blame her. I'm also sure that the problems in this city are not going to be solved so easily."

"I agree. We will have to defend ourselves as we always have. Such treatment of Jews cannot go unpunished. But I want to reassure you that your mother and Rivka will be taken care of. Clara and I are here for them."

Klein nodded. Either Isaac was so self-centred that he did not know how much he hurt his wife by his public display of affection for Freda, or if he he did, he ignored it.

"Have you heard from the police again?" asked Isaac.

"No. I don't expect to. They told me they are working on the case. But there were so many people that night. They'll never find out who killed her. What about your store?"

"It's a disaster, like the rest of Selkirk. You know they also nearly destroyed the *shul*. The damned *goyim*, they broke every window. Have you seen the papers today?"

"No, not yet."

"Of course. The *Free Press* wasn't too bad. Dafoe has always been a fair man. He's calling for the mayor's resignation. But the *Tribune* was very critical. An editorial actually blamed our people for the riot. Have you ever heard of anything so ridiculous?"

"I'm not surprised, considering it was the *Tribune's* fool reporter Maloney who spread the blood libel stories in the first place."

Hirsch pulled a clipping out of his inside coat pocket and began to read. "The Jew is by choice an outsider. This has over the years given credence to numerous beliefs and ideas about their secret religion and rituals. We do not know if Rabbi Aaron Davidovitch killed Anna Rudnicki for her blood, or even if he is guilty of murder. That will be for the court to decide."

"Yet the very existence of the blood accusation indicates the tenuous position of all those of Hebrew faith in Canada. Our message to our Jewish brethren would be this: assimilate. Become part of the community and you will find greater tolerance and understanding. Yesterday's riot was unacceptable, but placed in its proper perspective, it is easy to see why it happened."

"How much more Canadian would they have us become?" asked Isaac, placing the clipping back in his jacket pocket. "You mean it is impossible to be both a Jew and a Canadian at the same time? Nonsense, there has to be some middle ground."

"Ignore it," suggested Klein. "The newspaper's editors are merely repeating what they have heard Woodsworth say time and again: that a good immigrant is an assimilated one."

"Yes, yes I know. Why can't that preacher just be content with providing food and care for needy children. His opinions do nothing but stir up trouble."

For a change Klein agreed with Hirsch's analysis of the situation. Klein had adopted the customs and life of the Gentile world more than most Jews he knew, and yet he was not prepared to abandon it altogether. Influential people like J.S. Woodsworth, however, could not comprehend such desires because they began from a different premise: that Canada was and always will be an English-speaking country of British values, ideas and conventions. These were matters, however, best kept to himself.

"Now, let us speak about the rabbi," announced Isaac.

Klein threw his cigarette on to the step and stamped it with his boot. "Tell me again about how the rabbi's *teffilin* wound up around that girl's neck."

"The rabbi says that there was a robbery at the synagogue a few days before the murder and that he reported it to the police," explained Isaac. "He never said a word to me about it. In any event, the police say there is no report. Why? Did you find something?"

"Maybe. You know how I got this lump?" said Klein, pointing to the back of his head.

"I assumed by the mob on Selkirk."

"No. Two nights ago, I was supposed to meet a friend of mine, a constable, at nine o'clock in an alley behind the Brunswick on Main Street. He had phoned me to say that he had some information about the case. But by the time I got there, he was nearly dead from a knife in his chest. His last words were that he was sorry about something. Before I could figure out much more, I was attacked and knocked out. I presume it was by the killer or someone working for him."

"My God! I just read about that murder. He was found by a cleaning woman who works at the Brunswick. The assumption was that he was a victim of the riot. Have you told anyone about this besides me?" asked Isaac.

"No. I wanted to send an anonymous message about the body. The guy had a wife and kid. But with all the trouble on Selkirk, and then finding Rivka, I didn't do anything about it."

"You think he knew something about the rabbi's police report?"

"It has crossed my mind."

"So what are you going to do now?"

"I am going to pay a visit to Bob's wife tomorrow morning. I know she and Bob were close. Maybe he told her something. This whole thing stinks."

"I have another favour to ask of you. I was supposed to see the rabbi's lawyer, Alfred Powers this afternoon. But with all the trouble, I've delayed it for a day. Can you come with me tomorrow? You should probably speak with him."

It was late when Klein returned to Melinda's. Business was slower than usual. The riot, at least for the moment, had stifled Winnipeg's night life. Except for a few men in the main parlour, the house was quiet.

Klein slipped through the house and into his room. The curtain was drawn on his window and the small room was dark. At first, he did not see her.

"I'm sorry about your sister," said Sarah from his bed. "Will she be all right?" Sarah's hair hung down over her naked shoulders.

"What are you doing here?" Klein asked casually, reaching for his cigarette case.

"I thought you might want some company."

"Actually, I think I want to be alone."

"Are you sure?" she asked, her fingers playing with her hair. "I could help you relax."

"Don't talk like a whore to me," Klein snapped.

Sarah blinked.

Klein closed his eyes. "I'm sorry, Sarah. It's just ...."

Before Klein could finish speaking, Sarah stood up and moved close to him. He could smell her perfume and the scent of her hair.

"Sam, let me help you," she said as she lightly brushed his cheek with her fingers.

She took his hand and their fingers intertwined. Neither of them said a word. She pulled his face close to her and they kissed. Her mouth parted and their tongues touched. Then she took a few steps back and stood silently, her arms at her side. After years of working every day with heavily made-up whores dressed in clinging lingerie, Klein thought he had become immune to sexual temptation. But seeing Sarah standing naked and unadorned before him, her body trembling in the night cold, moved him deeply. Without a word, he reached and pulled her body against his. Her skin was silky and soft, her scent intoxicating. He kissed her again, harder. His fingers first ran through her hair, and then roamed all over her, touching and caressing every part of her. Finally, he led her to his bed.

Sarah still said nothing, but her twisting movements urged him on until he entered her. She stopped after a long satisfying minute, pushed him sideways and deftly moved on top of him. The smoothness of the movement spoke of much practice and for a moment Klein's mind filled with the image of a thousand other gasping men lying under her. But then Sarah leaned down and kissed him gently on the mouth. His mind cleared instantly. Closing his eyes, he reached up to fondle her firm breasts as she rocked up and down on him. Then, suddenly, before he was ready, it was over. He gasped with a pleasure he had never felt before.

They collapsed into the tangled sheets, their arms wrapped tightly around each other. He opened his mouth but before he could speak, Sarah held a finger to his lips.

"Don't say anything, Sam," she whispered. "Think whatever you want, but don't say anything."

It was four in the morning when Sarah returned to her own bedroom. The last customers had already left and the house was quiet again for a few hours. It had been wonderful with Sam, just as she knew it would be. So why did she feel so lousy? As they lay in each other's arms, she had almost told him about the trouble she was in, but couldn't quite bring herself to do it. She had gently fondled him until he was ready to enter her again. This time, he had lasted longer and the sensation was exhilarating. Later, exhausted, Sam had fallen asleep. But she could not. As much as she tried to relax, cuddled next to his warm body, sleep would not come. Restless and confused, she finally left his bed.

Back in her room, she tried desperately to sort things out. She was in love with Sam, she knew that now. Yet she was not prepared to forgo her share of the money that was promised to her and that she had earned. Nor was she even certain that she wanted to give up her lucrative work at Melinda's. She knew Sam, at the very least, would demand that of her. She had just poured herself a glass of whisky when she heard someone attempting to pry open her bedroom window. Startled, she moved towards her door. "What the hell," she whispered.

"Open the window," the familiar voice cried out. "I have to speak with you now."

"Are you crazy?" asked Sarah with anger in her voice. "What are you doing here? What if someone should see you?"

Ignoring her, the man climbed through the window into the room. He reeked of cheap liquor and tobacco.

"You're drunk, aren't you?" she asked. "I thought we agreed we'd meet tomorrow."

"I want you to hide this for me. Take it, quickly," he ordered, handing her a black book.

"What is it?"

"My insurance."

"What?"

"It is names, dates and amounts, that's all you need to know," he said, running his fingers through his black greasy hair. "Now do as you are told, you Jewish whore." He raised his hand to her face, but did not strike her.

"You wouldn't dare. Not here. Not with Klein in the next room."

"You think he's going to save you. We're going to deal with him in our own way."

"What are you talking about?"

"Nothing. If you want your money just do as you're told."

Sarah took the black book and placed it under a loose floorboard by her bed.

"Satisfied?" she asked him.

He nodded as he reached for Sarah's bottle of whisky.

"There is something else," she said, "I want to know, have you got someone following me? Because if you have...."

"I don't what you're talking about," he replied. But the weakness of his response suggested otherwise to Sarah.

He swigged the whisky back and sat at the edge of her bed. "There are many tragedies in life," he began, his mood clearly changed, "but none more than the death of a child. So innocent, so helpless. They don't deserve to die young."

"What the hell are you talking about?"

"What am I talking about? I saw that little girl get murdered. The life choked out of her," he blurted out. "That's what I'm talking about. And I can't get her face out of my head."

For a moment, Sarah was stunned. "You mean you were there? You know who killed that Polish girl in the alley? It wasn't the rabbi they have arrested?"

"You stupid whore," he said dully.

"Hey Maloney," a group of *Free Press* reporters standing at the bar of the Royal called out, "stop drinking and get back to work. Maybe this time, you can start a war." The men laughed loudly as they reached for their beer mugs.

Maloney ignored them. He just wanted to be left alone with his whisky. Everything had been going so well. The blood ritual story had been sensational. The Trib's circulation broke new records. He had done a great job, everyone in the newsroom had told him. Then the riot had erupted. One person had been killed, a cop no less. A Jewish woman had been injured. Dozens of homes and shops destroyed. And they were blaming him.

Telegrams flooded into the *Tribune* office from across the country. "Winnipeg, the city that advertises itself as the 'Gateway to the West', the place in Canada were there is room for everyone," declared an editorial in the *Vancouver Sun*, "was the scene of a riot against Hebrews last night, no different than the pogroms of Russia. Add the city's name to the long list of towns and villages in the Czar's Empire where Jews no longer feel safe: Odessa, Aleksandriia, Berislav, Kishinev, and now Winnipeg. Blame for the outbreak of violence must fall squarely on the shoulders of the *Tribune* and Mr. John Maloney, for writing what amount to a slanderous attack on the Hebrew community."

It was the same story in the *Montreal Gazette*, the *Edmonton Journal*, the *Calgary Herald* and the *Ottawa Journal* — Winnipeg's reputation was tarnished, the citizens angry and scared, and it was all due to the irresponsible reporting of John Maloney.

He stared at a telegram sent to him by Jack Bryant, an old friend and reporter with the *Globe* in Toronto. "Thought you might want to see today's headline. RIOT IN WINNIPEG LINKED TO TRIBUNE REPORTER, JEWS TARGETED BY MOB, NEIGHBOURHOODS DESTROYED. Have a nice day. Jack."

"He was an asshole when we worked together five years ago," Maloney muttered, "and he still is." He threw the papers on the floor.

"Maloney, take it easy," said Jimmy Seville, the Royal's bartender.

"Just give me another whisky," demanded Maloney, "and mind your goddamn business."

"Sure thing Maloney. But listen, you can either feel sorry for yourself or do something about it. That's free advice."

Maloney turned away clutching his glass. So he had been caught up in the excitement of his scoop. Who the hell cared? He never thought for a moment that his stories would set off a bloody riot. This was Winnipeg, after all. In his mind, he was just serving the public interest and doing a damn good job of it. If the aliens wanted to kill each other, so be it.

Christ what a mess, he thought. Suddenly he felt nauseous. He needed some air and quickly.

Bob Stewart and his family lived in a two-bedroom house on Lipton Street, about a block from Portage Avenue. It was a typical middle-class neighbourhood with small wooden bungalows that resembled one another. Unlike the North End, however, the streets and sidewalks were paved and during the summer the lawns were painstakingly manicured.

The curtains were drawn at the Stewart home. Klein knocked on the front door. He had only met Bob's wife Amanda once before, many months ago while shopping at Eaton's. He doubted if she'd remember him. After a few moments, a thin woman with short black hair came to the door. She was clutching a white handkerchief; her face was drawn and her eyes red.

"Mrs. Stewart, my name is Sam Klein. I was a friend of Bob's. I don't know if you recall meeting me at Eaton's."

"Sam, yes of course. Please come in. You'll have to excuse the mess, I..."

"Please accept my sincere condolences. Bob was a good man and a fine constable. Could we talk for a few minutes?"

She led Klein into the dark living room. Bob's funeral had been yesterday, she told him. He had been killed in the line of duty, Chief McRae had informed her. Yet there were no details, no clues. She sat down on the couch, Klein took a seat opposite her on one of the chairs.

"It doesn't make any sense. What was Bob doing in that alley? He told me he was meeting a friend," she said, close to tears. Klein shifted uncomfortably. "The next thing I know," she continued, "the police chief is sitting where you are telling me that Bob was murdered. Bob and I talked about such a thing happening. All part of his job, he used to say. But, well, you never think it could happen to you. Our son, Garth, is only five years old, Sam. All he knows is that his daddy didn't come home from work yet. He won't even remember him. A little boy should not have to grow up without a father, don't you agree?"

"I do, Mrs. Stewart. I lost my father when I was a young boy. Don't even know what he looked like. You never really accept it, but you do learn to live with it."

"I'm sorry."

"Don't be, it was a long time ago, another lifetime. Now please listen, I know we don't know each other but I believe I can find out who killed Bob."

"What do you mean? Wasn't it one of the rioters?"

"I don't think so."

She stared at him for a moment. "Bob was going to meet you, Sam, wasn't he?"

"Tell me, in the last few weeks, did you notice anything unusual about Bob?"

"He was a little jumpier than normal. He kept losing his temper with Garth. When I asked him about it, he said he was having some problems at work. I didn't think much about it though. Why?"

"Was he ever more specific?"

"No, not that I can recall. But you know the day he died, he did say he was going to fix whatever it was that was troubling him."

"Do you mind if I ask you a more personal question?"

She shrugged.

"Were you and Bob having any financial problems?"

"Depended who you spoke to."

"What do you mean?"

"Look around you, Sam. I know this is no castle, but I like it. Honestly, I could live here the rest of my life and it would not bother me in the least. For Bob, on the other hand, it was different. He was never satisfied. Always wanted more clothes, more toys for Garth. He wanted a bigger house. He used to talk about one day owning one of those mansions on Wellington Crescent and travelling to London for a holiday. He had read somewhere that the bankers William Alloway and Henry Champion had made a bundle buying and selling land on Portage Avenue and he would tell me how he too was going to make thousands of dollars investing in city real estate and farm land. That one day, Bob Stewart would join James Ashdown, Sir Daniel McMillan and Nicholas Bawlf as one of Winnipeg's millionaires. I told him he was being foolish."

"I hadn't known. When ever we played poker or had a whisky together, he didn't talk much about such things. It was strictly cards and booze."

"I'm not surprised. There was a part of him which was proud to be a police officer, but he was embarrassed to talk about his wages."

"From where I sit, he wasn't doing too bad."

Amanda shrugged. "All I know is that Bob was never happy on pay day and it probably got him killed."

"Why do you say that?"

"I don't know. You tell me that his death was not related to the riot and I believe you. But if Bob was murdered for another reason, I would wager it had something to do with money."

"If you'll trust me, I will see what I can find out. Would you mind very much if I took a look at his private papers?"

"I suppose not. Come follow me, he kept stuff in a wooden box in our bedroom."

Klein followed her through the hallway to the bedroom. A black and white photograph of Bob in uniform hung on the wall.

"It was the day he became a constable. I don't think I ever saw him more proud of himself or happy. He didn't worry about making millions in those days."

She bent down and lifted a brown crate on to the bed. "Here it is. You have a look and I'll fix us some tea."

Klein pulled out a pile of papers. It was funny what people saved. There were yellowed clippings of cases Bob had worked on, letters he had written to his wife when he had been out of town, ribbons and honours he had received as a constable, and a variety of advertisements and business opportunities. There was land for sale in Oakdale Park and a venture in North-West real estate offered by Alloway and Champion. Another small piece of wrinkled paper announced an auction of furnishings and art donated by the local business tycoon, Augustus Nanton. Each scrap of paper wasn't much by itself, meaningless scraps, but taken together they reflected a man's goals, objectives and achievements. In Klein's hands, in short, was the tangible spirit of Bob Stewart's life and dreams. One piece of paper caught Klein's eye.

Ten minutes or so passed before Amanda returned with some tea. She handed Klein a cup.

"Did you find anything?" she asked.

"Not what I was looking for. In fact, there is nothing very unusual except this," Klein said holding up the piece of paper. "I didn't know that Bob was much of a grain speculator."

"He wasn't, at least he never told me about it. What is that?"

"It's an invoice for $330.10 from Peter Tooley, grain broker. Do you know anything about this?"

"Nothing. I've never heard of him. Bob looked after our finances and he didn't tell me much. As I told you, he was always thinking of ways to make some more."

"Well maybe he thought he found it. Do you mind if I hold on to this for a little while?"

Amanda shrugged.

"Also, do you have a recent photo of Bob that I could borrow?"

"I think so."

Amanda returned a few minutes later with a smaller version of the picture that hung on the wall.

Klein smiled awkwardly as he took the picture. "Bob and I were not that close, but I know he was a good man."

Amanda nodded her head slowly. "No matter what you find out, Sam, remember that. He was a good man."

Klein was back downtown after a thirty-minute streetcar ride. He had promised Isaac that they would meet at noon in Alfred Powers's law office to discuss Rabbi Davidovitch's case. As luck would have it, the lawyer's office was in the new Grain Exchange building on Lombard Avenue, close to the corner of Portage and Main. Klein figured he could first meet with Powers and then try to find the broker Peter Tooley.

Since the next day was Good Friday, it was busier than usual. As he moved through the crowd of afternoon shoppers, businessmen and secretaries scurrying back to the office after lunch, Klein had the distinct feeling that he was being followed. Several times, he stopped and glanced behind him but saw nothing unusual.

A small group of people near Garry Street were standing around watching workers high above repair a telephone wire. Young boys off from school for a few days darted back and forth across Portage in between horse-drawn wagons and electric streetcars. A light freezing rain made walking slick. Klein reached Portage and Main and turned quickly to his left. Still nothing.

About a hundred feet away, a cart driver steadied his feisty horses by pulling back hard on the brown leather reins. The two black mares, eyes blazing ahead, coughed and snorted. Foamy spittle spewed on to the muddy street. The driver could see his target about to cross Portage. He would have to time it perfectly. The orders had been clear. First, no one other than Klein was to be hurt; second, make it look like an accident.

Klein could see the seven-story Exchange building in the distance. Caught in the middle of a mob of pedestrians, he moved onto Main Street. As he did so, the driver eased up on the reins and urged his horses forward with a light whip of the straps. When Klein reached the mid-point of the intersection, the driver snapped his whip hard and the horses picked up speed, their muscular legs moving in tandem, heeding the call of their master. Faster and faster they came, bearing down on their intended victim.

"Watch out, runaway horses!" screamed a woman on the other side of the street. "Get out of the way!"

Seeing the charging horses, the group of people crossing Main Street ran in every direction, pushing and shoving each other. An elderly woman standing directly in front of Klein was nearly trampled. She lost her balance and fell. Quickly, Klein moved to her and helped her up. Now the horses were less than twenty feet away. They were coming hard and fast, aiming for him. As he ran forward to get out of their path, the driver veered the horses to keep them on track. Ten feet. Five feet. Klein could see the rolling whites of their eyes. There was nowhere to go.

Then at the last possible moment, a hand from the crowd found Klein's jacket collar and yanked it hard, jerking him from the wagon's path. The horses raced by and headed down Main Street, their driver pulling his hat low over his head.

Klein looked up from the ground as John Maloney smugly wiped the dirt from this hands. "You don't look very grateful, Klein. I could've let that wagon run you over."

Klein scrambled to his feet. "Have you been following me?"

"I could lie and tell you it was only a coincidence that I happened to be here. But it's not true. I've been following you since you left Stewart's house."

"What the hell are you up to? First that stupid story —"

"— Maybe I got a little carried away." Maloney's shoulders rose in a shrug.

"And when did you figure this out?"

"A few hours ago, I was sitting drinking at the Royal, feeling sorry for myself. You think I don't feel terrible for what's happened? I may be an irresponsible asshole, but I'm not a murderer."

"Go to hell, Maloney." Klein turned to walk away.

"Wait."

Klein stopped but kept his back to Maloney. "What is it you want from me? Do you want me to forgive you? Fine, I forgive you. Now go on living your pathetic life."

Maloney darted in front of Klein, so that the two men were facing each other. "I used to be a pretty good reporter. I know I've done a lot of damage here. I'm not trying to make excuses. But I've been down to Selkirk Avenue and seen the destruction. If what you say is true, that I am partly to blame for this riot, then I'd like to make amends."

"Yeah, well, I'm sure my sister would be happy to hear that."

Maloney said nothing.

Klein sighed. "What exactly do you want to do, Maloney?"

Maloney narrowed his eyes. "I've heard you're trying to find the real killer of that little girl. It's all over the streets."

"You mean you don't think the rabbi was after her blood?"

"I guess I don't."

"So, what are you going to do for me? You expect me to trust you?"

"No, not now, but maybe later."

"Yeah, much later."

"Listen to me, I know a lot of people in this city, including some of the big shots. I think I might have a better chance of figuring some of this out because...huh...well," Maloney shifted uncomfortably.

"Because you're not a Jew."

"Something like that. You might not want to admit it, but it is bound to hamper your investigation."

"Don't worry, I know better than you what it means."

"Fine then, so let me help. Besides, you got enough problems already."

"What do you mean?"

"That wagon. That was no runaway. The driver aimed his rig directly at you. When you moved forward, he changed directions."

"Maybe."

"No maybes about it. That guy wanted to kill you. You need someone like me around. I can watch your back."

"I feel safer already." Klein pursed his lips. Maloney did offer some advantages. He could go some places Klein couldn't. "Okay, Maloney, you can help me on one condition."

"And that is?"

"Nothing about this investigation gets into the paper until it's completed. Then you can have the whole story, no matter who the real murderer is. And so help me, if I read one word in the paper before that time, I'll kill you myself. Do you understand?"

"I do. So where do we start?"

"Not so fast. There is one last thing I want you to keep in mind."

"I'm all ears."

"Don't misunderstand my invitation for anything other than what it is. We are not pals. I'm using you, Maloney, the way you use people all the time. You can get me through some doors. After this is over, we part company. Got that?"

The reporter nodded.

Klein looked at his watch. It was too late to meet Isaac. "We're going to try to find a grain broker by the name of Peter Tooley. Ever hear of him?"

"Tooley. No. I know a lot of the boys at the Exchange, but not Tooley. I know where to look, though."

"Good. Let's go."

They turned left on Main Street towards Lombard Avenue.

"By the way, Klein, do you know what's happened to Amy? I was at Melinda's last night and no one has seen her in days."

"That's our next job. I'm afraid your favourite girl is mixed up in this mess. I just don't know how."

7

Klein may not have admitted it, but he was thankful to have Maloney accompany him. They were about to enter a strange Anglo-Saxon world that made Klein uncomfortable. On the streets, he knew how things worked. But there were different rules for the rich bankers and grain dealers of the financial district.

They reached the corner of Rorie and Lombard and stood in front of the Grain Exchange, the largest, grandest building in the city. A grey brick structure that rose seven stories high and stretched for one city block, its Italian Renaissance palazzo style gave it the appearance of a European monument rather than an office building. Finely hand-carved floral patterns were etched into the brick at each corner. No Winnipegger who passed by its archway entrance with the words "Grain Exchange" embedded in the stone above could help but be impressed by its grand design. "Wheat is King," the citizens of the prairie city were fond of saying. And the new building was a fitting home for the powerful grain barons who controlled trade in the commodity that had made Winnipeg famous throughout the Empire.

"Come on, Klein, follow me," said Maloney as he opened the thick door beneath the archway entrance. "Have you ever seen the trading floor?"

"Never been here in my life," replied Klein, affecting nonchalance.

Maloney led him down a spacious hallway, past dozens of offices and up the stairs at the back. At the top, they passed through another door and stepped onto a gallery platform overlooking the trading floor.

It was one o'clock, fifteen minutes before the market closed for the day, and the action was frantic. In the corners, phones mounted in a row of booths were ringing non-stop. Beside them, well-dressed men sat in big leather chairs filling out order forms. On the opposite side, underneath three large windows which filled the room with light, a group of telegraph operators tapped away, oblivious to the chaos around them.

In the middle of the vast trading floor were three octagon pits. Inside, a mass of human bodies vied for space in the limited area. Yelping brokers waved their hands to signal buyers and sellers across the other side. Beside them, standing on a thin platform, were young men in blue jackets who marked each price shift in white chalk. Grain prices from markets in Chicago and Minneapolis were designated on an adjacent board.

"Have you ever seen anything like this before?" Maloney asked, trying to shout above the noise. "Free enterprise at its most raw, that's what it is." Klein nodded, mezmerized by the action.

Railways and grain had first put the city of Winnipeg on the map in the late 1870's. And nothing was more illustrative of this powerful partnership than the Grain Exchange. It was here in its huge, crowded pits, that millions of bushels of rich western Canadian wheat were traded so it could be marketed all over the world. The deal-making was swift and not for the faint-hearted. It was a high risk game where thousands of dollars changed hands with a wave of a finger.

Alongside the elite of the city's financial community — grain elevator company owners and shipping magnates who lived in mansions on Wellington Crescent — were brokers and traders all trying to make a fast buck. Their clients were speculators, anonymous players, 'bulls' and 'bears' gambling their fortunes on the wild fluctuations of the grain markets.

It was a world unfamiliar to Klein, a part of the city well beyond the immigrant population. True, there were a few older, more established Jews doing business here. Charlie Goldstein, a broker with Bruce McBean, had been able to purchase an Exchange seat a few years earlier. Yet for the most part, the Exchange, like every other institution of any importance in Winnipeg, was closed to people like Sam Klein.

Was it surprising that Jews regarded themselves as outsiders? They were barely welcome as customers in downtown businesses and certainly not as club members and neighbours. Even wealthy English and German Jews were barred from the posh, stuffy Manitoba Club and the elitist Canoe Club. Nor did they attempt to buy property at Victoria Beach on the shores of Lake Winnipeg where large signs in bold black print declared "NO DOGS OR JEWS ALLOWED".

At precisely 1:15 p.m. a loud bell clanged. Paper flew in the air as the trading on the floor instantly came to a stop. Maloney tugged at Klein's jacket sleeve. "Let's see if we can find Tooley," he said, his voice suddenly loud and echoing.

They exited through the same door they had entered and went back down the stairs. This time, they turned to their left and down another narrow hallway. A young man sat in front of a closed door directly in front of them.

"John Maloney, Tribune. I'm here to see a broker named Peter Tooley."

The young man looked Maloney up and down and then gave Klein the same treatment. "Who's he?"

"Cub reporter. I'm trying to teach him the ropes. Now will you let us through please."

Satisfied with Maloney's credentials, the man opened the door which led on to the floor itself. Standing right in the middle of it, the trading area seemed even larger to Klein. Maloney searched the faces in the crowd, immediately recognizing an Exchange secretary named Gertie Franklin. He walked to her desk with Klein following right behind.

"Gertie, how are you doing?"

"What the hell do you want?" the woman demanded as she closed a file and put it in her out tray.

Klein laughed. Obviously Maloney was a popular fellow. He guessed Gertie was about thirty. She was wearing a tight calf-length gray skirt and a polka-dot blouse. Her blonde hair was tied back in a severe bun. She wasn't beautiful, but she was attractive in a severe, matronly way.

"Gertie, you're not still mad about that little misunderstanding are you?"

"Damn right I am. You left me sitting in that restaurant for three hours. I felt like a fool."

"I told you how sorry I was. There was a fire, I had to cover it. What could I do?"

"What you could do is go to hell." she said, turning away.

"Ma'am, we need your help," said Klein quietly.

Gertie paused. "And who are you?"

"No friend of his, I assure you. My name is Sam Klein."

"You a cop or something."

"I'm not a cop. Just helping out a friend."

Gertie took a good, hard look at Klein. "You're kind of cute. You sure you're no friend of Maloney's?"

"Oh, for God's sakes," said the reporter.

"I barely know the guy," said Klein with a grin.

"Okay," said Gertie, returning the smile, "what can I do for you?"

"I'm looking for a broker named Peter Tooley. You know him?"

"Not well, but we've talked. He's about as pleasant as Maloney. Except he likes fine suits and expensive jewelry."

"Go on."

"To be honest, he kind of gives me the willies. He has this black slick hair that he always greases down."

"So where can we find him?"

"Well, he has a small office on the third floor, but don't bother checking. He hasn't been there or on the floor for about five days. I heard he may be traveling in the States. Between you and me, I hope he never comes back."

"One more thing. You wouldn't know where he lives, do you?"

"He has a room at the McLaren, the last I heard."

Klein thanked her for the information.

"Thanks Gertie, I'll be in touch," said Maloney as the two men left.

"Please don't!" she called back.

"So what do you think?" Maloney asked Klein once they were back in the main lobby.

"I'm not sure, but don't you think it's rather suspicious that Tooley vanishes within a day or so of Anna Rudnicki's murder."

"I do. Why don't we go have a look in his office just to satisfy our curiosity?"

"Maloney, I'm surprised. I was thinking exactly that."

Maugham at eighteen, when he entered medical school.

St. Thomas' Hospital and Medical School in London, which Maugham attended.

Maugham at nine. A year later his father died and the boy was sent to Whitstable.

The Vicarage of Whitstable, the home of his uncle, where Maugham spent the latter part of his boyhood. This photograph, taken soon after young Maugham's arrival from Paris, shows the boy holding the hand of his uncle, the Reverend Henry Maugham.

They walked up three flights of stairs and began searching for Tooley's office. The hallways and offices were quiet; after the market closed it was time for lunch and beer before an afternoon of paperwork and phone calls.

"Look," said Maloney. He pointed at a small black sign with white printing beside room 304. "Peter Tooley. This is it."

Klein turned the handle. It was locked. He knocked on the door. There was silence. He looked at Maloney. "You sure you want to stay for this?"

"Go ahead, Klein. I've seen it before."

Klein hesitated for a moment. He checked the hallway one more time. Then when he was certain no one was around, he grabbed the door handle and shoved hard with his shoulder. It opened easily.

"Very nice, Klein. I take it you've done this before."

"Yeah. Sometimes at Melinda's clients try to lock the girl's rooms. You know, people who drink too much do that sort of thing."

Maloney sighed impatiently. "C'mon, let's do it."

The office was dark. There was only one window and the curtains were drawn. Klein moved inside slowly and his foot caught something on the floor. In fact, the entire office was littered with debris. He maneuvered his way to the desk across from the window and his right hand found a small desk lamp.

"Damn, what a mess," said Maloney, who was right behind him. "I guess someone has been here first."

The office was indeed in a shambles. Tooley's file cabinet had been opened and ransacked. The phone had been pulled right out of the wall and the drawers in the desk almost destroyed.

"What are we looking for?"

"Not sure," replied Klein, picking up some papers, "but I'll know when I find it."

Klein tried to open one of the desk drawers but it was either locked or jammed. He pulled out a pocket knife that he always carried with him, a Christmas present from Melinda, and jimmied the lock open.

"You're wasting your talents at Melinda's," Maloney observed.

Klein ignored him. Inside the drawer he found blank trading forms and invoice sheets, the same kind he had discovered in Bob Stewart's papers.

Digging deeper, underneath all the forms were two black bound binders and a small notebook. He flipped the pages of the binders. There were columns of figures and names.

"Must be his account books," said Maloney, looking over Klein's shoulder." Could be useful. We would have to take a closer look."

"Yeah, I know someone who might be able to help decipher this."

"Who?"

"Later. Let's see what else we got here."

Klein picked up the small notebook. It was Tooley's appointment book. He quickly turned to the second week in April.

"Maloney, look at this. April 10, the night of the murder. Meeting 9 p.m.'"

"So Tooley had a meeting at nine o'clock the night the girl was murdered. It doesn't prove much."

"Maybe."

Klein turned five or six pages back. His chest tightened. "This can't be," he muttered.

"Klein, what is it?" asked Maloney. "What's written there?"

Klein ignored Maloney, his eyes glued to the page. Wednesday, April 5. Call Sarah B.

Klein walked slowly down Main Street carrying the two leather binders he had taken with him from Tooley's office. Maybe there was an explanation. Maybe it was nothing at all. Maybe she wasn't even the Sarah B. listed in Tooley's book. Yeah right, who was he trying to kid? His insides churned.

He stopped at Higgins. He felt dizzy. But he kept on moving, trying to shake it off. The closer he got to Melinda's, the madder he became. If she was involved in this, if she was somehow responsible for the riot, for the attack on Rivka...

He walked quickly up the path leading to the front door of the house. It was open.

"Sam, darling where have you been?" asked Darlene, lying on the plush maroon couch in the parlour. She was wearing nothing but a black lace corset and black silk stockings. At any another time, Klein might have flirted with her for a few moments, but not today.

"Have you seen Sarah?" Klein snapped. She could've been dressed in work overalls for all he cared.

"Can't say I have, darling. Why don't you come keep me company."

There was a small wooden table with a lamp to his right. His fist swung hard at it, smashing it to the floor. A piece broke off and nearly struck Darlene in the face.

"Sam, take it easy!" Darlene yelled in alarm.

Melinda came running from her back office.

"What's going on?" she demanded. "Sam, what happened?"

Klein stood, his fists clenched. He took a deep breath. "Melinda, where is Sarah? I have to talk with her."

"She left early this morning. Something about going shopping at Eaton's. Said she'd be back by six. Now, come to my office and tell me what's going on."

Klein sat down opposite Melinda's desk while she poured him a stiff shot of whisky.

"Thanks, Melinda," Klein said, downing the whiskey in a gulp. "I need your help. Have you ever heard of a Peter Tooley? He's a grain broker. Wears fancy suits."

"Tooley. Can't say that I have. Why?"

"I never heard of him either and I know most of the regulars here."

"So what does he have to do with Sarah?"

"I found her name in his appointment book."

"And?"

"And he might be involved in that little girl's murder."

"I see," said Melinda, pushing a strand of hair back from her face. "That could be a problem. You know, honey, it might be something else. I tell my girls not to work on the side, but I know it goes on. Maybe she was trying to make some extra cash."

"Maybe."

"Why don't you give her the benefit of the doubt?"

"I suppose I..."

The phone on Melinda's office wall rang.

"Hello," she answered. "McCreary? What the hell do you want? Where? I see. Yeah, I could be down there in thirty minutes. You don't mind if I bring Sam Klein with me? Well, too bad."

Melinda hung up the receiver. "Shit."

"What is it? Where are we going?"

"That, as you may have gathered, was Bill McCreary. The police just pulled Amy's body out of the river."

"I would say," mused Dr. Jock MacDonald, "from the marks around her neck that she was first strangled and then thrown into the river. She might've been still alive and drowned. But I'd have to do an autopsy to be absolutely certain."

Dr. MacDonald was a 63-year-old general practitioner who specialized in forensic medicine. From his small, dingy office in the McIntyre Block, he had been helping the Winnipeg Police Force solve crimes for more than two decades.

"Go ahead," said McCreary, "we'll be out of your way in a minute." The detective looked over at Melinda and Klein sitting on the other side of the cramped examination room. He was still angry at how Klein had treated him that night at Melinda's.

"Klein," he barked, "I hear you were visiting Bob Stewart's widow."

"Yes, I was there. Bob was a friend of mine. But how do you know?"

"I got my sources."

"I bet you do. You got even a vague clue who killed him?"

"Not yet, but Stark and I are working on it. Don't worry, we'll find the son of a bitch who did it."

"Right, I'm sure there's another rabbi you can arrest. Or maybe you can find some priest."

"Listen, McCreary," said Melinda. "Do you want me for something or did you bring me down here so you can chitchat with Sam?"

"No. Come over here, Melinda. For the record, I want you to officially identify the body."

Melinda stood up with a white lace handkerchief covering her mouth. The odor from the body was a combination of rotting fish and ammonia. There was no doubt in Melinda's mind who it was. Before her on a slab of wood lay Amy Christopher, a woman who could please any man and entertain as many customers in a night as Melinda ordered her to. Her long elegant fingernails that, until two days ago had satisfied her clients most basic urges, were now embedded with the mud and green weeds of the Red River.

"It's Amy," Melinda said under the handkerchief.

McCreary laughed. "What's wrong Melinda? You never seen a dead whore?"

"McCreary," said Klein, standing up. "Why don't you shut up."

"Are you threatening me?"

"Take it easy, Sam," said Melinda.

"Because if you are," continued the detective, "I'll run you in right now. You can share a cell with that murdering Jew rabbi of yours."

Klein had had enough. He knew McCreary was trying to provoke another fight, one where he was in uniform and in front of witnesses. Before he lost his temper completely, he had to leave. Klein raised his hand in a sarcastic salute and headed for the street.

"I don't know what it is, Stark," McCreary said to his partner, "but that Hebrew troublemaker Klein gets under my skin." He shuffled some papers on his cluttered desk, searching for his box of cigars.

"That's because," said Stark sitting opposite him, "he isn't your average North End foreigner that you can walk all over. He's a clever son-of-a-bitch who knows his way around this city as good as you. And..."

"And what?" demanded McCreary.

"And he doesn't lose his head drinking whisky."

McCreary's face darkened.

"That's right," continued Stark, "I heard about your night at the brothel. It's not the first time, is it?"

"None of your damn business. You're my partner Stark, not my wife. I handle my whisky fine. It was that slut Sarah Bloomberg who had the problem. To be honest, I don't know why the men in this city make such a fuss about her. Yeah, she's a beautiful woman, but she's still a whore, and a Hebrew one at that."

Stark turned away with a frown.

Smirking, McCreary pulled out a cigar and lit it. "You know why there was trouble," the detective declared. "Because, I hear she's Klein's bitch. He just couldn't take it that I had had her."

"That's not the way I heard the story," shrugged Stark. "I heard you hit her and he hit you a lot harder. And as for anything happening in the bedroom..."

McCreary leaned forward. "You know what I think, Stark. I think you actually like that Jew. In fact, the way you've been acting during this entire investigation, interrupting my interrogations, tampering with the evidence, I'd say that you've become a Jew lover. You like Klein and you feel sorry for the Hebrew killer we have behind bars. Do you hear that?" yelled McCreary. "Our friend Stark here is a Jew lover."

For a moment, typewriters stopped clicking and ringing phones went unanswered. A few chuckles resonated through the smoky office.

"What's going on?" asked an intoxicated man dressed in gray coveralls and a black flat cap. He had been picked up for causing a public disturbance. "Who's a Jew lover?"

Stark shook his head in disgust. "The show's over," he declared. "Bill's just having a bit of a tantrum. Why don't you all get back to what you were doing."

"Listen McCreary," Stark continued in a lower voice. "Maybe we should just concentrate on solving the murder of Amy Christopher before another body turns up. Personally, I could do without another lecture from the chief."

McRae usually left McCreary and Stark alone when they were working on a case. But the publicity surrounding the murder of Anna Rudnicki had given the city a black eye. Even with the arrest of Rabbi Davidovitch, Mayor Sanford Evans had been hounding the chief. Evans, the owner of the *Winnipeg Telegram*, wanted to be reassured that the evidence against the rabbi was solid. Like many citizens of Winnipeg, the mayor wasn't sure what to make of the blood ritual charges; at this point, he didn't care. "Make sure you have the right man on trial and for God's sakes make the case stick," he had ordered the chief. "I don't want to read again in the Toronto Globe that Winnipeg is persecuting its Hebrews."

McRae, in turn, had been on his detectives' backs to check and recheck their facts. "Talk to that peddler one more time, re-interview witnesses, check with Hicks about fingerprints," he had told them. "And find out if these killings are connected in some way. I have a nasty feeling that they are."

"One goddamn murder after another," Stark muttered to himself, "What has happened to this city?"

"Stark," McCreary said, butting out his cigar in a tin ashtray. "I think you're going senile in your old age. What's the problem? We got the Hebrew in jail. That case is as good as closed. Stewart was in the wrong place at the wrong time. No big mystery there. And our young whore? What is there to tell? She obviously met a client who she didn't quite satisfy. We'll ask around at the houses and bars. Trust me, give it a week and our man will turn up."

"Right," Stark grumbled, returning to the papers on his desk. McCreary had a well-deserved reputation as an intuitive detective. Except on this occasion, thought Stark, he had things all wrong.

Like most bars on Main Street, the one at the Brunswick Hotel was frequented by all types: drunks, thieves, hustlers, pool sharks and workingmen from the railway or nearby factories. The damp wooden floor was covered in sawdust and several spittoons were conveniently located by the bar. The rule was that if you didn't stay awake you might end up with brownish-yellow tobacco juice in your eye. The noise from the pool players at the back and the shooting gallery next door was loud and boisterous, day or night.

Klein sat down beside a smiling Maloney. The reporter had been at the bar for a couple of hours, comfortably settled into that uniquely Irish drunkenness that combined maudlin reflection with the urge to philosophize. Maloney shot back his whiskey and peered at the young Jewish bouncer. "So, Klein, tell me about that woman of yours. What makes her so special?"

"Maloney, I think you should mind your own business."

"Listen, there are lots of beautiful women in this city, especially at Melinda's. So, I ask again, what makes her such a prize? I mean, I could speculate."

"Maloney, you are an asshole, do you know that?"

"Yes," Maloney nodded sagely, "I have been told that."

Klein laughed, in spite of himself. He lit a cigarette and exhaled to the ceiling. "Am I going to read about this in a newspaper column?"

"You really don't trust me, do you Sam? You don't mind if I call you Sam? You can call me John."

"To be perfectly honest, Maloney, no, I don't trust you. I've known a few newspapermen and in my opinion, you're all the same. You would sell out your own mother if you thought it made a good story."

Maloney shook his head and raised his right hand. "If it will make you happy, I'll see if One-arm Eddie has a Bible I can swear to."

"Just remember what I said."

"I'm all ears."

Klein took a deep drag on his cigarette. "About two years ago, in the middle of winter, I found her lying in the snow on Melinda's doorstep. She was wearing nothing but a ragged dress. Her body was black and blue with bruises. At first, she wouldn't even tell us her name. But Melinda nursed her back to health and she gradually revealed to us the details of her life."

Klein paused to sip his drink.

"And?" asked Maloney.

Klein shrugged. "She said she was sent to Canada from Lodz, a city in Poland. She was to be the wife of a Jewish immigrant named Meyervitz, who had been in Winnipeg for about three years and supposedly was the owner of a hardware store in the North End. There was a house on Magnus awaiting her. The marriage had been arranged by her stepfather, the bastard. I don't even think he got more than fifty dollars."

"And let me guess? There was no store or house."

"Exactly. Meyervitz was nothing more than a pimp who brought young women over from the old country and forced them to be prostitutes. If they didn't obey his rules, he beat them silly. As Sarah later told me, Meyervitz never asked questions first. What could she do? She didn't speak English. She had no friends."

Maloney nodded sympathetically.

"Each night for almost two years, he sold her like a piece of meat and beat her if she didn't listen to him. He took all the money she earned.

Christ, he barely fed her. Finally, after he beat her so badly that she couldn't endure anymore, she ran away and wound up at Melinda's."

"That's it?"

"About a month later, Meyervitz shows up at Melinda's looking for her. He is this stocky bald guy, real ugly. I give him a few shots to the face and let's just say, he's never returned to bother her again."

"So everything turned out for the best."

Klein smiled bitterly. Right, he thought. He fell in love with a beautiful whore. Melinda wasn't holding Sarah prisoner. She could quit if she wanted to. Walk away from it all. Truth was, she didn't; in fact, and this was the most difficult thing for Klein to accept, he believed Sarah reveled in her work. She liked the attention; she enjoyed her clients. Worst of all, there was a decent and innocent man in prison right now and Sarah Bloomberg was somehow involved. He could feel it.

"Maloney, what time is it?"

Maloney glanced at his gold pocket watch which he kept in his vest. "Four o'clock. Why?"

"I've got to go."

"She's not back yet?"

"No, and I'm getting worried. Amy is dead and now Sarah is missing."

"So how can I help?"

"Are you sober enough to ask around if anyone has seen her?"

"Don't worry, Klein, you wouldn't believe what I can do with a bottle of whisky under my belt."

"One other thing —"

The reporter raised an eyebrow.

"As soon as you can, I want to you to start researching every blood libel trial for the past hundred years. Talk to that professor at the College. I'm sure he can assist you."

"How will that help?"

"Just do it. I don't have time for explanations. And remember to meet me at the corner of Logan and Main about eight o'clock this evening and we'll see if we can sort out what Peter Tooley was up to."

Despite the fact that Rivka Klein was back on her feet, the house on Flora Avenue was crowded again when Sam arrived. There were a dozen women huddled around Freda Klein and a group of men sitting around the dining room table. They gossiped in Yiddish about Rabbi Davidovitch's plight, drank Passover wine, and talked about better times.

Freda remained seated on her stool in the middle of the room. Clara Hirsch sat beside her. Klein watched as Isaac walked up to both women, whispered into Freda's ear, smiled, and then ordered one man near the front of the table to pour him a glass of wine.

"Why do you embarrass me like this, Isaac?" asked Clara in Yiddish.

"Pardon?"

She slightly raised her voice. "Everyone knows how you feel about Freda. Everyone talks about it. I hear them whispering."

"Clara, please....," Freda said, "Not here. Not now."

"I am his door mat, you know that, everyone knows that."

"Clara, be quiet," ordered Isaac.

"I won't. Is it because I could never give you children? Is that it? Have I not been good to you? Please Isaac, tell me."

Hirsch turned to look at Klein for a moment. Then, suddenly, he raised his right hand as if he was intending to slap his wife across the face.

"Isaac!" exclaimed Freda.

For a long moment, the room was silent. Finally Isaac dropped his hand to his side. Clara stood up, glared at her husband and then marched out of the house.

"Isaac, how could you?" admonished Freda.

Hirsch said nothing. He turned and walked towards the men. "Quickly, where is my cup?" The man who had poured the wine handed the cup to Isaac who drank it down in one gulp.

Hirsch called to Klein to join them, but Klein just stared at his mother's friend.

"Shailek, did you hear me?" repeated Isaac. "Come have some wine with us."

Klein hid his shock over Isaac's bizarre outburst and joined the older men. After he drank a glass of red wine, Isaac led him through the crowd of people to the back of the house and into his old bedroom that he had shared with Rivka for so many years. It was a small room with one window. Rivka's possessions, her books, newspapers, and clothes remained exactly as they had been the day he moved out. When Rivka had turned twelve, Freda had hung a white sheet in the middle of the room, so that both Klein and his sister could have their privacy.

"You don't approve?" asked Hirsch.

"What do you mean?"

"The look on your face. I can tell."

"Perhaps you are feeling guilty."

"Someday, you will have a wife and understand. A man has the right to discipline his wife. That is the way of the world. Besides, I didn't actually strike her, did I?"

Klein hardly saw the distinction, but did not belabour the point. "I am not going to argue with you, Isaac. Just don't ever attempt to do that to my mother."

"Please, Sam, don't threaten me."

"I'm not. I'm warning you. There's a difference."

Hirsch laughed. "Enough of this. Let us talk about other matters. I thought you were going to meet with me at the lawyer's office."

"I know. I tried. But let's just say I was delayed. How did the meeting go?"

"Fine. Powers is a real gentleman, though I don't think he's had many Jewish clients before. I doubt, in fact, if he's ever even been beyond the CPR tracks. Nonetheless, he has agreed to take the rabbi's case. The man is a legend in the Winnipeg legal community. You know he was mayor of the city when he was only thirty, a King's Counsel by thirty-six."

"That's fine, but how is he in court?"

"He'll be wonderful. I guarantee it. He says he is so disgusted by what has happened that he is willing to take the case for free. Of course, I refused the offer. He's already heard that the special Crown prosecutor will be Timothy Jarvis and that we shouldn't be too surprised when he raises the blood accusation. The judge will no doubt rule him out of order, but if the case goes to a jury trial, which he thinks it will, the blood libel will obviously have an impact. So what I'm telling you Shailek, is that we have to stop this thing before it starts."

"That's easier said than done."

"I know, but we don't have a choice. Mark my words, if this goes further, there will be more trouble, maybe bloodshed. The preliminary hearing in Police Court is on Tuesday and Powers thinks he'll have another ten days or so before the trial begins. The mayor, the police chief and the attorney-general want this business to be completed and quickly. One way or another, Anna Rudnicki's murderer is going to be brought to justice."

Hirsch leaned forward. "And now tell me, have you found out anything yet?"

Klein considered telling Isaac about Amy, Tooley and the attempt on his life. But some instinct told him to keep the information to himself. "Nothing yet, but I may have something after tonight."

Hirsch smiled and patted Klein's arm. "I had better see how your mother and Clara are doing."

Joe James was exactly where he always was. Maloney had got to the corner of Logan and Main first. Klein showed up a few minutes later.

"Anything turn up, Maloney?"

"Nothing. I asked around at a few bars, the McLaren and Leland, but no one has seen her."

"Keep looking and don't forget about that research."

"I haven't forgotten. Believe me, my editor can't wait for more blood ritual stories. He's on my back. The Trib's circulation has never been higher. We're finally giving it to both the *Free Press* and the *Telegram*. I hear both Dafoe and the Colonel are beside themselves. You want to tell me what I'm looking for?"

"I'll let you know when you find it. Just dig."

"Dig. Right."

"I don't mean to break up your tea party, gentlemen, but what can I do for you?" asked Joe, with his trademark bowler hat sitting smartly on the top of his head.

"Sorry, Joe," said Klein. "We need a favour. I hear you know your way around the grain business. Is that true?"

"I used to a long time ago," said the old man. "What do you have?"

"Maybe we should go inside somewhere and sit down," said Klein.

There was a coffee shop across the street. The three men walked in and found a table by the window. Except for an old woman in the corner and two men sitting at the counter smoking cigarettes and drinking coffee, the place was empty. Mixed in with the smell of tobacco, the aroma of fresh warm apple pie and hot coffee lingered in the air. A waitress brought them coffee. Klein pulled the two black binders out of a canvas bag he had brought with him.

"Joe, I'd like you take a look at these. They belong to a grain broker Maloney and I are trying to find..."

"And?" interrupted Joe.

"And we think he's as crooked as a penny pretzel. See what you think."

Joe studied the pages and sipped his coffee. Casually, he took a brown paper bag from his inside coat pocket and poured some clear liquid into the coffee.

"Want some?"

"No thanks," said Klein.

"I'd love some," said Maloney, then he glanced at Klein, "but maybe later."

"Suit yourselves."

Every so often Joe grunted, then returned to the books. Fifteen minutes passed, then thirty, then forty-five. Klein and Maloney had already drunk three cups of coffee and still Joe said nothing.

"Joe, the anticipation is killing me," said Klein. "Is there anything there or not?"

Joe snickered. He signaled the waitress to bring him more coffee. "There's something here all right. I can't be positive, you understand. But I'd say that your broker has been stealing money from his clients. In the neighbourhood of roughly $750,000 would be my best guess."

"Are you certain?" asked Klein.

"Here, see for yourselves."

Joe shifted the two books. "This binder on the right, I presume, was the one he showed his accountants and customers. The other one is where he kept track of his winnings."

"So what did he do?" asked Maloney.

"Patience," said Joe. "It's really quite an ingenious but very simple operation. Let's say a client comes in with $5,000 and an order to buy 10,000 bushels of May wheat futures. He tells your broker to sell as soon as the price moves five or six cents. Your man goes into the pit at the Exchange and buys the contract at say 90 cents a bushel for $9,000. You still with me?"

The two men nodded.

"A week later," Joe further explained, "the price goes up six cents so he sells, except he tells his client that he sold the contract when the market was only three cents higher. It's a difference of $9,600 versus $9,300. On a daily basis, prices change so fast, what is the average client going to know? So he credits his client's account with $300 and his own personal account with the other $300. It doesn't sound like much, but you do this over a few years with more than four hundred customers and it adds up. Better still, let's say the price goes down. He calls for more margin money than is required and again pockets the difference."

"Look at these two columns," said Joe, pointing to the two books. "On September 29, 1909, he bought 15,000 bushels of November wheat futures for a client named L. King at $1.05 per bushel. Five days later, he sold the contract for $1.09, except in this ledger the price is listed as $1.065. Look over here in the other book at this account marked 'S.B.'. On September 29, S.B. is credited with $375, the difference between 15,000 bushels at $1.09 or $16,350 and the same amount of wheat at $1.065 or $15,975. Hardly a day goes by when something is not deposited into S.B.'s pockets."

Klein grabbed the books and quickly skimmed the pages. Joe's assessment appeared to be correct.

"Is there anything else?"

"I think so."

Joe flipped the pages ahead to March 12, 1910, nearly a year earlier. "Around this time, this guy starts to get greedier."

"How so?" asked Maloney.

"If you examine the figures, he starts to take more and more. Now we're talking maybe six to seven cents per contract. It's hard to believe no one noticed."

"Maybe they did," said Klein.

"Starting on that date," said Joe, "in addition to the 'S.B.' account, there is a new account right below it listed as 'M.S.'. And if you follow it through it grows pretty fast until about three weeks ago, when both 'S.B.' and 'M.S.' drop to almost nothing."

"So what happened to the money in those accounts?" asked Maloney.

"That, my friend, is a good question and one only your broker can answer. You guys need anything else?"

"No, that's it Joe. Thanks, you've been a big help," said Klein. "Here, for your trouble." He shoved a five dollar bill in Joe's coat pocket.

"Always a pleasure, Sam."

Joe finished his coffee and left the cafe. Maloney kept studying the account books while Klein stared out the window.

"Klein, I know something is bugging you," said Maloney. "Out with it."

"You don't get it, do you?" Klein snapped.

"Get what? Tooley was a goddamn thief. That's what I get. Maybe he killed the little girl."

"Maybe. But it's staring at you right in the face."

"I'm sorry, I still don't get it."

"Christ, Maloney, are you blind? 'S.B.', what the hell do you think that stands for?"

"To be honest, I haven't the vaguest idea."

Klein gritted his teeth. "Sarah Bloomberg. That's the only name that fits."

8

As she hurried into the soaring main hall of the CPR station on Higgins Avenue, Sarah glanced over her left shoulder. She was certain that she was being followed. Earlier in the day she had changed from her usual attire — a brightly coloured dress and matching hat — and opted for something more drab, more common. Now wearing a white silk embroidered blouse and a navy skirt, she nearly fit into the crowd of newly arrived immigrants, travelers and tourists milling about in the city's bustling train station. She only hoped that no one would recognize her, especially none of her clients. It was the first time in a long time that she had no desire to be noticed.

Even this late in the evening, the station was a beehive of activity. Since it had been built in 1905 (the third CPR depot in Winnipeg's brief history), this imposing structure had been the entry point for hundreds of thousands of immigrants bound for western Canada and their free 160 acres of rich prairie farm land. The British and their western European neighbours from Scandinavia and Germany had arrived first. They were eventually followed by newcomers from Russia, the Ukraine and other eastern European locales. Processed by overworked and underpaid federal authorities at the nearby and perpetually crowded Dominion Immigration Hall, a dingy and unsanitary centre, many of the foreigners opted to stay in Winnipeg. Quite naturally, they tended to congregate among people who spoke the same language and practised the same customs. Thus within a few years, the city was divided into a number of immigrant quarters. The most visible and most impoverished area was the North End, but there were others as well in the Weston area and in Fort Rouge.

As usual, a Babel of languages echoed through the station's large waiting area. Several businessmen in fine dark suits and bowler hats chatted in English, while their wives in long dresses and wide-brimmed hats gossiped and kept an eye on their noisy children. A group of newly arrived Norwegian farmers, blond and broad-shouldered, talked amongst themselves about their future plans. They were headed for homesteads north of Minnedosa. And in the far corner of the station, a Ukrainian family, a husband, wife and their two children dressed in worn clothes and boots with holes, sat patiently counting the seconds until the ten o'clock train arrived from Toronto. Sarah could overhear and understand their conversation. They were expecting the woman's sister from their home village of Ghermakivka in Galicia whom they had not seen in five years. Another poor soul coming to find her fortune in the ragged slums of the North End, thought Sarah.

She clutched her train ticket and found a chair in a darkened area of the large room. Her train for Winnipeg Beach, fifty miles north of the city, was scheduled to depart in one hour. Scanning the station one more time, the sinister face she was searching for was nowhere to be seen. A little more relaxed, she set her small suitcase on the floor and collapsed in the chair. She found her gold cigarette case in her purse, took a cigarette out and lit it. Sarah didn't normally smoke, but she always kept her gold case in her handbag should the craving for a cigarette arise. At that moment, exhausted and on edge, the tobacco was a much needed tonic. As she deeply inhaled the cigarette, her mind raced over the events of the past twenty-four hours. She tried to make sense of it all, but one image kept clouding her thoughts: Amy was dead and she was to blame.

She remembered the scene vividly. Tooley had barged into her bedroom at four in the morning, drunk and menacing. He had given her a black book to hide, presumably a record of the clients he had bilked. She felt like such a fool for becoming mixed up with him and his greedy scheme. Worse, she knew now that he was somehow involved in the murder of that young Polish girl.

Then, Amy had walked into her bedroom, awakened by the noise. She was wearing a loose fitting black silk night gown. In the chill of the night air, the nipples of her round breasts protruded forward. "Oh you have company," she had said.

Sarah had tried to get rid of her, but seeing her standing there nearly naked had aroused Tooley.

"How long have you been at the door?" he had asked her with a wolfish smile.

"Only for a minute or two," Amy had answered him slyly. "But long enough to see that you are a man to be taken seriously."

"You don't know the half of it," Tooley had said. "In fact, now is as good a time as any to show you."

Sarah had protested, but neither of them had paid any attention to her. As Tooley led Amy into her own bedroom, he had warned Sarah to keep her mouth shut.

In the morning, she had tried to find Amy, but no one had seen her. A few hours later, she had heard that the police had pulled Amy's body out of the river. It was then that she had known she was in real danger. Her instincts had told her that either Tooley or whomever he had hired to follow her would be back. She had no other choice: she had to leave Melinda's and quickly. She had packed a few things and had thrown a suitcase out her window on to the ground. In a rush, she had announced to Melinda that she would be shopping all day and would return later that evening.

All morning and afternoon, she had kept out of sight. For a few hours, she had wandered down back alleys behind Portage Avenue and eaten a slow lunch at an out of the way diner near Portage and Lipton Street. Two or three times, she was certain that she had seen the bearded man from the Walker Theatre again. Overwhelmed with guilt about Amy's death, she had began to wonder if the money was worth all of this. Conflicting emotions had risen from within. She had worked so hard for the money, wasn't she entitled to her fair share?

At about six o'clock, tired from a day of running, she had made her way to the grand Royal Alex Hotel, next to the CPR station. There, a trustworthy bellhop who occassionally sent clients her way allowed Sarah to hide out in a room used by the hotel's daytime cleaning maids. Finally at about 9:15 p.m. she had left the hotel and made her way across the street to the station.

Winnipeg Beach was the perfect place for a brief respite. Sarah knew that Klein would be notified when she did not return to Melinda's. But she knew as well that he would never think to search for her at the Beach.

For him, the world stopped on the outskirts of the city. She glanced at the large square clock above the ticket counter. Only twenty minutes more until she could board. She had already sent a telegram to her friend at Winnipeg Beach, a girl named Lind Olsen, who lived in the small town on the shores of Lake Winnipeg. She was certain Lind would meet her at the train platform when she arrived at a few minutes past midnight.

A tall blonde, Lind had worked at Melinda's for about a month last year, before deciding that the life of a Winnipeg prostitute was not for her. Instead, she had returned to her family home at the Beach. In her brief stay in the city, however, she and Sarah had become close. Sarah did not have many female friends. Perhaps it was her independent and stubborn streak; maybe she was just too busy working. She liked Darlene, Michelle, and Amy, of course, and Melinda treated her like a sister. But Lind was different. She was truly interested in Sarah's life and problems. Sarah had met few women who were as sincere or genuine as Lind. It seemed natural to turn to her, now that she was in trouble.

Last summer, Sarah had spent a weekend at the beach with Lind. The fifty mile train ride from the CPR station was short and the weather hot and muggy. The Olsen family lived in a small frame house not far from the lake. Unlike the fast pace of life in the city, the beach was quiet and serene. Sarah had found the cool breeze off the water soothing and the woodland setting comfortable. There wasn't much to the town — a general store, a Chinese laundry, a run-down hotel and a few restaurants along the main street opposite the lake.

Sarah and Lind had lazed in the sand by the water during the day and danced in the new pavilion at night. There were no clients to please and she didn't have to feel guilty about how Klein felt about her work. She hadn't talked with Lind for many months, yet she knew that her friend would help her out.

Sarah's thoughts were interrupted by the cry of the conductor.

"All aboard," yelled the middle-aged man in his navy blue uniform. "Train for Selkirk, Winnipeg Beach, Gimli and Riverton now departing on track number three."

Sarah gathered up her belongings and moved into the middle of the small group of people walking towards the track. Instinctively, she glanced behind her one last time. Then she saw him at the other end of the station. It was the same husky man who had followed her at the Walker. From across the room, her eyes met his and a sly smile crossed his face. He started to move towards her. But Sarah did not panic. Quickly she pushed her way to the front of the crowd. She walked through a large double doorway and scurried up the stairs where the train was waiting, its great steam engine idling. Patches of white smoke covered the platform. She could hear heavy footsteps not far behind her. What could she do? She knew that if she boarded the train, he would have her. She had no other option. She ran as fast as she could to the front of the engine and leaped blindly on to the track. This close, the smoke was dense as the engineer inside continued to stoke the furnace. In the confusion, the heel of her black pump splintered. She grabbed both her shoes and threw them on to the ground.

"Miss, where do you think you are going?" It was the voice of the CPR conductor. "Charlie," he shouted to the engineer. "Get that woman out of there."

But before the engineer could descend from his car, Sarah had leaped on to the platform on the other side of the train, climbed up the stairs and ran out the side door of the station. Terrified, her heart beating faster and faster, she searched the blackness of the night. Less than a block away a streetcar, on its last run of the evening, was about to pull out.

"Wait," she shouted. In her stocking feet and still carrying her suitcase, she ran over the wooden sidewalk and on to the muddy street. The streetcar operator had heard her. She reached the car out of breath.

"You in trouble or something, Miss?" asked the driver.

Sarah shook her head. "I'm fine. Please just go."

"Sure thing Ma'am."

She stood up for a moment and looked back towards the station. There was no one there. The streetcar travelled south down Main Street and proceeded west along Portage Avenue past Wesley College. At this late hour, Portage was silent, except for the odd drunken straggler on his way home. The streetcar stopped at Sherbrook where Sarah transferred to the last SRTC train going into St. James that night. Twenty minutes later, she was at the corner of Portage Avenue and Queen Street, a few steps from the St. James Hotel.

Fortunately, she had packed another pair of shoes in her bag. She put them on and decided it might be a good idea to stay at the hotel for the night. Somehow, she would have to get word to Lind in Winnipeg Beach. She hoped that when she didn't turn up on the midnight train, her friend would assume that she got busy with some work for the evening.

More tired than scared, Sarah pushed opened the brown wooden door of the hotel. Inside, several kerosene lanterns flickered near the windows. There was a table with six chairs to her left and a dark coloured couch on the far wall. Both of its pillows were ripped and the cotton stuffing protruded through the small holes.

Ahead of her was the front desk behind which a gray-haired woman sat dozing.

"Excuse me," she said. "Could I have a room for the night?"

The elderly woman opened her eyes. "Yes, of course, my dear. I was just resting. It'll be two dollars."

Sarah forced a smile, reached into her purse and handed the woman the correct amount of cash.

"Now, please sign this."

Staring at the blank page of the hotel register book, Sarah momentarily paused and then she signed it as Megan O'Connor — the same name as an American singer from New York she had once seen at the Orpheum Theatre.

"That's funny, dear," said the woman, "you don't look Irish."

Sarah shrugged and said as little as possible. Despite having been in Canada for more than three years, there were still traces of a Polish accent in her voice. The woman gave her a key to room 104, down a narrow, dark corridor.

The room was small with one single bed and a dresser. A copy of that day's *Free Press* sat on the top of the bureau. Immediately, she walked to the room's single window and peeked out into the darkness. Except for the chirping of crickets by the banks of the Assiniboine River, a short distance away, the evening was silent. Feeling more secure, she sat on the edge of the bed. Damn that Tooley, she thought. She did not know the man who was chasing her, but was certain Tooley had to be involved. About a month ago, he had casually mentioned to her that he had acquired a partner. No names were used and Sarah didn't ask for any. Under the circumstances, it did not make any difference. Her life was in danger. She needed to think of a plan.

From the moment she had left Lodz, Sarah Bloomberg had rarely looked back, especially since she had escaped from Meyervitz. She knew what she wanted: money and lots of it. She was prepared to do whatever it took to acquire it. She had had everything figured out — except for Klein. She had not counted on falling in love with him. From the first day she had met him, she had been excited by him. He was strong, handsome and rugged. She loved his quiet manner and his dry sense of humour.

A loud knock on the door interrupted her thoughts. Startled, she grabbed her handbag and reached for the small pearl-handled razor inside.

"Miss O'Connor," wheezed the little old lady from the other side of the door. "Are you there, Miss O'Connor?"

Sarah breathed easier. She undid the door latch and opened it. The lady from the front desk was standing before her with a cane in one hand, and a plate of food in the other.

"You looked hungry, dear. I thought you might like this."

"Thank you. That's very thoughtful."

The woman handed Sarah the plate which contained a slice of bread, a piece of cheese and a chopped carrot. She peered curiously into the room. "Well, you enjoy the food."

Sarah shut and bolted the door again, and sat at the end of the bed eating the food. The woman had been right; she was hungry and the food made her feel slightly better. After eating, she tried sleeping, but could not. She lay in her dark room, once more trying to sort out the events of the past few months.

She had had a good thing going with Peter Tooley. True, he was as sleazy as any man she'd met. He had made advances towards her more than once, but she had made it clear from the beginning that it was to be strictly business between them. Tooley had reluctantly agreed.

She was clearing about five hundred dollars a month from her business with him. It was simple work. She entertained his clients and softened them up; he would take their money. Then, six months ago something happened. Tooley was nervous and he started drinking much more than usual. He kept promising to pay her, but each time he was supposed to deliver the cash, he had one excuse or another.

Annoyed and frustrated, Sarah had given him an ultimatum: either pay her what he owed her or she was going to the police with the details of his swindle. It was a risky and dangerous bluff and she now knew that he did not take kindly to threats.

Maybe she should phone Klein to let him know where she was. She got out of the bed and started to dress, then abruptly stopped. What was the use, she asked herself, he would never understand. She sat down at the edge of the bed, lit another cigarette, and reached for the newspaper on the dresser.

She flipped through it quickly. The news from Ottawa on the front page hardly interested her. A local story about Charlie Johnson caught her eye. She knew Johnson; she had slept with him more than once.

Johnson was no fool. About a decade ago, he had started buying up tenements in the North End. But he kept them barely livable. Few of them had proper sewage hook-ups or running water. When his tenants complained about rats or vermin, he usually laughed off their complaints. Until one day last month, the city health authorities caught up with him. Not surprisingly, he refused to comply with their orders to clean up his houses. The city had him arrested and his day in court did not go well. As Sarah read, Johnson was fined $250 and given two weeks to comply with the city's ruling. She laughed out loud. Serves the bastard right, she thought. Below the Johnson story was another one that drew her attention. It was a small item:

Prominent Winnipeg lawyer Alfred Powers announced today that he was appointed the attorney for Rabbi Aaron Davidovitch. The Free Press *has learned that Rabbi Davidovitch will be charged in the murder of Anna Rudnicki. Mr. Powers had no other comment to make at this time.*

She reread it several times, before lighting a cigarette. She drew heavily on it, thinking that maybe the time had come to make some changes in her life. The truth was that she was not terribly happy with herself. She had renounced her Judaism many years ago, but she didn't think she could stand by while an innocent man, a man of God, was wrongfully accused of a horrific crime.

She toyed with the idea of going directly to the police, but that seemed too dangerous. Perhaps she could speak with Alfred Powers.

Mrs. King rarely went to bed before two in the morning. It was an old habit she had acquired ever since her husband Fred had died five years ago. She missed him.

It had been a large responsibility taking over the management of the hotel. At first, the bank manager wouldn't even consider it.

"A woman running a business by herself! It'll never happen as long as I'm in charge here," he had declared. "My wife informs me she wants to vote, my daughter wants to attend university instead of getting married, and you tell me I should trust you with my bank's money. I don't know what's happening in this world, but I do know I don't like it."

Mrs. King, however, wore him down. She and her husband had been loyal customers for many years and the amount of the mortgage yet to be paid off was quite small, only $1,000. With support from some of her neighbours, the bank manager had agreed to let her try for a period of six months. That was more than four years ago. She had met her obligations to the bank and kept the hotel in good shape.

The water was boiling when she heard the thud on the front door.

"I'm sorry, we're closed for the night," she said as loud as she could.

"Please Ma'am," said the voice on the other side, "I'm from out of town and I really need a place to stay. Could you please open the door?"

Mrs. King thought about it for a moment. "Oh, all right. Wait a minute, please."

She unbolted the main door of the hotel and pulled it open. No sooner had she done so when a large fist smashed into her frail face. She had no time to react. Her nose exploded in blood and she fell to the floor unconscious.

The man stood over the Mrs. King, her fragile life in his hands. Not now, he thought, first the girl. He walked briskly to the front desk and found the register book. There were only four paying guests that night: four males and one female, Miss Megan O'Connor.

He took the master key from a hook under the desk and moved towards the corridor. He reached into his pocket and pulled out a thin but very sharp razor.

The man put the key into the lock of room 104 and slowly turned it. The door opened half-way and then stopped. Sarah had latched it with the small chain from inside. He tried to reach it, but his hands were too large.

Sarah had finally fallen asleep, confident that she was about to do the right thing, something Klein would've approved of. Now, under the covers, Sarah stirred. A narrow beam of light from the hallway lantern hit her eyes and awakened her.

She saw his hands. Her first instinct was to scream, though she did not. She slipped off the blanket and with her right hand picked up her razor she had placed on the floor beside the bed. She moved out of the light and eased her way to the door.

His left hand was now fumbling with the chain. She slashed at it with her blade.

The man cried out. "You fucking whore, I'm going to kill you for that," he shouted.

She did not recognize his voice.

He tried to get his hand out of the door, but he could not move fast enough. She slashed at him again, drawing more blood. He cried out once more. Finally, his bloodied hand was free. He pushed as hard as he could with his shoulder and the chain gave way.

"Come here you little kike bitch," he said. "I've had enough of this."

Sarah stepped back, keeping her knife in front of her. He moved towards her, the floorboards creaking with every step. With his distinctive black beard, she easily recognized him as the same man from the train station and the Walker Theatre.

"Who are you? What do you want from me?" she yelled. "How did you find me? Get away."

Then with as much strength as she could muster, she screamed. There were voices raised in alarm from the other rooms. For an instant her eyes met those of her attacker. She was terrified but stood her ground, waving the knife in his direction. As a man shouted from down the hallway, he turned and ran out the door.

An elderly farmer, another guest at the hotel, was at her room first. "Are you okay Miss? What happened?"

"I'm okay."

"Help me, please help me." It was the voice of Mrs. King in the lobby.

"You go to her," Sarah told him. "I'm all right."

The farmer ran down the hall.

Sarah knew she had to get out of there. The police would be called. She grabbed her few personal belongings and ran towards the window. She pushed it open and climbed outside into the cold, damp night. Within moments, she had vanished into the darkness.

Peter Tooley awoke with an aching head. He could not remember how much he had drank the night before, or even where he had drank it. But there was no question about the throbbing pain in his head.

From his bed, he surveyed the room. He had thrown up sometime during the night and the residue remained plastered on the floor. Yellowed wallpaper was peeling from the walls and the white ceiling was covered in black soot. A small grey mouse scurried across the floor. He wondered where the hell he was.

Tooley threw off the blanket and attempted to stand. He was still wearing his white shirt and black suit pants, now stained and crinkled. For Peter Tooley that was not acceptable. Appearances always mattered, which was why he spent so much money on fine clothes. He shopped at Bristol's on Portage Avenue, the most expensive men's clothing store in Winnipeg, where a suit could run you as high as thirty dollars. It was a small price to pay, he reasoned, in order for him to keep up his debonair image.

Holding his head with one hand, he struggled to remove his shirt. He tugged at the left sleeve, then the right. As he laid the shirt over a chair, he noticed something curious. There were dry, encrusted spots of blood near the bottom of both cuffs. He sat down on the edge of the bed, with the shirt in his hands. Several minutes passed until the events of the past several days returned. Then he remembered most of it.

Two nights ago, he had been at Melinda's house with Sarah when another girl — Amy, Sarah had called her — had walked in on them. He recalled that he was quite drunk on Meyer's dark rum before he had arrived and then had had a few swigs of Sarah's whisky. He wasn't sure what this whore Amy had heard, but he could not afford to take any chances. He had decided right there and then that she had to be eliminated, yet not before he had indulged himself. He had left Sarah after giving her his client book and returned with Amy to her own room. She was lovely and shapely. He ordered her to remove her clothes. He had then had his way with her while sitting in the middle of the room in a large wooden chair with black satin-covered pillows.

When it was over, he had told her to meet with him two hours later near the river and he would pay her triple what she made in an average evening. For Amy, the temptation was too great.

She had arrived at the banks of the Red at the end of Hallet Street, a short walk from Melinda's.

"So where's the cash, mister?" she had asked Tooley.

"Patience my dear," he had told her. "All in good time."

He had demanded that she sit on top of him again. She hiked her skirt and reluctantly complied. After it was finished and Tooley had quickly relieved himself, he suddenly turned and hit her hard on the head with a rock he had concealed in his left hand. It was then that her blood had splattered on to his jacket and shirt. He threw her body into the river, and resumed his drinking at another bar. He hadn't stopped, he figured, for the next twenty-four hours.

It was a shame, he now thought, to have done away with someone so lovely and with so much style. But as his partner had made plain, either he cleared things up or he himself was destined for the river. Tooley hardly needed any more problems.

His partner was beyond placating. After he had seen what the man was capable of doing, Tooley knew that he was no longer safe. At their last meeting yesterday, they had argued — about money, about Sarah, about the future. He had promised him that Sarah could be trusted. She was too beautiful to kill, he had joked. It had always disturbed him that Sarah had refused to succumb to his charms. Yet she was so adept at her job, so slick with his clients, that he could not so easily replace her.

His friend, however, was skeptical. "She is a liability," he had told Tooley. "If you will not deal with her, then I will let Smitty handle it."

Further protests were futile. Tooley knew that once his partner's mind was made up, there was little he could do to change it. Besides, only Sarah knew that he had been the last person to see Amy alive. She might get ideas about talking. Let his partner do as he pleased, he thought after reconsidering the issue. Assisted in no small way by several quarts of rum, he forgot about Sarah Bloomberg.

But now, with a groan, he remembered. Tooley finished dressing and wandered out into the hallway. As it turned out, he found himself standing in the lobby of the Dufferin Avenue Hotel, the cheapest establishment in Winnipeg. Located at the corner of Dufferin and Main, the Duff was the hotel for vagrants and other dregs of society. Rats stayed away from the place.

"So you're finally awake," said a voice from behind the front desk. The clerk was as gaunt a man as Tooley had ever seen. He was probably about forty years of age, but appeared to be much older. He was wearing a pair of baggy brown pants and a loose fitting green sweater. He was bald, except for two pieces of thin hair which he draped across the front of his head. His dark beard was unkempt and Tooley was certain that there was something dripping from his nose. He thought he was going to be sick again.

"Yeah, you sure tied one on," the man said laughing. "You kept calling me Amy. Told me you were sorry."

Tooley tried to smile. "I talk a lot of nonsense when I drink too much. But thanks for helping me out. What do I owe you?"

He paid the man fifty cents for the room and got out of there as fast as he could. Tooley desperately needed to wash himself, before he could begin another day's work. He had arranged to meet with his partner in his office the next day, Good Friday. It would be quiet and he hoped they could iron out their differences.

So many needless complications, the man thought. First the young girl, then Smitty had stupidly lost his temper with Bob Stewart, now the prostitute. It was Tooley's fault. All of it. How he had allowed himself to become the grain broker's partner was beyond him. There were times in the past few days when he wondered if the money was truly worth this aggravation. And he couldn't forget about the biggest problem of all: Sam Klein.

He admired Klein's tenacity and sense of purpose. He had watched the way Klein handled himself at the whorehouse; it took a certain kind of personality to successfully negotiate with drunks and deal with men who had sexual pleasure on their mind. He knew Klein had a temper, but usually kept it under control unless someone got out of hand. In short, Klein was no fool.

If he were honest, he never really thought that Klein would've been scared off by the runaway horse. It had been wishful thinking at best. Yet, maybe there was another angle to explore. He had heard that Klein fancied the whore. She had eluded his man at the CPR Station and then in St. James. But she would be found again, his man had promised him. Perhaps after she had been dealt with properly, Klein would then stop his search for the truth.

Sarah was alive, but she knew she was not out of danger. Thus far, she had eluded her stalker on at least three occasions — at the Walker Theatre, at the CPR Station, and then at the St. James Hotel. She had walked through the night, using side streets to make her way to Portage and Main. In the cold and windy darkness, she crossed the bridge into St. Boniface and huddled in an alley behind the hospital until morning.

She tried hard to fight the fear. It had taken such a great effort over the past year to gain the self-confidence that had made her into a woman of style, grace and spirit. Sarah prided herself in, as Klein put it, "taking shit from no one."

So what was happening to her? She had thought she had seen the last of that poor immigrant girl who had been shipped across the Atlantic like a piece of undesirable cargo only to be abused by that ogre Meyervitz. That Sarah Bloomberg no longer existed, or so she believed. During the last forty-eight hours, she found herself slipping back and it made her ill. How she detested that meek and helpless girl.

Daylight brought the warmth of a shining spring sun and some much needed relief. She found a cheap room in a boarding house on Rue St. Joseph a block from Provencher. For a dollar a night, she had a bed, washing facilities and breakfast. Here in the French quarter, she felt safe. The house belonged to an elderly couple named Gauthier, who didn't ask questions. Sarah began to relax.

Sarah slept for most of the morning. A hot meal of pancakes and syrup was awaiting her in the dining room. She gobbled up every morsel while Mrs. Gauthier quietly knitted. Absently, Sarah then lit a cigarette and stared out the window.

"If you would like to talk about it dear, I am a good listener," Mrs. Gauthier said.

Sarah turned around, startled. "It's that obvious?"

"It's your hands. Those lovely manicured fingers are not the fingers of a waitress. I'd guess you do something much more glamorous than that."

"Some might argue." Sarah smiled. "I'll be fine. I promise I'll be back later, and then you can show me how you knitted that lovely sweater you're wearing."

"It would be my pleasure, dear."

A Provencher streetcar had Sarah downtown in ten minutes. She was determined to speak with Alfred Powers before the day was out. It would be good to rid her conscience of this unwanted burden. Did she care about Peter Tooley? Now more than ever, she knew he had to be the one trying to kill her.

She found Powers's office on the fourth floor. The walls were white and a plush, rich red carpet covered the floor. Several large oak chairs stood ready for clients and a stack of magazines sat on a glass table. Directly in front of her was a medium-sized mahogany desk, occupied by the receptionist, a blonde woman with glasses and a hint of perfume. She was busy typing when Sarah approached her.

"Excuse me, Miss. Would it be possible for me to speak with Mr. Powers?"

The receptionist peered at Sarah over her glasses.

"Do you have an appointment?"

"No, but I..."

"I'm sorry. Mr. Powers is extremely busy today. I doubt if he will have the time."

"Please, it's very important that I see him."

"Could you tell me what its about?"

"I'd rather talk to him directly. It's urgent."

The secretary sighed. "All right, Miss...?"

"Bloomberg, Sarah Bloomberg."

"Have a seat, Miss Bloomberg and I'll see what I can do."

Sarah sat down in a chair beside the wall and flipped through a Maclean's magazine. An article about the Prince Edward Island school teacher and writer Lucy Maude Montgomery, the author of the best selling book Anne of Green Gables, caught her eye. But she did not have the patience to struggle with the small English language print. She placed the magazine back in the pile and reached for another one. An hour passed and still there was no sign of Alfred Powers. She started to get nervous again. Not only was the Exchange building a busy place where she might be recognized, but Tooley's office was one floor below.

As the minutes ticked by, she grew more agitated. Every so often, the receptionist would look up at her, then return to her typewriter.

"I'm sorry," Sarah said to the woman. "I can't wait any longer."

The woman shrugged indifferently.

Sarah was already out in the hallway and heading towards the stairs. She rounded the corner and reached for the door that led to the main lobby.

"Hello Sarah."

"Tooley! God, you scared me."

Peter Tooley had washed up and changed his clothes. He was now wearing a navy suit and his greasy black hair was matted down as usual. The heavy smell of his cologne made her ill.

"What are you doing here?" she demanded.

Tooley stared at her with strange expression on his face. "I might ask you the same question."

"I...I was looking for you. I want to know what you did to Amy, you son-of-a-bitch, and I want to get out of the city with the rest of my money."

"I see. First of all, forget about Amy. She doesn't concern you."

"That night, she didn't hear anything. You didn't have to kill her."

Without warning, Tooley raised his right hand and slapped Sarah across the face. "Shut up, you slut. Never speak like that again or you'll be..."

Tooley gasped as Sarah grabbed his testicles and squeezed hard. "I'll be what? You bastard, I know you've sent someone after me. Well, that animal has not succeeded in killing me yet."

"I don't know what you're talking about," Tooley rasped through gritted teeth. "Now, do you want your money or not?"

Sarah let her hand drop. Damn. Always it was the money. Her cheek was throbbing with pain, but she tried to ignore it. "Bastard. Of course, I want it. I earned it."

"Good." Tooley straightened his pants. "As it turns out, I've managed to come up with the cash. Return here tomorrow to my office after two o'clock and I'll pay you everything I owe you."

"Fine, but you had better be telling the truth."

Tooley laughed. "There is only one condition."

"What?"

"You remember that book I gave you the other night for safe keeping?"

"Yes."

"I need it back."

How could Sarah possibly retrieve Tooley's book in time for tomorrow's meeting? It was still under the floorboard in her bedroom at Melinda's. And she wasn't about to go walking in there, until she had her cash. He would have to wait for it. As long as she still had his black book, she figured, there wasn't much he could do to her. Peter Tooley was the least of her problems.

She had returned to St. Boniface via the streetcar, but had taken precautions to ensure that she was not being followed. She had initially hopped a car going north down Main Street towards Melinda's. Just as the car was leaving the stop across from City Hall, she leaped out and ran to a southbound streetcar. She was back in St. Boniface fifteen minutes later without any trouble.

Madame Gauthier had prepared a roast chicken dinner with boiled potatoes and gravy. Sarah hadn't feasted so well in weeks.

After dinner, she went into the kitchen to help Madame Gauthier wash up. They quietly washed and dried the dishes. As she polished the last of the glasses, the older woman smiled at Sarah.

"So my dear. You still look troubled. A man?"

"There is someone, but...let's just say I've made a mess of things."

"Does he love you?"

"He did."

"Why not give him the benefit of the doubt. Men can fool you."

They both laughed. She was such a kind woman and Sarah was desperate to speak with someone about her problems.

"Madame Gauthier," she began slowly. "As you have guessed, I am in some trouble. I can't get into all the details, only that my life is probably in danger. If you and your husband want me to leave, I will understand."

"Don't be silly. You are free to stay here with us as long as you wish."

"Thank you," said Sarah giving the woman a hug.

"Now, are you sure I can't be of some assistance."

Sarah did have an idea. A hour later, Madame Gauthier returned from the store with a pair of sharp scissors and some dye. Sarah sat in a chair in the middle of the kitchen while Madame Gauthier cut her long black hair. The last time her hair had been that short was when she was five years old. The cut was followed by a dose of red hair dye. When Sarah looked at her reflection in the hallway mirror, she hardly recognized herself. Madame Gauthier also had purchased her a long flowery dress, not the kind Sarah usually wore.

"It's amazing, my dear. A complete transformation."

Feeling much better, Sarah decided it was time to phone Klein. She knew he would be worried; she owed him at least a phone call. Then it was time to collect her money.

9

Sam Klein had difficulty sleeping that night. Again, for the second time in as many days, his childhood dream had returned. And once more, just as the man in the black beard surrounded by a hostile mob was about to speak to him, he awoke suddenly in a cold sweat. Damn, he thought, why now? Why has this tormented man come back to haunt him? He tried to get back to sleep, but it was hopeless. He tossed and turned as the images of his childhood fused with those of the present.

There had been still no word from Sarah. Klein had spoken to as many people as he could — on Main Street, in Point Douglas, and downtown. He called in long forgotten favours. But the answer was always the same: No one had seen Sarah Bloomberg in days. She had vanished. It was as if Sarah had never existed.

George, the doorman at the Eaton's, a tall black man in a majestic uniform, couldn't recall seeing her on the day she claimed she went shopping. Melinda wanted to ask the police to help in the search, but Klein wouldn't hear of that. He would find her by himself.

Klein also had heard from Maloney, but he had nothing to report. The journalist promised Klein that he would begin the blood libel research Sam had wanted within a day.

"You look terrible," Melinda said to Klein over breakfast the next morning.

It was Good Friday. The streets of Winnipeg were quiet. Businesses and shops on Main Street were closed for the holiday and the farmer's market across from City Hall was silent. A slight drizzle melted the last bit of snow away. Since Melinda's was closed for the day (Easter and Christmas were the only other days she shut down) many of the girls were either asleep or had left the night before to be with friends and family.

"So what's next, Sam?" asked Melinda, sipping a cup of coffee.

"Not sure yet. I was thinking of speaking to people who work around the Grain Exchange building. Maybe they've seen Sarah."

"You're certain she is involved with that broker. What is his name?"

"Tooley, Peter Tooley. I'm quite sure." He lit a cigarette and reached for a cup of coffee.

The phone rang. Klein jumped to his feet and answered it on the second ring. But it was only Isaac. Alfred Powers had called him trying to find Klein.

"He wants you to come by his office at three o'clock."

"On Good Friday?"

"That's what he wants," said Isaac. "Says he has a family dinner later in the evening, but plans to work on the case all day."

"I'll be there."

Klein hung up the phone and lit another cigarette. The phone rang again.

"Isaac, what did you forget?"

"Sam, this isn't Isaac," said the familiar voice at the other end.

Klein's heart raced. "Sarah, are you all right?"

"As well as can be expected."

"Where are you?"

"Please Sam, I needed to get away for a while. It's safer that way."

"Sarah, Amy is dead. Drowned in the river."

There was silence at the other end of the line.

"Sarah, did you hear me? Amy is dead."

"I know, I'm sorry, I...."

"Sarah, please tell me where you are and I'll be there as soon as possible."

"I can't. You'll have to trust me."

"Trust you! You must be joking. How do you know Peter Tooley?"

"Sam. Please, stay away from him. I'll explain everything soon. Just leave me alone. I have to go."

"Sarah."

The phone went dead.

It was still raining when Klein left for Alfred Powers's office at two o'clock. The streetcars were not running because of the Easter holiday so Klein was forced to walk the few miles to the Grain Exchange building. He didn't mind because it gave him time to think.

As he walked, he kept reviewing his conversation with Sarah, searching for some further explanation. The only thing he was certain of was that she was scared, even terrified. It was the uncharacteristic tremble in her voice. It reminded him of how she had been when he first found her in the snow outside Melinda's. Like a frightened child. He knew he had to find her before Tooley did.

He was at Bannatyne and Main when he saw it. It was a law office, next to a Bank of Montreal. The sign on the door read 'Fineman and Katz, Barristers'. The front glass window had been smashed and scratched across the wood door in bright red was painted: "JEWS KILLERS OF CHRIST MUST DIE TONIGHT!' It wasn't over yet, Klein thought. How could it be? Rabbi Davidovitch was still locked in jail, an innocent man caught in an ancient feud. When you considered the terrors of the past — the slaughters, humiliations and expulsions — it was a wonder that there were any Jews left in the world at all.

He crossed Main Street and picked up his pace, moving towards the Grain Exchange. Isaac had told him to use the side entrance on Rorie Street which Powers would leave open. He found the right door and walked up the stairs to the lawyer's office in room 407.

As soon as he walked in, Klein knew he had entered a different world. The office of Alfred Powers was a far cry from Peter Tooley's one floor below.

"Hello, anyone here?" he called out.

Within moments, a tall, distinguished man in a blue three-piece suit stood before him. His gray hair was perfectly combed and trimmed and

Klein noticed that the nails on his hands were manicured. His black leather shoes glistened in the sunlight shining through the window from the back office. Klein recognized the lawyer immediately from his newspaper photographs.

"Powers," he said, extending his hand. "I'm Sam Klein."

"Sam, good of you to come," said Powers shaking Klein's hand.

There was no more capable lawyer in the city than Alfred Powers. Over the past twenty years, he had defended more murderers than any lawyer in Winnipeg and his success rate was high. He was an important leader of the city's elite, a member of the Manitoba and St. Charles clubs, and a director of several corporations, including the Bank of Montreal and the Great-West Life Assurance Company.

Nevertheless, he made Klein feel entirely at ease. "Please, come into my office, we have much to talk about."

Powers's office was even more luxurious than the outer waiting room. Klein figured that it was about the size of his mother's home. A magnificent view of Main Street could be seen out a large picture window. Not far away, Winnipeg City Hall in all its ornate splendor stood proudly, looking as imposing as it did in penny postcards Klein had seen. And directly behind it was Market Square, the grand and bustling headquarters of Winnipeg commerce. The walls were covered in original paintings and there was a door that led to a small private bathroom. It was difficult not to be impressed.

Powers sat down in his chair. "You don't mind if I smoke this cigar, do you Sam? My wife hates them. I like to smoke while I'm working."

"Go ahead," said Klein, pulling out his cigarette case.

The lawyer reached for a thick file and laid it open on the desk.

"This is it, everything they've got on the rabbi. Statements he made to the police, eye witness accounts and most damaging of all, the rabbi's personal possessions found at the scene of the crime."

"He can explain those."

"Yes, I know. They were stolen and he reported it to the police. But the police cannot locate any report."

"I can't prove anything yet, but I can tell you with near certainty that there was a report and I have an idea what happened to it."

"All speculation, my friend," said Powers, taking a deep drag on his cigar. "We need a lot more than that. Isaac Hirsch says you know your way around the city. Is that true?"

"I know a few people."

"Sam, I've defended many murder suspects in the past and I don't like the smell of this one. The Attorney-General wants this case to disappear, and quickly. That's why he's brought in Timothy Jarvis as special prosecutor. He could've used one of his regular lawyers, but opted for Jarvis instead."

"You sound worried."

"I'd be a fool if I wasn't. Don't be concerned, Jarvis is good, but I'm better. To be honest, though, I could use some help."

"I'm working on it. Can you give me a little more time? I'm sure I'm getting close."

"I can give you about a week. The preliminary hearing will be on Tuesday of next week before Justice Mathers. There is enough evidence for a trial. Mathers and Jarvis will want that to begin as soon as possible, probably a week to ten days later. So if you're going to save the rabbi's bacon, pardon the expression, you'd better come up with something."

"How's he doing?"

"Not great. His family and Isaac have visited him nearly every day, but he was extremely upset when he heard about the near destruction of the synagogue. He fasted for two days."

"He's a strong man. He'll come through this."

"Tell me Sam. What do you know about Stark and McCreary, the two detectives in charge of the investigation?"

"There's not much to say about Stark. I hear he's honest and forthright. He's extremely competent at his job. A family man, and I hear he'll probably be head of the department some day. As for McCreary, well, that's another story."

"Oh?"

"Let's put it this way: if McCreary had to arrest his own mother, he would and it wouldn't bother him. Why do you ask?"

"Nothing. I was just curious. Actually, I've dealt with both of them and my assessment would be much the same."

"Now, there's something I'd like to know."

"Yes?"

"Why are you doing this? You didn't have to take this case. Isaac would've found a Jewish lawyer to defend the rabbi. Why are you spending your holiday time here?"

"It's my job. Is that a good enough answer?"

"Not really."

"Well how about this? I don't like injustice and I don't like racism, plain and simple. I've been living in this city since 1878 and I think its still big enough for Jews, Christians, Chinese, whatever."

Klein laughed. "I wouldn't have expected such an opinion from someone like you."

Powers chuckled too. "Just because I happened to be a *goy* and a powerful one at that."

Klein laughed harder.

"One more thing," said Powers. "Do you know a woman named Sarah Bloomberg?"

Klein's smile disappeared. "Yes. Why?"

"Nothing really. She was here yesterday and demanded to...."

"Sarah was here in your office!"

"Yes. That's right."

"What did she want?"

"As I was trying to tell you, she demanded to see me, but I was tied up for most of the day. She was gone by the time I was available."

Klein had arranged to be at Maloney's apartment later in the afternoon. The reporter had promised Klein that he would call as many contacts as he could for leads on both Tooley and Sarah.

Klein left Powers and told the lawyer he would be in touch before Tuesday's preliminary hearing. He was down the stairs and at the front door when he stopped. Why not check out Tooley's office one more time? Maybe he and Maloney had missed something. Abruptly, he turned around and headed back up the stairs to the third floor. As soon as he reached the hallway leading to Tooley's office, he heard the noise.

He stood perfectly still, his ears listening to every sound. Two people were arguing, perhaps three. He thought he could make out one male voice, possibly two. Then a high-pitched scream and pleading. "Please, don't, don't", a third voice shouted. It was Sarah.

His legs instinctively moved towards the screaming. They were coming from behind the door of office 304. Klein turned the knob and eased the door open. It was difficult to see anything through the crack so he pushed harder. Then he saw him by the window. There was a man in a navy suit. His shiny black hair was greased back. Tooley. He was holding something in his hands, a blackjack. Klein looked down and saw her on the floor, blood was flowing from her head. Her hair had been cut and dyed red, but he was certain it was Sarah. The man raised the jack, as if he was about to strike his victim again.

Without waiting, Klein bolted through the doorway and dove across the desk, grabbing on to Tooley's suit jacket. He swung the man hard against the wall. The grain broker's right hand went limp and the club fell to the ground. Tooley tried desperately to push Klein away, but he could not. Klein clenched his right hand and drove it into Tooley's face. Blood spurted from the broker's nose. He pulled back his fist one more time. Tooley was barely conscious. Klein arched his shoulder and then, suddenly, an explosion of light and pain filled his head and sent him into blackness.

"Tooley get the hell up, you fool," ordered the large man. He glanced at both Klein and the woman on the floor of the office.

Tooley slowly stood up and wiped the blood from this face with his handkerchief. "Don't you think we should make sure she's dead?"

"Look at her, even if the bitch is alive she'll remember nothing."

"What about Klein?"

"Leave him. Without her, he'll never figure any of this out."

"I don't know..."

"You don't know what, Tooley? Just do as you're told. Now come on, we have to get out of here."

"And leave them here in my office?"

"Dump them in the hallway if it'll make you feel better. In any event, I've decided that it would be best if you disappeared for a while. Your career in the Winnipeg grain trade is over."

"And what about your money?"

"What about it? I haven't forgotten about one penny. You're going to get it for me out of town. Now, no more talking. Let's move, before Klein wakes up."

Klein came to slowly. The back of his head was pounding where he had been struck. He got to his feet and stumbled over to Sarah. She was not moving. A pool of blood circled her head. Klein put his ear to her heart. She was still breathing. He picked her limp body up in his arms and carried her up the stairs one flight to Alfred Powers's office. Blood from the deep gash on the side of her head dripped on to the floor as he walked. He kicked the door of the lawyer's office with his boot.

"Quick, call an ambulance," ordered Klein as Powers rushed forward.

He lay Sarah down on the red carpet. Powers telephoned for an ambulance and brought bandages from his storeroom. The lawyer kneeled beside Sarah and bound her head.

"Sam, what happened?"

He was still groggy from the hit on his own head.

"Klein, did you hear me," the lawyer repeated, "what the hell is going on? Who is this woman?"

"She was at Tooley's downstairs," he said, out of breath. "There were two of them and Sarah. They were going to kill her. Snuck up on me from behind. I didn't see the other man."

"This woman is Sarah Bloomberg?"

Klein nodded as he picked up Sarah's right hand and cradled it in his own.

"Do you think she'll live?"

"I don't know. She's lost a lot of blood."

Klein wiped the blood from her face and then Sarah's eyes opened. "Sam," she whispered. "I think I've made a mess of things."

"Don't talk. You're going to be fine. You have to be."

The horse-drawn ambulance arrived. The two attendants placed Sarah on a stretcher and whisked her away to the General Hospital.

"Why didn't they kill her when they had the chance?" Powers asked Klein.

"I'm not sure. Why didn't they kill me?"

The two men were sitting in the main waiting room of the Winnipeg General Hospital. There were a few chairs and stools, surrounded by white walls and wood floors. Other than a man patiently waiting for news of his pregnant wife's delivery, Klein and Powers were alone. Because it was a holiday, only a bare minimum of the staff was working.

Klein leaned back and ran his hands through his hair. "Are you an expert on women?"

Powers chuckled. "That's an odd question, especially coming from you."

Klein nodded ruefully. "I thought I knew Sarah. But now with all this, I don't know."

"She'll be fine, Sam. You mark my words."

"I think I should call Melinda. Let her know what has happened," said Klein, standing up.

He was about to search for a phone when a man wearing a white coat approached them.

"Are you the two who brought in Miss Bloomberg?"

"Yes," said Klein. "How is she?"

"I'm Dr. Mackenzie. Miss Bloomberg has suffered a serious concussion. A scalp laceration caused all the bleeding, but we stitched that up. Nevertheless, she was hit very hard. The blow was approximately here," said the doctor pointing to the front left side of his own head. "We believe that there was no further internal damage, but in such cases it may be days before we know for certain."

"So, she is not going to die, in other words."

"No," said Dr. Mackenzie. "She is in a semi-conscious state right now and may suffer some memory loss when she awakes. With luck, you might be able to speak with her briefly in a few hours."

"You see, I told you everything would be fine," said Powers, patting Klein's shoulder.

"Yeah, great. But what if they try again?"

"Here? Never," said the lawyer, "but if you're worried I have an acquaintance who can help. Give me a minute."

Powers walked over to the nurse's desk and asked to use the telephone. He returned moments later.

"My friend is an ex-cop, Frank Delaware. He'll be here in thirty minutes and he's agreed to stand guard by Sarah's room."

"Thanks, I appreciate it."

"What about the police? Do you want me to notify them?" asked the lawyer.

"Absolutely not. That's all I need is to have McCreary showing up. Let me handle this in my own way. First, I have to find out where Sarah fits into all of this. Then, we will worry about the police."

Two hours passed, then three, then five. Still, Sarah remained comatose. She lay in a bed in a special section of the hospital on the second floor, her head wrapped tightly in white bandages. Every so often, her eye lids would flutter, but nothing more.

Klein refused to leave her side. He had convinced the nurse on duty to allow him to remain in the room. Powers had long since gone home and Melinda had stopped by for a short visit, bringing Klein some food and drink. As Powers had promised, former Constable Frank Delaware had arrived earlier in the day to stand guard outside Sarah's room.

"Don't worry, son," declared the burly ex-policeman. "I've never lost anyone yet."

Delaware was sixty years old, bald except for two strips of gray hair on the side of his head, and still muscular. He had retired from the Winnipeg force three years earlier after he had been shot in the left upper part of his leg, which was why he now walked with a noticeable limp. His presence reassured Klein that Tooley and his partner would have their hands full if they tried to get close to Sarah.

Sitting beside her, Klein could not stop reviewing the events of the past few days, sorting, reconstructing, and sorting again. And each time he arrived at the same conclusion: Peter Tooley was the key to unraveling this entire mess and Sarah was the link to Tooley. He had so many questions to ask her.

By midnight, with no sign of any change, Klein required a break. A new nurse had come on the night shift and offered Klein some coffee. He got a cup for Frank Delaware and pulled up a chair beside him.

"How's your friend doing?" the former constable asked.

"No changes, yet," said Klein. "But they say by morning she should be better."

"Good, that's real good. I'm glad I could be of service."

"Me too, especially on Good Friday."

"Think nothing of it. Doesn't mean much to me. Never has. I'm not the religious type."

"Me neither. You miss being on the force?"

"A little. I enjoyed meeting people, but there are many things I don't miss."

"Such as?"

"Where to begin? How about the terrible hours, the lousy pay, the drunks and hoods on Main Street, finding my partner in a whore house, and let's not forget dealing with detectives like Bill McCreary."

"You know McCreary?"

"He's a bastard as far as I'm concerned. Why?"

"Oh, let's say that he and I don't get along."

"McCreary doesn't get along with a lot of people. You see my leg all chewed up by a bullet?"

Klein nodded.

"Well, that bullet was intended for McCreary. We were investigating a murder and robbery at a house on William Avenue, not far from here. Anyway, there's me, two other constables and McCreary. He's in charge. We knock on the door of the house, but there's no answer. So McCreary tells me to bash the door down which I do. We go inside and its dark, real dark. Suddenly from nowhere this half-cocked kid is pointing a rifle at McCreary, telling him to stand where he is or he'll kill him. But McCreary's no fool. He leaps behind me just as the kid pulled the trigger. The bullet caught me right above the knee. Lucky I didn't lose my leg. You think McCreary could've at least acknowledged that I got hit instead of him. Nothing. Not even a visit while I was laid up here on the third floor."

"Sounds like McCreary. And what do you know about Stark?"

"Michael Stark? A bit strange but a good cop."

"What do you mean strange?"

"He keeps to himself a lot of the time. It's funny, I worked on many cases with him but I couldn't really tell you much about him. Never talks about himself or his family. Still, I'd trust him with my life if I had to. He's the kind of cop who'd watch your back, if you know what I mean."

"I do. Now one more thing about something else I'm working on."

"I'm all ears."

"Let's say someone files a report with the police about a robbery. Is it likely that the report would disappear without a trace?"

"No. Chief McRae runs a pretty tight ship. He's real careful about paper work and that sort of stuff. I'd say that if the person reported the incident, the only way it could disappear would be if the cop at the desk wanted it to disappear."

"I see. Thanks, that's helpful."

The two men sat in silence for a few minutes, finishing their coffee. Klein felt comforted by Delaware's kindly bulk. He didn't seem to care about whether or not Klein was rich or poor, Jewish or Gentile. He was there to watch over Sarah and that made Klein feel good.

Two days later Sarah's condition had not changed. The doctor told Klein and Melinda that there was more internal damage than they had first thought. They would have to wait, he told them, and pray if they were religious. There wasn't much else they could do. He hoped that within time she would awaken. He promised no miracles.

At first, Klein refused to leave the hospital. He was prepared to sit beside Sarah's bed until it was over — one way or the other. But sitting alone, hour after hour, had allowed him to review all the facts of the case. Then he remembered something Frank Delaware had said to him. "If the person reported the incident, the only way it could disappear would be if the cop at the desk wanted it to disappear." Jesus, Klein thought, it had been staring him in the face the entire time. He had been so obsessed with Sarah and finding Tooley that he had missed the obvious. He had to see Rabbi Davidovitch immediately.

It was a short ride on the streetcar from the hospital to the police station on Rupert Avenue. Klein walked through the main entrance of the station. This time there would be no trouble. He had spoken to Alfred Powers about gaining access to the Rabbi. The lawyer had called the attorney-general's office and had been assured that Klein would have no problems. A letter would be sent by messenger to the police station immediately.

"I'd like to see a prisoner, Rabbi Aaron Davidovitch," announced Klein to the duty sergeant at the front desk. Both men recognized each other from Klein's last visit to the station.

"I thought I told you, Klein, no one but his lawyer and close family members gets in to see him."

Klein restrained himself. "I think if you'll check, you'll find a letter about me that makes an exception."

The sergeant looked down at the pile of paper on his desk and pulled out a white envelope. "You mean this, I presume?"

"Why don't you just read it?"

"Already have." He threw the letter on his desk, shrugged, then pointed at the stairway leading to the cells.

"Thanks, sarge," Klein sang out, "Say, let's go for a beer sometime." The sergeant started to snap something back, but changed his mind and returned to his paperwork.

Klein was proceeding up the stairs when he suddenly heard a gruff, distinctive voice behind him. "Hello, Klein, are you here to see the rabbi?"

Michael Stark stood in the shadow of the stairwell.

"That's right. You have a problem with that?"

"No. In fact, I'll take you to him. Follow me."

Stark led the way through the dark hallways. "It doesn't look good for him, you know that?"

Klein shrugged. He had nothing to say to cops.

"Too much physical evidence tying him to that little girl. And all that other stuff about the blood killing. He had a motive. The jury will believe it all."

"Maybe. Maybe not."

Stark stopped. "I've seen guys hanged with less evidence against them than we have on the rabbi. It's the way it is. People in this city have vivid imaginations. By the end of the trial, none of those twelve jurors will have any doubts that the blood ritual accusation is true."

"Yeah, I've read the newspaper."

"No, I'm quite serious. When I was younger, I travelled throughout Europe."

"Fascinating."

Stark ignored Klein's sarcasm. "I remember as a young boy visiting a small village in the Tirol, in the Austrian Empire. There was an old Catholic church, beautiful architecture and stain glass windows. The people who ran the church had preserved the bones of a young girl said to be the victim of a Passover ritual murder hundreds of years ago. They had dressed her up with a gold leaf crown. It was very strange. I think the Church actually canonized her at some point in the 1700's."

"I wouldn't call the Catholic Church a friend of the Jews," said Klein.

"Maybe so, but you'd have to admit it is possible that there was, or is, some secret Hebrew organization somewhere in the world that practises this blood ritual. Maybe not here in Winnipeg, but in some small Russian or Austrian village. Why not?"

Klein was not sure what to make of Michael Stark. He had generally agreed with Frank Delaware's assessment: Stark seemed like a decent and honest detective — everything McCreary was not. He had a good reputation in the department. And yet, something about Stark troubled Klein. It always seemed as if Stark had more to tell him. The question was, why was he holding himself back?

As Klein pondered this question, Stark led him down the damp, dark corridor to the rabbi's cell block.

"He's just down here," said the detective. "So Klein, you're sure he's innocent?"

"Of course. He's the most gentle man I know. He is incapable of committing the crime you have charged him with."

"I suppose we will find out soon enough."

Rabbi Davidovitch was sitting on his cot, reading the scriptures. He had lost some weight, and his skin was paler, but otherwise he appeared to be fine.

"Sam, is that you?" he said, squinting his eyes through the darkness. "I'm so glad you've come to see me."

Stark opened the cell door. "Just yell when you want out. There's someone on duty down the hall." The cell door clanged shut.

"Come in, sit down, Shailek," said Rabbi Davidovitch in Yiddish. "I'm sorry about your sister. I feel like it is my fault."

"Nonsense, rabbi. If anyone is to blame for all this trouble, it's certainly not you."

"But the synagogue, dear Rivka, the blood accusation." The rabbi shut his eyes. "God must have a reason for such tragedies. Maybe he is testing my faith."

"Rabbi, I don't know about that, but I want to help you get out of here before your trial even starts. There is something I have to know."

"Anything."

"Tell me about the day you filed the police report of the synagogue robbery."

The rabbi frowned. "Let me see. It was about a week or so before that little girl was murdered. I had gone into the *shul* for morning prayers when I noticed the main door was opened. At first, I thought nothing of it, but later when I could not find my *teffilin* and ritual knife, I assumed someone must have broken in and stolen these objects. What value my *teffilin* could be I don't know. The knife might be worth a little."

"Go on."

"A few hours later, I walked down to the police station on Magnus and Charles and reported the incident to the constable on duty."

"Do you remember the officer you spoke with?"

"He was tall, with a reddish moustache. I don't know, Sam, I'm not very good with faces. All the policemen look the same."

"Do you think it might have been this man?" Klein asked, handing the rabbi the photo of Bob Stewart that his wife had given him.

The rabbi studied it carefully. "I think I know this policeman. He showed me to my cell the day they put me in here."

"Is it possible, he was also the constable on duty who took your report? Please think back. It's very important."

The rabbi stared at the photo again, shaking his head and shutting his eyes. "Yes. It might have been him, Sam. In fact, I recall now that I felt I had met him before. Where is he? Can you talk to him. Perhaps he will testify in court for me."

"That will be difficult. He was murdered a few days ago."

"Murdered! What has happened, Sam? Who could do such things? And why?" The rabbi sat back on his bunk. His fingers slowly stroked his beard.

Klein was now certain that it had been Bob Stewart on duty at the time the rabbi had filed his report. That it had been Bob Stewart who had later destroyed it. And that Bob Stewart had been murdered because of it.

Rabbi Davidovitch stood next to Klein and kissed his forehead, blessing him in Hebrew. Klein thanked him, then called for the constable to let him out. As the door of the cell was banged shut again, the rabbi called to Klein.

"I was thinking that sometimes a man has to reveal another's secret if it is absolutely necessary." He hesitated, his face troubled. "It says in the Talmud that...."

"Rabbi, what are you trying to tell me?" asked Klein.

"I believe that Detective Stark may be of assistance to you."

"Stark? Why? He is quite certain that you are guilty."

"Talk to him."

"But why?"

"He is one of us."

Klein's eyes widened. "Stark is a Jew?"

The rabbi nodded.

"How do you know?"

"There is an old expression in Yiddish, *men ken derkenen dos pintele yid* — you can always recognize that essence of Jewishness."

"I am sure you know better than me, but I had never thought about it until now. After all, he's a cop."

"Trust me Sam, *foon undzere*, he's from our tribe. In fact, I confronted him with this and he more or less admitted it. Seems he was born in the town of Lida in Poland. If you listen closely, you can still hear the accent even though he has made a great effort to disguise it. Now if you'll excuse me Shailek, it is time to *daven*."

Klein opened his mouth to say something, then stopped and shrugged. As he turned and left the cell, the rabbi faced east and, in a deep melodious voice, began to chant his mid-day prayers.

10

Three days before the opening of the trial, Klein left the hospital and met John Maloney for a glass of beer at the Brunswick. The two men sat in a secluded corner of the bar smoking cigarettes, each sipping a mug of barrel draft.

"Not a bad article today, Maloney, but what about that research you promised me?"

"I have our librarian working on it, but with the trial I haven't had the time to finish yet."

"Make the time, Maloney. My gut feeling is that we will find some connection in the past to what happened here."

"Sounds like a wild goose chase to me."

Klein butted his cigarette. "How would you like an exclusive interview with the rabbi?"

"Would I?" exclaimed Maloney, "Every reporter in Winnipeg wants that story."

"You got it if you want it."

"I want it. Let's go."

"Not now, meet me tomorrow at the jail about two o'clock."

"Your sure this is okay with Powers?"

"Whose idea do you think it was!"

Rabbi Held Over For Trial

Winnipeg April 18 — Rabbi Aaron Davidovitch will stand trial in provincial court for the murder of Anna Rudnicki, the young Polish girl whose body was discovered last week. Appearing today in Police Court on Rupert Avenue before Magistrate Thomas M. Daly, Special Crown Prosecutor Timothy Jarvis argued that Rabbi Davidovitch brutally murdered Miss Rudnicki in what may have been a ritual murder. Evidence presented by the police puts the rabbi at the scene of the crime. Possessions belonging to the accused were found wrapped around the body of the victim.

Lawyer Alfred Powers, acting for the defence, asked that his client be released on $10,000 bail. The request was denied by Magistrate Daly who ruled that in light of the recent violence in the north end of the city, Rabbi Davidovitch would be safer if he remained in custody.

The magistrate, however, did approve Mr. Powers's request that his client be kept at the Rupert Street jail. It is customary for defendants in trials held at the law courts building on Broadway Avenue to be transferred to the Vaughan Street detention jail. Mr. Powers argued that given the rabbi's dietary restrictions (among numerous other rules, Hebrews do not eat pork) and the fact that his wife must bring him his food each day, it was imperative that the rabbi remain as close as possible to the north end of the city.

Many prominent members of Winnipeg's Hebrew community, including businessman Isaac Hirsch and Rabbi Judah Kahn were present in court, offering their support to the rabbi and his family.

Outside the Rupert station, a group of a dozen or so men and women marched carrying signs which read: "PROTECT OUR CHILDREN FROM JEWS" and "OUR BLOOD IS NOT FOR JEWS".

In general, the north end of the city has been tense. According to Mr. Hirsch, Christian and Hebrew neighbours who have been friends for many years are no longer speaking to each other and Hebrew children are afraid to walk the streets alone.

There have been several isolated incidents of violence since last week's outbreak of violence on Selkirk Avenue.

Chief McRae first doubled, then last night tripled the number of constables on duty in the area. Nevertheless, new windows installed on the street within the last few days have already been smashed. Private guards have been posted around synagogues.

At city hall Mayor Evans has threatened to read the riot act if the situation does not improve.

J.M.

Rabbi Claims He is Innocent

Winnipeg April 24 — Rabbi Aaron Davidovitch charged in the murder of Anna Rudnicki maintains that he is innocent.

In an exclusive interview yesterday afternoon in the rabbi's jail cell where he has been kept for more than two weeks, Rabbi Davidovitch spoke candidly with the Tribune about his ordeal.

"I am incapable of committing such an act. It is not in my nature," the rabbi said.

Asked about the physical evidence discovered by the police, he simply said that he has no idea how the objects in question were found at the scene of the crime. "As I have maintained from the beginning, they were stolen from my synagogue and reported to the police."

During the rabbi's preliminary hearing, Mr. Timothy Jarvis, the Crown prosecutor, maintained that no report existed because there was no report filed. Last night, Mr. Jarvis and Winnipeg police detective Michael Stark refused to comment further.

Since last week when Magistrate Thomas Daly decided to hold the rabbi over for trial, Rabbi Davidovitch has refused to eat. The police have permitted his wife and family members to bring him kosher food, but he has not touched very much of it. As a result, he has lost a great deal of weight. His face is thin and his eyes hollow.

"I don't think I will be able to look at food until this ordeal is over," he said.

As a last word, Rabbi Davidovitch, stroking his long gray beard, said, that "forces of evil have long attacked the Jewish people. Somehow they have managed to survive it all. Throughout history, there have been brave Jews, tortured and killed, all in the name of their religion and identity. If God should so choose that I be one of them, so be it."

J.M.

Hebrew Trial Opens Today

Winnipeg April 25 - - The trial of Rabbi Aaron Davidovitch opened today at the Provincial law court. Judge Winston Graves of the Court of King's Bench presiding.

Most of the day's agenda was taken up with the swearing in of the jury. Of the twelve men finally chosen, four were identified as "foreigners". There are three Galicians and one Russian man who is a teacher at a North End school. The remaining eight men include among them, a clerk from Eaton's Department store, a railway porter and a grain broker.

Defense attorney Alfred Powers questioned the fact that no Jewish jurors were chosen, but Judge Graves ruled him out of order.

In his opening statement, Mr. Timothy Jarvis argued that he will show that the accused willfully sought out the victim and killed her as part of a blood ritual in which Jews are said to use the blood of Christian children in their Passover celebrations.

The trial continues tomorrow.

J.M.

Rabbi's Phylacteries Found Around Girl's Throat

Winnipeg April 26 — The courtroom was quiet today, as the peddler Ben Goldberg related how he discovered the body of Anna Rudnicki behind his wood shed on the morning of April 10.

Each time Anna's name was mentioned, her mother Eva Rudnicki let out a whimper. Few in the room, including the members of the jury, could not help but be moved.

Asked by Mr. Jarvis to identify the thin leather strap found around the neck of the deceased, Mr. Goldberg began sobbing. After several minutes, he told the court that the straps were called tefillin, or in English, phylacteries. They are used in the morning prayer each day, except on the Sabbath. In the Hebrew religion, Sabbath is celebrated each week on Saturday.

Next on the stand were detectives Michael Stark and William McCreary who each described for the court their investigations and discovery of the murder weapon, a large ritual knife, usually used to slaughter kosher cows according to Jewish ritual.

Dr. Jock MacDonald testified that his examination of the body revealed that the victim had been strangled and then cut with the knife. He said that the stab wounds on the body seemed to have been made in a peculiar circular pattern which accounted for the excessive blood loss.

Since the day the trial started, a small group of protesters have remain outside near the entrance to the law courts chanting slogans against the accused. Judge Graves has ruled that as long as they do not constitute a disturbance, they may remain there.

Isaac Hirsch, a spokesman for the city's Hebrew community, said he was disappointed by the Judge's decision.

J.M.

Rabbi Takes Stand in Own Defence

Winnipeg April 29 — Rabbi Aaron Davidovitch took the stand today in what many legal observers regard as an act of desperation by lawyer Alfred Powers. Faced with an abundance of physical evidence which links the accused to the murder of the young Polish girl, Anna Rudnicki, Mr. Powers had little choice but to allow the rabbi to speak on his own behalf.

Earlier, Professor Leon Fredericks of Wesley College attempted to refute Crown Prosecutor Timothy Jarvis's assertion of a blood killing. According to the learned professor, the blood accusation, which has haunted Jews for centuries, has never been proven to be true. For this reason said the professor, most serious scholars refer to it as the "blood libel". It always has been, he added, a defamation and a misrepresentation of Hebrew religious customs.

Asked by Mr. Jarvis if such a killing was nevertheless possible, the professor answered that it was possible but not likely.

In his own defence, Rabbi Davidovitch told the court that he did not kill the little girl who was killed. Several times the accused, who has refused food, broke down and nearly fainted.

Under cross-examination, the rabbi was unable to answer Mr. Jarvis's question about the alleged police report he made concerning the objects found on or near the girl's body.

J.M.

II

"Come on you two, the jury will be out for a while. I'll take you to lunch," Alfred Powers said to Isaac and Klein. "I'd be willing to bet that neither of you have ever eaten at the Manitoba Club before."

Isaac Hirsch frowned. "I've heard they are not very fond of our people."

"Nonsense. I'm a former president. No one would dare say a word."

Klein was not so sure. Located since 1905 near the corner of Broadway Avenue and Fort Street next to the site of old Upper Fort Garry, the Manitoba Club was the gathering place of the province's Anglo elite. On its roster were the leading businessmen and politicians of the day: the grain men of the Exchange and the Conservative supporters of Premier Rodmond P. Roblin and Robert Rogers, his chief henchman. It was as white, Anglo-Saxon and Protestant as the Church of England.

They rode the short distance from the court to the club in Powers's horse-drawn carriage. The seats were a soft black leather and the floor covered in a red carpet. The driver, a tall and silent Scotsman named McKinley, had worked for Powers for more than twenty years. And the two horses, huge black shire geldings that the lawyer had imported from England, were said to be the finest in the city.

"I still like this way of travelling," said the lawyer. "I know automobiles are the thing of the future, but you can't surpass this for comfort."

"Can't argue with you on that," said Isaac, who seemed to be enjoying himself.

"You're awfully quiet, Sam," said Powers. Klein simply nodded. He had not yet told Hirsch or Powers about Michael Stark's Jewish background and he was not sure yet if it was even a relevant issue. So what if Stark was a Jew, he reasoned, what did that have to do with Anna Rudnicki's murder? At that moment, as he rode along Broadway, he made the decision to concentrate on finding the link between Bob Stewart and the missing police report. That, he believed, would ultimately lead him to Peter Tooley.

"Don't worry about the rabbi," assured Powers over the clip-clop of the horses, "The jury looked at him when they left. That's usually a good sign. Besides, I think I proved the evidence is circumstantial."

"I hope so. The other day, I spoke with someone who has been attending the trial. He has less confidence in the jury."

"You mean Kowalski?" asked Isaac.

Klein nodded.

"I wouldn't put a lot of stock in his comments. He's no lawyer. Besides, I've asked around, he's not as popular in the Polish community as he thinks. The odd thing is, I could swear I've met him somewhere before."

"Both of you, have some faith in my abilities," interjected Powers. "Now Sam, tell me about Sarah's condition."

"No change. The doctors don't know when she'll wake up."

"And you still think she's involved somehow?"

"I do. But let's leave it at that until I have a chance to speak with her."

The carriage continued along Broadway. The avenue, wide and grand, was an impressive sight. Giant elms, not yet in full bloom, lined the boulevard as far as the eye could see. On both sides of the street, magnificent homes and apartment blocks towered over the trees.

"A man could retire on a street like this," laughed Isaac.

"Agreed," said Powers. "Sam, what do you think? You like to live here one day?"

Klein shrugged dismissively.

McKinley stopped the rig directly in front of a large brick edifice. A canopied entrance led into the building. A man dressed in an ornate uniform held open the thick oak doors.

"Afternoon, Mr. Powers."

"Good afternoon, Ben. How's things today?"

"Just fine, Mr. Powers."

The lawyer led Klein and Isaac into the main lobby. As they passed through the entrance, Isaac removed his *yarmulke* and stuffed it in his pocket. Klein had never seem him do that before. He thought it was odd, but said nothing.

The carpet was a thick plush blue, the ceilings high and the room surrounded by oak pillars. To their immediate left was a wide staircase. And at the top, looking down at them, was an imposing stained glass window depicting Queen Victoria.

"Installed in 1898 to honour her Diamond Jubilee," Powers pointed out.

"Very impressive," said Hirsch.

While Isaac seemed in good spirits, Klein felt uncomfortable. Dressed in his old pants and jacket, he did not feel he fit in with the grain barons and bankers strolling the hallway. He decided that he would eat as quickly as possible and get himself back to Main Street.

Powers checked his coat and walked up one flight of stairs to the second floor dining area. The room had a long, beautiful well-stocked bar, much fancier than those on Main Street. The floor was a glistening hardwood. The dining room was filled with mahogany tables and highback leather chairs. A score of men, dressed in black suits and white shirts were eating lunch, drinking French wine and smoking cigars. For the past decade or so, the club had ordered its cigars directly from the Anglo-Egyptian Cigar and Tobacco Company of Cairo. They were the finest gold-tipped cigars you could find in the city.

Powers waved to one or two of the men and directed Klein and Isaac to a table by the window. Many of the men stopped talking and watched. Someone in the corner said something Klein could not quite make out and a loud chuckle could be heard across the room.

Fifteen minutes passed before a waiter dressed in a short red jacket and black pants walked over to the table.

"Excuse me, Mr. Powers, Mr. Stephens would like to have a word with you."

Powers frowned, then got to his feet. "One minute, gentlemen."

The lawyer walked over to the bar where he was greeted by the manager of the club. Klein shifted in his chair and lit a cigarette.

"I have been a member of this club for more than fifteen years," Powers shouted loud enough for everyone in the room to hear. "And I'll be damned if you can tell me who I can and cannot bring here. I want to eat my lunch and I want it now. Is that clear?"

Stephens glanced at the other members and reluctantly nodded his head.

"Anything wrong?" asked Isaac when the lawyer had returned.

"Nothing. Seems a few of my fellow-members are not thrilled about having you chaps in here."

"Maybe we should leave," said Klein.

"Nonsense. I brought you here to eat lunch and that's exactly what we're going to do."

At the table next to them, a man puffing on a cigar blew the smoke in their direction. "You see, gentlemen," he said in a loud voice. "The problem in this city is that immigration is not working. We've ended up with our North End becoming a home for mongrel Canadians. They can't speak English and I hear they rarely take a bath. If you ask me, the Galicians are the worst. Why, I've heard that the police are now required to be in attendance at their weddings, otherwise someone is likely to get killed."

The other men around the table nodded their heads in agreement.

"It's the truth. And next to the Galicians are the Jews. Rag pickers and bottle collectors."

"Oh, I'm not so sure," said another man sipping a glass of wine. "I hear they pretty much mind their own business. They might have a lot of strange customs and all, but they hardly ever break the law, not like the rest of the horde."

"If that's the case, how do you explain the murder of that little girl?"

The other man shrugged.

"And I'll tell you another thing. Anyone who defends such a crime must deep down be a Jew himself."

Klein gripped the arms of his chair.

"It's all right, Sam," Powers remarked, "he's a fool and it's best to ignore such people."

"I can't do that. We're not wanted here and you know it," Klein said, getting quickly to his feet. "I have work to do. Isaac, are you coming?"

Hirsch shifted uncomfortably in his seat. "I think I'll finish my lunch first."

Klein headed for the door, then stopped abruptly. He walked back to the table next to Powers and Hirsch.

"May I help you —?" asked the man who had been doing most of the talking. Before he could finish his sentence, Klein picked up a glass of red wine from the table and slowly poured it over the man's crisp white shirt.

"You know," he said conversationally, "I don't recognize everyone here today from Melinda's place, but I sure remember you, Mr. Massey. Melinda told me it took her half an hour to find your dick and another twenty minutes to get you to half-mast. I guess that's why all the whores on Main Street call you Half-Mast Massey."

"Good for you Sam," cheered Powers, exploding with laughter, as one of the city's most prominent grain dealers acquired a new nickname.

The gray marbled corridor outside of the second-floor courtroom was crowded with newspaper reporters and spectators eagerly awaiting the decision. Klein recognized a few faces, including Maloney, who was standing at the other end of the hall. As more and more people arrived the noise grew louder. And still the door of court remained shut. Small groups of lawyers talked loudly; others joked and laughed as if they were about to attend a vaudeville performance. The atmosphere, Klein thought, resembled Melinda's on a busy Saturday night. Expecting the worse, he had no patience for such revelry. He inhaled deeply on his cigarette, his thoughts clouded with images of Sarah and Bob Stewart. Time is what he needed to make things right. No matter what happened today, he told himself, he was not going to stop his search for the truth.

The jury had been deliberating for nearly three hours when the court was suddenly ordered to reconvene.

"Isn't that a little quick?" Klein asked Powers who had just returned with Isaac from their luncheon at the Manitoba Club. They were standing a few feet from the door.

The lawyer shrugged. "Doesn't necessarily mean anything. I've seen juries convict after four hours and acquit after less than two. You can never be sure. Anyway it doesn't matter now. We'll know where we stand in a moment."

"I'm glad you can be so calm."

"Who says I'm calm? It's just that I have been through this before."

"You must have faith," reassured Isaac. "They'll never convict a rabbi."

"Yeah, well, I need a cigarette," said Klein. He turned and pushed his way to a corner of the narrow hallway.

"There she is," one of the reporters called out. Klein peered over the mass of people to watch in disbelief as the newspapermen, like a swarm of angry bees, surrounded Rabbi Davidovitch's wife, Chana, and Clara Hirsch. The *rebbetzin*, cowering from the sudden attention, held on tightly to the hand of her eleven-year-old daughter, Laya.

"Do you think the verdict will be guilty?" one of the reporters yelled.

"Have you talked to your husband?" another one asked.

"Please, I must get into the court room," she pleaded.

Klein began to push his way through the mass to help when there was a sudden commotion behind him.

"Doors are open," someone called out.

The crowd of journalists surged into the courtroom. Isaac Hirsch escorted Clara and the Rabbi's wife into the courtroom. Klein followed and took a seat in one of the wooden chairs in the first row.

The spectators' gallery was separated from the main court area by a marble divider. In fact, the entire room was resplendent with gray marble. From the judge's magnificent dais at the front, to the boxes reserved for the jury on the left and the accused in the middle of the room, shiny marble dominated the court. The room was not large, but the stained-glass windows on one wall and the high vaulted ceiling left the impression that this was no ordinary courtroom.

Both Alfred Powers and Timothy Jarvis were already seated at their respective desks. A door at the back of the room opened and two constables entered with Rabbi Davidovitch, his hands bound by handcuffs. The crowd grew silent. Dressed in his traditional black suit and coat with the white fringes of his *tsitsis* visible at the bottom of his *kopte*, the rabbi, frail from a lack of food, hardly looked like the child-killer he was accused of being. At least, that was what Klein thought. As he shuffled towards the defendant's small enclosure in the middle of the room, he glanced in the direction of his wife and eldest daughter and forced a smile. Chana Davidovitch began to cry softly. Sitting beside her, Clara Hirsch gently touched her shoulder.

"It will be fine Mama," young Laya said. But there were tears in the child's eyes as well.

Seeing his client, Powers quickly walked towards him. "Are those cuffs really necessary?" demanded the lawyer.

"Chief's orders, sir," replied one of the constables.

"Well, I want them removed now."

"As soon as he is seated in his chair."

"I have never seen such...."

"All rise," said the bailiff.

Everyone in the courtroom stood as Judge Winston Graves, wrapped in his black gown with his white hair flowing, marched to the raised platform. For a moment, he peered out into the crowd and then took his seat in the high-back leather chair. The spectators and lawyers sat down.

"Call in the jury," the judge announced.

Immediately, the bailiff walked to the same door where the judge had entered and vanished into the adjacent hallway. Within a minute, he returned, followed by the twelve-man jury. Led by Frank Harrison, the middle-aged real estate broker who had been appointed foreman, the members of the jury stared straight-ahead, avoiding eye-contact with the rabbi. They took their seats in the box to the right of the judge. No one in the room said a word.

"I understand the jury has reached a verdict," said Graves.

"That is correct, my lord," replied Harrison, his voice steady. He handed a small piece of paper to the bailiff who in turn handed it to the judge.

Graves examined the paper. "Will the defendant please rise," he said. The rabbi got to his feet, his eyes fixed steadily on the judge.

"Rabbi Aaron Davidovitch," the judge declared, "By a jury of your peers, you have been found guilty of murder in the first degree."

A collective gasp could be heard throughout the room.

"No, no," cried Chana Davidovitch.

Powers walked to defendant's enclosure and reached for his client's arm. But the rabbi seemed to have regained his strength. He turned to look at his family and friends and began to recite the words of the *Shema*. "Hear O Israel, the Lord is my God, the Lord is One."

"Order," demanded Judge Graves.

The court grew silent. It was as if everyone in the room suddenly decided all at once not to breathe. Klein glanced down the row of seats at Isaac. He was holding the *rebbetzin's* right hand, looking like a man who was still confident everything would work out for the best. But as Klein stared more intently at his face, he could see a haunted look within. At that moment, it was a sentiment that he too shared. A great injustice was about to happen and Klein was powerless to stop it.

"I will now pronounce sentence," said Graves, placing a piece of black cloth on his head. It was an English custom dating back generations when judges wore black caps on top of their white wigs while delivering a sentence of death. For everyone in the courtroom, its somber meaning was clear.

Graves looked directly at the rabbi. "For your crime, this court rules that you are to be taken to the Vaughan Street Jail, and that you be there confined as the law requires until Friday, the fifteenth day of May, 1911, and on that day, between the hours of one o'clock and five o'clock in the morning, you be taken from your place of confinement to the place of execution and you be there then hanged by the neck until you are dead. And may God have mercy on your soul."

"Papa," young Laya Davidovitch whispered.

The rabbi turned to look at his daughter, but there was nothing he could say.

Klein sat motionless in his seat. How was such a verdict possible? At best, the evidence was circumstantial. How could the members of the jury not have had a reasonable doubt? The answer was obvious, though Klein refused to accept it.

Joseph Kowalski's earlier assessment had been correct. As they watched and listened to Rabbi Davidovitch over the past week, the jury members would not allow themselves to see the religious leader that Alfred Powers had tried to portray, a man incapable of murder. Rather, in their eyes, the rabbi was nothing less than the representative of a strange and bloodthirsty cult, an anti-Christian willing to do anything and kill anyone to satisfy his evil desires. In the end, Powers could do little, because there was no known defense to counteract hatred, bigotry and superstition.

As Klein joined Hirsch in the lobby, Michael Stark suddenly appeared in front of him. Klein could not restrain himself.

"Turning your back on your own people, Stark. How do you live with yourself?"

"What are you talking about?" said the detective, clearly flustered.

"What are you scared of? Being called a Jew?"

"No man who works in a whorehouse should have anything to say. Now, get out of my way."

Klein stood in front of the detective. "C'mon, Stark. How does it feel to be a party to the lynching of a rabbi?"

"Go to hell."

"What do you know about the missing police report?"

Stark frowned.

"You didn't tamper with any evidence did you, detective?"

Finally, Stark pushed Klein aside and strode out of the lobby.

"What was all that about?" asked Hirsch, his eyes narrowed.

"Nothing," replied Klein. "I was trying to stir things up a little. This is not over yet."

"You should have put me on the stand. I could've told them about Stewart and the police report," argued Klein. He was pacing back and forth in Alfred Powers's office. Isaac Hirsch sat dejected in a chair beside the desk.

"Based on what?" asked the lawyer, puffing angrily on a cigar, "A hunch? Jarvis would've killed you."

"Maybe, but it would have been better than this. What are you going to do now?"

"File an appeal. But to be honest, I don't have much room to maneuver."

"Well, I'm not going to let an innocent man hang at the end of a rope."

"Sam," said Isaac, staring out the window "you've done all you could. Face facts, there is nothing more we can do. There is nothing more any of us can do."

Klein turned around to look at his friend. "How can you say that? My God, you're giving up. Isaac, it's not like you to quit. There's still Tooley and I know Sarah can help us."

"If she ever wakes up."

"She will."

"Who knows what she will remember."

"So what would you have me do," Klein's voice rose in irritation. "Forget about the rabbi? Get on with my life, go about my daily routine, and pretend this never happened?"

Hirsch shrugged. "Maybe it's best."

"You can go to hell! Last night, they broke more windows on Selkirk and tried to break into another synagogue. I tell you, this is not going to go away, even after the rabbi is dead. And you Isaac should know better than anyone. Don't you remember what life was like in Russia, always afraid, always waiting for the worst to happen."

"This is not Russia."

Klein strode forward and pointed his finger at Hirsch. "I'm tired of being an outsider, someone who doesn't fit in. We have as much right to live in this city, to be protected by the law, to raise a family in peace. This is 1911 and there is a man about to be hanged because the world out there still believes that Jews drink the blood of Christian children on Passover. And you both say relax, do nothing! Well, believe me, I will do something!"

"Michael, I was worried about you. It's nearly ten o'clock. You told me you'd be home hours ago," said Julia Stark.

The detective kissed his wife's cheek. In her day, Julia Stark had been a beautiful woman. Tall, with wavy brown hair and a soaring singing voice, she could have been on the stage, a career her preacher father strictly forbade. Despite the wrinkles and gray hair, at age fifty-three, she retained her youthful glow and sparkle.

"I am sorry Julia," said the detective. "I lost track of time. It's this case. You know how it has been bothering me lately."

Indeed, in twenty-five years of marriage, Julia Stark had never seen her husband fret over a case as much as he had the murder of the Polish girl.

"But it's over, Michael. The man you arrested is guilty."

Stark walked to the bar and took down a bottle of Scotch.

His wife frowned; Stark rarely drank during the week. The poor man, she thought, he can't forget the sight of that little girl lying dead. "I got a telegram from Christopher today," she said in a bright voice. "He is planning to visit in the summer."

"That's great news," Stark replied. And he was happy that his only child, who had recently obtained a civil service job in Ottawa in the new department of labour, was planning a trip home. The last letter he had received from Christopher indicated that he was enjoying his work preparing reports on trade union activity, although he had noted that his boss, William Lyon Mackenzie King, was a rather odd man. Christopher had even shaken hands with Prime Minister Laurier.

Stark sighed heavily as he poured himself a glass of whisky. He was carrying more than the weight of the girl's murder. What would Christopher and Julia think of him if they knew the truth of his past? He had kept the secret of his Judaism hidden for so long, he was not sure who he was anymore. He was a man with no past; no shared history to guide him in these difficult times.

Events had unfolded as he thought they would. But could he stand by while an innocent man was hanged? He had been taught as a young child in Poland about the virtues of *tzdakah*, of charity and righteousness. His recent actions had displayed none of this. He could not recall when he had been so self-absorbed. He had allowed McCreary to hijack the murder investigation and then helped him convict the rabbi on circumstantial evidence.

"Your dinner is ready, Michael," his wife called from the kitchen.

But Stark wasn't paying attention. Sitting in a chair by the window, he sipped his whisky and contemplated a future as murky as his past.

12

Simeiz, Russia
On the Coast of the Black Sea
April 30, 1911

Not even the warm spring breeze from the Black Sea could improve the General's disposition or physical condition on this beautiful morning. Sitting in a large wooden chair a few feet from his small but palatial *dacha*, he could not stop coughing. And as he spit into his handkerchief, he noticed that his phlegm was redder than usual. The majestic view of the Crimean mountains that swept behind him and the shimmering sea in front, hardly mattered. He had little time left, he knew that.

Five years ago, doctors had diagnosed him with tuberculosis. He had been forced to retire from his high-ranking position in the Okhrana. Soon after, he had left the cold magnificence of the Imperial capital for this dacha in Simeiz, only thirteen miles west of Yalta. His cousin, General Pavel Zavarzin, had been generous once again. The property, both the two story brick house with its seven rooms and the elegant estate which surrounded it near the water, had been in Pavel's family for many years. But with radicals threatening to overthrow the old order at every turn, his cousin had little time for leisure by the sea. There were anarchists to arrest and revolutionary presses to shut down. The *dacha* was his as long as he wanted it, Zavarzin had assured him.

All his life, his cousin had protected him, often at great risk. He had ensured his promotion to St. Petersburg from Odessa, where he had admirably served his master Alexander III, defender of the old order and protector of Russian Orthodoxy. He had enjoyed the night life in the capital then, the vodka flowed freely and there were many young women at his beck and call. There were also the whores of the Haymarket to toy with.

A grimy slum neighbourhood, the Haymarket was only a few blocks from the Winter Palace. In its narrow streets and alleys, the air was foul, a mixture of grease from outdoor cooking pots, urine, and *makhorka* — the cheap tobacco of choice smoked by the thieves and whores who resided there. He grew both excited and agitated as he remembered his numerous trysts with the *marukhi*, the local whores who for twenty kopeks satisfied his unusual sexual desires.

Yes, he owed Pavel much. Who else but his powerful cousin could have made that mess in Odessa vanish? True it had been his own fault. He had been careless and sloppy. Still, matters would have been resolved favourably, if not for that meddling agent. He had caused him much trouble and then the agent had disappeared before he could answer for his insolence. On the other hand, the punishment for the crime had been rightly meted out to the Jew, as it should have been. Justice had been served after all.

He placed his damp handkerchief back in his jacket pocket and reached for his morning newspaper. But after a few minutes, he threw the newspaper to the ground in disgust. Nicholas II is nothing like his father, he thought. So weak, so timid. He has no mind of his own. He listens to his wife Alexandra and that filthy monk Rasputin. How many times had he wanted to travel the short distance to the Royal Family's summer palace at Livadia and offer his counsel. Regretfully, he knew that Nicholas was more interested in hunting deer than in running the country.

"General, is something wrong?" asked Sergei who had walked up from behind. He was carrying a silver tray with a bottle and glass. Under his left arm, held tightly to his body, was a brown envelope.

"The usual, Sergei. It is the Czar, he has no mind of his own. All this talk of change, of becoming modern. I refuse to accept it. And you know who is to blame?"

"Who sir?" asked Sergei, knowing full well the answer the General would provide.

"The Jews. They are the distraction that has burdened the military. They are both Bolsheviks and financiers. What place can there be for them in the Empire? Remember Czar Alexander's words, Sergei, 'Russia should belong to Russian people.' I wish they would all go to America. Let them destroy that country instead."

General Mikhail Perov's speech was cut short by a fit of coughing.

"Here, calm yourself, sir, I have brought you vodka." The tall servant, his gray hair neatly combed and long black coat pressed, poured General Perov a cup of the clear but potent nectar. The General grabbed the glass with a gesture of urgency and with one quick movement of his right hand, he swigged down the liquid. Drops of vodka lingered on his gray moustache.

"Ah, I can always count on you, Sergei. How many years have we been together?"

"Twenty nine years."

"A long time. Then I had some real power in the Okhrana. I made a difference, didn't I Sergei? Destroying the radicals, closing down their news rags, chasing the Jews from Moscow."

"You may be retired, sir, but let me remind you that you do still have some influence. The Sacred Guard is not yet dead. True, it is not as powerful as it was, but I am certain that today the remaining few will rise up against the radicals and anarchists. They shall be defeated. There remain opportunities and men loyal to General Zavarzin and yourself."

"You are right, of course, but the situation is not good. I am afraid that the voices of moderation are becoming louder. Now show me what the mail has brought today."

"I have taken the liberty of opening it, sir. It is from the London office, a recent news story from the *Times*."

As part of his training many years ago, the General had learned to read and write English. It was one of the few skills he possessed. He took the envelope from Sergei's hand and perused it quickly.

"You will note the similarities, sir, as I did."

"Indeed, Sergei. It says that a rabbi has been arrested and the authorities are proceeding with a murder trial. There is talk in the Canadian city of blood rituals. Excellent. First Beilis in Kiev, now this in North America."

"You are not concerned then?"

"Of what? That a Jew has killed another Christian child. He will pay as Schiff did and as Beilis will."

"So you don't find it odd that the victim in ....what is the name of the city?"

"Winnipeg."

"Yes. That the victim in Winnipeg was murdered in precisely the same fashion as the woman in Odessa twenty-eight years ago."

"A coincidence. That is all. My conscience is clear about Odessa. There is nothing to worry about," asserted Perov, his voice rising.

"You are correct, of course. I was only thinking...."

"Still, there would be no harm in investigating further. If I am not mistaken, we have a retired officer there. An intelligent and loyal man. You know who I am talking about, Sergei. Send a telegram to St. Petersburg, to General Zavarzin's office. Some one there will have the address in Canada, but take the usual precautions."

"As you wish, General."

"Now leave me the bottle and go about your business. I have grown weary."

Sergei placed the silver tray with the bottle of vodka beside the general and returned to the *dacha*. The servant indeed knew who his master was referring to. The man could be of some service. But as for being loyal to the General, Sergei knew better.

13

Damn, he thought, why can't they leave him alone. It was not that he was no longer loyal to the cause — he was. He was aware that the radicals were a threat to the Empire. He also understood that democracy would never work in Russia as it did in North America because of the large number of illiterate peasants. How could a man whose father was a serf comprehend the complex affairs of the state? How could such a man vote in an election? It was preposterous. But time had taken its toll and he wanted to be left in peace. He had lived in Canada for many years and had retired from the service more than two decades ago. He had built a life for himself and was respected in the community. More importantly, no one knew anything of his past, not even his wife.

He reread the telegram from General Zavarzin's office in St. Petersburg several times and then placed it in a metal ashtray on his desk. Of course he had noticed the similarities between the two crimes. But unlike that fool Perov dying in Russia, he knew precisely how it happened.

He recognized the former agent immediately after he settled in the city, but decided not to pursue a relationship with him or to tell anyone in the service that he had seen him. That could have only led to more questions. Knowing the man as he did, however, he was equally certain that the young girl's death must have been an accident, and that the blood ritual had been used to disguise the murder. It was the way it had always been with such killings in the past. The man was clever. And there were no better scapegoats than the Jews.

What the perpetrator did not know, of course, was that someone else in Winnipeg knew about the incident in Odessa, the mysterious circumstances of the murder there, and what had transpired in St. Petersburg when the agent had reported Perov's transgression.

In his youth, as an officer of Okhrana, he had been much braver and, he now realized, more foolish. At the time, though, he had no fear. Once Sergei, the General's servant, had confirmed the true events to him, he had decided that he could not stand idly by while a good agent died for no reason. Out of a sense of honour and justice, he had saved the former agent's life. Now he had the choice of betraying the man he had once helped or ignoring the whole affair. It was a dilemma.

He wasn't certain what Zavarzin and his Sacred Guard would prefer: the execution of a Jew, guilty or not, for a blood ritual—this would undoubtedly aid their case against Beilis and possibly quiet foreign objections— or the name and whereabouts of the former agent who had attempted to indict Perov and then fled. Revealing the latter, of course, might also jeopardize his own position.

At the same time, he was growing increasingly uncomfortable with the thought that an innocent man was about to be put to death. Already there had been a riot that had caused great damage. Perhaps he had been living in Canada far too long. He had become weak and this matter of the rabbi troubled him greatly. Still, how could he reveal the truth without also revealing his own secret? He would have to ponder this problem further.

He struck a match and placed it gently into the ashtray. Within seconds, the telegram was nothing more than a pile of black ash.

Klein was now a man possessed. Using every contact, friend, bartender and drunk he knew, he searched the streets for Peter Tooley. Nothing turned up. He posted look-outs at the railway station. He had Maloney write a missing person's story with a photograph. With Melinda's backing, he offered a one thousand dollar reward for information leading to the grain broker. Still, there was no trace of him.

"Sam you're exhausted. You need some sleep," said Melinda. "When was the last time you had something decent to eat?"

"You are beginning to sound like my mother." Klein was back for a brief rest at the house before continuing his search. Alfred Powers had already filed his appeal for a stay of execution on some legal technicality that Klein did not understand. He expected a decision within a week, four days before the rabbi was scheduled to be hanged. Provincial officials wanted this entire episode over quickly and within days of the conclusion of the trial had set the date of the hanging for May 15. Ironically, this coincided with the first day of *Shavuot*, the Feast of the Weeks, a religious holiday that celebrated the spring and the giving of the Ten Commandments to Moses on Mount Sinai. Members of the Winnipeg Jewish community were aghast that the Roblin government could be so callous. So far, requests that the date of execution be changed had fallen on deaf ears.

"Have you ever stopped to consider that perhaps Tooley has left the city or is dead?" asked Melinda.

"I have, but I don't buy it. Call it intuition, call it what ever you want. I'm telling you not only is he still alive, but he's in the city, somewhere."

Melinda stood up and walked over to him. She ran her fingers through his hair and gently kissed his cheek.

"What was that for?"

"You're a good man, Sam, with a good heart."

"Yeah maybe so, but it hasn't helped me so far."

"I think it has, you just don't know it."

Darlene, dressed in a white robe, ran into Melinda's office. "Sam, there's a little bald man here at the front door. Says he knows you and he has to talk to you, right away."

Klein found Joe James waiting for him.

"Joe, what have you got for me?"

"Plenty. But not here. Can we talk somewhere more private?"

"Sure, this way."

Klein led Joe through the parlour to his bedroom at the back of the house. The girls giggled as the old man tipped his bowler hat at them. Darlene casually reached out for a glass as Joe passed, and as she did, her white robe fell open. Joe's mouth dropped.

"Come back later and you can touch them," she said.

Joe nodded dumbly.

"Darlene," Klein said firmly. "Not now."

"I was just having a little fun, that's all."

"All right Joe, out with it," Klein demanded as he shut the door to his room.

"I think I know where that broker you're looking for has got himself hid."

"Where?"

"I was at my corner as usual, when those two detectives come by. You know them, McCreary and Stark."

"Yes?"

"And they were having an argument. One of them, Stark, is saying that they have to check it out. McCreary is very angry. 'Look', he says, 'it's over. The Jew is going to hang. Let's leave it alone. I don't care if you think you know where he is.' I try to move closer to hear better. Then Stark says, as loud as can be, 'I'm telling you, Tooley was spotted at his sister's house on Aberdeen Avenue.' That's what he said."

"He's here, right in the North End. I knew it. Do you have an address Joe?"

"After I hear this, I make a few calls to some of the boys downtown at the Exchange. They tell me, Tooley mentioned having a sister who was married to a street car operator named McWilliams. So I check in the Henderson's directory and sure enough there is a Tom McWilliams at 773 Aberdeen Avenue."

Klein grabbed his friend's shoulder. "Joe, you did well. You did real well. Thanks. I owe you one."

"Well, there is something I haven't had in a long time," Joe said, smiling nervously.

Klein laughed. "Wait here."

A few moments later, Darlene appeared at the door of Klein's bedroom. Her robe was low on her shoulders. She offered Joe her hand. "Come on, old man, we'll see if you're still alive. It's on the house."

Klein made one phone call before he left. He wasn't sure whether this was a smart move but he made the call anyway. He knew it was a calculated risk.

Klein then hurried to Selkirk Avenue and hopped a west-bound street car. It took ten minutes to reach Arlington Street and another ten minutes to get to Aberdeen Avenue. Number 773 was a small but well kept house near the corner. It was enclosed by a white picket fence. There was a veranda and porch in the front. Klein stopped for a moment. The house looked deserted.

"Nobody home," said a gray-haired man, next door. He was sitting on a rocking chair in his front veranda.

"What's that?" asked Klein, walking over to him.

"The McWilliams are gone. I haven't seen them in more than a week. Heard they went to visit relatives down east."

"I see."

"You a friend?"

"Yes. A friend of the family. I know Mrs. McWilliams's brother Peter. I'm a little worried about him. He said he was sick."

"Don't know him. Though I did see a stranger poking around here last night. Big man wearing a brown suit. Maybe that was him."

"Could be. Mind if I take a closer look?"

"It's a free world. Go ahead."

As the old man had said, there did not appear to be anyone home. He turned the knob on the front door; it wouldn't budge. He tried opening the window, but it was locked from the inside.

"Try the back door," shouted the old man, "I don't think they lock it."

Klein walked around to the back of the house. There were some children's toys and a sandbox. Someone had also fastened a rope to a large tree so that it could be used as a swing. Klein turned the handle and sure enough the door opened.

"Hello. Anyone home?"

There was no response. Klein took one one step inside the kitchen when the odour hit him. It was powerful and putrid, like nothing he had ever smelled before. He took out his handkerchief and covered his nose. His instincts told him to get out of the house. He hesitated for a second and then continued walking farther into the house.

"Hello," he again called out. And once more, there was no answer.

The closer he moved toward the bedroom directly in front of him, the stronger the smell. The bedroom door was open. He peered in, his hankerchief over his nose. There was blood everywhere. On the floor and on the walls. A red patch covered the white sheets on the bed.

On the other side of the bed lay Peter Tooley. By the look of the deep gash on his neck, Klein figured that the grain broker's throat had been sliced with a sharp razor. Whatever secrets Tooley had stored away, whatever he knew about the murder of Anna Rudnicki, he had taken with him.

Klein looked around for a scrap of paper, a clue, anything that could explain all this. But he could find nothing. There was a small enclave to the right of Tooley's body with a bureau. He walked towards it. Each drawer had been pulled out and its contents — clothes and other personal items — thrown about.

His eyes glanced upwards for a moment and it was then that he saw the writing. There was an oval mirror above the top of the bureau. On it, scrawled in Tooley's blood, was a message for him: 'Klein, stop now or this will be you and your family.'

At that moment he felt something hard jab into his back.

"Hands in the air, pimp," a voice ordered.

Klein turned around slowly with his hands above his head.

"Hello, McCreary," said Klein. "Who do you think called you?"

"Now why would you do that?" asked the detective, slightly easing back his finger on the trigger of his black pistol. "You hate my guts."

"Yes. But even though you're a racist, I think you're probably a honest cop."

"I'm flattered, Klein."

"It doesn't matter how I feel about you. I called you here because I figured either Tooley killed that little girl or he knew who did."

"And?"

"And it was the latter. The man's in there," said Klein, pointing at the bedroom door, "with his throat slashed. Go see for yourself. If you look, you will also see a message on the mirror meant for me."

The detective said nothing. "Turn around," he told Klein finally.

"What for?"

"Just do it."

Klein reluctantly did as he was asked. McCreary grabbed Klein's right wrist, placed one ring of his handcuffs around it, and attached the other to the door handle.

"What are you doing?"

"A precaution, that's all. You wait right here. I'd like to see this mess for myself."

After a few minutes, McCreary returned. The smirk he usually wore on his face had been wiped away. Silently, he unlocked the handcuffs. "I don't like you Klein, but I never figured you for a murderer. I still don't."

Klein rubbed his wrists. "So does that mean you will help me?"

"That's funny, Klein, you coming to me for help. This killing probably has nothing whatsoever to do with the Rudnicki murder. And let me repeat, I don't like you or your kind and I certainly don't trust you."

Klein knew that he was at a crossroads. Either he was going to have to beg McCreary for his assistance, or he would have to walk away and depend on luck. He would've preferred to ignore McCreary. In his view, the detective represented everything he detested about the Gentile world: the intolerance, the bigotry, the condescension. And yet, he knew if McCreary were to be convinced, the battle to save Rabbi Davidovitch could be won. As he stood there before the detective, Klein realized that he had no choice at all.

"I know you would like me to beg, McCreary, but I'm not going to do that. Instead I'm going to appeal to your sense of justice. We both know that the rabbi's conviction was circumstantial. That the accusations were nothing more than a blood libel. You don't like Jews, I can accept that. But I figure you are smart enough to spot a witch-hunt, especially when it's so blatant."

McCreary shrugged.

"I can't explain yet how the rabbi's possessions were at the scene of that murder," continued Klein, "but I know as sure as I know anything that he is telling the truth about the synagogue robbery. There was a police report."

"So what happened to it?" asked McCreary.

"Bob Stewart got rid of it."

"Stewart? What does he have to do with this?"

Klein looked at the detective for a moment. He had gone this far, he thought, he might as well play the whole thing out.

"The night Stewart was killed he was meeting with me. He had called to let me know that he had something important to tell me about the Rudnicki case. But by the time I got there he was nearly dead. All I heard him mumble was it was his fault and that he was sorry. At the time I didn't know what for. When I visited his house, I found, among his papers, an invoice from Tooley. So the two men knew each other. I'm convinced more than ever that Stewart destroyed that report and that somehow his connection to Tooley played a part in this."

"You're reaching Klein. Stewart was as straight as they came. Why would he do such a thing?"

"Believe it or not, for money. It's that simple. Bob was an unhappy cop who wanted a lot more out of life and he ran out of patience. I figure he became involved with Tooley who promised him a treasure, and one thing led to another. For some reason, Tooley wanted that police report to disappear and Stewart was paid to do the job."

"Is that it?"

"No, there's more." Klein had gone this far, there was no point holding back. "Tooley also knew Sarah Bloomberg. I found her half-dead in his office. She's in the hospital right now in a coma. And I'm positive that Amy's murder is tied up in this as well. So it all comes down to this. There are only two people left who know the truth about that night in the North End: the killer and Sarah — and she's not talking yet. I think that if I was the murderer, I'd keep a close eye on that hospital bed. Right now, there's a guard at the door but he's only one man. He might not be able to stop the person who sliced Tooley's throat."

McCreary slowly clapped his hands. "Klein, that is the greatest fairy tale I've heard in a long time. There are so many holes in your story, I lost count. You know what you got?"

"What?"

"You got shit! You got a hunch and you barely have that. I should arrest you for leaving the scene of a murder, a policeman's at that." McCreary paused. "But you are right about one thing. I don't believe you or the rabbi drink the blood of young Christian children. On the other hand, you still have not convinced me that we have the wrong man in jail."

"What will it take?"

"Something that will stand up in court. As I see it, there are two leads here, one to Bob Stewart, the other to Tooley and the girls. Let's say for the sake of argument that Stewart did indeed destroy that report after the girl was murdered, a time difference of perhaps a week or more. He would've had access to the files at the North End station so that part would've been easy. However, about ten months ago, the department's administrative rules were changed. Since then, a carbon of every report is also sent to the chief's office. After we had arrested the rabbi, I checked both the North End Station and Stark went to the chief's office. We both came up empty. There was no report."

"Which means?" asked Klein.

"Which means, Klein, if Stewart got rid of that report, someone in the chief's office had to have helped him. Assuming it was not the chief himself, that could only leave one other person."

"Who?"

"Let me call in Tooley's murder and then we'll go downtown and I'll show you."

Within twenty minutes, a swarm of police wagons and cars had surrounded the McWilliams's house. Michael Stark had been called at his home to handle the investigation. McCreary and Klein were waiting outside on the porch for him when he arrived.

"Bill, what's going on? You're the last two people I would've expected to find together," said the detective.

"We kissed and made up," said McCreary with a smirk. "Now listen, Michael. My new friend and I have to check something out downtown. That's why I had them call you at home. The house belongs to the victim's sister. The family is out of town in Hamilton, I believe. Maybe we should try and find them. They're going to love the new decor in their bedroom."

"Christ McCreary, try not to be so sensitive," said Stark. "What's so important downtown anyway?"

"Oh nothing much. Klein here," he said pointing his finger at Sam, "has this wild idea that we got the wrong man for the Rudnicki murder and I've decided to play along with him for a bit."

"Is that so? What have you got?"

Klein stood silent. "You really want to have this conversation now, Stark?"

"What have you told McCreary?"

"Nothing, for the moment."

"Will someone tell me what is going on?" demanded McCreary.

"No," replied Klein, "it's between me and Stark."

14

Neither Klein nor McCreary said much as they drove down Main Street towards the Rupert Avenue station. As he stared at passing pedestrians and shops, Klein's mind was filled with images of Sarah. Not the way she was now lying in a hospital bed bandaged and nearly dead, but sitting beside him at the Walker, laughing, happy and beautiful.

That was the last intimate evening they had spent together. Three weeks ago, they went for dinner at Angelo's and then a hilarious vaudeville show at the theatre. Nothing pleased Sarah more. There was a singing juggler named Nello who did fantastic feats with a dozen white plates. He was followed by the Sullivan comedy team, three brothers who could sing and dance as well as any performers Sam had ever seen. Away from Melinda's, it was almost as if they were a normal couple. That was to be the night he would ask her to leave Melinda's. Yet when the right moment presented itself, he could not find the words. Perhaps it was because he knew what her answer would be.

Then, Anna's murder had turned his life upside down. His sister beaten, Bob Stewart killed, Sarah mixed up with Tooley. Now he was personally involved. He wanted desperately to save Rabbi Davidovitch, yet at the same time, he was wary, even fearful, of the truth he might uncover.

"You think the murderer will try to kill Sarah?" asked Klein, as the car pulled up in front of the station.

"Hard to say," said McCreary. "Especially since I'm not sure I believe your story to begin with."

"Humour me, please."

"Do I think he'll kill her? First of all, why are you so certain it is a single killer we are after? For all we know, he may have hired someone to do his bidding for him. In this city, with all the riffraff on Main Street, it's not that difficult to find someone to do your dirty work for you. It's clear, however, that he's desperate, but not stupid. Assuming everything you have told me is correct, I doubt whether he or his man would try to get at her in a hospital, especially if she is unconscious. Why take an unnecessary risk?"

"And if she wakes up?"

"I'd say we have a problem."

The two men entered the station. It was quiet. The constable at the front desk was taking a statement from a Chinese man and was having difficulty understanding him. He waved to McCreary.

Klein saw the look of disdain in the detective's eyes.

"You really hate us, don't you?" he asked.

"Who you talking about?"

"Us. Immigrants. Newcomers."

McCreary shrugged. "I don't know if hate is the right word. It's just that I think God meant for this country to be British and white and somewhere along the line, the train went off the track, so to speak. There are some people in this city that believe everyone can be transformed into God-fearing Canadians. I don't have that much faith."

"You've never been deprived of your freedom, McCreary, have you?"

The detective rolled his eyes.

"You've never had people stare at you with hate, real ugly hate in their eyes. It's amazing really. They don't know you. They don't know anything about you. But they hate you, nonetheless. Why? Because you talk a different language, dress in different clothes and eat different food. That's reason enough to hate. Explain that to me."

"Sorry Klein, I don't have all the answers. All I know is that people like you are never going to be changed and that's going to lead to a lot more conflict and tension in the future. Because there are too many people like me who are never going to accept that."

They reached the second floor and walked down the hall to the chief's office.

"McCreary, how are you doing?" asked Molly Austin. "If you're looking for the chief, you just missed him."

Molly was forty years old and prematurely gray. She was the only woman to be employed at the police station. A spinster, she was related to McRae's wife and had worked for the chief for a number of years. There had been some talk that the station was no place for a lady, but the chief quickly put an end to that discussion. So Molly kept her job and became an accepted fixture.

"Actually, Molly, I'm here to speak with you."

"Me? What can I do for you?"

"Molly, I'd like to introduce you to Sam Klein. I'm trying to help him out with a problem and we thought you could help."

"Sure," she said, nervously patting her hair.

Klein stood back and watched McCreary go to work. He was calm, meticulous but probing — like a big cat stalking its prey.

"Do you recall a few weeks back when Detective Stark asked you about an alleged copy of a police report?"

"Do you know how many reports I deal with here? Every day dozens..."

"I know, Molly. But this one was important. It involved the Rudnicki case and the arrest of that rabbi."

"I'm...I'm not sure."

"Think hard, Molly," said McCreary, his voice becoming sterner. "Stark asked you if there was a report filed from the North End station involving a theft at a synagogue."

"Oh yes, I remember now. I checked but I couldn't find anything for him."

"Yes, he told me." McCreary glanced at Klein. "But you see, Molly, it's like this. The rabbi says he filed the report with Bob Stewart and Klein here has convinced me that the rabbi is telling the truth. What do you think of that?"

Molly's lip was trembling, but she remained silent.

"Did you hear what I'm saying?" demanded McCreary. "If the rabbi is telling the truth, that could only mean that someone is lying. My guess is that someone is you."

She was softly crying now. But McCreary refused to let up.

"Molly, I want you to tell me what happened to that report. Did Bob ask you to get rid of it? What did you do with it?"

Klein wanted to tell him to stop. The woman obviously had had enough, but he sensed, as McCreary did, that she was about to talk.

"Molly, we're both waiting. You can either do it here or we can go downstairs."

"No," she cried out. "Please give me a moment."

"Take all the time you want," said McCreary, his voice calmer. He knew he had broken her.

"Yes, it was me! I lost it," she said, raising her chin defiantly.

"Spill it, Molly."

Molly's eyes blazed for a moment, then dimmed. With a sigh, she turned to Klein. "It was a favour for Bob. That's all. It was a favour for Bob. He called me one day in a panic. Said he couldn't explain, only that he was in some sort of trouble. He asked me to destroy the theft report. I don't know, he was a nice guy, always brought me coffee and pastry. Treated me with respect, not like a lot of the other guys. So I did it. I found the rabbi's theft report and burned it, just like he asked."

She glanced away. "I'm sorry. I didn't mean to hurt anyone, especially a man of religion."

"You must have known we needed that report," McCreary insisted. "Why didn't you tell Stark about it when he came?"

"Bob was dead. I was scared whoever killed him would come after me."

"And so you were going to let an innocent man die."

The secretary burst into tears. "Please don't tell the chief. I couldn't bear it."

"Shut up, Molly," McCreary said wearily, "Just shut your mouth."

"Don't look at me like that," said McCreary as they walked down the hall.

"I didn't say anything."

"Yeah, but I know what you're thinking. Did you want to know the truth or not? I learned a long time ago that compassion gets you nowhere in this business. I know you might find this difficult to believe, but I used to be a nice guy. I was also a shitty detective. Ruthlessness, Klein, and fear. You build up a reputation for yourself as a mean son-of-a-bitch and nobody stands in your way. You think Molly would've told us what we wanted to know if I would've come in there sweet-talking her. We would've got nothing."

"Listen McCreary, I'm making no judgments. You got to do your job the way you see fit. I just happen to think you can have it both ways. There's nothing wrong with compassion as long as you know when to use it and when not to. To be honest, I happen to think you handled that woman the right way."

McCreary slowed down. "I'm glad you approve of my methods. We might almost be pals some day."

"I doubt that."

The detective laughed. "You're a pistol, Klein, a real pistol. I didn't know you people could be so funny."

"Oh yeah, us Hebes can be a real hoot." Klein stopped. "Listen, now that we know that the rabbi was telling the truth, why not just go to the judge and tell him? We're running out of time. In four days, Rabbi Davidovitch is going to be hanging at the end of a rope."

"We could do that. Except what will that do? Think about it. The judge will order a new hearing. Molly will testify about the destroyed police report and your friend will probably be exonerated. It'll be the front page story in all the papers. And what about your girl friend lying in the hospital? The real murderer will still be out there waiting for her. Face it Klein, her life and yours are never going to be back to normal until this guy is caught."

"So what do you suggest?"

"I say we try to flush this asshole out into the open. What if we get the word out somehow that Sarah is about to talk to the police about what she knows. Our man is bound to make his move then and we'll be waiting for him or for whoever he sends in to do his dirty work."

"I don't know."

McCreary pulled out his pocket watch and ostentatiously checked the time. "I got lots of other work to do."

"I should be getting my head checked for listening to you." Klein stared at McCreary for a moment. "Okay, I'll go along on, with one condition."

"What's that?"

"I have to let Alfred Powers and Isaac Hirsch know what's going on. I owe it to them."

"I think that's a mistake."

"I'll take my chances."

Once the decision had been made, the two men moved quickly. They were the most unlikely of partners. One, a Scottish-born detective, so bitter and full of hate that he had forgotten how to feel for others; the second, a Russian Jew searching for his rightful place in the world.

They would never be friends. Yet, against all odds, Sam Klein and Bill McCreary somehow came to an arrangement, and their audacious plan was set in motion. Both Alfred Powers and Isaac Hirsch were initially furious when they heard what Klein had in mind. But he convinced them, as McCreary had convinced him, that it was the only way. It was agreed that Powers would prepare all the paperwork so that when the word came, he would be ready to file his new evidence.

"You're gambling with an innocent man's life, Shailek," Isaac warned him.

"You're the one who got me involved in this to begin with," replied Klein. "You're going to have to let me finish it."

Seventy-two hours before Rabbi Aaron Davidovitch was to be executed, a brief article appeared in the *Tribune*:

Winnipeg, May 12 — Police announced late last night that Sarah Bloomberg, who had been assaulted last week by an unknown assailant, has made a full recovery. Doctors at the General Hospital expect Miss Bloomberg to be able to speak about her ordeal this morning. Police are confident Miss Bloomberg will be able to explain what happened to her.

Maloney arrived at the *Tribune* building on McDermot Avenue bright and early. He was sober and ready to work. His white shirt was pressed, though he wore his wrinkled navy suit and scuffed black laced boots as usual. But that hardly mattered. As he crossed Main Street, the warm April sun brightly shining on his face revitalized him.

He was glad that he had been able to help Klein. He had no idea what his Hebrew friend was up to and had been startled to discover him working with McCreary. Still, he figured that Klein knew what he was doing. He promised him that this morning, he would finally prepare the historical research Klein had been patiently waiting for. If it could be of some assistance in Powers's appeal, so much the better. It was also another way for him to relieve his guilty conscience for all the trouble he had caused.

"Jesus, Mr. Maloney," remarked Henry the doorman. "It's only seven o'clock in the morning. What are you doing here?"

"I'm always here this early," said Maloney with a grin.

"I've been working this door now since the paper moved in here way back in 1900 and I swear on my mother's grave, may God bless her soul, that I never seen you here before ten."

"Henry, you're looking at the new John Maloney."

The elderly doorman laughed out loud. "You have a good day."

"And you too, Henry."

Maloney's desk was located at the far end of the second-floor newsroom among a sea of other desks, chairs and typewriters. A pile of newspapers covered the top of the table which was hardly visible to anyone passing by. Maloney couldn't recall the last time he had bothered to clean it up. "Keep the desk a mess," he used to tell other reporters, "and the editors will think you're doing something important."

At this time of the day, the newsroom was relatively quiet. A few younger reporters eager to get an early start to the day waited impatiently for their assignments by the city editor's desk. But their boss, a hard-nosed journalist named John Moncrieff had yet to make his appearance. The wooden floor, normally strewn with copies of the *Free Press*, *Telegram* and yesterday's *Tribune*, was still clean and the air was still free of cigarette and cigar smoke. But by nine o'clock, Maloney knew he could expect a lot more noise from phones and typewriters as the hunt for the day's events began in earnest.

"Hey, Maloney," one of the younger reporters shouted, "the sun isn't even up yet. You coming straight from the bar or something?"

"Don't you have an obituary to write?" he replied. "You go about your work, I got a real story to write."

The other cub reporters by the city editor's desk roared with laughter.

Maloney opened the bottom drawer of his desk and pulled out a thin file of clippings he had retrieved from the newspaper's small clipping library. "There isn't much in there," Gail Morrison had told him. "But you got every story on Hebrews we have."

Mrs. Morrison, as she was known around the newsroom, a fifty-year-old red-haired widow who favoured bright polka dot dresses, had worked for Richardson's *Tribune* since the paper had been founded back in 1890. Her job was to scour both editions of the paper each day as well as the *Free Press* and *Telegram* as often as she could. Using a large pair of metal shears, she clipped newsworthy stories and filed them in thin brown cardboard folders. It was a thankless task that required patience and organization, skills which Mrs. Morrison fortunately possessed. If you needed some background on Quebec politics or a biography of a former city mayor, she could supply it to you within moments. For reporters she was an indispensable asset.

Maloney threw the file on his desk and reached deeper into the drawer for two thick books loaned to him by Professor Fredericks at Wesley College. One was the second volume of the English translation of *The History of the Jews* by Heinrich Graetz published in Philadelphia in 1891; and the other was a recently-published collection of essays by Fredericks' friend, the noted Oxford University scholar Arthur Caldwell. Entitled *The Medieval and Modern Jew*, it contained one essay which traced the history of the blood accusation.

Maloney stared at both tomes and shook his head. These were hardly the kind of books he normally read. He'd recently plowed through J.S. Woodsworth's new book, *My Neighbour*, but it had not impressed him. It was a typical Methodist catalog of the evils of urban life and Maloney was hardly an advocate for using more money, public or private, to assist impoverished foreigners. Let them solve their own problems, he thought, or let them go back to where they came from. Out of curiosity, he had also started reading the novel *Sowing Seeds in Danny* by local writer Nellie McClung. But after fifty pages, he couldn't stomach its preachy tone which, in his opinion, overly glorified pioneer life and portrayed all rural women as saints. How it had become a Canadian bestseller, Maloney had no idea.

All Klein had told him was to compile as much information as he could about blood ritual cases that had taken place in the past hundred years. In the solitude of the newsroom, Maloney leaned back in his chair and picked up the file marked "Hebrews". Inside, he found about a dozen yellowed clippings and a short magazine article from a spring, 1910 *Maclean's* magazine issue entitled "The Jews of the Northwest" by Toronto journalist Paul Smythe. He knew Smythe quite well and was familiar with his writing. A freelancer, Smythe usually had steady work from *Maclean's* or *Saturday Night* magazine. He was also a typical easterner, a bit of a snob who boosted Toronto every chance he could get.

"One hundred years from now," he told Maloney the last time he visited Winnipeg, "'Hogtown' will be the greatest thing this country has ever seen. As for your 'Chicago of the North', you'll be lucky if the population will have doubled. You've reached your peak here, Maloney. There is no where else to go but down." Maloney merely laughed his comments off, insistent that Winnipeg's prospects were unlimited.

Maloney glanced at Smythe's introduction. "Twenty-five years ago," the article began, "there were no Jews in the Northwest. Now you can't travel ten miles without arriving at a Jewish settlement. At such locales as Edenbridge, Wapella, Lipton and Sonnenfeld, Hebrew pioneers have miraculously built communities, complete with synagogues and schools. The huts they live in are nothing to look at, but they call it home. For many this is a vast improvement over the living conditions they endured in Russia."

The article continued for another two pages with Smythe's insights into the Jewish character. Maloney turned to the last page. "For better or worse, the Jew is now here to stay, a permanent resident of our cities, towns and neighbourhoods. But it is imperative that we keep in mind that if he is treated fairly, the Jew will respond in kind. It is common wisdom that every country has the type of Jew it deserves. As Canadians, therefore, we must decide what type of Jew we want."

Maloney nodded his head in agreement. Whatever Smythe's failings, he knew his business. These were sentiments that Maloney concurred with: Keep the country's Jews in line, encourage them to assimilate and the world will unfold as it should. He doubted, however, that Klein would agree. It was his impression that Klein was not open to discussion on the subject of Jews and their future in Canada. Each time he had raised the issue, Klein had told him to mind his own business. "Jews in the North End or anywhere else in the country will decide for themselves how to fit into their new home," he had said. Maloney was not about to argue. Best to leave this out of his report, he thought.

He placed Smythe's article in the back of the file and began to examine the clippings. The first few were old *Tribune* stories from the 1890's about the arrival of Jews from Eastern Europe and how they planned to fit into the community. They had little but the clothes on their backs but were prepared to work hard. Another, from August, 1893 noted the dedication of the Rosh Pina Synagogue on Henry and Martha Street, a replacement for an earlier building destroyed in a fire.

A third dated September 24, 1902, was an article via the wire service from New York. It was the obituary of a German Jewish dry-goods merchant named Levi Strauss. The obit noted how Strauss, who had immigrated to the United States in 1848 from Bavaria, had made his way to California in 1849. There he had become a great financial success marketing blue denim overalls with copper rivets. Strauss's pants, simply called Levi's by the locals, became the favourite uniform among the horde of miners who had ventured west in search of gold.

All very well, thought Maloney, Jews are a resourceful people, he already knew that. But there was still nothing he could use. He continued to sort through the pile until his eye caught a *Free Press* story of April 10, 1903 which reported on the Winnipeg Jewish community's reaction to a brutal pogrom in Kishinev, Russia. As he read the clipping detailing the outbreak of violence in the Bessarabian city, Maloney's face turned white. My God, he thought, the pogrom was provoked by the writings of a newspaper editor named Krushevan who used the spectre of a ritual murder to incite the local population.

Apparently, the body of a fourteen-year-old peasant boy had been found several months earlier in the nearby village of Dubossary. The boy's distraught grandfather later claimed his grandson had been murdered by a group of Jews who wanted his blood for making Passover *matzoh*. No Jew was ever arrested for the crime, but Krushevan, a notorious Jew-hater, nonetheless, used his paper, *Bessarabets*, to spread vicious lies.

On Easter Sunday of that year, hundreds of rioters went on a rampage in Kishinev. Jewish women were raped, their husbands and children butchered as the police stood by and watched. One Jew by the name of Mottel Greenspoon attempted to save a group of women He was seized by the mob who first castrated him and then beat him to death. Maloney's stomach turned. He thought about his own front page story and the subsequent riot on Selkirk Avenue.

Finally, he reached the bottom of the clippings and took note of a small yellow article dated April, 1883 with a byline from London, England. It was marked "Sun files" and as Maloney knew, Richardson, the former city editor of the *Winnipeg Sun*, had taken some of that newspaper's files with him after the *Free Press* had bought the paper and shut it down in 1889. Richardson's intense hatred of the *Free Press* was said to have started that day.

There was no indication as to which newspaper the old clipping had originated from, but Maloney didn't care. It was the title of the piece which attracted his attention: "Jew killed in aftermath of Blood Ritual Accusation".

The Jew in question was a grain trader in Odessa named Max Schiff. He had been accused of killing a fifteen-year-old girl as part of a ritual murder. Following his arrest he was taken to the local jail, but somehow, a mob broke into his cell, took him into the main square and hanged him. Maloney wrote down the details of the case in his notebook and stared at the small grainy black and white drawing of the victim which accompanied the piece. It was only a rough sketch of Schiff, whose face was covered by a thick black beard. But it was his eyes and the shape of his long nose that Maloney noticed immediately. There was something familiar about it.

Distracted by more commotion in the newsroom, he placed the undated clipping on the top of the pile and closed the folder. Now, Maloney decided, it was time to tackle the two books. Volume two of the Graetz history was his first choice. For an hour Maloney worked undisturbed. He found references to the same twelfth and thirteenth century blood libel trials already described to him by Professor Fredericks but not much more. He jotted down notes about the Black Death that had begun in Europe in 1348 and the fact that Jews, then regarded as allies of the Devil, had been accused of poisoning the drinking water in the wells. Despite the intervention of Pope Clement VI who proclaimed their innocence, thousands of Jews were nonetheless slaughtered.

He grew more uneasy as he read how Christian merchants in western Europe and in the Kingdom of Poland had promoted the blood ritual charges as a convenient way to halt Jewish competition. It was brilliant strategy, thought Maloney. They spread rumours among the ignorant peasants that Jews had murdered Christian children for their blood, and stood back and gloated while their Jewish competitors were eliminated for good.

"Maloney, there you are. I'm waiting for a follow up on the blood ritual. Maybe something on the coming execution," boomed a familiar voice. John Moncrieff was a slight man with a black drooping moustache, but when he talked *Tribune* reporters jumped. He was a few feet from Maloney's desk wearing his customary crisp white shirt and black vest.

"Tomorrow, I promise," said Maloney. "I'm just doing a little research."

The editor noticed the books on Maloney's desk. "In those? What news do you expect to find in there? I want to know what's going on in the here and now, not two hundred years ago."

"Have I ever let you down before John?"

"You don't really want me to answer that, do you?"

Maloney turned away. "Can't talk anymore, John, got work to do."

Next, he opened the Caldwell book. The inside cover had been autographed: "To Leon, with my deepest respect and admiration. From one scholar to another, Arthur." Maloney quickly scanned the table of contents. The book contained six essays, "Rituals of Blood and other Stories" was the fourth one, following "A Glimpse of the Life of Jews in Frankfurt in 1456". He turned to page 143 and started to read.

According to Caldwell's research, there had been seven blood accusations between 1800 and 1904: one in Lemberg in the Austrian-Hungarian Empire, another in the village of Fulda, north of Frankfurt and five in Russia. Maloney was already familiar with two of them, Odessa in 1883 involving the Jewish grain merchant Max Schiff and the Kishinev pogrom of 1903.

As far as he could determine, the seven cases were nearly identical. In each instance, a Christian boy or girl approximately aged eight to fifteen was found dead, usually with their throat cut. A local Jew was arrested on the flimsiest of evidence and ordered to stand trial (except in Kishinev where the entire Jewish population paid the price). In all but one case, that in Lemberg where the accused Jew, a merchant named Simon, was acquitted, the other Jewish victims were killed either by the authorities or in a pogrom before the legal proceedings even began. That was what had happened in Odessa.

Caldwell had little to add to what Maloney already knew about the murder case in Odessa and the arrest and killing of Schiff, although there were more facts about the police investigation. He studied that section of the article carefully. There was something about the case which troubled him. But what? He reread the details of the incident several times: a fifteen-year old girl named Katrina had been found murdered behind a grain shed belonging to Schiff. Her body had been mutilated, her neck slashed, and a circular pattern carved into her torso. That was it. He checked the facts of each case listed by Caldwell. In none of the others had a circular pattern been found on the body. A circular pattern...Maloney began to sweat. He lunged for the pile of newspapers on the shelf by the window until he found his story of a few days earlier in the Trib Extra edition.

"The body of young Anna Rudnicki had been found in an alley behind Dufferin Avenue. All Chief McRae would say at this time is that the young victim's throat had been slashed sufficiently to allow a great deal of blood to drain from her body. The phylacteries belonging to Rabbi Aaron Davidovitch were found around her neck. The Chief also commented that an odd circular pattern had been carved into young Anna's body. 'In all my years on the force,' said McRae, 'I've never seen anything like this before.'"

The similarity between the murder victims in Odessa and Winnipeg was striking. The identical circular incision had been made on the bodies; the victims' necks had been slashed in a similar fashion; and the blood had been drained from their neck in the same manner. Perhaps it was merely a coincidence. After all what could a murder in Odessa in 1883 have to do with one in Winnipeg nearly three decades later?

Still, Maloney's journalistic instincts told him something was not right. He would have to find Klein immediately to report his discovery. Klein would know what to make of this. He quickly picked up the clipping file prepared for him by Mrs. Morrison and opened it. On top was the unmarked news story about the Odessa case. He stared at the drawing again. Take away the beard and a few pounds, he thought, and it was an uncanny resemblance. As absurd as it seemed, Max Schiff and Sam Klein had the same face.

15

Another telegram had arrived from Russia that afternoon. This time a lengthy coded one from officials in St. Petersburg who wanted to know what was going on in Winnipeg. They had received a message from Simeiz. It was from Sergei, the servant of General Perov. During the previous night the General had finally succumbed to his illness. Sergei decided to clear his conscience and revealed everything to them about his master's sordid life. They now knew for certain of the General's various criminal activities and of his cousin General Pavel Zavarzin's complicity. General Zavarzin, had been dismissed from his office and exiled to Siberia. His cherished Sacred Guard, protectors of the old order, had been dismantled. The time had come, military officials determined, for Russia to handle the radicals by different methods. The secret ways and harsh means of Czar Alexander III no longer worked in the twentieth century.

Sergei had also provided complete details of how Perov had murdered the woman in Odessa in 1883 and then blamed the Jew Schiff. The role of the agent had been related as well and how he had managed to escape General Zavarzin's men.

"Your own actions in warning this former agent are being considered," the telegram concluded. "If you know the whereabouts of this renegade and deserter, send this information at once. We have decided that he should be demoted to tie up all loose ends. We would also like more details on blood ritual killing in Canadian city. Comply immediately."

A bead of sweat ran down the man's face as he placed the telegram on his desk. He knew full well what the word "demoted" implied. He had been given orders to kill the former agent—if he knew where he was, that is. Such a mess, he thought. He could stall for another day or two. But there was still the matter of the rabbi's impending execution. Perhaps, he thought, it was time to confront this former agent he had helped in the past. Then he would know what to do.

Klein and McCreary decided to work out of Melinda's house. When the two of them arrived together, Melinda was speechless. She was reluctant to even allow McCreary inside, until Klein persuaded her that the detective would behave himself.

"We wait here for a few hours so that our man has had enough time to read the paper and figure out that he's about to be exposed," explained McCreary, sitting on a velvet plush chair in Melinda's office. "I've already talked to the hospital and they've moved Sarah to another room. Delaware is still with her, but I've ordered my two constables to keep guard over the phony room. As soon as you and I get there, I'll get rid of them."

"And?"

"And the rest is up to our killer."

"It sounds too easy."

"I know, that's the beauty of it. The less complicated these things are, the better they work out in the end."

Time passed quickly. They ate lunch and McCreary, under Melinda's disapproving eye, flirted with several of the women.

"How do you do it, Klein?" asked McCreary, his eyes flickering back and forth.

"Do what?" asked Klein, pretending he didn't notice the detective gawking at the half-clad women sitting around the kitchen table. Most were wearing nothing but satin negligees of various colours and lengths.

"Live here among all of this. How do you keep your hands off them? I don't think I could do it."

"That's the difference between you and me. It's business. I was hired to do a job and I do it. It's as simple as that."

McCreary shook his head. "And your hands never wander? Come on Klein, you're human aren't you?"

Klein shrugged. As long as as he could remember, he had always adored women; he liked the way they smelled after a bath, the way their hips moved when they danced, the way their soft skin felt next to his in bed. The real difference between him and McCreary, however, a difference that the detective would never have understood, was that Klein did not take women for granted. He did not treat them as inferior beings.

Why shouldn't women be able to vote and be treated as equals? In Klein's opinion, that included the rich ladies from River Heights, as well as the working mothers of the North End and the prostitutes on Rachel Street. Perhaps it had been his mother's influence and the many years he had watched her toil for her family, or his admiration for Melinda, but Sam Klein respected women in a way that McCreary, a creature of his time, found impossible.

"So are you going to tell me your little secret or not, Klein?" asked McCreary.

"Nothing to tell. It's just the way I am. Now don't you think we'd better get to the hospital?"

"Sam," shouted Melinda from the other room. "I forgot to tell you, there were two phone calls for you. That reporter Maloney phoned several times. Says he has something important to show you. And the other was from a Joseph Kowalski at the Holy Ghost Fraternal Society. He insisted that you should contact him immediately. Sounded kind of nervous to me."

"Kowalski? What the hell does he want? Well, both of them will have to wait. If Maloney calls again, tell him I'll call after I'm finished with McCreary. I'll deal with Kowalski after that."

As the two men drove to the hospital, Klein marvelled at how quiet the notorious saloon strip along Main Street was. Police constables were out in force, breaking up any collection of more than five people. Even the usually overflowing bars near the railway station were nearly empty, as regular patrons opted to stay home. One riot had managed to accomplish what legions of prohibitionists couldn't.

There was, however, a more vivid reminder of the terrible events that had unfolded over the past few weeks. Near the corner of Higgins and Main, someone had erected a large sign. Painted in black was caricature of Rabbi Davidovitch, his nose accentuated, with a noose around his neck. Written below the picture were the words: 'Salvation is Almost Here. Death to the Child Killer'.

"Don't worry, Klein," said McCreary, "I promise this will all work out."

Klein nodded. In the past forty-eight hours, he had decided that McCreary did have a few redeeming qualities, though he still was not comfortable working so closely with him. There was no getting away from the fact that the man was a boor, but after watching him put their plan in place, he respected McCreary's skills as a detective.

Klein pulled up the collar of his jacket to shelter himself from the evening cold. He urged McCreary to drive faster, now concerned more than ever that they would not reach the hospital in time to prevent another tragedy.

When they arrived, Klein immediately ran through the front door ahead of McCreary and up the stairs to Sarah's new room. Delaware was dozing in a chair outside the door.

"Frank, wake up."

"What? Oh Sam, sorry, I was just catching a few winks."

"Everything okay?"

"Not a peep out of anyone."

"Is she the same?"

"Afraid so."

Klein opened the door of the room and peered in. Sarah still lay motionless. Klein walked up to her and brushed his hand against hers.

"See, I told you everything would be fine," said McCreary as he walked in.

Frank Delaware rubbed his eyes. "I must be dreaming, seeing the two of you together."

"It's a long story," conceded Klein, "when this is over I'll explain everything to you over a beer."

The former policeman nodded, but eyed McCreary suspiciously.

"Frank, how's the leg?" laughed McCreary.

Delaware said nothing.

"Come on, Klein," said McCreary. "Leave Delaware here with her. We've got work to do. I've dismissed my two men from outside the other room. Why don't you plant yourself inside and I'll stake it out from the down the hall. All we have to do is wait until our man shows up."

"Just watch your back, Sam," added Delaware.

"Always do," said Klein.

Two hours passed. Sitting alone in the dark, the smell of sickness in the air, Klein felt disoriented. Images flashed through his head. Anna Rudnicki lying in the mud strangled in *teffilin*. Bob Stewart's last breath before he died. The bloodied and beaten face of his sister. Sarah in a coma. Nothing was going to happen, he thought desperately, because no one was coming. McCreary's plan was ridiculous; it was doomed to fail. Skillful detective or not, he was a fool for becoming involved with him. The man was nothing but trouble. He got to his feet and went to the door.

"McCreary," Klein hissed as he peered down the darkened hallway, "This is a waste of time."

There was no answer.

"McCreary, where are you? It's time to wrap this up for the night."

The detective walked out from around the corner.

"McCreary, there you are. Listen, I..."

Before Klein could finish a sentence, the detective stumbled forward, collapsing to his knees. "Klein, I..."

A small trickle of blood was running from his mouth. His eyes met Klein's as he fell to the floor. Klein rushed over to him.

"Nurse, nurse. Someone get over here!"

Shoved into Bill McCreary's back was a knife, the kind used by a *shochet* in the ritual slaughtering of animals; the same type of knife that had been found near the body of Anna Rudnicki.

Within seconds two nurses and a doctor arrived. They placed the detective on a stretcher and hurried him to the operating room. It was then that Klein thought of Sarah. He ran down one flight of stairs and through the corridor. Delaware's chair was empty. Klein tugged at the handle of the door and threw it open.

"Sarah!"

She was lying quietly in the bed, her chest rising calmly with each breath.

"Sarah, thank God."

Klein glanced down and saw Delaware lying on the floor. He was trying to stand up. "Frank, what happened? Are you all right?"

The former cop lifted himself from the floor. "Yeah, fine. I was hit from behind. I heard McCreary shout and went down the hall to investigate but

I didn't see anything. When I returned I came in here to check on the lady and that's when I got popped," he said rubbing the back of his head. "Where's McCreary?"

"They took him away, I don't know if...."

"Sam, is that you?" whispered a voice. "Please stop all that talking. You're giving me a headache."

Klein turned and looked into the open eyes of Sarah Bloomberg.

"Sam, what am I doing here?" she asked, trying to sit up.

He took her hand and kissed it. "Sarah, I thought I'd lost you."

"No. Still here. That a friend of yours?" she said pointing shakily at Delaware.

"Sarah, I'd like you meet Frank Delaware. He's been watching out for you. May have just saved your life, as a matter of fact."

"Nice to meet you, Frank," she said weakly.

Delaware smiled. "Ma'am."

"I guess I've caused a bit of trouble."

"You could say that."

"How long have I been here?"

"Almost a week. I found you nearly dead in Peter Tooley's office. You had run off. I was so worried. Sarah, what's going on? How did you know Tooley?"

"Where is he?"

"As dead as Amy and maybe Bill McCreary."

Sarah shook her head in disbelief. "Give me a minute and I'll tell you what I know. I promise."

"You'd better hurry because we don't have a lot of time. If I don't figure out what's going on or who really killed that young girl, the rabbi is going to hang and soon. To be honest, you should be dead too. I must have scared off whoever was in here."

"Sam," Sarah said softly.

He looked at her.

"I love you."

Klein flashed a quick smile. "I know you do. But we have to find the killer first. Tell me what happened."

Sarah looked so helpless. Klein wanted to reach out to her, but he forced himself to hold back. A narrow beam of sunlight blazed through the window illuminating her face. The beating she had received at the hands of Tooley and his partner had taken its toll, yet her face was as beautiful as ever; her presence as daunting.

"I need to know everything, Sarah. Start with Tooley."

"I met him maybe a year and half ago in a bar," said Sarah, awkwardly propping a pillow behind her back. "I was trying to make some extra cash and he bought me a drink. Before the night was out, he had asked me if I wanted to make some easy money, and lots of it."

"Go on."

"It was no big deal. Every so often, I'd have to be at his office to entertain one of his clients."

"You mean…"

"Yes. He set me up in a hotel not far from his office at the Exchange and I'd keep these guys happy. He said that way they didn't ask as many questions. And once a month, he'd give me about five hundred. And that was it."

"You didn't wonder where the money was coming from?"

"Believe it or not, I did want to get out of Melinda's and this was the only way. I didn't ask questions. Tooley was not the most pleasant person. This went on for about six months. Then things changed. I'm not quite sure what happened, but I think one of his clients found out what he was doing and threatened to go to the police. After that he became more desperate. He started drinking much more than usual."

"Do you know who this client was?"

"No, and he didn't say. I'm not even sure that I ever met him. Anyway, about a month ago before all of this trouble, I told him I had had enough and was not going to do him anymore favours. He was drunk and became very angry. He said he had made a big mistake, that he had lost some money and that his partner was not going to understand. He promised me if I stayed on for a little longer, he would pay me two thousand dollars. I couldn't say no."

"Of course not!"

"Don't judge me, Sam. Do you know what it's like to be poor, I mean really poor?"

"As a matter of fact I do."

"Well then, try to understand. He was offering me, and you I hoped, a new life. I was forced to sleep with these two big Swede farmers, stupid enough I guess to entrust their hard-earned savings with Tooley. He assured me my pay-off was coming. I waited a few days, but did not hear from him. By this time, that little girl had been murdered. I was walking down Main Street when I saw him. We spoke for a few minutes. He even hinted about the girl's murder, but at that point, I didn't think anything of it. Then, we had a big argument. He said he had to leave the city on business and I would get paid later. I told him that I'd expose his swindle, if he didn't pay up. He said he had to see me later that night and he was going to come by Melinda's to straighten everything out."

"Where did this conversation take place?"

"I don't know. I think around Logan and Main. Why?"

"Jesus, it was you, not Amy, who Joe saw."

"What are you talking about?"

"Nothing, go on."

"A few nights later, in fact, it was the night we were together." Sarah stopped and reached for Klein's hand. Their fingers lightly touched, then Klein pulled his hand away.

"Sorry," she said, suppressing a smile. "That night, at about four in the morning, there's a knock on the window and it's Tooley. He's drunk and talking nonsense. He crawls into my room through the window and tells me he has to give me something to watch while he's away. I ask him what's wrong and he starts babbling about that little girl. Says he was there and saw who did it. 'Why did he do that?' he keeps saying over and over. He was making such a racket, I thought everyone at Melinda's would wake up — except only one person did."

"Amy?"

"Yes. She stumbled into my room and saw Tooley sitting on the floor. She was half-asleep. She didn't hear anything. But Tooley became very angry. He asked me who she was so I told him. I told him! He took her out of my room. But I didn't think he'd harm her. When she didn't return the next day, I had a bad feeling about it. That's when I took off."

"Where were you?"

"I planned to leave the city for Winnipeg Beach, but was nearly killed by some stranger who was following me. I made it to a hotel in St. James where this man found me again. I was lucky to get out alive. Then I moved to a boarding house in St. Boniface. I was confused. I had read about Powers handling the rabbi's case. I don't know Sam, I suppose I felt guilty. That's when I went to see the lawyer. But it took so long that I panicked. I was running out the building and who do I run into, but Tooley. He seemed calm. I asked him what he was doing in the city. All he said was that everything was fine. He refused to talk about Amy, and..."

"And you didn't pursue the matter?"

Sarah shut her eyes. "No I did not. He promised me that I would get the money he owed me. The next day I met him...and well you know the rest. I didn't mean for any of these terrible things to happen. Sam, you have to believe me, please."

"I believe you. I'm not blaming you. I just wish you would've come to me in the first place."

"I thought of it. I didn't think you would understand about the money."

"Oh, Sarah," Klein moved closer to her and kissed her cheek. Then his lips found her mouth. He held her in his arms as tightly as he could. For a few moments, neither of them said anything.

Finally, Sarah sat back against the pillow. "Sam," she said quietly, "why didn't he kill me when he had the chance?"

Klein nodded. "That question also has been going through my mind. Tell me, what did Tooley give you to watch for him?"

"It was a black bound book, a book with names."

"Where is it?"

"Where it's always been, under a floorboard in my room at Melinda's."

The knife had narrowly missed McCreary's lungs. The doctor on duty managed to stop the bleeding and, after a few stitches, pronounced the policeman on the road to recovery. Had McCreary not been in a hospital when the attack occurred, however, there was no doubt he would have bled to death.

Two hours later, Klein was still at the hospital. Michael Stark's arrival had slowed him down. There were questions to be answered and police reports to fill out. Stark did everything by the book. This time, Klein tried to be patient with the detective's queries.

Did he see the attacker? No. Did McCreary say anything to him? No. Did he find any objects by the body? No. Was the knife removed from McCreary's back the same kind used to kill Anna Rudnicki? Yes. Why did Sarah Bloomberg require a former Winnipeg constable as a bodyguard? He didn't know.

Pacing back and forth in an empty hospital room, Klein answered all of Stark's questions as honestly as he could, though he was not prepared to share with the detective the details of Sarah's involvement. Let McCreary tell him about it if he chose.

Finally, Stark closed his notebook. "You're hiding something, aren't you Klein?"

"That is pretty funny, coming from you."

Stark sighed and nodded his head. "It's time we talked about it, I suppose," he began slowly, "You want to know why I hide the fact that I'm a Jew?"

Klein nodded.

"When I was a young boy growing up in a Polish village, I saw how my grandfather was beaten by local thugs. He was a beautiful, innocent man. A Talmudic scholar. We buried him when I was eight years old. I ran away from home seven years later. When I made it to Canada, it seemed easier to hide my other life. Life as a Jew in a Gentile world was too damn hard. Do you think I would've ever been accepted into the force if they had known the truth?"

"I don't know."

"Not on your life. I would have spent my days like old Ben Goldberg, selling rags and bottles. No thanks."

"And you've never regretted it?"

"Occasionally, but I am not the type of person to dwell on the past. My wife and son don't even know. I'm not sure how they would react."

The two men stared at each other, seeing the different possibilities fate has to offer.

"You think what's happened here will save the rabbi?" asked the detective.

"Yes. I believe it will."

"And you know who did kill that little girl?"

"Not yet, but I will soon. I am certain of it."

"Then everything should work out for the best. Good luck, Klein. I sincerely mean that."

After an awkward moment, Klein extended his hand and Stark grasped it. The detective then turned and left.

Klein decided the fastest route to Melinda's was by foot. It was dusk and the streets were relatively quiet, except for the steady stream of horse-drawn wagons. It had been market day at Derby and Dufferin and the farmers who had sold their produce for the past ten hours were finally heading with their wagons and animals to the barn on William Street. They kept their horses there overnight before making the return journey into the country. Klein knew that if they had had a profitable day, several of them might find their way to Melinda's for some fun. What their wives back on the farm didn't know would not hurt them, they'd roar as they marched into various bedrooms with an assortment of scantily-clad women. Melinda always liked market day.

He had reached the corner of Main and Jarvis, when he saw Maloney walking towards him in a great rush. He had a sheaf of papers under his arms.

"Klein, finally," said the reporter out of breath. "I have been trying to find you all day."

"I know. I was at the hospital. Sarah's awake and I have a better idea what is going on, but I have to get to Melinda's and I haven't got time to chat."

"Wait, I found something that I think you had better see."

"Well, what is it?" asked Klein impatiently.

"Here," said Maloney pointing towards the stoop of a nearby shop. "Sit here and look at this." He opened his papers.

"Maloney, I don't have time for this," said Klein still standing.

"I know, you already said that. But I did the research you asked. It's all in this report," said Maloney, handing Klein some papers.

"All right," Klein sighed. "Anything useful?"

The reporter nodded. "Well, I'm not sure what it means but there was a murder of a young woman in Odessa, Russia back in 1883 that resembles the killing in Winnipeg."

"Odessa? In 1883?"

"Exactly. They found the same circular pattern on the body in Odessa as they did on Anna Rudnicki's corpse. But that's not the most interesting part."

"I'm all ears."

"Here, look at this picture," said Maloney giving Klein the 1883 news clipping.

"What is it?"

"I know it's a little old, but look closely at the drawing."

"Yeah, who is it?"

"Name was Max Schiff. He was accused of the blood ritual in Odessa and eventually murdered by a mob. That name mean anything to you?"

"No. Why should it?"

Klein stared at the sketch of Max Schiff. A shiver went through his body as he looked more closely.

"It's remarkable, isn't it," said Maloney. "That face. Without the beard, it's you."

Klein said nothing. He wasn't certain if the drawing resembled him or not. What he saw staring back at him, however, was the man in the black beard who had haunted his childhood dreams.

At this late hour, the Holy Ghost Church on Selkirk Avenue was nearly empty. Its rising steeple could be seen for miles around, a testimony to the impressive Polish presence in the North End. Inside, a row of burning candles near the front of the dais illuminated the wooden cross set high above on the back wall. A few parishioners seeking solace and salvation prayed near by.

Next door in the darkened office of the Fraternal Society, a lone figure sat on the oak chair by a large desk, its wooden top tightly sealed. Behind him, two large maps adorned the wall: one of the Kingdom of Poland established by the Congress of Vienna in 1815; the other of the Canadian Dominion with Polish settlements, from Halifax to Vancouver, marked in black. Large circles were drawn around the cities of Toronto, Winnipeg and Edmonton.

Joseph Kowalski reached inside his jacket pocket for a small key. Grasping it, he unlocked the bottom drawer of his desk and took out a blue silk sack. His hands were shaking. He reached inside and pulled out the dusty pistol. It was a single-action Colt revolver that he had brought with him from Europe. In this younger days, he had been a crack shot and few of his friends could match his skill with the weapon. But that was long ago, he thought.

He took his handkerchief from his pants pocket and wiped the narrow steel barrel. He then snapped opened the empty cylinder and thoroughly rubbed each chamber with the cloth as well. Finally, when the revolver was cleaned to his satisfaction, he reached inside the silk bag and pulled out a small box of cartridges. He took out six, carefully inserted them into the cylinder, and snapped it back into position.

He pointed the loaded gun towards the wall, but his hand was not steady. My God, he thought, I have become useless in my old age. It was one thing to deal with immigrant labourers and their wives, quite another to threaten a man with a gun. Angry with himself, he placed the pistol back into the blue sack. I must do this, he thought, no matter how I feel. I must.

16

Klein's mother was the only person who could answer all his questions; the only one who could tell him why the image of Max Schiff had disturbed his sleep for so many years.

With the news clipping Maloney had given him tucked inside his jacket pocket, Klein walked swiftly towards his family's home. He found his mother where she usually was: bent over her sewing machine in the corner of her kitchen. A kerosene lamp flickered beside her barely illuminating the room, as the machine clicked the stitches into another pair of leather gloves. She had not heard him enter the house. He stood and watched her for a few moments. She had been through so much in the past month. He hated to bother her, but he had questions that needed answers.

"Ma," he said.

"Shailek, what are you doing here? Come sit down," she said to him in Yiddish. "Rivka is out with friends, I was just doing some work."

"We have to talk," he answered in the same language.

"What's wrong? Has someone died? Please Sam don't tell me that someone else has died."

"Ma, calm down. I have to ask you some questions."

"Questions?"

"Yes, about the past."

Freda Klein stood up and walked the short distance to the stove. "I was just making tea," she announced. "We will have some tea and then you'll tell me about your day." She picked up a piece of wood from the small pile on the floor, opened the black steel trap door on the stove, and threw it in.

"Ma, did you hear me? I need to know some things."

"What things?" The kettle was boiling. Freda picked it up from the stove and poured the steaming water into a pot.

"I want to know about my father."

"What is there to tell? He died so many years ago. Thank God, Isaac helped us get out of Odessa..." She suddenly stopped herself. "Here, have some tea."

"Odessa? When were we in Odessa? I thought I was born in Mezherich."

"Forget it. I shouldn't have said anything. Come have some tea."

"No, I won't forget it. Tell me about Odessa."

"Really, it's nothing. Your father and I lived in Odessa for a few years. After your father was killed, Isaac helped us move to Mezherich. You wouldn't remember, of course, you were only a baby. I was pregnant with Rivka then."

"Why didn't you ever mention this before?"

"I don't know, Shailek, it wasn't important." With a shaking hand, Freda poured herself some tea.

"Why did you have to leave Odessa?"

"It was after the accident, Isaac thought it was best if we left. He worked for the government and was able to secure the right papers and pay our way."

Klein frowned. "Ma, you remember those bad dreams I used to have when I was younger, of the man with the beard being chased by a mob."

She nodded. "Oh how I remember. You used to wake up so frightened."

"You know, ever since I have been hunting the killer of that little girl, they have returned. It is the oddest thing."

Freda remained silent.

"And more importantly, I believe I know now who that man is. The poor man who has pleaded to me to save him for so many years."

"You do?" his mother asked as she sipped her tea.

Klein reached into his coat pocket and pulled out the yellowed news clipping given to him by Maloney. "It was my father wasn't it, Ma? My father was Max Schiff?"

Freda was holding her cup. It fell out of her hand and smashed to pieces on the kitchen floor. "Why are you doing this to me?" she asked, her voice trembling. She began to pick up the pieces of the cup.

"Ma, please stop for a moment, look at this picture." He pushed the yellowed clipping in front of her. "This man, Ma, this face, it's me. It is the face of my nightmares."

Freda took the newspaper from his hands and she stared at the picture. "It's been so many years. Yes, that is your face." She looked deep into Klein's eyes. "Yes, my dear Shailek, Max Schiff was your father."

"Why didn't you tell me sooner?"

"I know I should have. I just wanted to forget that horrible time. Klein was my family's name. I changed it after we left Odessa."

"All these years you told me that my father was killed in some sort of rail accident. But that's not true is it?"

Freda stared at the ground.

"Max Schiff was accused of murdering a girl in a blood libel accusation. The newspaper says that he was killed by a mob before he was even brought to court. This is the vision of my dreams, isn't it?"

Freda covered her eyes with her apron. "Yes, it is true, all of it. We had been married only a few years. Your father was a grain merchant in Odessa, as his father had been before him. It happened such a long time ago...They took him right in front of me. But you were so young. When you first told me of your bad dreams, I found it hard to believe that you could remember such a terrible event. I was so happy the day that dream stopped."

"Well, it has returned. Ma, please I must know everything."

"There was a murder in the city during Passover in April of 1883," she said slowly. "The girl was discovered behind one of our warehouses. It was just a coincidence. Your father had nothing to do with it. But a few nights later the police came to our house and arrested your father. He was put on trial. I went to visit him at the jail with you the day the mob came..."

Klein embraced his mother and hugged her. "You should've told Rivka and me about this."

"It was such a terrible memory, I tried to wipe it out. We came to Canada to start a new life. Why would I want to ruin it with such a terrible memory? I decided many years ago that if I didn't have to share it with you, then maybe it didn't happen after all. And Isaac assured me that it was for the best."

"Isaac has told me that he knew my father."

"Yes. They were friends. As I said, Isaac worked for the government and he visited Odessa from time to time. He would eat with us. He and your father would play cards."

"What did he do? Which department did he work for?"

"I don't know. Something very high up, though. He knew many important people. One of the few Jews to hold such a position in the Czar's government. It was a real honour."

Klein said nothing. Now he understood the significance of his dreams and the tragic death of his father. The question that still needed to be answered, however, was what all of this had to do with the murder of Anna Rudnicki in Winnipeg nearly three decades later. And, more importantly, how did Isaac Hirsch fit in? Why had he not mentioned the link to Odessa? Perhaps he was merely protecting Freda.

He reasoned that there was no sense upsetting his mother further with his suspicions. He bid her farewell and headed towards Melinda's where he was certain he would find the final missing piece of the puzzle.

As soon as Klein entered the house on Rachel Street, he could see that it was busy. Must be market day, he thought. About twenty labourers, regular customers whenever they were in the city, had arrived on the five o'clock train from Saskatchewan, thirsty for beer and yearning for fun. They were joined by a half dozen farmers from Treherne and Glenboro. It was so crowded that Klein could barely make it through the front room.

Pushing past the crowd, Klein raced up the stairs to Sarah's bedroom. Other than a large bed, dresser and mirror, the room was sparsely furnished or decorated. Nevertheless, Klein could smell her presence in the air. It was a warm and sweet odour that moved him. He stood still for a moment, his head swirling with images of her face and body. Then his eye spotted the flimsy floor board at the side of the bed. He grabbed at it and flung it across the room.

The black book was there. He pulled it out of the hole in the floor and opened it. It was Tooley's client list. Names. Addresses. Phone numbers. Dates. Amounts of Money. There were hundreds, all bilked in a simple but profitable grain-trading swindle. Klein flipped the pages, his eyes scanning and searching for a clue that would explain the killing and destruction of the past month. But there was nothing until he reached page twenty-nine.

First he saw scrawled 'Bob Stewart....$2500 deposited to account 723, Bank of Montreal. April 11.' So, he thought, Bob had indeed been bought off. This had to be the money he had received for destroying the police report. But why had it come from Tooley? Sarah had said that Tooley had only witnessed the murder, maybe he had lied to her. Maybe it had been Tooley all along. Klein was about to turn to the next page when his eyes saw the letters. His heart jumped. He stared it at the name for more than a minute, before the full significance of his discovery sank in.

"Son-of-a-bitch," he cried out. "How can this be? How can this be?"

Hearing Klein's anguished shout, Melinda ran up the stairs towards Sarah's room. She found Klein kneeling on the floor, his face white. "Sam, what's happened. What have you found?"

"I have been betrayed," he said in a choked voice.

Melinda moved closer to him. She took the black book from his hands and read the list of the names on the page. Bob Stewart. Jack Griswold. Frank Smith. Zachary Duncan. Joseph Robinson...Isaac Hirsch.

It was raining as Klein walked from Melinda's towards Selkirk Avenue. Klein was oblivious to it. He moved purposely through the mud and the puddles, his eyes straight ahead.

His head swirled with the images of his dead father — victim of a blood libel and ruthlessly murdered by a mob. His mother said that Isaac worked for the Czar's government. Why didn't he try to save him? Klein could not correct the errors of the past, but the present he could still rectify.

By the time he reached Hirsch's store, his initial astonishment and dismay had turned to anger. At first, he could not fathom how or why, Isaac Hirsch — his friend, his mother's companion, a leader of the community — could have been mixed up with Peter Tooley. The thought of Isaac committing murder, taking the life of another human being, and allowing Aaron Davidovitch to be convicted for a crime he did not do, was preposterous. There had to be a reasonable explanation. Perhaps Isaac was just another one of Tooley's customers who had been cheated.

And yet, he had a feeling he was missing something important. The closer he got to the store, the more intense it became. Even as a young child, he had sensed there was another darker side to Isaac. His quick temper and the dreadful manner in which he so callously treated his wife, were only the most visible examples. Status and money were always important to him, far too important, Klein thought. Even the other day at the Manitoba Club, he had revelled in the wealthy environment, forgetting his roots and people. Yes, Klein finally decided, it was possible for Isaac to have been mixed up with Tooley. But as for being a murderer, that was impossible.

Selkirk Avenue was nearly deserted. Since the riot, stores were closed by seven. Even the Queen Theatre, offering this week a popular Yiddish rendition of The Jewish King Lear starring Mordechai Tenenbein, had opted to begin its evening playbill an hour earlier. Most Jewish merchants and shopkeepers had replaced broken windows and replaced damaged stock. Yet now large wooden shutters covered almost every building.

Klein stood for a moment in front of the Hirschs' store, thinking of the past, of family dinners at Rosh Hashana and Passover, of sharing the secrets and problems of his life with Isaac.

Beyond the shutters the store was dark and still. Klein tried to peer through the window, but could see nothing. His right hand reached for the door; it too was bolted shut. He moved through the narrow pathway beside the building to the back. There were old, wet pieces of wood and boxes of junk strewn around the yard. As he reached the small door leading from the alley, he could see a light flickering from inside.

"Isaac, it's Sam," he called out, "I need to speak with you."

The light vanished.

"Isaac, is that you? Please, can we talk?"

Silence.

Klein put his shoulder against the side door, eased back, and shoved as hard as he could. The door gave way with a loud crack. He peered into the dark. The gloom did not bother him. He had been at the store so often over the years, that he could easily navigate it without light.

The table in the back room was exactly as it had been that day only a few weeks ago when Isaac and the synagogue board members had asked him to help clear the rabbi's name. This whole charade troubled him. Why had Isaac involved him in this mess and then tried to have him killed?

He walked through the curtain and into the main store area. The rows of nails, tools and metal paraphernalia of every type and kind were neatly stocked as they always were.

"Isaac please, I know you must be here somewhere. Let's talk."

From behind the front counter, Klein heard the striking of a match. A candle flickered before the face of Isaac Hirsch. He looked different to Klein — older, grayer, sadder. There was something disturbing about him; a light of fear in his eyes. This man was a leader in the Jewish community, an astute businessmen, and a confident and prosperous citizen. Yet standing there with the candle flame close to Hirsch's face, all Klein could see was the man's confusion and dread.

Klein took a deep breath. "Tell me this is all a mistake and I'll believe you. I want to believe that you are not involved. That you had nothing to do with the death of Anna Rudnicki. That you can explain your business dealings with Peter Tooley. Can you tell me that, Isaac?"

There was a long silence. Klein could hear the music of a phonograph somewhere in the distance. "I cannot, Shailek," Isaac whispered finally.

"Don't call me that!" Klein shouted. "You have no right. I want to know the truth. Are you capable of killing?"

The light flickered over Hirsch's face. "Like you, Shailek, I craved to belong and to be respected. Not as an outsider, not as a Jew, just as a man."

Klein winced to hear his own words thrown back at him. "At any price, Isaac?"

"I was having some financial difficulties in the store. People owed me money, creditors were knocking at the door. Clara was starting to suspect. I had to do something."

"Enter Tooley."

"Yes. I heard he was a grain trader who knew how to cut corners. And for a while, things were working out perfectly. I had invested five thousand dollars with him and he was paying me steady dividends. It was a perfect relationship. Until one day, I caught him trying to cheat me. Cheat me, Isaac Hirsch! He told me about his little game of skimming off the top. I don't know what came over me, desperation maybe. But I decided that he and I were going to go into business together. He had your whore Sarah working for him, enticing clients to keep them happy."

Klein's fists clenched. "Did you ever meet her?"

"No, not then. No one but Tooley knew that I was involved. We were doing wonderful. I don't know, forty, fifty thousand in a few months. It was beyond my wildest dreams," he laughed bitterly. "And then, Tooley, the fool, became a greedy *goy*. He wasn't satisfied. He had to make more. So he went long in a November wheat future and the price dropped. He lost thousands, thousands of my money, my future. That night a few weeks ago, we met in the alley. I can barely remember what happened. There was an argument. That little girl, I didn't want to hurt her, Sam, you must believe me. I didn't want to. But she was there. She heard. There was too much at stake."

"What did she hear? She barely spoke English, you fool. You didn't have to do anything to her."

"No, she heard our conversation. My position in the community. My life. There was too much money coming in and I needed every cent. She could have told the wrong people. I had to shut her up."

Klein shook his head. "What about the stolen items from the synagogue?"

Hirsch regained some of his composure. His fingers played with a yellow screwdriver as he spoke. "When it was over I had to do something. Tooley was fencing stolen property. Before he met me, he had received a box of stuff from one of the scum thieves he dealt with on Main Street, a man named Nicholas Smith. He knew they had come from a synagogue and wanted me to appraise the articles for him. I was going to get them back and return them to the rabbi. Once the girl was dead, I knew I had to cover myself."

"But why the blood libel? For God's sake, look at the destruction it has caused."

Hirsch frowned. "I never for a moment thought events would become so carried away. I thought that in this country we had moved to a new level of tolerance. I was wrong."

"You haven't answered my question," said Klein, his eyes focusing on the screwdriver.

"When I saw that little girl lying dead in the mud, all that came to me was an image from the past. It was many years ago, when I was in Russia."

"You worked for the government."

"Yes. How do you know?"

"My mother she told me everything. I know about my father, about the way he died."

Hirsch closed his eyes and nodded. "I always have been sorry about that terrible event. Maybe that's why I felt obligated to care for your mother. Max and I were friends. I couldn't save him. I tried..."

"Save the apologies, Isaac. But tell me what kind of position did you have in Russia? I'm curious."

"I was an agent for the Okhrana."

"A Jew in the Czar's secret service?"

"Yes. I had served in the army for several years and my commanding officer, General Pavel Delianov, took a liking to me. They were concerned about the growing dissident and terrorist movement challenging the Czar and believed that Jews were involved. Okhrana wanted an officer capable of translating Yiddish and Hebrew. General Delianov recommended me."

Hirsch laughed bitterly. "I think in the ten months I was in St. Petersburg I came across one letter written in Hebrew from a Jewish merchant complaining about his taxes. The poor man was arrested and beaten. After that I was much more careful about what I reported. In any event, one day in the spring of 1883, I was ordered to investigate a murder in Odessa."

"Behind my father's loading dock?"

"Yes. A young girl, fifteen years old, had been raped and killed. I soon discovered that the murderer was none other than the head of the Odessa Okhrana unit, a drunk by the name of Perov. He was notorious for his appetite for young women. When I submitted my findings, I assumed, at the very least, that Perov would be relieved of his command. I was wrong. Perov had much influence with a General Zavarzin, then head of the Okhrana. He supported Perov's decision to make the killing appear as if it had been a ritual murder committed by a Jew. Your father was arrested. I tried protesting, but it was useless. One night I received an anonymous message warning me of trouble. I had no choice but to flee the country."

"And so," said Klein, "you thought the blood accusation would work once again."

"Yes," snapped Hirsch. "But I never thought it would go this far." Isaac glared at Klein, the candle still flickering. "I will admit that matters got a bit out of hand. At the beginning, it was perfect. Once the rabbi was arrested and the blood libel was raised, I thought it was best to let things play themselves out. The police report was easy. Tooley knew Bob Stewart. He was one of his clients. All that was required was a little money and the report disappeared. Unfortunately, the constable got cold feet and threatened to expose us. He was dealt with by this *goy* Smitty that I hired."

"The man who robbed the synagogue?"

"Yes. He's a thief and a mean son-of-a-bitch who will do anything for cash. He was an acquaintance of Tooley's but ended up working for me."

"I see."

"Don't worry, he's left the city."

"I'm hardly worried. Smitty was supposed to deal with me as well?"

"Getting you involved was not my idea. It was the stupid members of the synagogue board. They were so adamant about you saving the rabbi's neck, that I had little choice. I had to go along with the idea. To be honest, I didn't think you were up to the job."

"So why then did you try to have me killed?"

"That was Tooley's idea. He was just trying to scare you off. He ordered Smitty to run you down. I told him it was a waste of time. That you were as stubborn as a mule."

Isaac shook his head before continuing. "The attack on Rivka is the only thing I really regret. The intensity of the hatred against our people, the riot shocked me as much as you."

"Spare me. You've been living a lie for years, maybe your whole life. I don't even know who you are. You were going to allow the rabbi to be executed. What kind of person would do that?"

"I never wanted the rabbi to be convicted. I honestly thought that there was enough doubt about his guilt that a lawyer like Alfred Powers would be able to get him off. Instead, the jury blames the Jews. By that point, I couldn't do anything about it, except try to control the situation. Tooley dealt with that young prostitute who heard too much and we knew that Sarah might present a problem."

"So you nearly murdered her as well?"

"I told Smitty to follow her, but he got carried away. In any event, she was lucky. Tooley made such a fuss about her. You know, he was infatuated with her. Can you believe that? We had a terrible argument about it, first in his office where you found her. I would've eventually had Smitty take care of her. She had become a liability, but Tooley fought me on this. And then later at his sister's house, we argued further. He pulled a knife on me, the *mishiginer*. What was I to do?"

"So you killed him too?"

"Yes. I had to."

"You had to. How many bodies, Isaac? How much blood on your hands?"

Hirsch said nothing. His hand tightened around the handle of the screwdriver.

Klein pressed on, his face hard. "Once Tooley was dead, why didn't you finish Sarah off when you had the chance?"

"I stood over her. She was breathing very softly. It would've been painless and simple. But for you, Shailek, I couldn't bring myself to do it. "

Klein stepped forward. "Enough talk, Isaac. You and I are going to find the judge and stop an innocent man from being killed tomorrow morning."

"I don't think that's possible, Sam," said Isaac moving out from behind the counter.

"And why...."

Before Klein could finish speaking, Isaac rushed at him, wielding the long metal screwdriver as a knife. He slashed at Klein's face, just missing his eye. Klein lurched to his left, drew up his right fist, but lost his balance. He stumbled for a moment and fell to the floor, hitting his head. He was momentarily dazed.

"Stop!" shouted a voice from the darkness.

From the far corner of store Joseph Kowalski walked into the light. He was holding his single-action Colt in his right hand. The hammer was cocked, ready to fire. His hand was steady.

"You. What are you doing here?" demanded Isaac.

Klein too was astonished to see the president of the Holy Ghost Fraternal Society standing before him with a revolver.

Kowalski smiled as he raised the gun to Hirsch's head. "Many years ago in St. Petersburg an Okhrana agent got himself into lots of trouble, accusing a high-ranking general of murdering a young girl."

"You were there," whispered Isaac. "At the courthouse the other day, I sensed that we had met. It was in the St. Petersburg office. You were an agent also. Isn't that right? But what do you know about the case with General Perov?"

"You are such a fool, Hirsch. Yes, I was there. Like you I had been recruited to deal with Polish radicals. I followed General Zavrzin's orders. But on the day you submitted your Odessa report, identifying Zavarzin's cousin Perov as the girl's murderer, I knew there would be trouble. Who do you think warned you the night Zavarzin's men were coming for you?"

"But why? We hardly knew each other."

"Perov was a pompous fat fool. More to the point, I thought you were a man worth saving for future use. Evidently, I was wrong. As soon as I read about the details of the murder of young Anna, I knew it had to be you. Who else would know about the circular pattern?"

Watching the two men warily, Klein got to his feet.

"Stay where you are, Sam," said Isaac firmly, waving the screwdriver in front of him.

"Kowalski," snapped Klein, "are you going to use that gun or is it just for show?"

"No. That is why I am here with this," he said raising his pistol. "I still have contact with the office in St. Petersburg. Perov is dead and Zavarzin is in custody. But, Hirsch, I should tell you that I have been ordered to demote you as a way to tidy things up. It seems that your former employers consider you a liability. You remember what that means, don't you?"

"Give me that gun, God damn it," said Klein. "I'll use it."

Kowalski momentarily lowered his pistol and in that split second Isaac quickly turned and raised the screwdriver, high above his head. "Please forgive me, Shailek," he whispered as he lunged towards Sam.

Kowalski's Colt boomed and Isaac screamed in pain. The bullet had caught him in his chest and knocked him down.

"Stay on the ground," yelled Kowalski, "or I'll fire again, Hirsch, I swear it."

But Isaac Hirsch would not get up again. As Klein knelt beside the man he had for many years thought of as a father, he could see Hirsch's vacant eyes staring sightlessly at the ceiling.

As he looked down at Isaac's body, Klein wanted to forgive him, but he couldn't force himself to do it. He thought of young Anna, his sister, Bob Stewart, lovely Sarah lying in a hospital bed, even McCreary. All that sorrow. All that blood. Because of one man's greed.

What would his real father have done in a situation like this? Klein thought he knew. He reached for a blanket, covered Isaac's body and whispered the words of the *kaddish*. "*Yisgadal, vyskadash sheme rabah....*" As he chanted this ancient prayer, something deep inside told him that he had seen the last of his terrible childhood dreams.

September was always a pleasant time in the city, the best time of the year to celebrate a wedding. The heat of the summer had passed and the frigid temperatures of the winter were still at least a month away. The leaves on the elm trees along Wellington Crescent were beginning to turn a beautiful golden brown and the autumn evening air was invigorating.

On the first Sunday of that September in 1911, Sam Klein took Sarah Bloomberg to be his wife, vowing to love, honour and cherish her until death parted them. The ceremony was held at the newly renovated Shaarey Shamim Synagogue. Rabbi Aaron Davidovitch presided over the service.

Freda, of course, had arranged the entire affair; she had made enough cheese *knishes* to feed a small army. Yet there had never been a wedding quite like this one. Much to Freda's dissatisfaction (but much to the delight of every man in attendance) Melinda and Darlene walked down the aisle alongside Rivka. Neither Bill McCreary nor John Maloney had ever stepped into a synagogue before. And for Michael Stark it had been a very long time. Nevertheless, all three men were more than willing to stand beside Klein, after Rabbi Davidovitch had approved the most unusual wedding arrangements Winnipeg's Jewish community had ever witnessed. Joseph Kowalski toasted the bride with words about healing and tolerance. To cheers, he declared that it was time once and for all to leave the problems of the past where they belong and to build a better future in Canada.

In his speech to his friends after the ceremony, Klein spoke of his late father and of friendship. He spoke of the dangers of greed and not being satisfied with what you have; he spoke of the importance of belonging to a community, of being a part of a people whose ancient bonds will survive long after the individual is gone. Looking directly at Michael Stark sitting beside his wife Julia, he spoke about knowing who you are and where you fit into the vast scheme of things. The detective nodded his head ever so slightly.

That was Isaac's real problem, Klein thought. Beneath the veneer of the community leader and merchant was a man who in the end coveted nothing but money and status.

Clara offered Klein the store, but after everything that had happened, he refused. Hirsch's hardware store went on the market. At least, Clara wouldn't have to worry for the rest of her life. She moved in with Freda and they kept each other company, remembering happier times from long ago.

Melinda told Klein that he had a job at her house as long as he wished. Sarah was leaving the business and Klein thought it might be a good idea for him to do so as well. They would visit her, they said, but of course they rarely did.

Sam and Sarah moved into a small apartment on McGregor near Burrows and Klein found an office for rent down the street. If anything good had come out of those terrible events, it was that Klein had discovered what he did best. Beginning in October, the "Sam Klein Investigative Services" was open for business. Before too long, Klein had more cases and clients than he knew how to handle.

Klein had made sure that John Maloney got the full story of Isaac's confession but decided to keep Kowalski's name out of it. McCreary reluctantly went along with that also. The detective sent word to the Mounties who eventually arrested Nicholas Smith in a Regina bar for the murder of Constable Bob Stewart.

In the wake of the riot, the city established a new council for immigrant relations and the leaders of the North End's various ethnic groups, including Polish, Ukrainian and Jewish, agreed that it was time to talk.

Across the ocean, storm clouds were on the horizon, however. The leaders of Europe had yet to learn the lessons of life that Sam Klein had learned so well that spring and summer in the New World. And many, many would perish before the lesson could be learned.